2156

—————

THE RELIFE PROJECT BOOK 1

C. M. DANCHA

OTHER BOOKS BY C. M. DANCHA

World War -The ReLife Project - volume 2

The Buttputty Gang - The Mystery Begins - volume 1

The Buttputty Gang – In Trouble Again - volume 2

The Buttputty Gang – Versus Evil - volume 3

Found-volume 1

Ten Light-Years to Insanity

This book was derived from my fertile imagination. However, there were several people who kept my imagination in check, making sure I didn't go too far and end up losing the reader. Thanks to my wife Cheri, Jerry, Pat and Linda.

PROLOGUE

NOT THAT MANY YEARS AGO, I went to see Mel Gibson's movie, "The Patriot". If you don't remember it, the story revolves around a Colonialist in early America who must decide if he supports the upcoming Revolutionary War with Britain. When one of his sons is killed by a Hessian mercenary, he joins the fight against Mother England and her allies.

I'm not sure what Hollywood thought of it, but I liked it. Then again, I'm easy to please when it comes to creative works of art. The more imaginary and out-of-the-box, the better.

Anyhow, back to the point. As I left the theatre, I had one of my "what if" moments. For whatever reason, a simple question popped into my brain. "What would happen if a Founding Father of the United States was brought back to life in modern times?"

From that one question, it was off to the races. What would the Founding Father think of today's America? Would he be impressed, sad or somewhere between? What would he think of our politics, dress, manners, morals, and behavior? The number of questions was endless.

I kept all these questions in the back of my mind until I got the chance to answer them in the ReLife books you are about to read. Of course, my predictions of the future are most likely way off base. If it were easy, I would have bought Apple stock before anyone knew people would use telephones for virtually everything.

So, without further chatter, grab a refreshment, sit in your favorite easy chair and enjoy this ride into the future.

CHAPTER ONE

THE WORLD COUNCIL came to power because of sex. Its rise and eventual takeover of the world had nothing to do with sexual preference or discrimination. A marriage of convenience between two powerful families wasn't the cause. And, the use of sex as a tool of influence wasn't at play.

The central government, which represented all peoples and geographic areas of the world, arose because of human fertility rates. They went haywire in the latter half of the 21st century and threatened the existence of mankind.

Most scientists picked 2055 as the year fertility rates started to shift from the 50-50, male-female rates which governed human reproduction since the dawn of time. Within ten years, the female birth rate fell to only 30% of all births. Five years later it hit its lowest mark of 12%. Also, total births were dropping precariously. By the time the female birth rate hit its low, the total birth rate had decreased by 50%.

At first, social scientists thought the shift in fertility rates was temporary and would correct itself within a couple of years. But as rates continued to trend downward, scientists, governments, and citizens became concerned and desperately sought a solution. The effect on societies was overwhelming. The fertility rate problem dominated world news and the attention of governments regardless of political doctrine. Very little else seemed to matter.

It wasn't long before the end of the world predictions began. It was easy to foretell the extinction of mankind if it could not replenish itself. Death rates crept by birth rates then accelerated to a hundred and finally a thousand times more. Countries and continents were dying a slow death.

To make things worse, men who were unable to find female mates turned to crime, drug addiction and war at an alarming rate. Male homosexuality increased, which led to new diseases and deadly viruses like the AIDS virus of the late 20th century. This reckless behavior amplified death rates and contributed to declining populations. Once thriving cities became ghost towns. Entire continents went from overpopulated to underpopulated within a couple of generations.

Governments throughout the world put most of their resources into finding a solution to the female fertility problem. It was classified as a plague and given the acronym FISS, which stood for Female Infertility and Selective Sex.

Every possible solution was explored with no conclusive results. A virus, bacteria and all other forms of infectious diseases were ruled out as the cause. Possible environmental changes, like air and water pollutants, offered no causal reason for FISS. Drugs, foods, farming methods, fertilizers, and a hundred other possible explanations were explored with no results. Scientists were unable to find a common denominator in women who stopped conceiving or gave birth to only boy babies. The answer and ultimate cure for FISS eluded the entire scientific community.

Couples who had children but could not procreate were of

major interest to the scientists looking to cure FISS. Hundreds of these couples were isolated and put through a series of tests to determine why they became barren. Was the problem related to the men or was it something affecting only the women? Not one study produced an answer. Everything in their lives, from the quality of the man's sperm to living conditions, appeared to be the same from when they brought children into the world.

Even though the campaign to find a cure for FISS was unsuccessful, cures for other diseases resulted from the intensive biotechnology research. The most noteworthy medical advancement was by a research scientist in Switzerland who stumbled upon a cure for cancer. What should have been earth-shattering news was hardly discussed after the initial press release. The attitude of most people was, *why get excited about a cure for cancer when mankind might be gone within 75 years?*

The inability of the scientific community to find a remedy led most religious leaders to put the blame for the FISS plague on the back of man. In their opinion, man's injustice and mistreatment of each other were to blame. Ignoring God's laws for hundreds of years finally resulted in dire consequences. He had enough of man's lack of faith and worship and decided to take revenge on his disrespectful creation.

End Times announcements became more and more common. Religious leaders pleaded with anyone who would listen. Their mantra was for everyone to prepare their souls for the end by coming back to God's commandments. Their pleas fell on deaf ears and had a negligible effect on creating new converts. Even former believers balked at returning to God and organized religion.

Most people ignored or rejected the idea that God's wrath had anything to do with FISS. The hell and brimstone answers offered by religion were not very appealing. Spending the world's last days in comfort and luxurious surroundings was more attractive. Many people gathered a huge food supply, grabbed weapons and headed to the fishing cabin they dreamed about for retirement. If it was End Times, they were going to spend it in comfort, doing whatever the hell they wanted. Most figured they could make last-minute amends with the Creator on their death beds.

Women became a commodity. Many were moved to isolated areas and hidden. There was a common belief that women could run away from whatever caused infertility and the lopsided male-female birth rates. The theory had merit, considering it worked with other plagues throughout history. It didn't take long to learn that hiding in remote locations had no effect on a woman's ability to conceive and become pregnant. Fertility rates for women in populated and remote areas were the same. The only people who benefited from taking women to remote areas were the men who accompanied them. They had available sex partners without having to fight other men for their affection.

Nearly 45 years after it began, the FISS plague subsided. Fertility rates and male-female rates started to trend back to normal. At about the same time, twelve young women from various regions around the world claimed they had the cure for FISS. They backed up their claim by making infertile women conceive and women who could produce only male children give birth to little girls.

How they accomplished this feat was never discovered because everything was done behind closed doors. The "Healers", as these women were called, took infertile women into a closed room for approximately four hours. At the conclusion, the women left and resumed their normal daily activities. There was nothing observably different about them. But within a month they became pregnant and 70% of them gave birth to little girls. When asked what the Healer did in the closed room, the response most often heard was, "she just talked to me; that's all." When pushed for a more detailed explanation, none of the women could remember specifics. No matter how much investigation was done, details of the Healers' methods were never uncovered. It always boiled down to "we just talked."

A larger debate soon developed. Were the Healers responsible for ending FISS or did it run its course and burn itself out? The Healers modestly took credit for ending the plague and increasing female births. But they refused to explain how they did this. Their critics claimed it was coincidence and the Healers happened to be in the right place at the right time. Their more passionate opponents believed the Healers were empowered by some sort of diabolical power.

The similarity between these twelve Healers was more than coincidental. In fact, it was shocking and somewhat disturbing. They were all in their late thirties to mid-forties, unwed and homeless. No two of them lived in the same area. They were spread out across the globe and there was no evidence they had ever met each other. They had no living relatives and none of their friends were considered close. Birth, immunization and school records could not be found for them. They worked alone and refused to let anyone help or sit in on their four-hour sessions. Their results were numerically the same regardless of the geographic location.

Their fame and notoriety spread with each successful female birth. Within two years, each of the Healers had a cult following like a celebrity. Their fans and supporters were fanatics who believed the Healers were somehow divinely inspired. Their detractors and enemies were few and far between. They had difficulty explaining their opposition other than accusing them of using some type of evil power. The supporters responded to this criticism by claiming it was nothing more than jealousy.

Intervention by the Healers was no longer needed after the fertility rates stabilized. By this time, they were the most recognized and respected people on Earth. Their supporters and opponents both wondered where the Healers would go and what they would do next. Most of the remaining population and government officials pleaded with the Healers to help rebuild society. The decimated infrastructures and economies needed their help and guidance.

Without any formal announcement or fanfare, all twelve Healers traveled to a small village north of London named Ickleford and established a help depot. The concept was simplistic and very much like a roadside travel plaza. Anyone, from the highest government official to the lowest ranking person in society, could stop in and seek advice from the Healers.

There were no limits or restrictions on the number or types of questions posed to the Healers. If the visitor was serious and didn't waste the Healer's time, he could ask about any subject. It could be seeking advice to personal problems, economic inquiries or love interests. More serious subjects like the differences between theologies were discussed. The Healers even fielded questions about foretelling the future.

Their advice was free and without any type of quid pro quo. Sometimes visitors were surprised by the answers. Other times it was exactly what they expected. Not all visitors agreed with what they heard. But none complained about how they were treated or claimed to have been intentionally misled. Many donated to the Healers' service. The poor and penniless always left with some food in their stomach or a few coins in their pocket.

For the next five years, the Healers dispensed advice and

information to all who sought their help. The world economy started to recover, families reunited and living conditions improved.

The Healers disappeared on the five-year anniversary date of establishing the help depot. They were replaced by a dozen other men and women. These new appointees claimed to be selected by the original Healers. People were dubious about these replacements and questioned their authority. The replacements seemed to have as much knowledge and wisdom as the original Healers. But there was an egotistic edge to their personalities which didn't sit well with many people. They immediately restricted visiting hours. The previous open-door policy was replaced by an appointment-only system.

For the next five years, the new Healers served the world as the top-ranking intellectuals, advisers, and seers. And, like the original twelve Healers, the replacements disappeared on their five-year anniversary. They too were replaced by another dozen people of various ages, races, and gender.

Each new group of Healers became more authoritative and self-serving. Early in the 22nd century, the Healer group name was replaced with the title of World Council. By this time, its purpose had changed from giving helpful advice to telling the populace what to do and when to do it.

Citizens no longer stopped at the Ickleford help depot to ask questions and seek advice. Contact with the World Council was now done by submitting an official inquiry. The newly devised Universal Communications Network (UCN) was used to submit all inquiries. Official decrees, rules, and laws replaced helpful, fatherly guidance. A network of World Council enforcers was put in place by the new world government. Any order of the World Council not obeyed resulted in immediate and harsh discipline.

The only people allowed to own a weapon were World

Council officials and enforcers. All other weapons were seized. Sports shooting and hunting were no longer allowed. Older weapons were destroyed. Newer ones, like energy burst guns, were issued to government enforcers or warehoused for whenever the government needed them. Keeping citizens safe was the reason given by the World Council to justify seizing privately owned weapons. Anti-firearm groups joined in lockstep with the ban. They enthusiastically participated in bounty programs to arrest people who still possessed weapons. As the no-weapon ban grew harsher, the underground economy in weapons flourished.

Prisons became unnecessary and were eliminated. Only holding cells existed to temporarily house violators. Once the sentence was issued, violators were dealt with in one of two ways. Repeat offenders or violent criminals like murderers were put to death immediately. Due process and appeals were deemed outdated thoughts from past legal systems. Minor violators returned to society with a reduction of their monthly world credits, which was the new currency for the globe. This penalty could last from two years to a lifetime. Many violators were unable to sponge from friends or find a way to make up for lost world credits. They ended up dying within a year.

All towns and cities over 10,000 citizens had an official "drug zone". The World Council began distributing mind-altering drugs to addicts free of charge. Supplying low-grade alcohol and narcotics was an uncomplicated way of controlling the populace and minimizing crime. The lowlifes of society migrated to the drug zones to get strung out. With these people herded into a defined area, it was easy to keep them under control. There was no reason for the addicts to rebel against the government because they had exactly what they wanted from life; a perpetual high. The only restriction was that drugs must be used within the boundaries of the drug zone. Any citizens caught with drugs outside the boundary faced immediate execution or discontinuation of their world credits. Most apprehended violators chose a quick death by overdose.

Each citizen got a series of injections to avoid contracting any number of contagious diseases. Information soon leaked that one of the injections contained a microdevice. This device entered the bloodstream and lodged in a kidney. The Council claimed this intrusive program would promote world health and prevent crime. It tracked future fertility rates, identify new plagues and prevented hostage-taking and kidnapping. To the average citizen, the security and safety features of this program seemed reasonable. Besides, it didn't cost anything and didn't hurt. Once it was in the body, it was forgotten. There was no reason for the average person to protest its implantation. What the average citizen didn't realize was the injected microdevice was part of a devious plan. With a device lodged within each citizen, the World Council could watch and track everyone.

World government replaced the individual as the most important piece of society. By the mid-22nd century, all countries and geographic territories acquiesced control and governance to the World Council. The average citizen didn't care for the heavy-handed tactics of the World Council but willingly followed its dictates to move beyond the horrific memories of FISS. Giving up a small bit of freedom and self-determination was easy when done in exchange for the security and safety provided by the World Council.

The entire world landscape made a radical change in less than one hundred years. And it all started with an unexplained change in human sexuality.

CHAPTER TWO

2156 A.D

RODOLFO SWEATS LEFT his office at Phoenvartis Corporation in Zurich, Switzerland, at nine o'clock and headed to a local restaurant for a late-night dinner before going home. Another twelve-hour day had left him exhausted. He was in dire need of a soaking shower and a restful night's sleep before returning to work early the next morning.

The thought of playing hooky tomorrow crossed his mind. Routine seventy-hour work weeks were too demanding and stressful. He was aging prematurely with gray hair, wrinkles, and stooped shoulders. At 36 years of age, he felt 65. Each time he stood in front of a mirror he could see the signs of aging which were catching up with his mental exhaustion in record time.

The money and prestige of working at Phoenvartis were fabulous. The world was in the midst of an economic recession and jobs like his were few and far between. As the senior vice president in charge of theoretical medical advancement, he was making over 350,000 world credits a year. On top of that were a healthy bonus, free housing, and vehicle. Compared to the boom years of twenty years before, his compensation was meager. But, compared to most corporate executives in 2156 he was doing very well.

When he compared his compensation to fellow Stanford classmates he was at the top. He was making three times more than the average alumnus in his graduating class. This wasn't due to a superior IQ, pronounced creativity or overwhelming greed. It resulted from choosing to work in Switzerland, one of the few areas left in the world with little interference by the government. The tiny country still operated under the mandates of capitalism. Government involvement in business and the lives of its citizens was minimal. And socialism was repeatedly rejected in favor of economic freedom.

Switzerland, along with three other geographic areas, formed the Free Zones of Cooperative Thought. Of the four, only Switzerland maintained the same borders it had for hundreds of years. The other three zones were pieced together from former countries or states. Texas and parts of Louisiana, former states in old America, formed Zone 2. Bangkok in southern Thailand to Phnom Penh in southern Cambodia became Zone 3. The country once known as South Africa with about 20% of southern Zimbabwe, also known as colonial Rhodesia, formed Zone 4.

All four zones were tolerated by the World Council. They were immune from the social and economic dictates issued by the World Council to the rest of the world. The Council viewed the Free Zones of Cooperative Thought as a necessary evil. They were the only areas which produced new and innovative ideas and products.

New ideas and products blossomed in the zones. These innovations included cures for infectious diseases, bio-technical advancements, and new housing systems. In exchange for this continuous stream of new ideas, the World Council allowed the zones to operate with unfettered autonomy. It was rare when they stepped in to override or punish the zones for being too independent or anti-government.

Rodolfo's decision to leave the former United States and work in one of the zones made perfect economic sense but was hard on his personal life. Most of his family and friends were still in the Macon, Georgia area of old America. It was difficult leaving them behind. What made matters worse was the reaction by many of his family members. Relatives who were staunch supporters of "papa government" were especially opposed to his decision. They didn't want any family member living in a location where the government didn't control each citizen's life from birth to grave.

Too many of his family and friends were dependent on the government-supplied housing, food and health care. In exchange for these free necessities of life, they swore allegiance and support to Papa. The freedom they sacrificed to get this lifestyle was given up in the name of security and safety. Anyone like Rodolfo was considered a traitor to papa government. His decision to move to a free zone was harshly criticized or considered good riddance by a few family members.

Even his brother considered Rodolfo's decision to move to a free zone as a slap in the face to the Sweats family. The family heritage had always been one of supporting big government. It started after the American Civil War when the central government in Washington D.C. reneged on its promise to provide former slaves with a mule and 40 acres of land. From that point forward, every member of the Sweats family supported the politician who offered the most in government handouts. It could be food credits, rent-supported housing or some other form of welfare. It didn't matter that they voted against President Lincoln's party which freed the slaves. All that mattered was getting their fair share of free hand-outs.

As the Sweats family helped to put more of these politicians in office in exchange for more government benefits, the central government grew in power and influence over every citizen. It was a vicious circle where citizens incrementally exchanged personal rights and liberty for more and more handouts. Old America and most other countries of the world became government dominated. This was all done in the name of fairness or the false pretense that no one person should have more or less than his neighbor. The real result was that this artificial equality left everyone, except the leaders of the World Council, equally poor.

From an early age, Rodolfo was the outcast of the Sweats family. He didn't want to live at the will of the government. He wanted to make his own way and receive compensation for his efforts. The thought of getting the same compensation no matter how much or little he worked was repulsive. Being told to share the fruits of his labor with someone else because it was the fair thing to do infuriated him. He wanted to be his own man, responsible for creating his own destiny. So the decision to enter the yearly lottery to get one of the few slots allocated for relocation to a free zone was a logical, rather than emotional, decision.

But, after ten years in a Free Zone, he was beginning to question his decision. Certain aspects of his life were unfulfilled with no solutions in sight. He lived in a geographic area which allowed, valued and encouraged freedom but was that true in all facets of life? He had the freedom of thought for economic advancements but did his personal life have the same freedom for self-enjoyment?

As he walked through the city center streets of old Zurich, he passed the enclosed garage where his company-provided hover vehicle was stored. This was a perfect example of the personal freedom question he was debating with himself. He never used the hover vehicle to go to or from work because he lived within walking distance of the corporate office. His demanding schedule left little time to take the hover vehicle and explore areas of Europe. Since moving to the zone, he had only been able to break free from the demands of his job to see Paris over an extended holiday weekend. On another mini holiday, he visited a half dozen small hamlets and towns in Switzerland. Otherwise, the hover vehicle sat in its stall collecting dust week after week.

But overriding everything else, the lack of free time was limiting his chance to develop a meaningful relationship. Not having a female partner was beginning to weigh heavily on his subconscious and affect his well-being. Sure, he had dated a few women since moving to the zone but none of those relationships lasted more than a month or two or got beyond the third date. He wanted to know exactly what the problem was. Was he not devoting enough time to building the relationship or was he ill-equipped to relate socially and culturally with European born and bred women?

A possible solution was to find an attractive American woman in Zurich. He quickly dismissed that thought for he knew no such creature existed in the Swiss free zone. He often joked with himself that of the three attractive American women in Switzerland, one was married and the other two were lesbians. The bottom line was that he was getting tired of spending time with available women on fantasy communication stations at a cost of 100 world credits per hour. He needed to discover how to relate successfully to European women.

His deductive mind went to work over-analyzing his dilemma. The first step was to assess the potential reasons why he was having such difficulty establishing a permanent relationship. Were his darker skin and minimal Negroid facial features the real reasons? Swiss women were supposedly refined and very liberal. But was it possible that they had yet to accept interracial dating and meaningful relationships between races? If that were true, why did they bother to go out with him in the first place? Could it be that they wanted only a free meal and entertainment at a local theater? Or, did it take them two to three dates to realize Rodolfo had Negroid ancestry?

Either explanation was plausible. Times were tough economically with high unemployment. For most Swiss women, dining at an upscale restaurant and enjoying exotic foods was a treat far beyond their limited budgets. If they could spend the night at the opera house or theater, that would be something they could remember for the rest of their lives. Plus, they could impress their friends at the next gossip session.

There was another feature which might explain the average Swiss woman's reaction to him. His body did not follow the normal features of European Caucasian men. He had a sprinter's body with long legs, massive thighs and lean yet tightly bound calves like a Cheetah. His upper chest and arms were overly muscled even though he didn't spend much time in the gym working out. And his butt was tight and well-defined compared to men of European ancestry.

There was nothing wrong with his body. In fact, Rodolfo liked the way he looked standing in front of the full-length mirror after showering. This chiseled frame served him well when it came to running track and playing wide receiver in high school and college.

He guessed that his time in the 100-meter sprint was the best in Georgia high school history. Also, his 32 touchdown catches as a high school senior had to rank in the top ten nationally.

Unfortunately, statistics and scores were outlawed under the "Everyone Is a Winner" law passed 115 years earlier. Rollie thought that not keeping athletic results was stupid. Every one of the athletes knew who was doing well and who wasn't. So what if some performed better than others? Wouldn't that entice everyone to train harder and improve?

He soon realized there were other people keeping unwritten notes of his performance on the track and football fields. The premier universities which still had athletic teams knew exactly what he could contribute to their teams. Stanford and several other universities were overly generous when recruiting him. Those schools didn't care if they broke the laws governing athletic competition. They were hot-beds of social-istic thought, so they made a quid-pro-quo deal with the government. Turn a blind eye to our athletic programs and we'll support everything the government creates.

Regardless of his athletic prowess, he accepted the fact that Swiss women may favor the physique of European men. Their lower butts and less muscled upper body might be appealing to these women. It was possible that his body build was too different or odd for Swiss women.

His last thought on this subject was that his name might also prompt women to think of his Negroid ancestry. European women were generally well educated, but were they savvy enough to know that Sweats was a slave name? That its roots were from cotton fields of early America and the sugar cane fields of the Caribbean islands during the 17th to 19th centuries? How many European men were named Rodolfo and had a last name which described a body secretion? Well, it didn't matter. It was a little late in life to petition the central government for a name change. Besides, they wouldn't allow such a thing for a frivolous reason like finding a girlfriend. His nickname of Rollie would be as close to a non-slave name as he was going to get.

The walk from his office to the Schwarzenbach Tavern was about a mile-and-a-half and took less than fifteen minutes. He could have taken public transportation, but he needed the exercise and fresh air. An early evening stroll along the Limmatquai Promenade, which hugged the east and west sides of the Limmat River, was refreshing and made him feel alive. Although he was jealous of the hundreds of people dining together on the outdoor patios, it helped to minimize his own personal problems. If these people could develop relationships, then he should be able to do so.

When he arrived at the Schwarzenbach Tavern the crowd was light compared to most weekday nights. He scanned the crowd hoping to see someone he knew so he wouldn't have to dine by himself.

He was still searching the crowd when the hostess approached and asked in labored English with a heavy German accent, "Good evening sir. May I show you to a table?"

Rollie thought about leaving the tavern but the idea of spending another night alone was too depressing. He needed to stay at the tavern to postpone the loneliness which awaited him at his apartment. It didn't matter that all the faces in the tavern were unfamiliar. Just having other people around was enough to make him feel like an important part of humanity.

"Yes, I'll take a table for two, please." There was no one scheduled to join him but telling the hostess a small white lie made him feel better and self-confident.

Rollie ordered a traditional Swiss entree and lager beer from the menu. He spotted the local Beobachter newspaper on a nearby empty table and started to thumb through it to pass the time. It was printed in German which he knew enough to figure out the main topic of each article. The Beobachter was one of only three newspapers left in the world which printed paper and electronic versions. Rodolfo liked reading paper newspapers. There was something comforting and controlling about holding it and manipulating the pages any way you wanted.

After a few minutes, he put the paper down and looked up. He felt eyes watching him. He looked across the tavern to confirm his intuition or cast it aside as a minor form of paranoia.

At first, he didn't see her even though her staring could not have been more obvious. He might have been expecting a man's gaze but not a woman's. For whatever reason, it took about a minute before their eyes locked.

Her gaze was so intense that he felt violated. He looked down again at the newspaper to break the contact. He wasn't reading the newspaper; he was wondering if he knew this woman and if she was really looking at him. He looked behind his table for anyone else who might be the object of this woman's attention. The only people seated behind him were two elderly women getting drunk on cocktails and chatting about the latest gossip.

His curiosity and confidence returned so he looked across the tavern toward this woman. He found her staring again directly into his eyes. This time she gave him a thin smirk. Otherwise, she did nothing to change her stare even though there were two women at the table trying, in earnest, to get her attention. He could almost read her thoughts. She had no desire to be with these two women and whatever they were talking about held no interest for her.

He wondered what to do. Should he walk over, introduce himself and save her from the two chatterboxes accosting her? Or should he sit tight and let her make the first move? As he pondered this question another observation caught his eye. This woman was dressed entirely in black. She wore a tight, tailored dress with black high heels which he could barely see below the table. The string of beads or stones around her neck were also black as coal. And the purse lying on the table in front of her was shiny black patent leather.

A black outfit was understandable on a dreary winter night, but worn on a summer's evening was unusual. Warmer temperatures normally brought out colorful clothes worn by men and women. Regardless, Rollie found the all-black outfit very sexy. It was the perfect match to highlight her rich black hair which flowed in curls past her shoulders. The final piece was her dark eyes which appeared to be ebony from across the restaurant.

This woman's continuous visual fixation was alluring and sexual. It made Rollie feel very self-conscious. So much so, he knew eating dinner with her eyes watching his every move would be impossible.

He got the impression that the other two women at her table would not allow any interruptions. They were so vested in holding the woman in black's attention that if he tried to interrupt, they would become hostile and tell him to shove off. They reminded him of two wolves who finally cornered their prey and wouldn't allow anything to interrupt their feeding frenzy. It was a no-win situation for him. If only the woman-in-black would take the lead and do something or give him a hint of what she wanted.

Nothing changed by the time his dinner arrived. He considered what he should do. There was a part of himself who wanted to stay and see what happened to the woman-in-black. And there was the other option of packing up and leaving. It was possible that he was misreading the situation, and going home to eat dinner was a wise decision. It might not be as interesting but at least he could eat without the intense scrutiny of a stranger's gaze.

"Waiter, I'm not feeling well. Can you put my dinner in something, so I can carry it home?"

The server transferred Rollie's dinner to an insulated

clamshell and then placed it inside of a medium-sized thermal bag. Rollie paid the bill, left a tip for the server and headed to the tavern's front door. He did all this without looking at the woman-in-black. But he couldn't help himself before taking the final steps into the night. He gazed one last time to the back of the tavern to where she was sitting.

She gave him a weak wave with her right hand and a modest smile. The other two women missed both signals and kept babbling like magpies.

Rollie ambled along the narrow side streets to his apartment. He couldn't stop thinking about the woman-in-black. Why was she looking at him? Did they know each other? Would they meet in the future? It would be some time before he knew the answers to these questions. For the moment, he reveled in the thought that he might be more attractive and desirable to the opposite sex than he believed at the beginning of the day.

CHAPTER THREE

SIX MONTHS LATER

"MR. EKSTROM, can you give us the latest results on the ReLife project?"

Rollie normally hated attending committee meetings devoted to updating new product development. They were boring and monotonous. It was aggravating listening to the snail's pace required to bring new products to market. But as Senior Vice President of this department, he needed to attend each update meeting. It didn't matter that 90% of the updates were not updates at all. Rather, they were excuse sessions for why projects fell behind schedule or came to a screeching halt. It was the 10% of updates with encouraging news to report which captured his interest.

But there was another consideration why he attended every product development meeting. Somehow, his boss, the CEO of the company always knew about each failure and success. There was no reason for Rollie to look like a fool simply because he missed the latest significant news.

The ReLife project was an exception to the rule. Rollie looked forward to each update meeting regardless of the latest reports. They were a welcome change of pace from the routine meetings about developing or improving drugs and devices to extend human life. Phoenvartis Corporation had a storehouse of drugs and devices in one phase or another of testing, development or approval. What it had only one of was the ReLife project which was a major leap forward in the recreation of human life. It was one step away from understanding how God and the universe worked.

Claude Ekstrom leaned forward in his chair, straightened his collar and glasses and then cleared his sinus cavities. The snorting sound he made through his nose was his trademark and object of repeated teasing. The snorting went on for two to three minutes. The other attendees either stared at him in disbelief or let their minds wander and daydream. A few who attended prior meetings with Ekstrom regarded this an unscheduled break. They walked around the conference room, poured themselves more coffee or ate a Swiss pastry.

Ekstrom's greased-back, golden hair reminded Rollie of the way men wore their hair over two hundred years before in old America and Europe. Old black and white movies were filled with actors wearing this hairstyle. Unfortunately, these movies were banned from viewing without special permission from the World Council.

As Ekstrom continued to snort his sinuses clear, Rollie couldn't help thinking about Dixie Peach. It was the sweet-smelling salve his grandfather used to grease back his hair. Besides making his hair smell like a summer meadow it shined like a patent leather shoe. It made his hair so rigid that even a hurricane wind could not move it. Rollie didn't know what Ekstrom used to get the same greased-back look but thought it would be fun to give him a small round, metal container of Dixie Peach. Of course, the gag wouldn't be complete unless he signed the gift, "from an unknown admirer". He dropped the idea because it would take forever to find a can of the salve. Just the thought of researching the central government's allocation network was exhausting. The network was supposed to make locating "hard to find" and frivolous items easy for citizens with a few extra world credits to spend. In reality, it was a royal pain in the ass. The network was hard to navigate and extremely outdated.

"Mr. Ekstrom, you can begin your report at any time." Rollie was hoping his slight jab would speed along the snorting routine but knew from experience he was fighting a losing battle.

Rollie wanted to fire Ekstrom years before. But there were two things which outweighed Ekstrom's annoying personality traits. First, he was incredibly smart. Rollie had no idea what his IQ was but it had to be far above any other employee at the corporation. Even more important than his brilliance was the fact he was the nephew of the CEO, Klaus Ekstrom. Rollie accepted years before that Claude was on his team until one of the Ekstroms died, retired or moved on to a different company.

Claude gave the final inhale snort which Rollie heard so many times before and began his presentation.

"Ladies and gentlemen, as you know, the ReLife project has been in development for several years. During the last two years, it has been my distinct honor and pleasure to lead this effort. We are on the brink of making a major breakthrough in medical advancement. This project will not only benefit mankind but thrust Phoenvartis Corporation to a position of leadership in ..."

Ekstrom's opening statement was so self-serving and grandiose Rollie couldn't take it. He was ready to interrupt for the sake of everyone's sanity. But before he could say anything, another senior vice president, Helmer Stanke, spoke up. "Claude, can you please get to the update information and statistics? Everyone here has very busy schedules today. We need to hear the key facts of your report before heading off to other meetings."

Rollie considered Stanke the best executive in the company. He was smart and hated corporate politics. He excelled at cutting through all the bullshit and getting to the point in record time. His direct manner put off quite a few of his peers. For Rollie, it was a refreshing change of pace in a company where politics was, at times, more important than producing ideas and products.

Stanke and Claude were well-established foes. Stanke took every opportunity he could to irritate Claude. The well-aimed barbs, like the one he shot across the room at Claude, always got under his skin.

Claude was annoyed with Stanke's interruption and gave him an "I'll remember this" look. Even though Stanke was number one on Claude's "shit list," the interruption did push him along to bypass the self-serving opening statement. He launched into the vital facts about the ReLife project.

"Rollie, and esteemed colleagues. My team has taken a major step forward in the ReLife project. I am pleased to announce that this week we recreated an entire field mouse from a severed foot of a deceased mouse. It appears that we have brought a version, or should I say, brought a cloned version of a dead mouse back to life."

Claude stopped to let his information soak in with the other attendees. He knew this breakthrough would vault him into the annals of medical history and probably put him in line for a major promotion. Dead silence now gripped the meeting. It was the same reaction he got two hours earlier when he told his uncle, the CEO of Phoenvartis, the news about the cloned mouse. He had been warned about going behind Rollie's back, but in this case, he didn't care. This news was too earth-shattering and momentous to worry about corporate rules and politics.

After the initial shock, Rollie immediately thought of his boss. Claude must have run to him already with the news about the successful cloning. It must be killing him to wait until Claude delivered his presentation to the ReLife committee. Otherwise, there was no other way to protect Claude, the snitch. He would have to control his reactionary personality a few more minutes. Then he could call the executive committee together to discuss the next step in the cloning project.

Rollie also knew his boss would want to bypass prescribed scientific methodology. He would demand going to the ultimate goal of the ReLife project which was creating a cloned human from a corpse fragment.

Before anyone in the room could ask a question or make a comment, Claude continued with his presentation. "From what I can tell, the cloned mouse is physically and mentally sound. Granted, it's been only a week, but all tests on the mouse have netted positive results. What we don't know is if the cloned mouse possesses the memories of the donor mouse or will develop its own memories during its life cycle. Then again, it might be a combination of both. I guess we won't know that until...."

"Claude, how long did the cloning process take and did you record it?"

Ekstrom hated interruptions but showed Rollie the respect of his position and answered. "The entire process didn't take long. Once the severed foot from the donor mouse was put into the CR47 incubator capsule the regeneration process started immediately. It took about an hour before the new mouse was born, so to speak. By the way, we named the mouse Eden, as taken from the fictional Biblical story of Adam and Eve. And yes, the entire regeneration process was recorded so each of you can watch it."

"I think we would like to watch the recording now, Claude. All of us can clear our calendars to watch this incredible break-through."

"Rollie, I'd love to show the recording to everyone now, but I've got a very important doctor's appointment which I can't miss. Can we do the showing tomorrow?"

Rollie put an artificial, concerned look on his face and responded. "Well, I guess you don't have to be here for the video showing, Claude. I can go up and get the recording out of the CR47 and play it for the group. And you can go to your doctor's appointment."

Rollie started to get up from his chair knowing Claude was formulating another lie to cover his first lie.

"Sir, I'd really like to be here for the group showing. I can add a lot to the video presentation and answer the questions which come up. I don't think the people in this room will understand exactly what is happening as they see each phase of the regeneration process. Again, can we play the recording tomorrow?"

Rollie wanted to call Claude out as a liar and discipline him in front of the entire group. The CR47 recording wasn't in its locked housing as it should be. It was in Klaus's office, exactly where Claude took it when he realized the regeneration process was successful. Claude couldn't admit the recording was with his uncle. It would be an admission that he went around the chain of command again which would result in disciplinary action.

Rollie made the snap decision to let Claude off the hook. Rather than be petty it was far better to let Claude have his ten minutes of glory. He could then wait to expose him for a sneaky little rat sometime in the future. And Rollie knew exactly how he was going to trap the rat.

"Okay, Claude, we'll have the recording review tomorrow. I'll have my assistant set up the meeting." Rollie looked at the meeting attendees and asked, "Tomorrow might be a better time to ask questions, but are there any which have to be answered today?"

None of the other four people in the room raised any questions. All of them congratulated Claude on his achievement as they left the room.

As an afterthought, Rollie added, "Okay, people, see you tomorrow. And please remember this is top secret. We have a chance to bring to the world the next great medical advancement since the cure for cancer. So let's keep our mouths shut until we know for certain if the process works."

Rollie left the room a minute or so behind Ekstrom on purpose. He wanted to see which way Claude headed. Would he go in the direction of his own office, out the door to the fictitious doctor's appointment or scamper back to his uncle's office?

It was almost comical watching Claude leave the building. The first thing he did was make a call through the government's Universal Communications Network (UCN). He didn't have to enter a number into a communications device. All he did was speak in a normal tone into a tiny micromic embedded into his clothing.

The micromics were unique to each citizen. They allowed each user to connect with any other citizen by simply stating that person's name or identity number. When the connection was made, the parties could talk to each other. If they wanted to see each other they chose the visual feature. This feature used a person's peripheral vision without blocking his forward vision. Somehow, it fooled the brain into believing that the other person's face was directly ahead when in fact it was offset to the corner of the eye. This split-screen effect allowed each person on the call to do something else without being hindered by the other person's image. It was common to see people driving a hovercraft or playing a sport while they communicated on a micromic.

The UCN was an incredible communications system developed a decade earlier by a corporation in Zone 3. It was also an incredibly efficient system to track the movement of every human on the planet Earth and the three colony planets. And the World Council did exactly that. If a citizen wore a piece of government issued, free clothing he was tracked regardless of when and where he went. If he wore non-issued government clothing, the injected kidney microdevice tracked his movements.

Monitoring citizens through the UCN plus the health injection program kept close tabs on nearly everyone. It also identified radicals and dissidents before they had a chance to be a disruptive force on society.

Wearing non-issued government clothing without embedded micromics was tolerated but not encouraged. Very few people outside the zones were wealthy enough to buy more than one set of non-mic clothes on the black market. Wearing "scrubbed" clothes was frowned upon by the government. It made those people stand out from his fellow citizens and appear to be special. It didn't matter that scrubbed clothes were better made and more attractive. What mattered was that no one citizen appeared to be superior to his fellow citizens.

Violations of the Standards of Living Codes could result in a penalty phase lasting up to two years. Wearing non-issued government clothing often or exceeding travel restrictions were considered violations. During a penalty period, the violator did not receive his full monthly allotment of world credits. This forced him to come up with other ways to get food, shelter, and the necessities of life. Many violators died during a penalty term, especially if they couldn't find a friend willing to share food and shelter.

A medical emergency during the penalty phase was a death sentence. Hospitals were barred from treating patients who were serving time for violation of the Living Codes. It was not unusual for many of the hospitals in larger cities to find human corpses outside their entrance doors each morning.

Rollie owned quite a few scrubbed items of clothing but didn't think much about where and when to wear them. He didn't buy them to avoid the government's tracking system but rather for his own vanity. Scrubbed clothes were always more fashionable than clothes with embedded micromics.

Rollie watched Claude from a third-floor window close to his office. The corporate office had environment windows which produced radiant heat in the winter and cooling during warm days. This environmental feature made the windows one-way and prohibited anyone from seeing into the office building.

For being such a brilliant scientist, Rollie couldn't get over how mentally clumsy Claude was in his normal life. As he watched Claude below, he couldn't help wondering why the fool didn't walk another fifty feet and duck behind another building. At least he would be out of sight from prying eyes at the Phoenvartis building.

Claude was talking wildly to whoever he had connected with on the UCN system. Rollie didn't know for sure but he suspected that the other person was his uncle, Klaus Ekstrom.

He could just imagine their conversation about the cloned mouse. He was sure Claude was also whining about almost being caught in a lie about the CR47 visual recording. He knew Klaus wouldn't have one bit of sympathy and wouldn't offer to help Claude if he got caught lying about the recording.

Rollie was sure Klaus couldn't stand his brother's kid. The only reason he befriended him was to have another pawn and informant.

Claude headed back to the corporate office building forgetting he should be walking the other direction toward a fictitious doctor's office. Rollie could see he was no longer talking into his UCN system. If the person on the other end of Claude's call was his uncle, then Rollie could expect a call from the boss within the next couple of minutes.

Almost as soon as this thought left his mind, Rollie's shirt micromic hummed, indicating he had an incoming communication. God, he hated the humming sound. For some reason, it irritated the hell out of him. His grandmother once said that it reminded her of scratching fingernails on a chalk blackboard. He agreed with her even though he didn't know what a blackboard was. He made a vow to find a way to change the activation sound of his micromic units.

"Rollie, Klaus here. What are you doing?"

"Hello, Mr. Ekstrom. I'm reviewing some communiques in my office and ..."

That's all Klaus needed to hear before interrupting with, "Rollie, I need you up here in the next ten minutes. We have some important topics to cover."

Rollie took advantage of the situation and had some fun by asking, "Anything in particular, sir?"

"No, I mean, yes. I'll explain when you get here. See you in ten."

Rollie slipped into his office to look at messages. He asked his assistant to complete a couple of tasks which he knew would be critical to the ReLife program. He could foresee where the project was headed. He might as well be out front of the illogical and outrageous demands his boss would soon be asking for and expecting.

As they discussed the assignments for the rest of the day, Rollie looked up just in time to see a woman walk by his office windows. The tight-fitting blouse and skirt caught his eye first. But when she turned and smiled at him, her piercing eyes grabbed his attention enough to make him stop talking in mid-sentence to his assistant.

"Who was that, Ingrid?"

"Oh, that's the new girl who took over the Archives Department. She's only been here a week or so. I ate lunch with her the other day. She's very nice."

Rollie didn't respond or go on to explain the assignments. He stood there thinking about the woman who walked by his office at a rather hurried pace.

Ingrid took the silence as an opportunity to poke a little fun at her boss. "Why do you ask? Do you think she's attractive?"

The tongue-in-cheek questions broke his concentration enough, so he looked again at Ingrid and responded.

"I know that woman from somewhere. I've seen those eyes before."

CHAPTER FOUR

THE BERLIN CELL

"I BELIEVE we finally have the answer to our leadership problem and how to move our plans forward."

Krieger was the unofficial spokesman for the Tiger Cell of the Black Cross movement. In his mid-thirties, he was older than the other cell members and a veteran of various terrorist campaigns throughout the world. His initial terrorist training started at age 16. He joined the Chin Flay Liberation Front to fight against the central government in Mongolia. From there he moved on to the Andes Mountains to join and fight with several right-wing rebel groups. In twenty years as an insurgent and rebel, the cause always remained the same no matter where he was in the world. Overthrow puppet governments put in place by the World Council.

German-born, Krieger tried to project an upbeat attitude toward the Black Cross movement. This was important to keep the younger members in line, prevent desertions and promote the recruitment of new members. It also played a significant role in attracting world credits from people who hated the World Council anarchy. These donors wanted change but weren't willing to get their hands dirty by fighting in an armed conflict against the Council's forces.

What Krieger kept hidden was that he was getting tired of being a target. He had enough of being shot at, wounded and living like a frightened puppy. Always looking over his shoulder and waiting to be sold out or discovered by a World Council employee or snitch wasn't much of a life. He was getting too old for this crap and knew he was on borrowed time. Every other terrorist he befriended through the years was dead. They were either killed in conflict or blacklisted from the world credits program and succumbed to starvation or disease.

He promised himself that this would be his last campaign. If it failed, he would do something else regardless of how insignificant it might be. He might end up washing floors or dishes or some other menial task in the underground economy because he had no legitimate resume. Plus, there wasn't a big demand for has-been terrorists.

The thought of living his remaining years as a flunky was repulsive, especially when he thought of the opportunity he wasted nineteen years earlier. His father, a wealthy executive in Zone 4, somehow bypassed the annual lottery and got Krieger a zone position. Being an over-energetic idealist at the time, Krieger rejected the offer and went on to become a full-time terrorist. In his opinion, accepting the zone position would be a silent vote for the World Council. At the time, it seemed like a perfectly sound decision to turn down the position. But now he looked back and mentally kicked himself in the ass for being so stupid.

Of course, the old man disowned Krieger. He would never get another opportunity to live in a quasi-capitalistic society. His chance at the "good life" evaporated into thin air like a wisp of smoke from his Cudis assault rifle.

"What do you mean, Krieger? What's going on?" The questions came from an attractive young lady who joined the Tiger Cell less than three months earlier.

"I don't know all the details yet, but we are being fed information about a Swiss company that has perfected human cloning. Our unknown source claims to have first-hand knowledge. Supposedly, a cloned human might be produced from a small cell sample taken from a corpse." Krieger purposely gave the group a vague explanation, so they thought the leak at the Swiss biotech company was communicating with someone higher up in the Black Cross organization. For his own safety, he thought it best that no one in the Tiger Cell know he was the contact person for the leak.

The group of twelve Tiger members sat silent for a couple of minutes digesting what Krieger said. Some of them pretended to understand the consequences of such a technology break-through. In reality, all of them were still confused by Krieger's announcement. What difference could artificial beings have to the Black Cross and its goal of bringing down the World Council?

"Krieger, I may be a dunce but what does this development have to do with our cause?"

"You're not a dunce, Trish." It was the same young lady who spoke up earlier.

"You just need time to think of what this innovative technology could mean to us. I've spent the last couple of days thinking about what we could do with this technology. The more I thought about it, the more possibilities I came up with. For example, what if our fallen comrades never die? We take their bodies and bring them back to fight again. Think of how your entire life as a Tiger would change. Instead of always be overly cautious, you could fight with reckless abandon knowing you couldn't die."

"That's pretty cool, Krieger, but do we know if the artificial clones would have the same dedication to our cause and want to fight? Do the replicants always come back with the same memories, ideas, and beliefs? Or do they come back as an empty slate which needs to be filled with new experiences and values? In other words, do they have to learn how to be human all over again?"

These insightful questions came from Ivan, the Croatian freedom fighter. He had the second longest tenure in the Tiger Cell behind Krieger.

"Great questions, Ivan. Unfortunately, no one knows the answers yet. From what we know so far, the Swiss company has only brought back one animal. They have yet to attempt human cloning. Until a human replicant is produced no one will know the answer to your questions. So in the meantime, we need to go about our business and wait to see if this technology is real and what value it has to our cause."

"How long is that going to take, Krieger?"

"I'm sorry Ivan, I don't have that information. Our contact in the Swiss company is being very cautious with the frequency and amount of information she releases."

"So our contact is a woman? Why is she feeding us information?"

"Trish, the contact is a woman, but I don't know why she is cooperating with us. I'm sure someone knows why, but I don't. She obviously has some sympathy for our cause or knows..." Krieger stopped, realizing his rambling wasn't based on facts but rather speculation on his part.

"Guys, the bottom line is that I don't know why she is giving us this information."

The group stopped asking questions when they realized Krieger couldn't offer any more information. They broke into smaller groups to socialize and kick around wild guesses and theories about interacting with clones.

As Krieger meandered from one group to another, he was pleasantly surprised by what he heard. There were great ideas raised on how this technology might be used by Black Cross and the Tiger cell to achieve their ultimate goals. He had no idea some of the cell's members were so creative.

One comment he overheard was that clones would be reborn without the micro-monitoring device lodged in their kidneys. It was such an obvious thought. So obvious that he overlooked it during the last couple of days as he thought through the ramifications of having access to a CR47 machine. What a wonderful alternative to having the microdevice surgically removed from the kidney. He still could see the scar from having this surgery done years before.

But he was more amazed that not one word was mentioned about using this technology to bring back leaders from history. The one thing most terrorist's groups lacked was strong leadership from a dynamic, intelligent individual who could plan and motivate the membership to a point of frenzied loyalty. A mediocre leader always led movements to destruction. A strong leader created fanatics who followed him blindly as though they were following a god. That's exactly what the Black Cross needed to overthrow the World Council; a human god.

CHAPTER FIVE

MACON, GEORGIA

IN A LOW RASPY VOICE, the old black woman spoke from the bed she was tethered to for over two months. "Georgie, why do you always have to argue with me? Can't you just once do what I ask?"

Grandma LeeLee's death bed request wasn't difficult. It would take about thirty minutes to do. All he had to do was wrap a small maple wood box in a protective shipping container, take it to a nearby transport station and send it to the Swiss Zone. It was a reasonable request from his dying grandmother except for one thing. He had to ship the box to his younger brother, Rodolfo, who he considered a traitor to the Sweats family and World Council.

M.C. Sweats, also known as Georgie to his 112-year-old great-grandmother, didn't want anything to do with his brother, Rodolfo. As far as he was concerned, Rodolfo died the day he left the family and moved to the Swiss Zone of Cooperative Thought. It didn't matter that Rodolfo sent hundreds of world credits to the Sweats family each month. He went out of his way to help them live a little bit better than most other families.

And it didn't matter that he also sent gifts to each member of the Sweats family. He never missed their birthdays or year-end commemoration of World Unification Week.

M.C. knew the year-end presents were really meant to celebrate the outlawed religious holiday known as Christmas. For the other members of the Sweats clan, it didn't matter one iota what the presents commemorated or celebrated. They loved receiving new clothes, toys, gadgets, appliances, and food-stuffs from Rodolfo. Everything they received kept them a step above poverty level. To them, Rodolfo was more benevolent and understanding than the central government which provided just enough to maintain a subservient existence. Rodolfo was a hero to all the Sweats except M.C. and a few distant uncles.

It burned M.C.'s ass that his brother enjoyed such respect and appreciation. Who ran off to live a life of privilege in a free zone? And, who stayed behind to confront the daily problems of the Sweats family? It was easy sending gifts from the other side of the world. But, the real sacrifice was taking care of and watching every step taken by a group of under-educated, naive people like the Sweats.

When Rodolfo's gifts arrived, the real challenge began for M.C. Each time he had to warn the family members not to flaunt their new gifts around town. Otherwise, they risked drawing the attention of government agents. The last thing the family needed was government scrutiny. M.C. had to make sure none of the Sweats appeared to have a better life than anyone else. It was important that everyone looked equally poor.

The gifts from the zone were easy to spot due to their quality. But when the Sweats bragged about their gifts it made things dicier. M.C. knew it was a matter of time before someone in the family was tagged for violating the Standard of

Living Codes. That person would most likely lose their allocation of world credits. Then, undue hardship would be placed on the remaining family members trying to keep the violator fed, housed and alive.

Each time a transport agent arrived at the Sweats family home with a load of packages, M.C. wanted to write "no such person—no forwarding address" on the boxes. He'd love to see Rollie's face when they were returned. But he had yet to develop enough inner strength and courage to do this. He knew he would get caught and that would lead to more family turmoil than accepting the gifts. Until he thought of a way to deal with this delicate situation, he would let his hatred boil over each time the gifts arrived or heard the name, Rollie.

M.C.'s thoughts about his brother were interrupted by LeeLee's wheezing and labored breathing. He didn't want to be at her bedside when she died but it looked more and more likely that was going to happen. Even though they argued often, he loved the old woman who was more of a parent to him than his own mother.

For M.C., it was much easier watching an acquaintance or stranger die than someone he was emotionally bonded to. In fact, there was so much death occurring in the Macon area he became detached and callous to it. Malnutrition and inadequate medical health services resulted in alarming death rates. He ignored the problem and only spoke about the dead when he was drugging it up with his buddies and they needed something to laugh about.

"Georgie, are you going to do what I ask, or do I have to send the Haints after you?"

"Grandma, I'll send the box to Rodolfo. Just for you, my dear, just for you." M.C. took her hand and stroked it gently hoping to ease the pain and open the door a little wider for her departure. After all, living to over a hundred was almost unheard of. Rationed food and few medical supplies and equipment had reduced the average life expectancy by 15 years compared to rates before the FISS plague.

She had lived a good life and it was now time to join her relatives in the afterlife if there was one. Besides, extending her life by using rationed drugs and technology was denying a young person of those lifesaving items. M.C. understood this philosophy but had difficulty explaining it to the rest of the family. They couldn't understand or agree with M.C.'s explanation of why Grandma's hastened departure would benefit the rest of society.

As he sat at her bedside watching her soul slip away, M.C. couldn't help thinking back to their time together. Each laugh, argument and silent moment they shared raced through his mind. He almost laughed out loud when he thought about LeeLee's threat to send the Haints after him.

He had been hearing about the Haints for as long as he could remember. She used them to scare kids, and sometimes adults, into doing things they didn't want to do. Grandma described Haints as departed souls who hung around Earth because they were having difficulty taking the last step into the spirit world. Having nothing better to do, the Haints made life miserable for anyone who was difficult or naughty by Grandma's standards. This was especially true of kids, who refused to do their chores or go to bed at night.

Grandma LeeLee started every Haints story the same. "This is the way your great-great-great-grandfather told the story. Ya all know he was a slave on a cotton plantation in Mississippi." She then launched into a detailed Haints story which took at least twenty minutes to tell. By the conclusion, the younger children were frightened out of their wits. The older kids begged to leave and get back to the important job of horsing around. Clever Grandma LeeLee kept them at her side until they agreed to do whatever chore she assigned.

Grandma's description and stories about the Haints were endless. M.C. couldn't ever remember hearing the same story twice. For him, her stories were entertaining, but he never considered the Haints as scary as real ghosts. What scared the hell out of him though was Grandma's LeeLee's belief in the existence of the Haints. She shuddered when she spoke about them and the look in her eyes was as convincing as the sky was blue.

At age 40, M.C. was agnostic toward the existence of Haints. He could argue all he wanted about the Haints being lies or fables. Grandma LeeLee always came right back with five reasons from Haints folklore proving they were real. After years of arguing he gave up and declared them a possibility.

At two o'clock in the morning M.C.'s mother, Frontane Sweats, took over sitting at Grandma's death bedside. M.C. crawled into bed to get a few hours of sleep before heading to the government distribution center where he was an allocation specialist. The four to five hours per day he spent at the distribution center were a great diversion from his boring life. It was so rewarding and fulfilling he wished he could contribute more hours per week to his post which was the socialist version of a job. But the government had strict rules about the number of hours each citizen could contribute. A mere 20 hours a week was all it took to maintain a person's *value to society* status. The last thing M.C. wanted to do was violate the government work code and blemish his perfect record.

After leaving the distribution center, M.C. headed to the transport station to send Grandma's box to Rollie. If Grandma LeeLee was still alive by the time he got home, he didn't want to face her cross-examination about whether he sent the box.

Before wrapping the box, he couldn't resist looking inside.

He wanted to see what was so damn important that it must be sent to the Swiss Zone at an outrageous expense to the Sweats family. As he suspected, there wasn't anything important inside the box. In fact, it was empty except for a brief note from Grandma LeeLee which read: **Rodolfo: what I promised you long ago. I've received word from Him that you need this now. Remember what I told you. The obvious isn't always obvious. Love Grandma.**

He was sure this woman was going to drive him crazy before she left this world. He knew she had strong religious beliefs but now she was communicating directly with God, the made-up Creator and Lord of the Universe. Who else could she be referring to when she used the word, Him? At least he got a little bit of humor out of this. He could see her in his cartoon bubble talking on a micromic communicator to the heavens or wherever God called home.

And, what was the comment, "the obvious isn't always obvious" supposed to mean? It wasn't enough that she spoke to the Creator of Man, she also used code language to talk with her favorite grandson. M.C. laughed to himself thinking about his brother reading this sentence. He could see Rollie scratching his head in Zurich trying to decode and figure out its meaning.

M.C. was tempted to toss the box in the trash, go home and lie to Grandma about having sent it to the Swiss Zone. As much as he wanted to do this, he knew he couldn't look her straight in the eyes and claim to have followed her instructions. Even with poor vision, she would feel his deceit. Somehow, she always knew when a kid was lying to her.

After the moment of reconsideration, M.C. wrapped the box, paid the transport fee and sent it on its way. He could now quit being irritated by the entire ordeal and face his grandmother with a clear conscious.

When he got home, he was surprised to find nearly all the

Sweats family members gathered throughout the dining and living rooms. At first, he took this mob of relatives to mean that Grandma LeeLee had passed away. But the jubilation, joking, and upbeat conversations indicated the opposite. Grandma LeeLee had not died but rather made a miraculous recovery. She was sitting in a recliner chair surrounded by a dozen or more of her descendants, relatives, and neighbors.

M.C. made his way through the crowd and got close to the recliner. He arrived just in time to hear LeeLee say, "Kids, God has given me a new lease on life. He came to me last night and said I had a few things left to do before joining him up above. So, I'll be staying right here pestering each of you as I have..."

That was all M.C. could remember from Grandmother's announcement that she was far from death's door. He was shocked by how good she looked and the energy she displayed at her *not-going-away* party. He was happy she recovered but there was something very odd about this turn of events. He could feel it in his gut; something just wasn't right. A few short hours before she was gasping for air and her body temperature was dropping like a rock. Now, she looked twenty years younger. How could such a radical recovery and change take place? It wasn't natural and defied the precepts of medicine. There had to be a logical explanation other than God told her she had more work to do on Earth. M.C. refused to believe that drivel. But, all the "Praise be God" and similar religious remarks indicated that those around her chair were more convinced than ever in the existence of a loving Creator.

"M.C. M.C. Boy, you come over here and give your Grandma a big hug."

His thoughts about his grandmother's remarkable recovery vanished. He put a big smile on his face and trotted over to hug and sit by her.

"Grandma, you look great. How do you feel? I can't believe how good you look. Did the doctor give you something ...?"

"M.C. calm down. I feel great and no one on Earth doctored me. My medicine came from above. I've told you all the time to trust in the Lord. And, if you do that, everything will turn out okay."

"Well, Grandma, I'm not sure how you made such a great recovery but I'm glad you did."

LeeLee gave one of her raspy chuckles, kissed M.C. on the cheek and added, "By the way M.C., thanks for mailing the box to Rodolfo. He needs that box bad. The next couple of years are going to be so exciting and he's going to be right in the middle of it. In fact, you will be too."

Thank God, he chose to send the box. If Grandma was going to be around for a while, as it now appeared, then he made the right choice. But what the hell did she mean by the next couple of years were going to be exciting and the Sweats brothers were going to be in the middle of things? Was this another secret communique from her God or did she have a screw loose and think she could foretell the future? M.C. had no idea what to think. If there was a God, then He was probably the only One who knew for sure.

For the next hour, M.C. sat at her side, welcoming, shaking hands and making small talk with the Sweats family members. He was pleased to see the number of neighbors who showed up for the festivities and free food. As the custom, they had brought the food and beverages to the celebration. At least he wouldn't have to foot the bill for feeding the entire crowd.

Finally, he excused himself to go to the buffet-style food table. All this celebration made him hungry and he was a soft touch for the home-cooked dishes made by the women in the neighborhood.

As M.C. stood behind the food table eating a little bit of

every dish, he scanned the room. He wasn't looking for anyone in particular but rather taking inventory of the guests.

For the first time in his life, he realized something that was so obvious it had slid by his conscious mind for decades. He stopped eating and stared at his grandmother and the relatives standing and sitting around her.

Grandma LeeLee looked a lot like his younger brother, Rodolfo. She had the same light complexion and chiseled nose and lips. The only prominent Negroid feature was the tightly wound hair on her head. He guessed that if he could find a picture of LeeLee from eighty years before the two of them would appear to be brother and sister.

He had never seen or paid attention to this resemblance in the past. It was probably the darker-skin Sweats now standing around her who highlighted the differences. Most Sweats had medium or very dark skin with broad noses and lips. Even the color of their hair was several shades darker than the color of LeeLee's and Rodolfo's hair.

He wondered if anyone else in the family had noticed these differences. He was reluctant to say anything about this to any family member. There was no sense creating another family dispute. But he decided to do a little snooping and try to figure out how this happened. Was it due to normal breeding and genetics or reflect something more secretive or sinister?

CHAPTER SIX

COMPANY AND CAREERS ON THE LINE

"GOOD AFTERNOON, Helga. You're looking stunning as usual."

Klaus Ekstrom's middle-aged assistant blushed and gave a faint school girl snicker in response to Rollie's pointed and exaggerated compliment. He loved watching her turn from the CEO's stern sentry to a radiant wallflower each time he praised her appearance in one way or another. It didn't get him any special treatment from Helga, but it did brighten his day a bit seeing the joy he added to her life.

"Oh Mr. Sweats, you say the nicest things. I bet your mother taught you how to be such a gentleman."

"It was my grandmother, Helga. She spent a lot of time making sure the girls in our family acted like ladies and the boys knew how to treat them properly. For Grandma, there was no such thing as equality among the sexes. Boys learned how to become men and girls learned how to become ladies. And each sex had their own rules and values which were not shared with the other sex."

"That's quite an interesting take on child rearing, Mr.

Sweats. You and Helga can continue your conversation some other time." Klaus Ekstrom turned and walked back into his office after eavesdropping on their conversation. Rollie looked at Helga and gave her an exasperated smile before following his boss.

Of the three chairs in front of Klaus's desk, Rollie sat in the one to the right. He learned from experience that Klaus spent a great deal of time looking to his right as he thought about what to say to guests in his office. Not being in his direct line of sight was a break from the pointed and confrontational discussions with Klaus.

Seven years earlier, when Klaus was selected the new CEO, it took Rollie two meetings to understand his management style. It was a dictator rather than a benevolent and concerned leader. There was no horse-play, laughing or screwing around in Klaus's world. He was direct, to the point and expected results. Failure was not a word in Klaus's vocabulary.

During his first month as CEO, one-half of the upper Phoenvartis management staff looked for new careers. Most were let go after they were unable to write a convincing one-page memorandum explaining why they shouldn't be fired. Rollie could still remember when he got this assignment. After two days of worrying about what to write, Rollie knew there was no right answer. So, he decided to be blunt and as honest as possible. He wrote in big bold letters across the letter-size paper, **MR. EKSTROM: YOU SHOULDN'T FIRE ME BECAUSE I'M DAMN GOOD AT WHAT I DO. I DON'T ACCEPT A CHALLENGE UNLESS I PLAN TO BE THE BEST AT IT. IF I CAN'T BE THE BEST, THEN I WON'T TAKE THE ASSIGNMENT.**

AND, I LIKE TO WORK; ALWAYS HAVE AND ALWAYS WILL. Signed ROLLIE SWEATS.

Rollie was packing the personal belongings in his office when he received an unexpected incoming call on his UCN. It was from Klaus Ekstrom and was short and to the point. "Mr. Sweats, welcome to my team. Please contact my assistant, Helga, to arrange our first meeting. Be prepared to explain your current projects with a detailed timing and action. Also, I will want to know what we can do here at Phoenvartis to make the company more successful."

Rollie was relieved to survive the first reduction in management positions but knew this wasn't going to be the last. There was no such thing as having a safe and tenured position in a Klaus Ekstrom regime. Your performance was constantly under examination and evaluation. At any time, the boss could let you go because he decided you weren't of enough value to the company.

That day, six years earlier, Rollie decided to play by Klaus's rules and see what the future held at Phoenvartis. Since then, he was satisfied with his decision to stay at Phoenvartis and work for King Klaus, the unofficial nickname many people at the company called Ekstrom. After all, how many people had the chance to take part in medical breakthroughs like the replication of life?

"Well, Mr. Sweats, it appears that your idea from a couple of years ago has finally paid off. Congratulations. Now, what do you see as the next step in this project?"

It was true that Rollie had suggested looking at the possibility of creating life by cloning. But, if the truth be known, he never expected it to become a reality. When he brought it up as a possible project, he considered it a creative way to keep his job. If the boss bought the idea, he was guaranteed at least a couple of years of further employment. The years had raced by.

Now, he faced the bigger problem of where to take the replicant life project. The successful cloning of a simple creature had changed his life. And, most likely, the future of the world.

"Mr. Ekstrom, I haven't had a chance to think through how this project should proceed. It was only an hour or two ago when I heard about the recent developments from your nephew, Claude. In fact, I still have yet to see the recording of the first cloning."

"Rollie, you've had over four years to lay out a Timing and Action for this project. There shouldn't be any doubt in your mind what the next steps should be in this project. And, as far as the recording goes, I think you'll like..." Klaus Ekstrom caught himself before incriminating his nephew's deceit with the recording.

"Never mind about the recording. It's not that important. Here's what I want, Rollie. By 8 a.m. tomorrow morning, I want on my desk a detailed T & A for the cloning project. I want to know what direction we'll be taking and how fast. The executive committee expects big things from this project so let's not disappoint them. Any questions?"

"No, I don't think so. I have a pretty good understanding of what you want."

Rollie stood up to leave. He started to reach out to shake Klaus's hand but withdrew it after seeing that his boss was already thinking about other things. To him, Rollie was already gone from his office.

Rollie walked past Helga's desk and let out a muffled whistle. He replicated the whistle young, attractive ladies on the street get from construction workers. He smiled to himself as he walked away hearing Helga's girlish snicker again. He wished that he felt lighthearted like Helga but couldn't ever remember leaving Klaus's office in a positive mood. He always left feeling like the loser in a one-round cage match with a wrestling bear.

By the time he reached his office, he knew exactly how he was going to handle Klaus and give himself at least a 50% chance of surviving this debacle. Unfortunately, he needed Claude Ekstrom's cooperation to pull off his plan.

"Ingrid, please find that dweeb, Claude Ekstrom, and tell him to get up here immediately."

"Is it okay if I call him a dweeb, Mr. Sweats?"

Rollie smiled to himself. "Ingrid, after what he pulled today, I don't care what you call him."

Fifteen minutes later Claude crept softly into Rollie's office. He knew he was on the hot seat for going around Rollie's back. He had been warned about communicating directly with his uncle, Klaus.

Rollie waved Claude to a chair, shut the door to the office and sat down across from the dweeb. He stared at Claude for two to three minutes, not saying a word but rather snapping his pencil on the desktop. Each successive snap was louder and more forceful until the pencil finally broke in two.

"Claude, you and I have a problem, a big problem called SOA. Do you know what SOA stands for, Claude?" Rollie didn't give Claude a chance to answer the question. He didn't care what Claude thought it meant and he didn't want him to utter a word.

"SOA stands for Save Our Asses. Let me repeat Claude, it stands for Save Our Asses. Or, put another way, how can we develop the cloning project in a scientific manner without getting fired."

Rollie could tell from Claude's expression that he didn't have any idea what this lecture was about. He stood up and walked to the back of Claude's chair. Leaning forward, he balanced himself by resting his hands on the chair's back.

"Claude, I spent a half hour with your uncle talking about the cloning project. He told me that he saw the CR47 recording of the field mouse cloning. He said he got the recording from you. And he has already run to the executive committee to share the good news."

At the mention of his involvement in the disappearance of the CR47 recording, Claude swung around in his chair to face Rollie. He rambled on trying to explain away his disloyalty and deceit.

"Claude, shut up! Don't say a word and don't even think about trying to deny giving the recording to your uncle. He already sold you out, so don't make things worse than they are already." Rollie's lie was having the desired effect on Claude. His bottom lip started to quiver, and he frantically looked around the room to find something or someone to help him get out of this predicament.

"You and I both know that putting together one lousy little field mouse is light years away from what your uncle wants. He wants to clone humans. That's where the money is and that's what will make him the most renowned scientist-CEO in the world. And, he wants to start the human cloning immediately. Are you starting to see the problem yet, Claude?"

Again, Rollie went on without waiting for Claude to answer. "Let me make this really simple for you. If we start human cloning now, without following scientific procedures, there's a 99% chance the first human clone will be a vegetable or some unspeakable freak. Your uncle might be able to explain away the first failure to the executive committee but he sure as hell won't be able to explain why clones two, three and four are mutants. And when that happens, you and I are toast. In other words, when he goes down with the ship, we go too. And instead of honor and notoriety, we'll be lucky to have jobs sweeping floors."

Rollie walked back in front of Claude and sat on the front side of his desk. "Claude, do you understand the problem you've created by running to your uncle and shooting off that big mouth of yours?"

This time, Rollie waited for Claude to respond which was a simple nodding up and down of his head. He then started his well-known nasal snorting to clear his sinuses and airways. Rollie felt like grabbing him by the neck and slapping his sinus cavities clear.

When Claude calmed down and stopped snorting, Rollie continued. "Claude, we have a choice. We're going to decide right now whether to do exactly as your uncle wants or put together a game plan which might save the cloning project and our jobs. Which one should we do, Claude?"

It didn't take long for the dweeb to reach a decision. "God, I really screwed up, didn't I?"

"Claude, that's water under the bridge. There's nothing we can do about that now. Again, what do you think we should do?"

Claude pushed back the glasses on his nose and answered. "I think we better take the scientific approach and not rush into human cloning. Like you said, Rollie, the odds of perfecting human cloning right away are probably a thousand to one. But, how are we going to put off my uncle? He's going to be furious if we don't start human cloning right away. Especially now that he has oversold the idea to the executive committee and told them it's as easy as the mouse cloning."

As Rollie suspected, Claude confirmed what Klaus told the executive committee. He had convinced them that bringing the cloning project to market was going to be as easy as baking a pie. And, by doing so, he had jeopardized the image and reputation of the company. But worse, the fallout and rumors of a failed human cloning project would work their way up the food chain. It would stop with the ultimate government overlords—the World Council. And that would be the end of Phoenvartis,

Klaus and Claude Ekstrom and Rodolfo Sweats. Rollie had to tone down Klaus's unrealistic enthusiasm and goals. His boss needed to eat a plate of humble pie to save the project, company and everyone's careers.

"Claude, it's better that Klaus gets really pissed off now rather than drag out one disappointment after another. In other words, we are going to hit him with every disaster I can think of in the next few days. And the first thing will be the death of the cloned field mouse."

"Rollie, I just checked on the field mouse. He's in great shape."

"Claude, wake up. You are going to go back to the lab and euthanize the mouse. In one hour, the mouse will be no more. And, by the way, kill it using some method or drug that isn't traceable."

"Well, what good will that do?"

"It will be the first step in convincing Klaus he needs to throttle down on the cloning project and realize it's not a sure-fire success. The unexpected death of the mouse will start him thinking the cloning process might be faulty. By the end of this week, he'll mellow on the project and start conveying his reservations to the executive committee. He's going to be really pissed at us for the next few weeks but that's a lot better than handing him one human cloning failure after another."

"So, let me see if I understand this. I'm going to kill the mouse and you are going to think of some fake setbacks to tell my uncle?"

"That's right, and I just thought of another one. The CR47 incubator is going to suffer an electronic and mechanical malfunction. A malfunction that we create. One that takes several weeks to fix."

Claude thought about Rollie's proposed plan and summarized it out loud to see if it seemed reasonable. "Okay, we pile these problems on my uncle and hope like hell he tones down his enthusiasm toward the project. If that happens, he'll temper his reports to the executive committee. And if we get really lucky, he'll make up some bullshit excuses about the project and tell the committee it will take an extended period to fix the problems. Have I got this right?"

"Yeah, that's the general idea. But you know your uncle. He's a loose cannon who might do anything. Only time will tell."

"So, what is our goal by making up these lies? What's the bottom line, Rollie?"

"We get the time needed to develop the cloning project correctly. We follow scientific standards and minimize potential failures. I figure the least amount of time we'll get is four months but I'm hoping for six months."

"One question, Rollie. What if he gets so upset, he puts someone else in charge of the project?"

Rollie thought for a moment before answering. "That's a good question, Claude. I guess that could happen, but I still think we can squeeze out the time we need even if he appoints a new supervisor. Let's face it, the new guy won't have a clue about how cloning is done. It will take him weeks, if not months, to figure it out. Of course, we'll be the ones teaching him what he needs to know so we can delay and sidetrack his training quite a bit."

Rollie and Claude looked at each other and for the first time in years found a sliver of respect for one another.

"Any questions Claude?"

"I don't think so. My first assignment is taking care of the mouse. I assume you want its body kept?"

"Yeah, we have to make this look legitimate so keep the body in cold storage."

Claude sat reviewing the entire plan in his head. He was

cautious and didn't want to leave until he felt comfortable with the sabotage he was getting ready to join. "Okay, Rollie, I'll wait to hear from you on what you want me to do and when."

Rollie was relieved reaching an agreement with Claude. But he knew this would be the easiest part of his plan. He ended their meeting with a short pep talk meant to strengthen Claude's commitment to the plan. "Claude, you have to hang in there no matter what your uncle says or does. When he throws a temper-tantrum let it roll off your back. And if he tries to bribe you with promotions, gifts, and world credits, just ignore him. Try to remember that perfecting a cloning procedure will be a hundred times more rewarding than anything he can offer you now."

Rollie and Claude shook hands and went their separate ways. Each of them still had reservations about each other and the plan but there was no turning back. To be on the safe side, Rollie recorded the entire meeting with Claude. It might come in handy if Claude got cold feet and wanted to renege on his commitment to their plan.

Over the next two hours, Rollie put together a comprehensive T & A for the cloning project. It showed immediate human experimentation which was exactly what Klaus expected and demanded. It would be on his desk by 8 a.m. the following morning. But by the end of the week, after he and Claude hit Klaus with one disaster after another, the T & A would go up in smoke and be worthless.

For the rest of the day and much of the night, Rollie replayed every word and nuance of his meeting with Claude. He meticulously looked for potential loopholes and problems. He also thought of a couple more disasters which could be combined with the death of the mouse and malfunction of the CR47, to delay the project.

At 3 a.m. in the morning, Rollie woke from a deep sleep

thinking of something he forgot to tell Claude. He made a note to himself to see Claude first thing in the morning. Once the reminder was on paper, he was able to get back to sleep.

For the next couple of hours, he dreamed about his Grandma LeeLee. He didn't know why his thoughts focused on her but there was some type of strong link occurring between the two of them.

When he awoke a couple of hours later, he could recall the dream so vividly that he thought it actually happened. Grandma LeeLee was standing on what appeared to be a theatrical stage and repeated the same thing over and over.

"Sunny Boy, I've sent help to you. It will be there soon. Sunny Boy, I've sent help to you..."

He sat on the edge of the bed and thought about what the dream might mean. Sunny Boy, he understood. It was Grandma LeeLee's nickname for him. But what was the help she sent?

CHAPTER SEVEN

THE FIRST STEP OF REVENGE

DATE HATTORI, a fifty-year-old farmer, lived outside the city of Osaka in the country once known as Japan. He loved tilling the soil on his tiny farm but was fed up. As he bent over to pull another weed, he decided to carry through on his plan of treachery against the central government. The central government he had unlimited hate for.

This wasn't a spur-of-the-moment decision. He had debated his illegal plan for years. His wife contracting cancer and dying a brutal death from the disease was all he needed to push forward with the plan. There was no longer a reason to worry about the possible consequences. He couldn't care less if he got caught and lost his monthly allotment of world credits. He had saved extra credits, one by one, for years and could now survive as a rogue in the underground society of criminals and misfits.

The government's refusal to give his wife the medical care and drugs she needed was immoral and scandalous. There was a cure for her type of cancer, but she was classified as a nonessential citizen. This meant that the drugs and attention she needed could only be allocated to those citizens who were deemed more valuable assets of the state. Date had no idea who these more valuable people were and didn't care to find out. All he knew was that she was the most valuable person in his life. A faceless bureaucrat, somewhere within the World Council organization, condemned her to a miserable, agonizing death. A death far beyond what any human should experience.

The final straw was when they sent him a communique informing him that his wife qualified for a free syringe filled with a death potion. All she had to do was inject the liquid death.

The syringe arrived two days later along with a nondescript sympathy letter. It described how the World Council was sorry to hear about his wife's terminal illness. They wanted to do everything possible to make her death a memorable event for friends and relatives. The bastards were heartless, and he couldn't wait to strike back.

Several times he considered killing her so she could escape this world and move on to a pain-free afterlife. Each time he worked up the courage to end her life something happened to stop him. Twice she passed out, silencing the agonizing screams. A third time she begged to stay with him for a little while longer. On his final attempt, she passed away seconds before he plunged the syringe into her arm. She was now with her ancestors and Date looked forward to when he could join her.

Date kept the death potion syringe. He knew sometime in the future it would come in handy as a tool of revenge.

Revenge wasn't his only reason for committing the criminal act of treason against the World Council. For years, he had studied and thought about his rich family ancestry as samurai warriors. According to his great-grandfather, Date was a direct decedent of the famous samurai, Hattori "the Demon" Honzo who lived during the 16th century. Honzo was one of the most well-known and respected samurai of his time. He fought and led his forces to victory in many battles during his short life of fifty-five years. He served and protected the upper echelon daimyos, also known as great lords. And near the end of his life was master swordsman and protector general to the shogun for all Japan.

Six hundred years later, the samurai code of honor and discipline still ran with fire through Date's blood. He couldn't stop thinking about resurrecting his intended position as a samurai to a great lord. It was part of his DNA and he needed to carry through on what he was put on this earth to do. Farming was an honorable profession but serving a great lord, politically and militarily, was more important. It was what he must do to be a complete man and honor his ancestors.

Date spent hours each night studying the samurai code of Bushido. He learned how to use all the weapons. He was most concerned with the dueling sword which true samurai believed possessed their honor within the tempered steel blade. After years of study, he was qualified to become a samurai. He could now serve a great lord by protecting his land and possessions and fighting his enemies. The problem was that he didn't have any idea who this great lord would be. The power elite of society was now protected by armed guards versed in modern warfare, weapons and military tactics. The elite of world government in the 22nd century needed a sword-wielding samurai as much as they needed to contract a contagious disease.

Date was confident his lord would reveal himself eventually and welcome his protection, advice, and loyalty. But if he had to spend a few years as a ronin samurai until his lord became known then that was also acceptable. Samurai history was filled with many glorious stories about unattached and unemployed samurai. They roamed the Japanese countryside protecting the less fortunate in exchange for food and a place to sleep.

When his wife was alive, he would lie awake each night thinking his way through how to pull off this criminal feat. A lot of time was devoted to avoiding detection and apprehension by the authorities. The late-night mental exercises were so intense and detailed there was little doubt in Date's mind that his plans were close to foolproof.

The part of his plans which he enjoyed analyzing the most was how to handle the extra income generated from selling his illegal product. He knew that there were two things which tripped up criminals. Most landed in the hands of the authorities because they couldn't keep their mouths shut. Date was amazed by criminals who felt they must tell someone about the crimes they committed.

The second stumbling block for criminals was living beyond their means. Several times a year Date got a good laugh from reading or hearing about criminals who beat the system and then tried to live far beyond their means. They spent outrageous amounts of world credits on luxury items. How stupid were these people? What could they be thinking? Did they think the authorities were blind and ignored people who spent far more than their allotted world credits? Every citizen was expected to live no better or worse than their neighbor. Spending excessive amounts of world credits was an immediate tip-off to some type of criminal activity. These people were also fair game for government snitches. These rats looked for and reported "excessive spenders" to the government. The central government's reward program provided for a 10% reward paid to snitches from the recovered world credits.

Date wasn't going to make the same mistakes. He planned to use his criminally-gotten income on his passion of collecting samurai warfare equipment. He would also support dissident groups intent on overthrowing the World Council. Enemies of the World Council were now Date's comrades-in-arms no matter how radical their tactics and ideology might be.

Built beneath Date's house was 15-square meter room used to keep harvested food fresh. It stayed in this naturally cooled room until it went to the government's agent for redistribution throughout society. Concealed and camouflaged in one corner of this room was a small opening which led into a tunnel. This tunnel twisted and turned for 50 meters under the nearby rocky berms on Date's property. At the end of the tunnel, Date used a blaster laser to create a 20-square meter room out of the solid rock. The room was equipped with a high-security entrance. There was a supply of natural spring water and light provided by well-hidden, miniature energy cells on the hill's crest. In this vault, Date would store and admire his collection of samurai weapons and suits of armor. Also, the black-and-white pictures he inherited from his grandfather would be honorably displayed. Each of them showed a different 19th-century samurai forefather in full battle gear. The pictures highlighted the military relics and weapons.

True samurai artifacts were still available on the black market but very expensive. An authentic samurai sword made by one of the famous swordsmiths of ancient Japan could cost as much as a family's yearly allotment of world credits.

Date already had a couple of samurai swords, but he knew they were cheap reproductions of the real swords of ancient Japan. They were nice to look at but wouldn't last two minutes in an actual duel. A real samurai sword would chop the fake in half.

Authentic samurai swords came in straight, curved, long and short versions. The most sought-after models were made of soft and hard steel folded over and hammered together many times during the forging process. This blending of different quality carbon steel created a blade that could hold a sharp edge yet not brittle enough to snap in battle. The blade was then polished for weeks using fine grain sand to create a mirror finish.

It was not uncommon for a high-quality blade to take a month or more to manufacture. When done, it was etched at the handle end with the sword master's name. The daimyo or clan he worked for and year were also etched into the steel. The hilt was tightly wound in quality leather and silk. It had to be long enough so the sword could be held and wielded with two hands. The hand guard and scabbard were also works of art. They were often decorated with silver and gold and carved from exotic woods or ivory.

The highest quality swords were tested often upon completion. It was common for the samurai who bought the sword to test it by slashing and stabbing a human corpse. In some cases, condemned convicts volunteered to be test victims for new swords. This was considered a more honorable way to die than nailed to a cross and left for days to endure an agonizing crucifixion.

Date began his search for the finest samurai relics available on the black market. There were several reputable brokers within a day's travel who specialized in finding the best relics. This included swords, crossbows, long barrel rifles, archery equipment, and battle armor. All this equipment was used during the thousand years samurai warriors were a political and military force on the island nation of old Japan. The 10% to 20% finder's fee he would pay the broker was well worth the expense. Having them track down and verify each relic would give him the time he needed to start producing and selling his illegal cloaking device.

Years before his wife contracted cancer, a rumor spread

that the World Council had a method for monitoring each citizen's daily movements. Date suspected this was more than a rumor. It was too much of a coincidence how often government agents showed up as crimes and civil disobedience occurred.

Date was very upset by the possibility that his whereabouts and activities were monitored by the government. It wasn't that he went anywhere important or tried to hide his travel destinations. For God's sake, how much intrigue could a farmer's life have? It was the principle that some faceless organization could know where he was 24 hours a day. As far as he was concerned, they didn't have the right to know his whereabouts at any time. The only right they earned was to know he was a solid citizen who didn't commit any crimes against his fellow man or the state. Beyond this, their over-involvement in his life was a violation of one of his basic freedoms granted by God's Natural Law.

It finally leaked out that the health injections contained a micro-monitoring device which lodged in a kidney. Date was infuriated. He swore to find a way to either disarm or cloak this device so he could move about freely without anyone knowing when and where he went. For the next several years he studied and read everything he could about the monitoring devices which were called trackers.

He paid close attention to stories about people who had their kidney and the monitoring device surgically removed. This seemed like an extreme step to take considering the person was classified as unaccounted for once his device was removed and stopped transmitting. The only way to survive was to live successfully in the criminal underground. Otherwise, the authorities would arrest the person and have another monitoring device injected.

Government news releases always painted apprehended citizens as members of one anti-government group or another.

Date knew this couldn't be true. Professional criminals had the contacts and knowledge to avoid apprehension once they fell off the government surveillance grid. They didn't necessarily belong to an anti-government element. It was easy to conclude that the government published these stories to scare average citizens away from having their monitoring devices removed. And if the government went to this much effort to scare the public then there were a lot of people, like himself, who wanted to be tracker free.

Besides studying everything he could find about the tracking devices, Date volunteered as a janitor at the Osaka central government hospital. He knew this regional hospital was responsible for giving the health injections which contained the monitoring devices to children when they reached five years of age. Any malfunctioning trackers were also surgically removed and replaced in this hospital.

After working a couple of months at the hospital, Date figured out where the monitoring devices were stored. He was amazed by the lack of security in this area. There were no video recorders in the room and the main entrance door was propped open much of the time. With these conditions, the eye identification, entrance system was worthless. Even though the room was designated a restricted zone, personnel from throughout the hospital and sometimes visitors came and went without challenge. The bottom line was that this room was unsecured and any security breach, such as theft, would go undetected.

New monitoring devices lay helter-skelter throughout this room. The surgically removed devices were thrown in a trash can rather than put in a secured hazardous materials container. The lackadaisical approach to maintaining the monitoring devices told Date that a computerized inventory of these devices was either not used or ignored.

Date helped himself to one of the discarded monitoring

devices in a trash container. He wanted to test his observations about the ineffective security procedures and practices. After two weeks, not one word was said about the missing device. Within a year, he acquired over a dozen new trackers and at least as many defective units. Also, he copied and took home dozens of electronic journals and manuals describing the use, implantation, and repair of the monitoring devices. At no time did anyone question him about the missing equipment and documents.

The hospital employees and the government bureaucrats responsible for the hospital didn't have any idea Date was a thief. At first, he was surprised by this lack of control. But it made more sense as he observed the daily operation of the hospital and its staff. He concluded that centralized government which attempted to control every phase of its citizens' lives controlled nothing. The abundance of edicts, laws, rules, and regulations enacted by the government led most citizens to complacency. The average person either ignored what the government wanted or found ways to work around their demands. And if anything went wrong, the overabundance of governance allowed plenty of wiggle room for the average bureaucrat to point the blame at someone else.

After a year, Date had stolen everything he needed to start developing a cloaking device. The goal was simple. Create a device which fooled the monitoring devices and misled the government which used them to track its citizens. He quit the volunteer position at the hospital. He used this time to experiment, reverse engineer and develop a simple, yet effective, way to make the kidney monitoring device useless.

Date possessed an intelligence which far exceeded what was needed to be a successful farmer. But his formal education was minimal. He never earned any degrees or certifications of achievement. What he did have was the best motivation of all; a burning desire to end government intrusion in his life.

At first, the information he accumulated and studied about the monitoring device was like reading a foreign language. Through trial and error, he came to understand the inner workings of the monitoring device. After two years of experimentation in his hidden underground chamber, he was an expert on the device. He knew more about how it was made and worked than anyone else on the planet.

Even with all this knowledge, a successful cloaking method was hard to discover. Several times, Date considered giving up his quest, especially after his wife became sick with cancer. Trying to juggle his time between farming, caring for his wife and reverse engineering the monitoring device was exhausting. As with many great steps forward in engineering and medical advancements, Date stumbled onto the solution by accident. Unfortunately, this step forward was at the expense of his wife's health.

His wife's cancer started in the liver and spread to the bladder and kidneys. It soon metastasized and attacked her bloodstream which changed the chemical composition of the blood cells. When this happened, Date and his wife had a surprise visit from a government inspector. He asked dozens of questions about her health and ability to perform daily tasks. Could she perform routine functions around the house like bathe herself and make meals?

Date wasn't fooled in the least. The government employee's concern for his wife's welfare was shallow. It was an obvious ruse. In fact, the inspector's attitude was so unemotional and caustic that Date wanted to throw him out the door. But his curiosity about the inspector's hidden agenda overrode the disgust he had for the man.

Date realized that the inspector's real goal was to find out why the signal from his wife's monitoring device started to malfunction. Date played the role of a simpleton farmer. He asked a few pointed questions which the pompous inspector eagerly answered to show off his self-importance. After a half hour, the inspector was convinced the change in the device's faltering signal was due to a terminal disease. He ended the interview, apologized for the inconvenience and left.

Date hated the fact that his wife was subjected to such mental abuse by the inspector. But the clues the inspector dropped during the interview and the answers he gave to Date's questions were very valuable. They were enough to point Date in the right direction to solve the mystery of the monitoring devices.

Within two weeks, Date figured out that the monitoring device was powered by the flow of blood through the kidney. If the flow of blood decreased for any reason like an injury or medical condition, the device lacked enough energy to send a correct signal. Also, each person's unique blood composition correlated to their monitoring device. In other words, the chemical makeup of each person's blood was unique. It was just like fingerprints. No two people had the same chemical composition. When the monitoring device was injected into the body it became linked to that person's unique chemical makeup of his blood. From that moment forward the monitoring device and the person's name and blood were all linked. Together they showed up as one bleep on the monitoring grid.

As his wife's cancer spread, the chemical composition of her blood changed. The ability of her kidneys to process and filter blood slowed down. Both changes caused transmitting problems for her tracker. That, in turn, triggered an alarm condition at the monitoring station. The only recourse the government had was to send out an inspector to find out why her monitoring device was malfunctioning.

With this information, Date invented a simple pump container which contained about a quart of donor's blood. When Date dropped one of his home-made monitoring devices into the container the pump turned on. It started to transmit a signal which was an exact duplicate of the signal already transmitting from the donor. The last step was to block the signal from the donor's kidney, so the monitoring station would see only one signal, not two.

After some trial and error testing, Date found that a thin sheet of lead leafing blocked the monitoring device signal. All that needed to be done was sew it into an elastic bandage. The bandage was then worn around a person's lower chest and over his kidneys. The lead blocking band was lightweight and no more of a nuisance to wear than a belt to hold up a pair of pants. Deactivating the cloaking system was as easy as activating it. The person simply removed the lead blocking bandage after turning off the blood circulation pump. The fake monitoring device signal then fell off the monitoring grid and was replaced with the signal from the person's real device.

Date wanted to have his system perfected before his wife died. He wanted her to share the enjoyment of putting one over on the government they both hated. She blamed the government for the death of her two children during the FISS plague and wanted revenge as much as Date. Unfortunately, she died several months before Date finished his invention.

After a week of mourning her death with fellow villagers and a few relatives, Date went back to work perfecting his cloaking system. He tested the finished product on himself. After wrapping the lead blocking bandage around his midsection, he dropped the new monitoring device in a container of his blood. He turned on the circulating pump and sat down at the kitchen table. He poured himself a cup of sake and waited for the authorities to arrive. There was no other way to determine if his system worked. The authorities would either show up and arrest him or never show up. If they didn't bust in his front door it was because they didn't know his real tracker was replaced with a fake one.

Three days later, Date was well pickled from the sake and still sitting at his kitchen table. He was free as a bird to go wherever he wanted without worrying about the watchful eyes of "papa government". To make sure his system was perfect he spent the next month traveling throughout Japan. Nothing in his life changed. His monthly allotment of world credits stayed the same and his travel was not red-flagged. He wasn't the subject of any government investigation. The government thought he was still sitting at the kitchen table even though he was hundreds of miles away touring a city or remote countryside.

Date found it comical that the government thought a person could sit at the same kitchen table for over a month. They didn't care if a person stayed stationary for long periods of time. All they cared about was if the signal disappeared, malfunctioned or moved far beyond its normal travel area. It was another classic example of the government's ineptitude and stupidity.

He was ready to move on to the next stage of his life. Date's wife and children were gone. There were no close relatives to embarrass in the event of his arrest by the central government. He didn't worry any longer about the dishonor associated with doing something illegal against the World Council. He just didn't care any longer. Things had to be made right for all the misery the World Council had brought down upon his family. And he needed to make his life right in the service of a great lord, whoever that might be.

He planned to sell his cloaking equipment to people who lived outside the rules and regulations of the central government. Those who pushed drugs, worked in prostitution and bought and sold in the underground markets. Date spent years learning who these people were and where they headquartered. In Japan, most of these criminals were decedents of the Yakuza, the masters of organized crime. They had dominated illegal activities on the island for centuries. They didn't know it yet, but they were going to be his business partners within a few short years.

But there was one thing which Date overlooked. There were countless groups around the world preparing to revolt and overthrow their master, the World Council. Each had their own reason for defying the central government. They all needed Date's technology to move forward against the enemy.

CHAPTER EIGHT

HEY, THAT'S MY DESSERT!

"GOD, I'm tired of supporting the lowlifes in this town. I work my ass off and have nothing to show for it."

"What are you talking about, Poppy? You don't pay or give anyone anything."

Miguel Santanez, the grandfather and father to the eight younger family members sat on the front porch. He could have lost his temper and criticized his grandson for making such a slow-witted comment. Instead, he decided to use this as a teaching opportunity. The fourteen-year-old needed a lesson about life and the world the Santanez family contended with each day. After all, the boy was still in government school learning nothing other than what the World Council approved and wanted him to hear. To a youngster like Ramon, what he heard in school sounded wonderful. But it was a pile of crap which kept everyone poor rather create a society with a decent standard of living.

Miguel, the family patriarch, was affectionately known as Poppy. He and his two older sons sat down to rest after their normal ten-hour day of clearing land in the Amazon basin. It would be so easy to sit back and enjoy a few restful minutes before falling into bed. They needed sleep to regain enough energy to face the next ten-hour workday. But he had to take advantage of this opportunity. Ramon and everyone else on the porch must understand the faults of an overbearing government.

"Ramon, your father, uncle and I don't work for ourselves. We work for the government. We get the same amount of world credits no matter how hard we work. The government takes our labor, and in return, gives us just enough to survive. And the guy across the street who doesn't work half as hard, gets the same as us. I'm sure you've heard of the government's Equal Allocation law. It says that no one citizen has the right to more than another citizen. And no citizen has the right to live better than his neighbor."

"I don't see anything wrong with that, Poppy. They teach us in school that everyone needs to help everyone else. If we help our neighbors then everyone will have enough food, shelter and health care. Everyone will have what they need. Not like before when this area was called Brazil. Then, some people had a lot and others had nothing. The poor relied on the garbage dumps and handouts from the rich for their next meal."

"Ramon, there's a difference between voluntary help and forced mandatory help. I want real money for my labor. I want to spend my pay any way I want. I don't want to be dictated to by a government bureaucrat who thinks he knows how to spend my money better than me. If my neighbor is truly in need of my help, I will happily pitch in and give him what he needs. But if someone like the bottom feeder across the street demands my help because he doesn't want to work hard, then forget it. That's not fair. He's stealing from me. It's wrong and immoral."

"I don't understand, Poppy. What you said sounds kind of greedy to me. It doesn't sound fair for someone to have more than someone else. Shouldn't I share what I have? Doesn't sharing show I love my fellow man? Maybe not everyone can work as hard as you, my father and uncle. Did you ever think of that, Poppy?"

Miguel paused for a moment. He wasn't sure how to respond to Ramon's questions and statements. He wanted to bring Jesus of the Bible into the conversation but didn't know if that would be wise. Religion was banned over a century before. There were harsh penalties for anyone who believed and worshiped a divine God. He decided to take a chance. He could only hope that Ramon wouldn't repeat this conversation in front of anyone outside the family. Especially his teachers. There were many government snitches throughout society. They gladly reported anti-government hate speak in return for a few measly world credits.

"Ramon, there was a very wise man many centuries ago who loved all men and did everything He could to help them. In fact, many believe He was put on this earth to die for the sins of all men. But this wise and kind man also believed all men who could work should do so. Otherwise, they wouldn't eat."

Miguel could see that Ramon understood the story so far but didn't agree with it. He was too brainwashed by nine years of government schooling to throw aside approved doctrine immediately. The concepts of capitalism and religion were like a foreign language to him. It was going to be very difficult convincing him that the World Council economic theories were ill-conceived. They didn't work worth a damn in real life.

The conversation was becoming heated. Miguel debated with himself whether to continue or drop the idea of trying to argue Ramon to his point of view. Miguel decided to drop the topic and turn to something more pleasant to discuss. At that very moment, he was presented with a golden opportunity to open his grandson's eyes to the inadequacies of World Council socialism.

The ladies of the house were finished cleaning up after dinner. They had a special surprise for the family members resting on the porch. It was a serving of Brigadeiros Durazno, the national dessert cherished by all people living in the Amazon basin. Brigadeiros Durazno, referred to as BD, was a delicious dessert consisting of ice cream laid on top of peach flan cake. It was then topped with chocolate and tiny bits of pineapple smothered in honey.

Everyone in the family was thrilled when given a bowl of BD. For the men, a bowl of BD was better than getting a day off from work. For the women, it was an emotional high seeing their men smile again as they savored each scoop of the sweet dessert.

Being able to enjoy a bowl of BD happened only once every couple of years because of the shortage of chocolate, peaches, and honey. It usually took a couple of years for the women to scrimp and save enough world credits to buy the ingredients needed for the delicious dessert.

"Ramon, can I show you an example of what I've been trying to teach you? I promise to show you nothing more than what the schools are teaching."

Ramon thought about his grandfather's request. He had a feeling this was some sort of trap, but he went ahead and agreed to whatever the old man was up to. "Sure, Poppy, go ahead. I want to see why you think the government is so bad."

With that, Miguel stood up and walked over to stand in front of Ramon's chair. He picked up Ramon's dish of BD from the coffee table and said, "Ramon, pretend this dish of BD is what your labor produces. All your work each day ends up in this bowl. Understand?" Ramon shook his head up and down indicating he understood his grandfather's explanation.

"Now, also pretend I'm the government. I make the rules and decisions which you must follow like every other good, law-abiding citizen. Follow me so far Ramon?" Again, Ramon nodded his head up and down.

"Watch closely, Ramon. This is how the government makes me live every day of my life." With that, Miguel walked Ramon's dish of BD over to his two younger sisters and gave them the dessert to eat.

"Ramon, I have decided you don't need the BD as much as these two young ladies." Miguel returned to his chair, sat down and started eating his own dessert.

Ramon was shell-shocked and didn't know what to do. After seeing his two sisters attack his BD he regained his senses and launched himself out of his chair.

"Hey, you two, that's my BD. Give it back to me." Ramon snatched his bowl from the girls and headed back to his chair to eat the meager scraps remaining in the bowl.

Everyone on the porch except Miguel and Ramon was hooting, hollering and laughing. The sisters were giggling nonstop while poking fun at Ramon. "Thanks, Poppy. Ramon's BD was delicious. Can we have his BD next time, too?"

"Well, we'll see. Next time someone else may need his BD more than you girls. Or, your BD might go to the needy neighbor across the street. How would you feel about that?"

In unison, the girls rejected this thought. "There's no way that guy over there is getting our BD."

Ramon tried to be mad at his grandfather but seeing his family laughing and having fun at his expense cooled his anger.

"Ramon, you should have seen your face when Poppy gave your dessert to the girls and they started eating it."

"Yeah, it was really funny, Father. I'm glad everyone had such a good time on me."

The family started laughing again at Ramon. It wasn't what

he said but rather the sarcastic way he said it that was so humorous.

Ramon looked over at his grandfather and said, "Poppy, I'll get you for this. When you least expect it, I'll get you." Everyone could tell by the smile on his face that this was an idle threat. He didn't have any intention of seeking revenge for what he just learned.

Miguel stood up again and walked his half-eaten bowl of BD over to his grandson. "Good news, Ramon. The government has reconsidered your case and decided you need more dessert."

Poppy handed his remaining BD to Ramon. "Here, this is yours now. Enjoy. And by the way, I give it to you freely. No one forced me to. I want you to have it because giving of my own free will makes me feel good."

Everyone smiled at Poppy's announcement and waited to see how Ramon would respond. This was a perfect example of why they loved the family patriarch.

"I get the point, Poppy. Thank you." Ramon shoveled the last few scoops of Poppy's BD into his mouth before anyone had the chance to take it from him.

That night, Ramon and Poppy laid in their beds thinking about the BD incident. Each of them still laughed on the inside remembering the happiness and fun created by one small bowl of sweet dessert. And both thought of the serious lessons and consequences derived from this event.

Ramon remembered vividly how he felt when Poppy took his dessert. He instantly felt contempt for the old man who took his food. If it had been anyone other than Poppy, he would have fought to get it back. Poppy was right. Government taking his food wasn't any better than a thief taking it. He realized the main lesson of Poppy's demonstration. The government could steal from its citizens. And it has the power of law to make it legalized theft.

Miguel knew Ramon was a smart young man who would see the underlying lessons of the BD demonstration. But there was one thing he didn't know. Could Ramon replace years of government indoctrination with the lessons learned that night? All he could do was hope for the best. And hope no one on the porch repeated to anyone outside the family what happened at the Santanez house. His family worked hard enough already. They couldn't survive should their allocation of world credits be reduced or eliminated.

Throughout the world, thousands of citizens were having the same thoughts and raising the same questions as Ramon and Poppy.

CHAPTER NINE

WHAT CAN GO WRONG NEXT?

"MR. SWEATS, I'm getting tired hearing why the ReLife Program isn't moving ahead. First, it was the mouse died. Then it was the CR47 incubation unit had to be re-calibrated. Then the incubator breaks down. Now, you're telling me the parts needed to repair the CR47 are out of stock and won't be available until the manufacturer comes back from holiday and begins manufacturing again. Exactly when will that be, Mr. Sweats?"

"Mr. Ekstrom, my understanding is that the manufacturer will be on holiday for another four weeks." There was a part of Rollie's personality which enjoyed giving Ekstrom bad news. He could see the CEO's face flushing with anger. He decided to pour a little more salt in the wound. "When they reopen after holiday it will take another three to four weeks to gear up and make the parts we need. As you know, the CR47 parts are all one-of-a-kind. So in total, we're looking at seven to eight weeks before we can move the project ahead."

Klaus got out of his desk chair and started to pace around the office. He was getting more annoyed by the minute and could feel a massive migraine coming on. He hated failure and didn't tolerate it among his staff.

"That's frigging wonderful. Another two months on top of the two months we've already wasted. What's next Mr. Sweats? Are you going to tell me there's a giant asteroid hurtling toward Earth and it's going to wipe us out before we perfect ReLife?"

Klaus didn't expect an answer from his subordinate and Rollie wasn't preparing one. In fact, Rollie was debating whether to tell Ekstrom the latest debacle with the ReLife project or wait a couple of weeks to surprise him. He noticed the streams of perspiration running down Ekstrom's red face. That was enough to delay the next bit of bad news. Rollie was having too much fun watching his boss unravel due to the news about the replacement parts. Plus, he didn't want Klaus to have a heart attack even though he despised the man.

Ekstrom's brain was in overdrive looking for alternative solutions to the ReLife predicament. He started talking to himself as he strutted around the office.

"I can't believe this. If I didn't know better, I'd say someone was intentionally sabotaging this project and wants me to fail..."

He stopped in mid-sentence when a possible solution appeared out of nowhere and raced through his head.

"Rollie, can we borrow a CR47 or the parts we need from another company?"

The relief and elation showing on Ekstrom's face was short-lived.

"That's not possible Mr. Ekstrom. We have the only CR47 in the world. We came up with the idea for the CR47 and had it built to our specs. There are pending orders, but they are dependent upon our results. Other companies are waiting to see our results before they commit to such a large capital expenditure."

Klaus Ekstrom fell into his desk chair, closed his eyes and

rubbed his forehead with his left hand. After a minute, he reached into the top drawer of his desk and removed a bottle of pain relievers. He popped two of them into his mouth and swallowed without drinking any liquid. He then reached across his desk and picked up a large piece of paper.

Holding it up so Rollie could see it, Klaus said in a voice weaker than his normal commanding tone, "Mr. Sweats, this is the T & A you gave me a few weeks ago. It's worthless now." With that, Klaus tore up the paper into several small pieces and threw them into the air.

Klaus refocused on Rollie who was sitting on the other side of his desk. "I don't have any more ideas how to kick start the ReLife project. Do you have any, Mr. Sweats, regardless of how off the wall they may be?"

Rollie gazed off into space doing his best to make Ekstrom believe he was thinking real hard to find a way to get the ReLife program up and running. He avoided looking at his dejected boss. He was afraid he would burst out laughing at a grown man acting like a spoiled brat.

"I can't think of anything we can do now other than wait, Mr. Ekstrom. I get sick every time I think about the delays. We are on the verge of making medical history and every time we turn around there's a delay. It's not fair, Mr. Ekstrom, not fair at all."

Rollie didn't know if Ekstrom bought his "I'm so upset I can hardly stand it" speech. Ekstrom's facial appearance didn't change one bit. He kept staring at Rollie with a hardened glare. Rollie never met any murderers but thought this might be the piercing gaze they gave their next victims.

"Okay, Mr. Sweats, we're done for now. Keep me appraised on any new developments about ReLife." Before Rollie could get out of his chair and start for the door, Klaus summoned his assistant to his office.

"Mrs. Brandt, would you get Claude on the communicator for me and then have Raul come to my office."

As Mrs. Brandt turned to leave, she asked, "Mr. Ekstrom, have you seen this morning's copy of the Beobachter?"

"No I haven't, Mrs. Brandt. I've been kind of busy if you didn't notice."

Ekstrom's sarcastic remark was typical when he was under a lot of stress. Until he found a solution to whatever new problem fell into his life, Klaus was the most miserable person she ever met. He was ill-tempered and treated everyone like dirt. During these episodes, he acted like he was the only person on Earth who faced difficult problems. But when a solution was found, his rotten personality subsided. It was replaced with his normal CEO personality. Not the friendliest or warmest corporate leader but rather a competent executive. He led by dictate rather than example. The staff was treated with respect only so long as they produced and lived up to his expectations.

Mrs. Brandt tolerated her boss and tried to make the best of their relationship. But she looked forward in earnest to the day he was replaced or retired.

"You need to look, Mr. Ekstrom. I'll put it up for you."

Before leaving the office, she swiped a small screen marked "News" mounted on the wall. A large hologram of the first page of the Beobachter appeared and floated in midair. It hovered there waiting to be read by Klaus Ekstrom. Mrs. Brandt had no idea where these holograms came from. They appeared magically. She loved their multicolored text and vivid images. And, the way they could be read and viewed from any place in the office was a mystery, far beyond her technical comprehension.

"There you go, Mr. Ekstrom." Mrs. Brandt scampered out of his office and closed the door as quickly as possible. He wasn't going to like what the Beobachter reported and she didn't want to be within eye-sight when he read the article.

The door shutting drew his attention from a report he was reading on his desk screen. He looked up to see the hologram projection on the other side of the office. In big, bold letters across the front page was, **"PHOENVARTIS MAKING HUMANS."**

Klaus's eyes damn near popped out of his head. He read and reread the headlines at least a dozen times. He hoped and prayed that he was either reading it wrong, it was a misprint, or some type of practical joke. He read the entire article twice before sitting back and taking a breath.

Klaus grabbed one of his favorite cigars and lit it as Mrs. Brandt announced Claude was on the inter-office communicator. Besides having a luxurious, sweet taste, the cigars were loaded with stimulating drugs. The smoker was intoxicated with a euphoric "high" from the first to last puff. There was no faster way to deliver drugs into the human body than by inhaling smoke. With the stress of his job, Klaus needed to smoke two to three cigars each day. Otherwise, he was an irritable mess, unable to focus on his executive duties. After reading the Beobachter article, he thought this would be a four to five cigar day.

"Claude, Klaus here."

"Good morning, Mr. Ekstrom."

"Yeah, sure. Good morning to you too. Claude, have you seen the morning edition of the Beobachter?"

Claude looked at his boss Rollie who was standing close by and staring out one of the office windows. Rollie turned to face Claude and silently shook his head from side to side. Claude took the cue and lied to his uncle.

"No, Mr. Ekstrom, I haven't seen the Beobachter this morning. Is there something about Phoenvartis in it?"

Klaus wished he had summoned Claude to his office. Without seeing his face and body reactions to his questions he had no idea if Claude was telling the truth.

"Yes, there certainly is. Read this morning's article about us and if you have any thoughts on it, let me know."

"Sure thing, Klaus, I mean Mr. Ekstrom." At times, Claude forgot to address his uncle as Mr. Ekstrom and used his first name. The surprise question about the Beobachter article was enough to make him temporarily forget the CEO's one simple rule. He demanded all employees, even those with family ties to address him as Mr. Ekstrom. They were never to use only his first name. Claude knew he would catch hell for this slip-up. But for now, Klaus continued as though he didn't hear Claude's mistake.

"Claude, I just had a meeting with Mr. Sweats, and he tells me the parts needed to fix the CR47 are at least seven to eight weeks out. Do you agree with that assessment?"

Claude looked again at Rollie to get the correct answer.

"Yes, I agree, Mr. Ekstrom. At least seven weeks."

"Claude, we need to get the ReLife project going. Can you think of anyone who has replacement parts or can fix our CR47?"

Rollie shook his head from side to side and then mockingly rubbed his eyes as though he were crying. Claude understood his mimicry and held back the urge to laugh.

"Mr. Ekstrom, we have the only CR47 in existence. The only people who can fix the regeneration incubator are here at Phoenvartis and the company we subcontracted with. The problem is that defective parts must be replaced. None of the technicians can fix these parts. Only new parts can get the CR47 working again."

Claude saw Rollie raise a thumbs-up as he continued to lie and patronize his uncle. "I've been trying to think of a solution for days but can't come up with anything. The other night I got physically sick because I couldn't think of a way for us to move the project ahead. We have a golden opportunity to make Phoenvartis the leading tech company in all the zones. But two little parts are stopping us from accomplishing this goal. Mr. Ekstrom, you can count on me. I'm going to spend more time thinking about our problem and maybe..."

Claude chattered on and on until he looked down and realized the communicator signal had been disconnected by his uncle.

"Apparently, he didn't like what I had to say."

Rollie snickered at Claude's sarcastic remark as he made himself comfortable in one of the office guest chairs. He found more amusement in Klaus's follow-up call to Claude. Klaus was so predictable. He always verified vital information, especially the latest problems, with another employee. Anytime he met with Claude, Rollie could expect a call from Klaus. And, anytime he met with Rollie, Claude could expect a similar call verifying Rollie's information. Rollie often wondered why he continued to verify everything he heard from them. Their stories never varied one iota. Why did he waste his time? There was only one explanation which made sense. Other employees Klaus dealt with couldn't keep their stories straight and tripped up on a regular basis.

Claude and Rollie were playing a dangerous game. There would be hell to pay if Klaus ever found out the two of them were cohorts in a plan to sabotage the ReLife project. With luck, Klaus wouldn't start wondering why Claude and Rollie were the only two employees in the entire corporation who always backed up each other perfectly.

Rollie was pleased that he made a detour to Claude's office after leaving the meeting with Klaus. Not only was he able to lead Claude through his uncle's questioning, but also learned something new. The Beobachter had written something which irritated Klaus.

"Claude, did you know about the Beobachter article?"

"No, I have no idea what my uncle is talking about. Let's look at it."

Claude brought up the same holographic article which Klaus read ten minutes earlier. He and Rollie were mesmerized and shocked by the contents of the article. It claimed that Phoenvartis had run trial tests on cloning human beings. The tests were successful and came from unnamed sources close to the project. There was information about when the project started and the results thus far. The article went on to make several speculative accusations relating to the ultimate goals of the human clone project. Some of the accusations were wild and without basis but the overall description of the project was accurate.

One of the wildest claims in the article was that the goal of human cloning was for military reasons. Specifically, the World Council wanted to know if the best military minds from the past could be brought back to life. Rollie didn't know whether to laugh at this or give it some serious thought. It wasn't anything he ever heard discussed since the ReLife project started at Phoenvartis. But it was such an off the wall assertion it might have some merit. Was it possible the World Council expected a major war which could threaten its grip on society? Did they fear the current leaders of the military were under-qualified? Were they capable of handling conflicts bigger than minor squabbles? Was the government's military prepared to fight a World War? He would have to give these possible scenarios more thought, but for now, he chose not to say anything about it to Claude.

"Claude, did you tell anyone at Beobachter about the ReLife project?

"Absolutely not. Did you?"

"No, of course not." Rollie furrowed his brow in deep thought for a few seconds before continuing.

"So if you and I didn't say anything, then who are the unnamed sources mentioned in this article? Where is this leaked information coming from?" Rollie went on, talking to himself to arrive at a plausible answer.

"I doubt it was Klaus. He seemed genuinely irritated by the Beobachter article. If he was the leak, then why would he waste time asking if you saw the article? No, it can't be him."

"How about someone on the executive committee?"

"Yeah, I thought about that. It's possible. The military part of the article sounds like something one of those guys would say but I still have my doubts."

"Why, Rollie? They would be my first choice."

"Claude, did you notice there wasn't one mention of the project name in the entire article? Every one of those guys on the executive committee knows the project name is ReLife. If any of them leaked information to Beobachter I'm sure they would tell the reporter the name of the project. I mean, if you were doing the story for Beobachter wouldn't you ask your source for the project name?"

"Well, I'm not a reporter but it does seem like a common-sense thing to do. Okay, if it's not me, you, Klaus or the executive committee, then who the hell is it?

"I have no damn idea, Claude. My experience in little mysteries like this has been that the culprit is always the most obvious person. So obvious, you don't think of them as a suspect. But for now, I can't see who that would be."

Both Claude and Rollie sat for a couple of minutes racking their brains trying to think of who the leaker might be. Finally, Rollie got up to leave Claude's office. "Claude, be careful with what you say and do. Someone around here has big ears and a big mouth, so be careful."

Rollie walked over to Claude, bent down and whispered in his ear. "I'm going to have a sweep done of our offices looking for electronic eavesdropping bugs. I'll see you tonight in the lab."

Even though Rollie's comment was the last thing he expected to hear, Claude nodded his head so Rollie knew he understood the whisper. Making a precautionary sweep of the offices looking for surveillance bugs never occurred to Claude. Thank goodness Rollie was a suspicious, big picture thinker who knew a good offense resulted from a great defense.

Claude locked his office door, so he could get a few hours' sleep in preparation for another night in the CR47 lab. Spending fifty to sixty hours each week systematically analyzing every aspect of the ReLife project was physically and mentally draining. If he hadn't been able to sleep during the day, night sessions in the lab would have been impossible. Fortunately, Rollie limited Claude's other assignments so he could be productive at night.

In the last few weeks, their arduous work was starting to pay off. A step-by-step, comprehensive and scientific plan was created. It analyzed every facet of ReLife in preparation for more cloning experiments. If Klaus could be put off a little longer, they would know if ReLife was a viable technology for cloning animals and humans.

The field mouse cloning was a good start, but it still left hundreds of unanswered questions. First was the question of whether more complex life forms could be reproduced. And if this was possible, what limitations, if any, would the replicants have compared to their animal and human hosts?

CHAPTER TEN

WHEN HE THOUGHT THINGS COULDN'T GET WORSE

KLAUS CONSIDERED ASKING Rollie if he read the morning edition of Beobachter but decided it was a waste of his time. If his nephew, Claude, denied knowing anything about the news article so would Rollie. And as soon as Claude read the article, he would call Rollie and tell him about it.

It was amazing how those two were so in sync. Ever since the field mouse cloning, it seemed like they had the same thoughts and opinions on every topic. It was a dramatic change from the past when they butted heads on everything. Now they seemed to not only agree but appeared to have more than a working relationship. If Klaus didn't know better, he would have guessed they were friends.

"Mr. Ekstrom, Raul is here to see you." His assistant's announcement interrupted his thoughts about Claude and Rollie. He made a mental note to devote more time later to their new-found friendship.

"Mrs. Brandt, get him a coffee or something to drink and send him in."

Two minutes later, a broad-chested man of approximately

45 years-of-age entered Klaus's office. He sat down after exchanging "good mornings" with his boss. Raul rarely said more than six words at a time. He was what Klaus referred to as a good listener. At six feet, four inches tall with a body builder's physique, Raul didn't have to say much to be imposing. To many, his presence was threatening.

Raul was one of the few direct-report employees Klaus kept after taking the top job at Phoenvartis. After reading his personnel file and interviewing him, it was evident Raul possessed the two major traits Klaus wanted in a security director. This man knew how to keep his mouth shut and was very loyal to his superior. In the past few years, Klaus's initial evaluation of Raul proved to be 100% accurate.

Klaus wished all his top executives were as effective and professional as Raul. It was amazing how Raul could collect sensitive information from within and outside of the company. Klaus never asked how he did his job. If Raul produced what he asked for, Klaus was fine staying at arm's length from his Security Director's methods and personal life. As a matter of fact, Klaus was so uninvolved with this man he couldn't remember his last name.

"Raul, I'll get right to the point. I want you to drop everything else and find out as much as you can about the company's ReLife project. You probably haven't heard anything about this project because..."

"You mean the project to clone animals and humans?"

That was the first time Klaus could remember Raul interrupting anyone who was speaking. But it wasn't as interesting as realizing Raul already possessed a basic understanding of the ReLife project. Klaus wondered how much more his security director knew about the project.

"Did you read the Beobachter article this morning?"

"Yes, but I've been hearing rumors and comments about it

for quite some time. What do you want me to find out about ReLife, Mr. Ekstrom?"

"Raul, I'm interested in everything you hear or see about ReLife. I'm specifically interested in the following questions." Raul took a note pad from inside his suit coat and began recording each of Ekstrom's key questions about ReLife.

"First, I want to know who the unnamed sources are, quoted in the Beobachter article. Or, put another way, I want to know if the leak is a Phoenvartis employee, and if so, who is it? Secondly, where did the reference to military objectives for ReLife come from? Did the news reporter make this up or did it come from someone inside or outside of Phoenvartis? Any questions so far, Raul?"

"No, sir. Continue."

"The ReLife project is treading water now. There's been one delay after another. Currently, the CR47 machine is broken and it will be at least seven weeks before we can get replacement parts. I need that machine up and running as soon as possible. I told the executive committee weeks ago that we would be cloning humans by the end of this month. Each time there is another delay I must go back to the executive committee and fabricate excuses. My original timetable is in shambles. It's embarrassing, and to be honest, the executive committee is losing patience with me. If the project doesn't get back on track soon ..." Klaus paused for a moment to select the words he was about to say to Raul.

"Well, let's just say, I don't want to think about what the executive committee might do if ReLife doesn't show a major step forward soon."

Raul knew exactly what the committee might do; throw Klaus out the front door. "What else do you want me to find out, Mr. Ekstrom?"

"Raul, I want to know if these delays are real or someone

sabotaging the project. And, I need you to find out if there is a way to get the CR47 working again in short order." For effect, Klaus stood up and pounded on his desk and shouted, "I need that damn machine up and running now! Do you understand, Raul?"

Raul waited for Ekstrom to settle down before responding. "Yes sir, I understand perfectly."

Raul understood Ekstrom's command to find out what was going on with the ReLife project. He also understood Ekstrom was an asshole. There were a lot of people Raul didn't care for but Ekstrom was at the top of the list. Without question, he had a lock on the title of number one jerk. Besides, he had worked for Ekstrom for several years and it was obvious the jerk-off didn't know his last name.

This was going to be an interesting assignment. It could provide him with the ammunition he needed to see Ekstrom replaced as the CEO. Time would tell. For now, he had to concentrate on his assignments and see what information he uncovered.

"Mr. Ekstrom, should I assume that Mr. Sweats oversees the ReLife project?"

"That's correct, Raul. He's the supervisor for now. By the way, my nephew, Claude Ekstrom, is also involved in developing ReLife. Don't give him any special consideration because he's my nephew. Treat him like everyone else. Understand?"

Raul ignored Klaus's comment about his nephew. He couldn't care less what Klaus thought about his relative. Personally, he didn't care for Claude but compared to Klaus, he was a knight in shining armor. Claude was a pathetic little nerd with an over-inflated ego. But at least he stopped short of treating people like scum.

"Raul, I want daily updates. So if you don't have any further questions, please leave."

Raul wanted to reach across the desk and smack Klaus in the face a few times. It took every bit of energy he could muster to stay calm and ignore Ekstrom's degrading dismissal.

As he walked to the office door, he debated whether to drop a news bomb on Ekstrom. He had intended not to say anything but Ekstrom's last caustic remark made him reconsider. It was a good time to make his boss a little more miserable.

As the door slid open, Raul turned around and said, "Mr. Ekstrom, a member of the World Council is coming to Phoenvartis next week."

"What did you say, Raul?"

"One of my sources let me know that a member of the World Council is coming to visit Phoenvartis next week. That's all my source told me. I don't know what day or which member is coming."

Raul watched as Ekstrom melted into his desk chair. It was great fun watching this pompous ass completely fall apart.

With a shaking hand, Ekstrom took a cigar from a wood box on his desk and tried to light it. Raul almost broke out laughing when Ekstrom finally put the cigar down because he couldn't fire it. His hands were shaking so violently the cigar and match never made contact.

Raul decided to take one last punch before leaving the office. "Mr. Ekstrom, if I had to guess, I'd say the World Council member wants to discuss the ReLife project. I'm sure everyone at Council headquarters has read the Beobachter article. Raul saw the last remnants of ego and bravado leave Ekstrom's body. He wanted to dance out of the office but turned and walked away like a professional manager. He left Ekstrom a quaking, pathetic mass of human tissue.

It took Klaus a half hour before he recovered enough to start thinking about what should be done. He knew the ReLife project was slipping away. If he couldn't find a way to make it a success, all the work and years of devotion to the project would go up in smoke. His entire future and career depended on this one project. He needed to be at the helm of Phoenvartis when ReLife became a reality. Otherwise, his replacement would reap the rewards and be known forever as the father of human cloning.

ReLife was out of control and Klaus needed to put in place some type of damage control. But, what else could he do? He was trying to speed up the CR47 repair. Raul was looking for the information leaker within the corporation. And there was an all-out effort to determine if sabotage corrupted the project.

Klaus decided to devote most of his mental energy to preparing for the visit by the World Council member. He wasn't sure how to do that because the World Council had not visited Phoenvartis while he was CEO. He guessed the least preparation would be to develop answers to possible questions the Council member might ask. He had two days to prepare. It was imperative the Council representative left Zurich happy. He must be confident in the direction of the ReLife project and Klaus's leadership. For the time being, all the other problems would be in the hands of Rollie Sweats, Claude Ekstrom and Raul what's-his-name.

CHAPTER ELEVEN

A MORNING OF SEX AND POSITIONING

ROLLIE WAS ABOUT ready to ask his assistant to find Raul Hakala when the security director rounded a nearby hallway corner and headed his way.

"Raul, I was just getting ready to contact you. Do you have a couple of minutes? I need to discuss something with you."

The two men finished shaking hands and walked into Rollie's office. Of all the employees at Phoenvartis, Rollie considered Raul a friend even though they spent very little time together. The extent of their interaction outside of work was a couple of unplanned dinners. They were both bachelors who lived in the same neighborhood. It was inevitable they would run into each other at a tavern or bistro and decide to dine together.

Although their backgrounds were vastly different, there was a natural bond from the first time they sat down and talked. Rollie was fascinated with Raul's military background. As a for-hire mercenary, Raul fought for whoever paid him the most world credits or under-the-table luxury items such as diamonds.

He had Rollie laughing hard one night at dinner when he admitted fighting for a case of sturgeon caviar.

Rollie probably knew more about Raul than the Employee Resource department at Phoenvartis. He knew his parents were an odd mix of Hawaiian and Western European. He was an only child given birth to by a mother in her early sixties after the FISS plague ended. His father was a descendant of Hawaiian royalty even though it netted the family nothing in inherited wealth or notoriety. Raul decided to become a soldier because tactics, misdirection, and fighting were the only things he excelled at as a young man.

The two men were only two of the six executives retained by Klaus Ekstrom when he became CEO of Phoenvartis. They seemed to share a lot of thoughts about the company without saying a lot about their own responsibilities. And neither of them were fans of Klaus Ekstrom even though they never openly criticized the loser who ran the company.

Raul always enjoyed speaking with Rollie. He found Rollie's background as a black athlete from the southern part of old America fascinating. He loved hearing about Rollie's extended family. Stories about the Sweats family were like attending a well-written play with an endless list of eccentric characters.

"How have you been, Rollie? It's been quite a while since we got together, hasn't it?"

"Yeah, it has, Raul. We should make plans to do something. Maybe hit the slopes for a ski weekend or at least go out to dinner. Why don't I contact you this weekend and let's see if we can arrange something?"

"Sounds good, Rollie. So, what's going on?"

"Raul, I have a favor to ask. I'd like you to do a sweep of my office and Claude Ekstrom's office looking for any type of eavesdropping devices. It can be visual, memory or sound type. And I'd like it done without anyone knowing other than you and me."

"That shouldn't be a problem. But tell me why you think it's necessary. Your input may help me know what to look for."

"Raul, there's no sense trying to bullshit you. I'm sure you've heard about the ReLife project which Claude and I are spearheading. It's a very sensitive project with immense potential for the company, providing we can make it work."

"What does "make it work" mean, Rollie?"

"In its simplest form, it means reproducing animals and humans from a donor's cell sample. Before you ask, we're not sure yet how much of a sample is needed. It could be as little as a single strand of hair or a dab of bone marrow, or as much as an arm or leg. That's one of the things we need to figure out."

"Okay, Rollie, go ahead with why you think you need me to check out your offices."

"In the Beobachter this morning there was an article about Phoenvartis creating human clones. Did you see the article, Raul?"

"Yeah, I sure did. Quite interesting."

"Yes it was, Raul. There was a lot of bullshit in the article but there were also a lot of facts which could have only come from someone within Phoenvartis. In other words, there is a leak within the company. That person is either intentionally or unintentionally leaking information about the ReLife project. I'd like to know who it is and think a good place to start is my office and Claude's office. I want to know if someone is eavesdropping on our conversations."

This was the second time within an hour Raul had heard about ReLife and the Beobachter news release. Whoever planted the seed for the news story sure stirred up a hornet's nest. All the executives associated with the project were very upset.

Raul thought it best to keep quiet about his meeting with Klaus Ekstrom. There was no reason for Rollie to know about the investigative assignment he was given by Klaus. He trusted Rollie more than Klaus, but his gut feeling was that both men were hiding vital information about the project. What it might be was anyone's guess. For whatever reason, both wanted to see if a nosy security director could unearth information to confirm their suspicions.

"Rollie, let me see what I can do. Just so you know, the halo detector hasn't shown any eavesdropping activity in the building for quite some time. But I admit, it's not a fail-safe system."

"Raul, refresh my memory, what is the halo detector again?"

"Rollie, the entire building is set up to detect any type of electronic bugging. It's like having a giant net over the building that is looking for certain frequencies used by bugging equipment. If one of those frequencies is detected, an alarm condition transmits to my office showing the location and time."

"Oh, yeah, I remember now. You told me about it one time at dinner. I'd say it's a pretty effective system."

"It's good, Rollie, but not infallible. The more sophisticated bugging equipment can get around the halo detector system. As the old saying goes, there hasn't been a safe made yet that can't be broken into."

"What's a safe, Raul?"

Raul let out a chuckle before answering. "It's a large metal box used hundreds of years ago to store valuables in. There were locks on the doors so only the person with the combination to the lock could get into the safe."

"It sounds like the large jar with a screw lid my Grandmother LeeLee keeps her valuables in. Believe me, no one has ever broken into her jar or even thought about trying. They know she'd figure out who it was and then there would be hell to pay."

Both men laughed at Rollie's description of his grandmother's makeshift security container. Mentioning her name again made Rollie remember that the package she sent should be arriving soon.

"Anyway, that's about all I can tell you, Raul. I want to make sure the leak isn't coming from our offices. If it isn't, then you might want to expand your investigation."

"To tell you the truth, Rollie, I already decided to look into this after reading the Beobachter article. I agree, there's too much accurate information in the article to be a fluke made up by some reporter. Someone is feeding information to Beobachter and I better find out who it is before things get out of hand."

"Well, I'll let you handle that, Raul. I've got enough problems of my own. Will you let me know if you find anything?"

"If you don't hear from me, it means that your offices are clean. I should know one way or the other by tomorrow afternoon."

"I hate seeing you work on the only day the company is closed, Raul."

"No problem, Rollie. I usually work seven days a week anyhow. Besides, there's an important guest coming next week from the World Council. I want to make certain our physical and informational security systems are perfect. By the way, the tip about the important guest is not for publication. It's for your ears only, Rollie."

"Thanks, Raul. I appreciate the inside info." Rollie stood up and escorted Raul to the office door. It opened automatically after scanning each man's facial features. The match of facial feature "reads" to authorized personnel file was instantaneous.

"Raul, I'll contact you tomorrow or the next day and we'll plan some type of get-together. Okay?"

"Make sure you do, Rollie. I could use some relaxation and fun."

Rollie gave Raul a slight pat on the back and both men headed to their offices.

As Raul walked the aisles of Phoenvartis he replayed in his head the meetings with Klaus and Rollie. He wondered if he missed any obvious connections between them. Most importantly, he tried to guess what information each man was keeping under wraps. If he could figure out what wasn't being said, he had a chance determining why these guys were being so secretive. Possibly his upcoming leisure time with Rollie would net more pieces to the puzzle.

When Raul got to the monitoring center for the building, he scrolled through several live video feeds. The images were from various locations throughout the building.

"Looking for anything, in particular, sir?" The agent monitoring the video screens knew it wasn't his place to question what his boss was doing but decided to offer his help anyhow.

"Nothing in particular, Jon. It's been a long time since I used this equipment, so I thought I'd see if it's working okay. Have you had any problems with it?"

Jon began describing a few minor problems with the equipment, but Raul didn't hear a word coming out of his mouth. He was too focused on two of the twenty-four images on the monitoring console. One image was outside of Klaus Ekstrom's office. Ekstrom was standing next to his assistant's desk giving her either a chewing out or detailed instructions. Ekstrom was obviously agitated. There were sweat stains under his armpits, and he paced and fidgeted as he spoke. Raul wanted to turn on the audio, so he could listen in on this conversation. But, doing so would bring it to the attention of his employee. It was better not to give Jon any reason to believe that he was snooping on the CEO of the company.

The second video image was Rollie's office door. What drew Raul's attention to this monitor was seeing Rollie leave his office dressed for the outdoor inclement weather. Ten thirty in the morning seemed like an odd time to leave the building for any reason other than going home sick. Raul was tempted to follow Rollie and find out where he was going. He elected instead to use the city's monitoring system to keep tabs on him.

It was illegal for Raul to use the city's video system. He only did it in unusual circumstances where the risk was worth the reward. Raul stepped into his office and contacted one of his paid sources in city government. This person was authorized to use the city monitoring system. He patched Raul into it without asking any questions.

Raul sat back and watched Rollie on the holographic screen in his office. His friend meandered through the city streets for ten minutes until he ended up outside a building. Raul recognized it as Rollie's apartment building. He watched Rollie vanish into the building. Raul thought about shutting off the video, but he was curious why Rollie would be going home at such an odd hour.

As he thought about possible explanations, he noticed an attractive, dark-hair lady enter the front door of Rollie's building. Even from a side-view she looked familiar, but he couldn't identify who she was or where he might have seen her. He waited another fifteen minutes for either of them to reappear on the street. When that didn't happen, he set the city system to record mode. He left his office went to the company's cafeteria for a cup of coffee. He hoped that a walk and some caffeine would clear his head, so he could see the best investigative avenue to take.

As Raul paid for his drink in the cafeteria, the dark-hair woman was taking off her black business suit and crawling into bed with Rollie.

She snuggled up to him from behind and started kissing him on the neck.

"Hi, do I know you, lady?"

Sophia gave Rollie a weak slap on the shoulder and pretended to be offended. "You better know who I am mister. I've spent enough time in this bed with you over the last couple of months."

Rollie rolled over, looked seriously into her eyes and said, "Oh, yeah, I remember you. You're that gal from Archives. The one I've been trying to meet for so long." Rollie's playfulness was endearing. It was the thing she needed to hear to feel romantic again on another misty, overcast day in Zurich.

As he stroked her backside, she asked, "Are you going back to work today?"

"No, Claude and I are pulling another all-nighter in the lab. So I'm going to get some sleep after you leave. How long have you got?"

"About an hour before they start wondering where I am."

"Well, in that case, Madam, we better get started." Rollie needed to catch up on his sleep but decided he had other needs which were more important. He pulled her closer and started to take her, beginning at her head and moving slowly to her toes.

Halfway into foreplay, a thought raced into Rollie's head forcing him to stop pleasuring her.

"What's the matter, Rollie? Why did you stop?"

"I'm sorry, Sophy. I just thought of something."

"Are you going to share it?"

Rollie ignored her request and went back to work with his hands and mouth. But he still had a figment of his earlier thought rolling around in his brain. There would be plenty of time later to dissect why Raul mentioned the special guest coming to Phoenvartis in an office which might be bugged. Unless he knew for certain there were no bugs in the office! Rollie smiled on the inside at his clever and sneaky friend.

CHAPTER TWELVE

DECEIT, MYSTERY AND ARETHA FRANKLIN

WHEN ROLLIE WOKE UP, the sun was dropping behind the mountains. The street lights were automatically coming on as darkness moved across the city. For the first time in several weeks, Rollie felt as though he had a few hours of quality sleep. Having Sophia come by for a mid-morning romp in the sack relaxed him enough to forget about the ReLife project problems. He was now refreshed enough to spend another ten hours in the lab with Claude. With luck, they would make considerable progress toward the goal of replicating animals and humans that were mentally and physically sound.

He had another two hours before meeting Claude. Rollie decided to clean up and have a decent meal at one of the local restaurants. His diet during the last couple of months was irregular and filled with junk food. He could see a bulge developing around his midsection and the jowls on his face growing plump. He had to get back to taking care of himself no matter how much stress the ReLife project caused in his life.

In a sudden burst of energy, Rollie dropped to the floor and did fifty leg lifts, sit-ups, and push-ups. He should have started an exercise program with fewer repetitions, but the words of his former football coach rattled around in his head. "No pain, no gain." He laughed, knowing that tomorrow there would be plenty of pain but little gain.

Slightly winded, Rollie got to his feet and went to the bathroom to take a shower. This was his time to listen to music from hundreds of years before. He loved classical music by Bach and Beethoven and a few other masters. If it wasn't classical, he had a real fondness for the music produced by Motown Records during the 1960s and '70s. There was something about the beat of these tunes which reached deep into his soul and made him want to dance like a teenager. He was one of the few people left on planet Earth who knew anything about Motown music. He knew where it originated and the artists who recorded on its label. He wondered if anyone, other than himself, knew what a record label was.

After drying off to Aretha Franklin pounding out "R-E-S-P-E-C-T," Rollie dressed and headed to the kitchen to see if Sophia left any notes. He had grown accustomed to finding her short notes on either the kitchen table or hanging on the food dispenser unit. None of them mentioned love but they all described her admiration and respect for various aspects of his life. He was usually amazed by how she could isolate a single facet of his personality and honor it. She described it as though he were the only person on earth who possessed that positive trait. Regardless of whether he agreed or not, Rollie always felt a little better about himself after reading one of her notes.

For the first time he could remember, Sophia didn't leave one of her gushing notes. She did, however, put a small box on his kitchen table with a note which read, "Found this outside your door. Contact me when you can. Want to see you soon. Love, Sophia."

Rollie stood at the table staring at the word love. Did she

mean love as in, I love you, or was this a pleasant way for her to end a note to a friend? Could it be she was falling in love with him or was she being the perfect girlfriend? Just as he was getting used to her personality traits she threw him a curve ball called love.

As Rollie unwrapped the box from Grandmother LeeLee, his thoughts turned to how he felt about Sophia. In a few short months, the woman in black who flirted with him one night in the Schwarzenbach Tavern had walked into his life as a lover and friend. She also got a job at Phoenvartis and became friends with his assistant. It was as if they were predestined to become enmeshed in an intimate relationship. And, nothing in the cosmos was going to stop it from happening.

Sophia's explanation for this rapid coming together was quite simple. She believed that the life forces of two people could be so attracted to each other it was inevitable they would meet and have some type of intimate relationship. This was one of several new age beliefs Sophia espoused. She also believed in reincarnation and described in detail being a slave girl in ancient Rome. At first, Rollie found her off-the-wall comments and stories comical. But he stopped laughing when he realized how serious she was about her beliefs. Was it possible that part of her brain short-circuited occasionally? Or was she one of those people who were so smart they couldn't help having thoughts most people found bizarre? Regardless of her strange beliefs, there was no question she was a tigress in bed.

For now, he thought it best to ignore the affectionate closing to her note. If she was really falling in love with him, it would come out again. As soon as the ReLife project stabilized he would take time to learn something about this woman other than her sexual preferences. Who was she? Where did she come from? What did she want from life? And, what was the real reason they met and became involved? Being a suspicious person, Rollie considered the life-force explanation a pile of malarkey. He guessed their union was somewhere between coincidence and sinister. But time would eventually lead to the real reason.

He removed the wood box from its container and placed it on the table in front of his chair. It was about twelve inches long by six inches high and wide. It was made of pristine maple burl, sanded and polished to a near-perfect, semi-gloss finish. The small, round bird's eyes in the wood glowed like the eyes of a live, winged creature. There were no nails holding it together. Rollie guessed the artisan who put this box together almost 400 years before used some type of interlocking dowel system to keep it solid. Whatever the fabrication and assembly method, the joints were impossible to see.

A capital "H" was carved into one large side of the box. It was in an old Roman English font and at a uniform depth of one-eighth inch. This lone letter was approximately four inches tall by two inches wide. It was detailed sanded and polished just like the rest of the box exterior. Rollie could not remember if his grandmother ever explained what the "H" stood for.

Rollie vaguely remembered seeing this box twenty to twenty-five years before. Grandmother LeeLee showed it to him one afternoon in her kitchen while the other kids were busy playing outdoors. He remembered her treating it like the most precious thing in her life. The only thing he could remember about that afternoon was Grandma LeeLee's words. "One day this will be yours, Rollie. So don't forget what I told you about the secret of this box." Now, years later, he wished he had paid attention to her. He could kick himself for not listening to her instructions. But as a young lad, he was too busy worrying about what his buddies were doing outside.

Rollie turned the box slowly in his hands. He hoped this would bring back the entire conversation with his grandmother from so many years before. He was ready to give up trying to find a way into the box when gravitation took over. The top swung open on a set of concealed hinges. A small piece of paper dropped out of the box and floated to the table.

Rollie put the box back on the table and picked up the note. It was from his grandmother and read: **"Sunny Boy: what I promised you long ago. I've received word from Him that you need this now. Remember what I told you. The obvious isn't always obvious. Love Grandma."**

He read and re-read her note several times. She was trying to communicate some type of encrypted message to him with her cleverly worded note. Now, he was very mad he hadn't paid attention to her so many years before. There was something special about this box. If Grandma LeeLee said he needed it now, then it was imperative that he remember its secret as soon as possible.

Thinking about Sophia, examining Grandma LeeLee's box and singing along with Aretha Franklin had consumed the extra time allocated for a decent meal. He had fifteen minutes left to walk to the lab and meet Claude. It looked like another night of eating second-rate food from the company dispensers. If he had known it was another night of junk food, he wouldn't have bothered exercising.

Regardless of how bad his next dinner would be, Rollie was excited about meeting with Claude. The first phase of animal testing was scheduled that night. With any kind of luck, there would be a few new cloned animals on planet Earth by morning. Fortunately, the company was closed tomorrow so they could work all night and into the next day if they wanted. Rollie looked forward to a productive evening, cloning simple animals like frogs and mice which took less than an hour each.

About the same time Rollie arrived at Phoenvartis, Raul Hakala was getting ready to go home and get some sleep. He had a big day planned tomorrow plotting access codes and times from critical areas of Phoenvartis used for the ReLife project. He planned to backtrack four to five weeks looking for any obvious patterns. Repetitious and odd behavior didn't necessarily prove someone guilty. But it often pointed to prime suspects and unauthorized or even criminal behavior.

Half a world away, Grandma LeeLee was rocking back and forth on her front porch swing. She had an unfiltered, hand-rolled cigarette hanging from her lips. She was warned a hundred times by her personal physicians to give up smoking but was never able to kick the habit. Yet, she had outlived the six or seven physicians who warned her about the evils of smoking.

She needed the calming effect of her cigarette this afternoon. She knew there was something wrong with her grandson Rodolfo. He was in danger of some sort. She could see in her mind's eye an evil and ominous cloud hanging over her grandson's head. It was black as night and threatened to injure her beloved Sunny Boy in some way. She knew the black cloud represented a person rather than an event or situation. Someone close to Rodolfo was planning to harm him.

As Grandma LeeLee worried about her kin, Sophia was communicating with her contact person at the Black Cross in Berlin. What she didn't know was Raul Hakala had already identified her as the woman entering and leaving Rollie's apartment building. A fast-forward scan of the city monitoring system gave him an excellent, face-first image of her leaving the building. He loaded the facial image into the company's identification system. After a quick scan of the database, it came back with a match to the new girl hired to run the Archives department. The system also told Raul she didn't live in Rollie's apartment building. It didn't take a genius to conclude that she and Rollie had something going.

Klaus Ekstrom sat alone at a table in the Faulkner Tavern pounding down shots of vintage Irish Whiskey. He was trying hard to forget the miserable day he just fought through.

CHAPTER THIRTEEN

A NIGHT IN HELL

FIFTEEN HOURS LATER, Claude Ekstrom and Rollie Sweats sat in the company cafeteria wondering why their animal testing was a bust. It had been a tough night filled with a few successes but plenty of failures. Rollie massaged his brow with his right hand, hoping to calm his splitting headache. The coffee he drank wasn't helping either. He promised himself to bring a container of whiskey to the next 'all-nighter' to either help celebrate or drown his sorrows.

Of the twelve animals they replicated, only five turned out physically sound. They had all their limbs and the internal organs were correctly positioned. There were no apparent maladies or disfigurements. Also, the five survivors appeared to be acting the same as non-cloned animals of the same genus.

The evaluation of their mental capacity was a guess based on a couple of hours of observation by Claude and Rollie. These animals, which consisted of two mice, one small dog, and two frogs, seemed alert and responsive to external stimulus. They over-ate just like their non-cloned counterparts. A brain scan of each revealed waves like those found in the same non-cloned species. Unfortunately, these observations and tests didn't guarantee the cloned brains were functioning properly. Until they could communicate with cloned animals or humans, the two scientists had no way of confirming the accuracy and functionality of replicated brains. Based on the pathetic results of the first round of cloning, the idea of communicating with a replicant seemed far in the future.

The seven animals who did not clone correctly were monstrosities. To refer to them as mutants or freaks was a compliment rather than a slur. Rollie could still see the twisted, deformed bodies of these pitiful victims. But what scared the crap out of him was the perverse expressions on their faces. If eyes were truly the windows to the soul, these things somehow knew they were hideous and not meant to live.

Fortunately, most of them died within an hour of being taken out of the CR47 incubator. The one which survived beyond an hour cried and writhed in terrible pain. It looked at Claude and Rollie with pleading eyes wishing to be shown mercy. Finally, Claude couldn't take anymore and put the pitiful thing out of its misery.

Only five of the seven failures were autopsied. Rollie and Claude realized examining every creature was a waste of time. There were no noticeable similarities in their deformities. The few external limbs and internal organs which appeared to be normal were not similar from one to another. Rollie was hoping the failed clones would show the same deformities in part or whole. Similarities among the failures might have revealed a clue about why some cloned replicants were a success and others were a disaster.

Simply touching the failures during autopsy gave Rollie the willies. He and Claude wasted no time and completed each examination within fifteen minutes. If they wanted to spend more time examining the bodies, they could review the autopsy videos later. Rollie couldn't wait to dispose of the bodies in the combustion chamber designed to incinerate hazardous waste.

The five successful clones were now critical to understanding if cloning in the CR47 could be done with a high rate of success. These five animals needed to be analyzed and evaluated thoroughly. If there was a common denominator among them which guaranteed successful cloning, it needed to be found. There had to be a common link between these clones which the seven unsuccessful clones did not have. Until it could be found, Rollie was hesitant to move ahead with more testing. He didn't think he could tolerate seeing more deformed and mutated animals.

"Claude, can you take the mice home and keep an eye on them? I'll take the puppy and frogs to my place."

"What do you want me to do with the mice?"

"Well first, take two other mice from the lab so you have two clones and two non-clones. Treat all four the same. Feed them the same food in the same proportions and at the same time. Put their cages side by side. Watch their behavior and put a recorder on the cages. Think of some tests you can put all four mice through. Maybe create a maze and see if the cloned mice can negotiate it as well as the non-cloned mice. Be creative, Claude, and use your imagination. There must be several tests you can think of to determine if all four mice act the same. Oh, by the way, mark the mice on their bellies so you don't get them mixed up."

"That sounds easy enough, Rollie. What are you going to do with your clones?"

"I'm not sure what I can do with the frogs, but I'll think of some tests to put the puppy through. I grew up with a bunch of dogs in the neighborhood, so I have a good idea of how to train a dog and determine its intelligence. One of the things we definitely have to focus on is the clone's ability to remember."

"What do you mean, Rollie?"

"It's critical to know if the clone can remember what it learns each day. In other words, does it have a memory? Let me give you an example. Let's say one of your cloned mice learns how to negotiate the maze and lowers his average time to five minutes. Then, you stop the maze test for a week before resuming it. Does the same mouse remember how to get through the maze in five minutes? Or, does he have to relearn the intricacies of the maze to get back to the five-minute speed?"

"Okay, that sounds reasonable. What else do we need to do?"

"For the next few days, we need to go through the autopsy results and analyze the blood, fluids and tissue samples. We need to run comparative tests on the chromosomes and DNA for all the clones. Bottom line is that we need to look at everything. We need to explain why some clones were successful and others were, well, you saw what they were."

Rollie paused for a minute to take another drink of coffee. After collecting his thoughts, he spoke. "Claude, if we're going to play God, we better be damn sure we know what we're doing because I don't have the stomach for any more results like tonight."

Before Claude could say anything, Rollie spotted Raul Hakala enter the cafeteria and look his way. He gave Rollie a half wave, went to the coffee dispenser for a cup and then walked over to the where Rollie and Claude were sitting.

"Oh, shit! Claude, don't look now but Raul, the security director, is heading over to our table. Let me do the talking, okay?"

"He's all yours, Rollie."

"Well, I didn't expect to find you two here this morning. Especially on your day off."

Raul sat down and began adding a sweet creamer to his coffee.

"Hi, Raul. Do you know Claude Ekstrom?"

Raul leaned over the table and shook Claude's hand. "Pleased to meet you, Claude. You have a popular last name."

Claude didn't know how to take Raul's remark. Rollie knew he was either kidding or wanted to see if he could get a rise out of Claude. Either way, the remark was of no importance. Claude kept his mouth shut and ignored the security director's comment.

"Funny, Raul. To answer your question, Claude and I were here all night working on the ReLife project. What are you doing here so bright and early?"

"One of my agents is sick so I thought I'd fill in for him." Raul's lie sounded plausible. And it was unlikely that Rollie would waste time trying to verify his story.

Neither man was going to admit what they were doing at Phoenvartis on a day the company was closed. Raul wasn't going to say that he came in to look for abuses in the ReLife project. And Rollie left out that he and Claude spent the entire night using a supposedly inoperable CR47 cloning machine.

For the next thirty minutes, the three men sat in the cafeteria discussing sports, women, family and any other subject they could wring a few laughs and thoughtful remarks from. As much as Raul tried, he couldn't get Rollie or Claude to open-up about their late-night vigil. Their silence would make his job of getting to the bottom of the ReLife project a little harder. But he was glad they kept quiet about highly confidential information.

"Well guys, I have to get home and get some sleep. Raul, it was a pleasure meeting you and I'm sure I'll run into you more in the future."

"'The pleasure was all mine, Claude. Say hello to your uncle for me."

Claude stopped shaking Raul's hand at the mention of his uncle and gave Raul a questioning stare.

"Yeah, sure. No problem. See you guys later." Claude turned and walked out of the cafeteria. On his way to the lab to get the mice, he wondered why Raul would make such an odd comment about saying hello to his uncle. Did he think his uncle was a close friend? As far as Claude knew, Raul reported directly to his uncle which gave him more access to the man than himself. When Claude got to his office, he was too tired to worry anymore about Raul. If he remembered, he would ask Rollie in a day or two what Raul was trying to do with the comment about Klaus. Otherwise, screw Raul.

"Claude was pretty quiet this morning, Rollie. I heard he was a loud-mouth, ego-filled dink. He sure didn't act that way this morning."

"Claude is a good guy when you get to know him, Raul. Plus, I worked him hard last night. I'm sure he's really tired like I am."

Not to be denied, Raul tried one last time to discover what Rollie and Claude were doing during the night. "Did you guys make any progress on ReLife last night?"

Rollie wanted to either laugh at Raul's question or tell him to knock off the bullshit. The repetitive questions about ReLife and their all-night vigil plus the wisecrack about saying hello to Klaus made it obvious he was digging for something. If he had to guess, Rollie put his money on Klaus instructing Raul to find out why the ReLife project was stuck in place.

Rollie made a mental note to himself to talk with Claude about Raul. Claude had to understand they now had a bloodhound on their trail. They would have to be extra sneaky and cautious from this point forward.

"Raul, I think we made some progress last night. We spent most of the time evaluating our progress thus far and laying out the best course of action for pushing the ReLife project ahead. You know, just scientist type stuff."

Raul gave Rollie credit for coming up with such a noncommittal, ambiguous answer. He was good at making nothing sound so important. With or without Rollie's help he would get to the bottom of the ReLife project one way or another.

"Well, I know you guys will figure things out soon. Hey, are we going to meet for dinner tonight?"

"Yeah, I'm glad you reminded me. Let's meet at the Raven's Lair at 7 p.m. I need to get a good nap this afternoon, so I won't bore you to death at dinner. Do you know where the Raven's Lair is?"

"I do. They've got great food. I'll meet you there at seven bells. Go home and get some sleep, buddy."

Raul patted Rollie on the back a couple of times as the two men left the cafeteria. Once in the main hallway, they went opposite directions. Rollie needed to get the puppy and frogs before going home. Raul's first stop was the monitoring central station to review recordings and look for unusual access code activity.

CHAPTER FOURTEEN

MR. SLICE

FINDING ROLLIE and Claude in the building early in the morning made Raul reprioritize his schedule for the day. The first thing he decided to do was find out if the CR47 room had monitoring equipment in it. If it did, he could determine who was using this room. He also decided to put an auto-search on the video recordings for Claude and Rollie's offices. The auto-search would do a fast review of the recordings and make a condensed version showing only the times someone went in or out of either office. By using this feature, approximately 30 hours of recordings between the two offices could be reviewed in less than 1 hour. By noon, Raul would know exactly how much time the two scientists spent in their offices the previous night. And if they weren't in their offices, then where the hell were they?

All the backtracking of access codes and recordings had to be done by 1 p.m. at the latest. Digging into the ReLife project and Rollie's activities were important but not as important as preparing for the visit by the World Council member. It was imperative that Raul check the building's physical security and emergency preparedness plans in detail. Were access systems used? Were employees trying to bypass these systems? Were there any signs of system break-ins from off-campus? Was each electronic access from off-campus by a registered and authorized person?

There were a hundred other things to look at before tomorrow morning. He planned to return to Phoenvartis after dinner and work through the night making sure his areas of responsibility were 100%.

When Raul walked into the monitoring central station, he was surprised to find a stranger being escorted around the facility. Raul watched as two of his agents described each piece of equipment to the stranger and gladly answered his questions. They were falling over themselves trying to be helpful to the stranger. Raul had no idea who this person was. This fifty-year-old with a full, bushy beard that matched his rotund physique certainly didn't work at Phoenvartis.

The more he watched the more upset he became. Who the hell was this stranger and what was he doing in his monitoring central station? Raul's internal thermometer was rising fast and close to bursting. He wanted to race over to the three-man group and haul all their asses out of the central station. On a military base, he would have these idiots arrested for violating security procedures in a top-secret, crypto area. Unfortunately, this wasn't a military zone so the best he could do was fire his two agents. Then the stranger could be interrogated to determine his identity and why he was at Phoenvartis. His answers better be damn good, or he would face criminal charges.

"Agent Murphy, can you tell me..."

This was as far as Raul got with his question before Murphy saw him and said, "Director Hakala. We've been looking for you. I'd like to present Mr. Slice from the World Council. We've been showing him around the facility ..."

The guest cut off agent Murphy's introduction. "Mr. Hakala. My name is Sedgewick Slice. As Mr. Murphy said, I'm a member of the World Council. How are you today? If I remember correctly your first name is Raul, isn't it?"

Raul was taken aback by everything he heard. He should have seen this coming. It was so typical of the World Council to use misdirection and show up on a different day. Of course, Raul couldn't act peeved about this unannounced visit. He wasn't supposed to know about Slice's visit at all. His snitch at the World Council had tipped him off to the visit. But, was the tip intentionally leaked to deceive Phoenvartis management? Regardless, there was a fat man with a red beard standing in his central station. Raul needed to put his anger aside and treat this guy with the respect due any member of the World Council.

"I, ... I mean, yes, my first name is Raul and welcome to Phoenvartis, Mr. Slice. I hope Mr. Murphy and Mr. Zeggler have been informative and answered your questions satisfactorily."

Raul turned his attention to Murphy and asked, "Mr. Murphy, did you check Mr. Slice's credentials?"

Brimming with exaggerated pride, Murphy responded. "Yes, Director Hakala. That was the first thing we did downstairs when Mr. Slice walked into the building."

Thank God Murphy followed the proper access procedures. "Mr. Slice, we have a double access verification procedure here at Phoenvartis. Could I see your credentials, too?"

Murphy and Zeggler looked at each other and then to Raul. They never heard of a double access verification procedure but were smart enough to keep their mouths shut. Their boss was up to something and they wanted to see what this was all about.

"Very efficient, Director. No problem." Mr. Slice flashed his holographic, multi-embossed and colored identification onto a nearby wall. Raul quickly memorized Slice's identification number. He would enter it later into the world security subsystem to verify it was a legitimate number. It would be interesting to see if Sedgewick Slice's name appeared and when the identification number was entered into the system. Or would it be blacked-out and labeled "Restricted Access Only."

"Thank you, Mr. Slice. I must admit, I've always wondered what type of credentials the World Council members carry.

"Now you know, Mr. Hakala. Interesting last name you have. Sounds Hawaiian. Is it?"

"You have a keen ear for the origins of names, Mr. Slice. It is Hawaiian. My father was Hawaiian, born and raised on the big island." Raul didn't believe for a minute that Slice could guess a person's heritage simply from his name and physical appearance. He bet that Slice spent a lot of time researching and committing to memory facts about the facilities and people he planned to visit. His unrestricted access to all company and government files was all he needed to make people believe he had the mental powers of a mystic. Raul wasn't falling for his act and hoped his men were smart enough to see his surprise comments for what they were.

"I want to apologize for showing up unannounced. I hope this minor interruption won't delay or negatively impact the important work you and the employees of Phoenvartis are doing. I meant to communicate my trip agenda to your central office, but my schedule has been so hectic I didn't seem to get around to it. I hope you and Mr. Ekstrom will forgive me."

Murphy and Zeggler nodded their heads up and down in full agreement with everything Slice said. Raul couldn't help thinking what a bull-shitter this guy was and hoped the amount of time he had to spend with him would be minimal.

Raul wanted to slap the big, broad smiles off his agent's faces but elected instead to excuse them. "Mr. Slice, agents Murphy and Zeggler should get back to their primary responsibilities. So, if you don't mind, I'll take over for them as your escort."

"Excellent recommendation, Mr. Hakala. Again, I don't want to upset the operational cart here at Phoenvartis. I'm sure these two fine citizens have more important things to do than waltz me around the building." Murphy, Zeggler, and Slice exchanged handshakes and parted ways.

Raul found it interesting that Slice used the term citizens rather than employees. But, coming from a person who didn't believe in socio-economic classes, it made perfect sense. In Slice's socialistic world, there was no such thing as an employer and employee. Everyone was the same. At least, that was the theory.

"Mr. Slice, what would you like to do? See the rest of the facility, or did you have something specific in mind?"

"Mr. Hakala, I forgot to mention. I think I saw Mr. Ekstrom's nephew leaving the building as I was talking with your agents in the lobby." Slice paused for a second but then continued, not giving Raul a chance to respond. "Why don't we go upstairs and look at the CR47. Is that a reasonable request?"

"No problem, Mr. Slice. This way, citizen."

Calling Slice, a citizen, was Raul's way of letting him know he wasn't fooling anyone. Raul and Klaus knew exactly why he was at Phoenvartis and there was nothing unplanned or sponta- neous about his visit. At least Raul gave Slice credit for not dragging out the charade before requesting to see the CR47.

"Would you like me to contact Mr. Ekstrom and tell him you are in the building?"

"That won't be necessary, Mr. Hakala. I don't think Mr. Ekstrom is feeling well today."

As they walked to the CR47 room, several questions were racing through Raul's head. How did Slice know the CR47 was on an upper floor of the building? Why did he think Klaus wasn't feeling well and what did he mean by that comment? Why did he mention seeing Claude Ekstrom and where did he know Claude from? And most important, how long was Slice going to continue with the parlor tricks? There were too many simple-minded people who would believe he possessed special powers and insight?

For the rest of the afternoon, Sedgewick Slice ran Raul ragged. He inspected everything and asked hundreds of questions. The examination of the CR47 room and adjacent lab alone took over two hours. For such a portly little guy, he had an immense amount of energy and was more inquisitive than a new-born kitten.

What bothered Raul about the man wasn't the number of questions, his inquisitive nature or running from one area to another without a break. Raul was put-off because it was obvious that Slice already knew the answer to damn near every question he asked. He asked Raul questions only to confirm what he already knew. Raul didn't like being tested, so he purposely answered one of Slice's questions with a made-up, bullshit answer. It was the only time during the entire tour when Raul saw Slice stop dead in his tracks. He flinched like he was hit in the head with a pitched baseball. He gave Raul an odd stare but didn't say anything.

Around 5:30 p.m., Sedgewick Slice thanked Raul for the tour of Phoenvartis and walked out the front door. He disappeared into the early evening foot traffic of couples and groups on their way to the theater, dinner and where lovers go. Raul wanted to follow him to see where he was staying but couldn't muster the energy. Slice wore him out physically and mentally. He was so exhausted he considered contacting Rollie and canceling their dinner. But the need to get off his feet and put something in his stomach overrode the cancellation.

There was no sense looking at access codes and recordings

and double-checking the company's security and safety regulations. It was too late now. Plus, Raul didn't have the energy to tackle one more thing before meeting Rollie and then going home to sleep. Yet, there was one more thing he must do.

When he got to his office, Raul entered Slice's identification number into the world security sub-system and waited for the results. For some unknown reason, it took almost three times as long to process Slice's information.

As Raul expected, the coded response came back, **"Restricted Access to This File."** The name Sedgewick Slice did not appear, and the normal picture of the individual was missing. The only other information for this identification number was an addendum at the bottom of the screen. In small print, it read, **"This citizen has been granted approval to access all domains and files."** Raul wasn't exactly sure what this meant but it sounded impressive.

CHAPTER FIFTEEN

HELP FROM MACON

AFTER COLLECTING his coat and umbrella from his office, Raul left Phoenvartis and started walking the mile to the Raven's Lair to meet Rollie. He was hoping the crisp air would reinvigorate him, so he wouldn't be a complete bore. Halfway there, he realized he was going to pass by Klaus Ekstrom's apartment building. He decided to stop and see if there was any truth to what Slice said about Ekstrom's condition. If Klaus wondered why he stopped, he could always use the excuse of telling him about Slice's surprise arrival and tour of Phoenvartis.

Raul showed his credentials to the front doorman and was immediately granted entrance to the building. Few apartment buildings had full-time doormen, but Klaus lived in one of the nicer buildings which housed many of the zone's top executives. Raul had been to Klaus's apartment once before for a cocktail party, so he proceeded to unit 302 on the third floor.

As Raul approached Klaus's apartment, he could see the door cracked open by about three inches. Music and light streamed from inside the apartment. Otherwise, there was no sign of anyone in the apartment. Raul froze outside the door for about thirty seconds to make sure he wouldn't bust in on Klaus in an embarrassing situation. His intuition said there was something wrong, so he took an energy burst gun out of his coat pocket. He knocked lightly on the door as he pushed it open to get a better look inside.

Face down on the living room couch was his boss, Klaus Ekstrom. From the smell in the apartment and empty bottles lying about it was a good guess Klaus was inebriated. The pool of vomit next to the couch confirmed that Klaus was not drunk; he was dead-ass drunk. Raul checked his pulse to make sure he was still alive and hadn't expired from alcohol poisoning. Thankfully, he wouldn't have to report a death this evening. Even though Klaus wouldn't be happy cleaning up the puke in the morning, vomiting and pissing himself had most likely saved his life.

Raul thought about leaving Klaus a note telling him about Slice but decided not to waste the time or effort. Let Klaus get the surprise of his life when he finally woke up and stumbled into work. But, to cover his own ass, Raul decided to make a couple of contact attempts to Klaus. He knew his drunk boss wouldn't wake up and answer the call. This would give him an alibi when Klaus wanted to know why he wasn't notified of Slice's arrival.

Raul took one last lap around the apartment before leaving. He wanted to make sure no one was hiding in the apartment and he hadn't overlooked anything suspicious. Finding nothing, Raul turned down the music volume and left the apartment. When he got to the street, he decided at the last minute to ask the doorman a couple of questions.

"Hey, thanks for letting me in the building. I went up to Klaus Ekstrom's apartment and tucked him into bed. He was pretty drunk." Raul made it clear he had been at Ekstrom's apartment, so the doorman would think he was honest and freely answer his questions. "Do me a favor and don't tell him that I dropped by. He would be embarrassed."

"No problem, glad to help you."

"Would you mind answering a question or two for me."

"Go ahead. What do you want to know?"

"In the last day or so, do you remember seeing or talking to a tubby little guy, about fifty years old with red hair and a big, bushy beard? He's a drinking buddy of ours and he said that he was going to check in with Klaus to make sure he was okay."

The doorman thought for a minute as he opened the door for a woman leaving with her poodle. "No, can't say I have. Believe me, I would remember anyone with a description like that. The guy must look like a leprechaun."

Raul forced a mild laugh and said, "Okay, thanks again. Here's a little something for you." Raul handed the doorman a free dinner coupon at one of the better local restaurants. Many of the restaurants came by the large corporations, like Phoenvartis, with incentives for the employees. It was part of their marketing strategy to increase business. To get their menu specials posted at Phoenvartis, the restaurant representative gave Raul's guys a couple of free dinner coupons. It was a nice perk for his guys who shared their bounty with the boss.

As Raul walked away, the doorman called out, "Hey, wait a minute. I just remembered something. A good-looking woman with long black hair came by yesterday afternoon and asked to see Klaus. I let her in and she went upstairs."

"Really? She sounds like Klaus's ex-wife. She's got black hair and is very attractive for a woman of over fifty?"

The doorman fell head-first into Raul verbal trap. "Oh, that couldn't have been her. This woman was in her late twenties or early thirties."

"Sounds like Klaus has been on the prowl and doing pretty

good for himself." Raul paused for a few seconds trying to assume the role of a buddy, jealous of Klaus's female conquests. "Now, I'm really curious to find out who this bird is. I wonder if I know her? Did this woman give her name?"

"No. When I contacted Mr. Ekstrom for his approval to let her in, he sounded like he was expecting a woman visitor, so I didn't bother to ask her name."

"Too bad, I'd like to know who he's seeing these days, so I can give him a hard time."

"Sorry I couldn't help you more. Make sure you don't tell Mr. Ekstrom that I told you about the girlfriend, or whoever she is. Okay?"

"My lips are sealed. Oh, by the way, how long did she stay with Klaus?"

The doorman was in deep thought for at least a half minute before answering. "You know, I don't remember her leaving. I usually see everyone, but I go on bathroom breaks every so often, so I could have missed her."

If he didn't have enough to do already, he added another item to his to-do list. Even though he suspected who this woman might be he wanted to confirm her identity using the city's monitoring system. It was too soon to go back and ask his city contact for access again to the system, so he assigned a low priority to this task.

His curiosity about the dark-hair woman was replaced by Slice's comment about Klaus not feeling well. If he didn't stop in to see Klaus, how the hell did he know Klaus was passed out covered with vomit and piss? Did he slip by the doorman like the dark-hair woman? Or, was there more to Sedgewick Slice than Raul thought? Raul was starting to question his intuition to size up a person's character and abilities. Could his first impression of Slice be that far off after spending almost six hours with him? If so, it would be one of the rare times in his life when the evaluator located in his gut was wrong.

About the same time Raul was checking on Klaus Ekstrom, Rollie was waking up from an afternoon sleep. He felt good for being up the entire night and working sixteen straight hours. He had about forty minutes to get ready and meet Raul at the Raven's Lair. The restaurant was only a five-minute walk, so he had enough time to shave, shower and put on clean clothes.

As he shaved, a vision started to form in his head. It was a memory of some sort. It slowly replaced his image in the mirror. He could see himself running through a field of what looked like tobacco. Overhead were two black and ominous thunderclouds spouting lightning, hail, and thunder. The thunderclouds stayed directly over his head no matter how fast he ran or what direction he went. They blocked out the daylight, so he couldn't see anything in the field.

Rollie ran, ran, and ran trying to elude the thunderstorm. Exhausted, he fell face first to the ground. He lay there trying to protect himself from the hail and thunderbolts hurled from the two sinister clouds. He realized if he stayed on the ground he would be pelted or electrocuted to death. He tried to lift himself off the ground, but his hands were locked onto something anchored to the ground. With the touch of his fingers, he could tell the item was a rectangular wood box. There was no use trying to see the item because everything around him was black as ink.

His hands worked themselves around the wood box, caressing the finely sanded grain. Soon, his hands felt as though they had found a long-lost friend. They knew every pore in the wood, each direction, and angle of the corners and all the microscopic flaws hidden in the grain. With a hand on each end, he held the box in an odd, yet specific way. He squeezed the box until he heard a slight click. He knew there was no reason to continue applying more pressure to the ends of the box.

The rain, hail, and thunderbolts stopped. A light appeared in the vision, so he could now see the field he was lying in and the box he held. A secret drawer of nearly a half-inch in height and almost the entire length of the box had popped out. He assumed the pressure applied at specific points on the ends released the lock holding the drawer in place and allowed it to spring open.

Rollie didn't have to look in the secret drawer to know what was in it. He now remembered Grandma LeeLee's instructions from a quarter century before about the box and what was inside the secret compartment. As the vision disappeared from the mirror like a wisp of smoke, Rollie smiled and realized what he must do with the box sitting on his kitchen table. He wanted to open the secret compartment but there were only five minutes left before his scheduled meeting with Raul. There was no rush. He could do it later after his dinner with Raul.

Half a world away, Grandma LeeLee was sound asleep in her front porch rocking chair when the thunderstorms started.

It was an unusually hot summer morning even by Macon standards. By 11 a.m., the temperature had already reached 93 degrees with 90% humidity. Grandma LeeLee appreciated the air conditioning in her home for sleeping at night but hated it during the day. It seemed so artificial and confining. With all the windows and doors shut tight to seal in the cool air, she felt like a prisoner in her own house. She needed to get outside for at least a couple of hours regardless of the weather.

By noon, she couldn't stand being cooped up indoors for one more minute. She went to the kitchen, made a pitcher of iced lemonade and headed to the porch to rock back and forth and wave at neighbors who drove or walked by her house. By 3 p.m., after three glasses of lemonade, the sweltering heat won the battle of wills and put her to sleep. During the next two hours, she slept through two massive thunderstorms. Each raged and spouted a barrage of rain, hail and lightning bolts.

Anyone seeing her sitting on the porch during the storms would have thought she was dead. There was no way anyone could sleep through the violent lightning strikes, howling winds and pounding hail and rain. Her trance-like sleep blocked out all the storms' violence. None of it broke through to her subconscious mind which was busy sending instructions to her grandson, Rodolpho. It was important that he know how to open the secret drawer in the maple box.

She was exhausted after waking. It was hard work using God's network to communicate His word half-way around the world. So hard, in fact, she felt like taking a nap. She got up from her rocking chair and started for the front door. It was then she noticed the lawn completely covered with small ice pellets. The bottom of her dress was sopping wet. What the storms delivered was interesting but not half as important as staying alive, so she could help Sunny Boy conquer evil.

CHAPTER SIXTEEN

GOOD AND BAD AT RAVEN'S LAIR

ROLLIE WALKED into the Raven's Lair ten minutes late. He spotted Raul sitting near the back of the dining area talking with a waitress. He found it humorous that Raul always sat far away and facing the front door in any public establishment. This was another of his military idiosyncrasies for staying alive. As Raul explained, "If someone is going to take me out in a public place then I'm going to make it as difficult as possible." It took Rollie a while to figure out what Raul meant. In his world, staying alive depended on seeing the enemy enter the building and being close to an escape route out the back of the building. Raul claimed that this simple rule saved his life a couple of times.

"Sorry I'm late, Raul. Been here long?"

"Oh, hi, Rollie. No, I just got here. I was giving Gretchen my drink order. Do you want something to drink?"

Rollie thought for a moment about what would taste good and quench his thirst. He opted to order one of the local beers and turned toward Gretchen to order. He hadn't paid attention to the waitress when he walked over to the table. When he turned to order, he was captivated with her beautiful face and figure.

Gretchen was a twenty-something beauty with long blonde hair and opalescent blue eyes. Her direct stare and beautiful smile caught Rollie by surprise. If he didn't know better, he would have thought she was flirting with him. It always amazed him how women wanted the guys who already had someone in their lives. Before he started seeing Sophia, he couldn't get a date, let alone establish a relationship with a woman. Now, he could feel the women looking him up one side and down another. It was as though they could smell Sophia's scent and decided immediately he was worth stealing from her.

"Oh, hi, Gretchen. Tell you what. Why don't you bring me a bottled beer; you pick it out. Surprise me."

Normally, Gretchen would come up with all kinds of excuses why she wasn't allowed to select an alcoholic beverage for a customer. But, in this case, she decided to play along with Rollie. He had such a warm smile and great body it was worth the risk of being caught doing a no-no by her boss.

"Well, did you get enough sleep today? You look a lot better than you did this morning."

"Slept like a baby. How did your day go, Raul?"

As Raul was ready to answer, Gretchen showed up with their drinks. She put down two napkins and then placed a drink on each. On the napkin in front of Rollie, he spotted a ten-digit number which he took to be Gretchen's communication number. He looked up at her and could tell by the look in her eyes that she wanted to hear from him.

"Is there anything else I can get for you gentlemen?"

"I don't think so. If you would, bring us menus in ten to fifteen minutes."

"I certainly will." Gretchen turned and walked away with both men closely watching her posterior.

"I think she likes you, Rollie. After you showed up, I became invisible to her."

"You're imagining things, Raul. Anyway, she's too young for either of us." Neither man believed that but acted as though it was an unwritten rule they had to follow.

"Well, she's probably too young for you Rollie, but she's still in my age bracket."

Both men laughed at Raul's ridiculous statement. "I don't know who you're trying to bullshit. As I recall, you're older than me."

"Yeah, but I look younger than you, Rollie."

As Rollie rolled his eyes, Raul took a drink and decided to hit Rollie with an unexpected question or two to see how he reacted.

"Besides, Rollie, you already have a girlfriend."

Rollie was taking a long draw off his bottled beer when Raul made the indirect reference to Sophia. It gave him the time to process Raul's statement and hold back any physical response which might give Raul a clue that his statement was true.

"You're wrong, Raul. I have several girlfriends."

Raul saw Rollie flinch a small bit and display a couple of other revealing responses. He tried to use a smart-ass response to cover up the truth, but his involuntary physical responses were enough to tell Raul all he wanted to know. The years Raul devoted to studying kinetics interviewing techniques once again paid off. Although he used these techniques hundreds of times to determine truthfulness, he was still amazed at how most people reacted physically when they lied. Unless the person was a habitual liar or on drugs, they all exhibited the same physical responses which screamed, "my answer to your question is a lie." To the trained investigator like himself, these techniques were more revealing than hooking the subject up to a truth verification device.

Knowing Rollie was seeing the dark-hair woman was the first step. Now, he needed to figure out why this woman was going to the homes of two Phoenvartis executives on the same day.

"Well, good. I'm glad to hear you're getting a lot of action. Do me a favor. When you get rid of one of your little friends, send her my way, Mr. Irresistible."

"Yeah, yeah. No problem. I'm sure any young lady would love to be interrogated and go through a background check before going on a date with you."

Both men knew this banter had run its course, so Rollie waved Gretchen over to get a couple of menus.

As each of them scanned the menus, Rollie went back to his earlier question about the day Raul had at Phoenvartis.

"Raul, you never answered my question about how your day went."

Without taking his nose out of the menu, Raul answered. "I spent the entire damn day with a member of the World Council. A guy named Sedgewick Slice."

Rollie's head snapped up like an explosion went off in the restaurant. "What did you say?"

"I said, I wasted an entire day escorting a World Council member around the Phoenvartis campus."

Rollie stared at Raul who was still previewing the menu in earnest. A hundred questions were swirling in his head, but he didn't know which one to ask first.

Before Rollie decided what to ask, Raul looked up and said, "I've decided. I'm going to have the garlic and cheese crusted cod dinner."

"Yeah, me too." Rollie couldn't care less what to eat after Raul's surprise comment about the World Council guy.

"I thought you told me the World Council guy wasn't coming until tomorrow or sometime this coming week?"

"That's what I was told. I was surprised to find this guy wandering through the offices and labs as though he owned the place. To make things worse, two of my guys gave him a VIP guided tour. They lapped up everything he said as though he was a god of some sort. They were eating out of his hand. I was so pissed, I kicked them back to their normal jobs and took over guiding this Slice character through the building."

"Don't you think that's a strange name, Raul?"

"Yeah, it sure is. The guy is a tubby little dude with raging red hair and a full red beard. He looks like a leprechaun but sure doesn't act like one."

"What do you mean by that?"

"The guy is super slick. He knows way too much about Phoenvartis and its employees. By the way, do you know if Claude has ever met this guy or any other members of the World Council?"

"I don't know. I guess it might be possible but if I had to guess, I'd say no. In fact, I'm sure he hasn't because Claude is the type of guy to brag about something like that. He's never said a word to me about knowing anyone in a high government position."

"Well, somehow this Slice guy knows Claude, or at least he claims to know him. He asked me if Claude was leaving Phoenvartis about the same time he arrived."

"That's very strange. What else did this guy want to know?

"Rollie, we spent hours looking at virtually every piece of equipment in the place. Get this, we spent about two hours in the CR47 lab. Slice looked at everything over and over and asked me a bunch of questions, most of which I couldn't answer. So, I recommend that you prepare for those questions. My guess is that he'll be at Phoenvartis early in the morning and the CR47 project will be at the top of his priority list. In fact, I think that's the real reason why he's here. He wants to know the status of the cloning project and when it will start producing results."

"What type of questions did he ask you about the ReLife project?"

"They were all science related questions. I had no idea what he was talking about. The only one I remember is something about chromosomal restructuring in different atmospheric conditions. Does that make sense to you? Oh, there was another question about how blood types and bone marrow composition affect the cloning process. Rollie, this guy was speaking a foreign language most of the time I spent with him."

Rollie thought about the two CR47 questions Raul remembered Slice asking about. At first, neither of them seemed pertinent to the cloning project. But he didn't discount entirely there was some relevance to one or both questions. He made a mental note to ask Claude if he could figure out why Slice might ask these two questions.

Rollie and Raul went over everything Slice did during the six-plus hours he spent at Phoenvartis. Rollie encouraged Raul to recall Slice's exact questions and comments. Raul did the best he could to remember the exact wording but couldn't help bitching about the time he wasted escorting the World Council member. He made sure Rollie heard several times his opinion of Slice. The man was a flimflam artist who tried to create the impression he knew much more than he did.

Rollie respected Raul's ability to correctly judge people. But in this case, he wasn't sure Raul made the correct assessment of Slice. He concluded that he would have to make his own assessment after meeting Slice.

Raul spent most of his time during dinner trying to decide if Rollie was concerned about Slice. Did Slice pose a threat to the CR47 cloning project or not? All his training with kinetics interviewing didn't help a bit trying to figure out what Rollie thought of Slice's surprise visit. Was Rollie thinking about side-tracking Slice's involvement in the project? The only conclusion Raul felt comfortable with was that Slice's primary goal was to find out the real status of the cloning project. Once he made that assessment, he could work on pushing the project ahead. Raul knew Rollie was too smart not to think the same thing.

By 9:30, Rollie and Raul had exhausted every subject they wanted to discuss. Neither man learned a lot about what the other knew or didn't know. It was time to go home and get some sleep. At the least, tomorrow would be interesting and stressful.

Raul paid the restaurant bill which would go on Raul's expense account. Rollie left Gretchen a generous tip and whispered in her ear as they prepared to leave, "I'll contact you. By the way, excellent choice on the beer."

The men left the restaurant as friends and walked together for a while before heading in opposite directions. When Raul was out of sight, Rollie sprinted the remaining distance back to his apartment. He needed to contact Claude and forewarn him about Sedgewick Slice and then open the maple box. And he needed to prepare for Sophia's visit. He had a lot to tell her this evening.

CHAPTER SEVENTEEN

I'LL DO IT MY WAY, THANK YOU!

"FOR CHRIST SAKES, I'm sleeping with both of them. How much more do you want me to do?"

"Catherine, I want to make sure you're doing all you can to get us up-to-date information on the ReLife project. This one technological breakthrough could be exactly what our cause needs to rid the world of the World Council."

Catherine, also known as Sophia, was beginning to question whether associating and feeding information to the Black Cross revolutionaries was a good idea. Her contact person was too demanding and implied constantly that she could do more to get restricted information. She was quite sure he never supervised a deep mole before. If he didn't knock off the outrageous demands, she would break ties with the Black Cross. She could easily sell her information to another group opposed to the World Council.

"Mr. Sun, if you think you can do better why don't you come to Zurich and show me how?"

"Okay, okay, I'm sorry, Catherine. I know you're doing your

best. I realize you can only push so fast for information without blowing your cover."

Krieger, using the code name Mr. Sun, wasn't sorry one damn bit. He kept pushing her for more information because she seemed to be enjoying her life at Phoenvartis a little too much. While he and his cell members were living like dogs each day, she was screwing two top executives at Phoenvartis, eating well and living the high life. Her marks were showering her with gifts and treating her like a princess in return for sex and the mistaken belief she cared about them.

"I am doing the best I can, Mr. Sun. You're not dealing with an amateur. I've been undercover many times. I've worked for groups wanting to do everything from steal information, blackmail important people and overthrow regional governments. So let me do things my way and get off my back. And by the way, I didn't see this week's deposit made to my world credit account. If that doesn't happen by 5 p.m. tomorrow afternoon, this will be the last time you hear from me."

Sophia broke the connection with Mr. Sun without any type of courteous or formal parting. That should get the point across that she was dead serious about being left alone. This constant hounding by Mr. Sun was irritating and didn't help her one bit. In fact, Mr. Sun's recommendations on how to work the marks were stupid if not downright dangerous.

His latest idea was for her to do a memory brain scan on one of her marks while he was sleeping. She couldn't believe he could be so naive to suggest this method of obtaining information. It was not only very hard, but many times damaged the mark's brain to the point of being left a vegetable. If she followed Mr. Sun's recommendations, she would end up dead or put away for the rest of her life.

And what was with the name Mr. Sun? What a foolish name. It was hard to believe the name had any significance.

And what was the reason for using the title, Mister? In the dozen or more undercover jobs she took part in through the years, not once did the contact person have a title not related to a military rank. It was usually Colonel, Commander or General. The brainchild at the Black Cross who came up with Mister must have thought it funny or clever.

This upset Sophia even more; almost to the point of calling off the entire operation. There was no room for this type of sophomoric humor in the undercover world. Being too cutesy or clever usually got people killed. She had no intention of being a victim because some idiot at the Black Cross wanted to make a name for himself. Starting tomorrow, her contact at the Black Cross was going to be treated like the amateur. And the first thing she would do is stop using the name Mr. Sun. If he demanded to be referred to by a name, Sophia thought either Dildo or Ass Face would be perfect.

She tested the temperature of her bubble bath and slipped off her clothes. As usual, the water was perfect. It would stay at the same temperature for the entire time she soaked in the bath. She needed time to forget that fool Mr. Sun, aka Ass Face. Time was too important to waste on him. It needed to be applied to handling and juggling her two marks at Phoenvartis. So far, neither Klaus or Rollie suspected she was seeing someone else.

Having two marks at the same company was risky but she had one thing in her favor. Both were high-ranking executives who signed a code of conduct contract. Bullet point number three on the contract explicitly stated that executives of the company would not fraternize or develop personal relationships with non-executive subordinates. Violation of this point or any others, like the rent Klaus paid for her trendy apartment, could result in immediate termination. This policy alone kept both guys at arm's length but close enough to be valuable sources of information.

Their relationship with Sophia was kept behind closed doors. By never appearing in public with either of these men it was easy to make each of them believe she was the committed property of only one man. She knew the day would come when one of these guys found out about the other, but it was way too early for that to happen. She needed to continue the ruse until the CR47 was working perfectly or found to be a failed pipe-dream. If the cloning project became a success, she could earn a huge bonus of world credits by figuring out how the Black Cross could access the CR47. She had no idea what they wanted to clone and didn't care to know. All she cared about was making enough world credits to live lavishly for many years.

The soothing warmth of the water and luxuriant, low pressure bubble jets relaxed Sophia enough to mellow her temperament. She remembered the upcoming date with Rollie in less than two hours. It was easy to be physically attracted to this man because he was gentle and such a good lover. Much more so than wimpy Klaus Ekstrom. Thinking about Rollie's lean and textured body and the way he used his mouth to work on her began to send chills of excitement throughout her body. She considered getting her dildo and pleasuring herself to the visual fantasies playing like an old black and white movie in her head. Her own fantasies were usually better and more pleasing than the touch of most men. But postponing her sexual gratification for a couple of hours with Rollie won out over masturbation. He always outperformed any make-believe lovers she created. Using Rollie was a lot easier than doing the work herself.

She left the warmth of the tub and went to the bedroom to select her evening wear without bothering to dry off. For some reason, she always felt sexy air drying in the nude as she prepared to meet a lover. It was another way to add more antici-pated excitement to the upcoming evening.

Sophia scanned the clothes in her walk-in closet, looking for the perfect outfit to excite Rollie. He seemed to prefer tight-fitting, dark business suits like the one she was wearing the first night they locked gazes in the Schwarzenbach Tavern. The memory of that night led her to select the same outfit. She knew he would like the tailored, black business suit worn over a ruffled white blouse and modestly adorned with a single chain of black pearls. Her black undergarments would consist of only a half bra to elevate her breasts and a garter belt to hold in place the ultra-sheer nylons. Open toe, four-inch stiletto type shoes, in black, completed the outfit. What she wouldn't wear this evening was a pair of panties. This should be a delightful surprise for Rollie and help get him hot and bothered. Anything she could do to make their lovemaking more adven-turous and satisfying made him open up about his job and the ReLife project.

She had nothing but grand expectations for this evening. She should leave Rollie's place knowing the latest about the ReLife project. Plus, she wouldn't have to worry about that dweeb Klaus trying to contact her. When she left him earlier in the day, he was so drunk and strung out on the drugs he wouldn't wake up until morning. Getting him high as a kite was the easiest way to get information from him.

As she slipped into her clothes, she thought back to the first time she was used as a sexual pawn in an undercover operation. She was only a girl of sixteen and stupid enough to believe her boyfriend loved her.

They grew up together in a small town located in the former country of Moldova. Their lives were filled with the benefits and perks derived from the two most prosperous and influential families. Her family owned several businesses including furniture manufacturing, retail stores, and coal production. His family had been buying and selling wholesale diamonds, gold and precious stones for hundreds of years. Their two companies monopolized commerce in that area of the world. The pending marriage between Sophia and her boyfriend would be the final move by the families to solidify their grip on the economy.

Unfortunately, the World Council moved into the area and set up a puppet government before the marriage took place. The entire political and economic systems in the region were turned upside down. The influence of the two families plummeted to nothing. The once prosperous families were targeted as enemies of the state. The new government confiscated their wealth and nationalized their businesses. In less than six months, the former powerful and wealthy families became pawns of the state with no more and no less than everyone else. They joined the ranks of the equally poor.

Even though Sophia's family accepted their fate, they continued to petition the government for the return of their land and assets. It never happened, and her father and mother died a pauper's death. Her brothers, sisters and their spouses were labeled enemies of the state and sent, one-by-one, to re-education camps. They refused to learn and follow the world government's dictates and ended up dying in the camps. Sophia was the only family member who went along with the government's propaganda. She played the role of a reformed citizen perfectly to gain her freedom. All the while, her hatred for the World Council grew day-by-day.

By the time she was released from the re-education camp, she was ready to strike back at the World Council. She sought revenge for the destruction of her family, the theft of her property and hijacking of her youthful happiness. It wasn't long before she united with other dissidents and formed a retaliatory strike force. Their goal was to do anything they could to cripple the central government. To assist in this effort, Sophia became the mistress of a high government official. It was her first experience as an espionage mole.

Her boyfriend's family reacted differently to the government's take-over. They fell in line with whatever the central government wanted from its citizens. They adapted to the new government and culture and learned how to survive in a highly regulated society. They used caches of diamonds to supplement and improve their standard of living by selling the stones in the underground economy.

She made the mistake of reuniting with her boyfriend. In the four years they were apart, each of them had changed quite a bit; more than either of them realized. Sophia truly believed his professed love for her. Her love was so deep she told him about the dissident group and her role as a mistress to help the group's cause.

Within two days, Sophia and everyone else in the revolutionary group were arrested. The government's justice was swift. The men in the group were executed. The women who were still a valued commodity after the FISS plague became servants and slaves to high ranking members of the local government. Sophia, who was beautiful by Moldovan standards, became the sex slave to a local magistrate. He treated her well, but she dreamed of the day she would escape and leave that area of the world. But not before slitting her ex-boyfriend's throat.

CHAPTER EIGHTEEN

A NIGHT OF LIES, WORRIES, AND PASSION

ROLLIE EXPECTED Sophia at 9:30 p.m. That gave him just enough time to contact Claude, put together a tray of finger-food and make sure there was an adequate supply of beverages.

"Mr. Sweats, how good of you to call. What can I do for you tonight?" Since making their secret pact to manipulate the CR47 project, Claude kidded around and poked fun at Rollie more and more.

"Claude, knock off the crap. I've got something important to tell you. Hang on a minute, someone is at the door." Rollie hoped he could get the call to Claude done before Sophia arrived. He wasn't quite sure it was a good idea to let her over-hear their conversation due to the sensitive topics. But, in this case, he couldn't see an overwhelming reason to keep her in the dark about what he was getting ready to tell Claude. Before opening the door, he made sure the visual option on his communicator was off so Claude couldn't see his guest.

His eyes bugged out when he opened the door. Standing before him was a goddess. Sophia had never looked so inviting and sensual. For a moment Rollie considered hanging up on

Claude and devoting all his attention to this gorgeous creature. He smiled, gave her a peck on the cheek and motioned for her to have a drink and sit down.

"Okay, I'm back. The next-door neighbor needed to return a serving bowl. Anyhow, I was told tonight that the World ..."

That's as far as Rollie got before Claude interrupted. "Let me guess, Rollie. The World Council has sent one of its members here to Phoenvartis."

"How the hell did you know that?"

"Believe it or not, I have a few friends at the company. I've already gotten two calls telling me about the World Council member who showed up today. They said he arrived sometime around noon."

"Well, your information is absolutely correct." Rollie paused for a moment to think about who Claude's contacts in the company might be. It was hard to concentrate considering how sexy Sophia looked in her tight outfit. "Hey, if you knew about this guy why didn't you call me?"

"Rollie, I did call you. I've been trying to reach you for the past couple of hours. Check your call log."

Rollie did a quick search and spotted several contacts from Claude. "Yeah, I see them. Sorry, I didn't answer. I must have had my communicator in *ignore* mode."

"Rollie, why do you think he's here and what do you want me to do?" Rollie could tell by the tone of Claude's voice he was very concerned and anxious about the visitor.

"I think he's here to check on the ReLife project. I don't know if he'll want to talk with you, Claude. But, if he does, stick to the same answers we've told Klaus. Nothing more and nothing less. I'm hoping he'll only question me and Klaus. It would be odd if he dragged you into the discussions. Anyhow, stay calm and either follow my lead if I'm in the room with you or stick to what we've already told Klaus. Very simple. Got it?"

Rollie didn't wait to hear Claude's response. Sophia was waiting and if he didn't end the communication, Claude would think of a hundred questions to ask. "Listen, I need to go. I'll see you in the morning around 8:30. Get a good night's sleep. We have a lot to figure out. By the way, how are your little friends doing?"

"I assume you mean the mice. They're fine. I've started testing them as you suggested. Nothing abnormal about them yet. They're acting like regular mice."

"Okay, good. I'll see you in the morning. Take it easy." With that, Rollie shut off his communicator and turned his attention to Sophia who was kneeling on the floor playing with the puppy.

"Rollie, whose dog is this? What a cutie."

Rollie smiled at the two of them wishing he had a recorder handy to capture the little guy licking Sophia's face.

"He belongs to a friend who went out of town for a couple of weeks. I got roped into dog-sitting."

Sophia knew Rollie was lying. He would never take on such a demanding task no matter how close the friendship. Now, she was very curious about where this little pooch came from and why Rollie had it.

"Well, he's a gem. Does he sleep with you?"

"The first night he didn't but then he got lonesome and cried until I let him sleep in the bed with me."

"Good, I'll have someone to snuggle with tonight."

Rollie rolled his eyes. "Real funny. You already have something to grab in bed."

Sophia put the puppy down and came over and gave Rollie a big hello kiss. "Can I get you something to drink?"

"Sophia, you're the guest. Go sit down and I'll make myself a drink. There are some hors d'oeuvres over there by the couch.

Oh, by the way, you look fabulous tonight. What's the occasion?"

"Absolutely nothing other than being with you. You're the best reason I can think of to get dressed up for."

It was the perfect answer. Rollie kissed her again before she went to the couch to get comfortable and he went to the bar to make himself a drink.

Between nibbling on the finger-food, Sophia asked, "Was that Claude on the communicator? Don't you guys talk enough at work? You have to talk at ten in the evening, too?"

Rollie walked to the couch debating whether to tell Sophia about Sedgewick Slice. "Yeah, that was Claude. I guess there's no reason not to tell you why we were talking. You're going to find out tomorrow anyhow." Rollie sat down, took a sip of his drink and announced, "Claude and I might be in trouble. A member of the World Council showed up today and spent nearly six hours touring the facility."

"Well, what's that got to do with you and Claude?"

"I'm pretty sure he's here to find out what's going on with the ReLife project. As a matter of fact, I'm expecting a real grilling tomorrow from this guy about the project."

Sophia half listened to Rollie. Her thoughts immediately shifted to the Beobachter article which detailed the cloning project at Phoenvartis. Was it possible this article alone was the reason why the World Council decided to send a member to Zurich? Was it enough of an embarrassment to force the World Council into investigating what was going on with the ReLife project? If so, then her plan worked. By feeding information anonymously to the news agency, the cloning project was exposed and could no longer be kept under wraps. This exposure brought a tremendous amount of unwanted attention down onto Phoenvartis. The result was a firestorm of interest by everyone directly or remotely involved with the project.

Most of these people wanted the ReLife project fast-tracked and given the highest priority. This was exactly what Sophia hoped would happen when she decided to feed information about ReLife to the Beobachter.

"Do you think you'll get fired, Rollie?"

"I don't know. All I know is what I was told. This guy from the World Council is super smart and sneaky. I guess the ball is in his court now. I'll have to wait and see what happens tomorrow."

"What does the ball in his court mean, Rollie?"

Rollie often forgot Sophia's eastern European upbringing. Her knowledge of sports jargon, especially from North America, was very limited.

"It means that my destiny, Klaus's destiny, Claude's destiny and the future of the cloning project is in the hands of this guy from the World Council. There isn't much of anything we can do at this point. The only thing we can do is try to convince him that we are still the best people to perfect the cloning system."

"Oh." Sophia thought for a moment about what Rollie said. "Sweetheart, you'll be fine. You and Claude are smart and know the ReLife project forward and backward. It would be stupid for them to put someone else in charge of the project."

Rollie looked over at Sophia, smiled and said, "Thanks. I'm glad I have at least one fan."

"Rollie, let me ask you a question. Are you and Claude going to get the CR47 machine working correctly or not?"

This was the same question Rollie had been asking himself for weeks. He looked away for a moment wondering how to answer her question. Finally, he opted for the truth.

"I don't know. I just don't know yet."

Sophia could see in Rollie's eyes that he was desperately trying to hide the fear which the World Council member created by coming to Phoenvartis. The beads of sweat on his forehead and slight quiver in his voice were completely out of character for Rollie. He was usually calm and collected and very few things got him rattled. Losing his job shouldn't upset him this much. He wasn't acting like someone who may lose his job, but rather like someone who committed a crime and was worried sick about being caught.

She stared into his eyes waiting to see if he would say anything else. When she realized his mind was somewhere other than in the room with her, she decided to change the subject to help him relax.

"Rollie, where did you get that wood box? It's beautiful and looks very old. Is it an antique?"

Sophia's question struck a chord and brought Rollie's thoughts back to the apartment and the lovely lady sitting next to him. "Yeah, it's an antique. My Grandma LeeLee sent it to me as a gift. She once told me it was around 400 years old."

"That's an odd gift for a guy like you. I could see your grandmother giving it to one of her granddaughters as a jewelry box but giving it to you..."

Rollie had to think fast. Sophia's observation and comment about the box being too feminine made a lot of sense. Frankly, he never thought anyone would question that aspect of the box.

"I loved to play with the box when I was a child. There was something about it which held my interest for hours as I opened and closed it and hid things inside it." Rollie looked at Sophia out of the corner of his eye to see if she was buying this explanation.

"Anyhow, I made her promise to give me the box when she..." Rollie caught himself before saying "died". He didn't want to think about the day when his favorite relative would be gone.

"I understand Rollie. You want something to remember her by."

Sophia slid next to him and cuddled under his arm as he nodded in agreement with her last remark.

Sophia didn't believe Rollie's explanation about why he received the box. It sounded a little too artificial for a guy like Rollie. Through the years, she learned how to evaluate people in short order. Many times, her life depended on this talent to accurately appraise new people she met. Rollie's explanations for the puppy and the box didn't match his masculine personality. He had an affection side, but it was reserved for select people, not animals and inanimate objects.

Sophia spent the rest of the evening trying to comfort Rollie. She did everything possible to take his mind off whatever consequences the man from the World Council might create in the coming days. By 11 p.m. they were in bed with the puppy. It was obvious Rollie wasn't in the mood to make love. He couldn't separate his physical desires from the problems at Phoenvartis.

Sophia had looked forward to a wild night of sexual pleasure. After all, she had decided against using her dildo in the bubble bath in exchange for the real thing with Rollie. "Oh well," she thought. "Things could be much worse." At least Rollie was talking almost non-stop, jumping from topic to topic. With a little prodding here and there, she got the latest information on the CR47 project.

Just before Rollie nodded off, Sophia asked, "Rollie, is the puppy a clone?"

"Yeah." He rolled over and fell asleep not realizing what he said to her.

Her suspicions were correct. There was another explanation for the puppy and this one made perfect sense. Sophia smiled to herself and rolled over to snuggle with the puppy.

Four hours later, Sophia awoke to the smell of smoke. Rollie and the puppy were gone. She got out of bed, put on one of Rollie's robes and walked out into the living room. Rollie was sitting at the kitchen table, smoking a cigar and fiddling with the antique box. The dog was obediently laying at his feet, half awake and half asleep.

From her view into the kitchen, she could barely see that the top of the box was standing upright in an open position. It looked like there was another slim drawer sticking out from the front side of the box. Rollie held the box at each end in an odd way. As she was about to ask Rollie what he was doing, the dog's head snapped to attention. He looked directly at Sophia as the slim drawer closed. It happened so fast she wasn't sure if her eyes were playing tricks. The light in the kitchen was so dim that what she thought happened might have been an optical illusion. Then again, it might have been real.

As the dog got up and moseyed over to Sophia, Rollie turned in his chair and smiled.

"Did I wake you?"

"No. I needed to go to the bathroom anyhow. I've never seen you smoke before. I would have never guessed you liked cigars."

"You know, I don't enjoy them much. I have about one a year. It's another bad habit I inherited by growing up in an area where a lot of tobacco is grown. I think everyone in my family, including my grandmother, has a cigar every so often. The bad thing is that the drugs they lace cigars with soothe the nerves but also make you sick to your head."

Sophia laughed as she sat down at the table. "Can I look at the box?"

"Sure." Rollie slid the box over to her and watched as she opened and closed the top lid several times. She ran her hands slowly over the exotic maple wood and the carved letter "H" in the lid. She turned it over several times to make sure she didn't miss one feature of the box. As hard as she tried, she couldn't feel or see where another slim drawer was hidden. If there was a hidden drawer it blended perfectly with the rest of the box's exterior.

"What does the "H" stand for?"

"I don't know. My grandmother might have told me, but I don't remember what she said."

Sophia could tell by the tone of his voice that he was telling the truth.

"This is very beautiful, Rollie. What are you going to do with it?"

"Not much, I guess. Maybe keep some personal stuff in it. Nothing expensive; just things which are important to me."

"Good idea. Make sure you don't lose the box. I'm sure you realize it's irreplaceable. Hey, can I have a puff off your cigar?"

Rollie looked at her with suspicion, not knowing if she was horsing around or not. Why would she want to suck on something that was stinky, wet and chewed on at the mouth end? Besides, it wasn't a good cigar from an area of the Caribbean which specialized in cigar tobacco and production.

Rollie handed over the cigar and watched her take in a mouthful of smoke and hold it for a couple of seconds before exhaling. From the way she handled the cigar and smoked it, he could tell this wasn't the first time she puffed on a stogie.

"Lousy cigar, Rollie."

Her assessment of the cigar's quality was 100 % accurate. There was no doubt in Rollie's mind that she had been around cigars and the people who smoked them before this evening. He was slowly realizing that her personality was as complex as her sexual desires. She surprised him often with the things she knew. Things the normal mid-level, female employee at Phoenvartis would never know. Things only a very educated and worldly person would know. He wondered if one day she would open up and tell him her true identity and where she came from.

"Let's go to bed, my dear." Rollie stood and led her by the hand to his bed.

For the next hour, they enjoyed each other in passionate love-making. When they weren't in the heat of passion, they were trying to reassure the puppy that their moans and groans were due to pleasure and not from hurting each other. They couldn't help laughing at the pup who tried to come to their rescue each time one of them had an orgasm.

Sophia fell back to sleep at about six in the morning. In another hour or so she would have to get up and prepare for work.

Rollie stayed awake for the rest of the night. He still had several things to worry about concerning Sedgewick Slice's visit and the cloning project. He also added another minor detail to consider when he got the secret drawer in the box open.

What was he supposed to do with the body parts he found in the hidden drawer?

CHAPTER NINETEEN

ACT NORMAL AND DON'T DO ANYTHING STUPID

KLAUS EKSTROM DRAGGED himself into Phoenvartis Monday morning at 9 a.m. He felt terrible and didn't look much better. A thirty-minute shower and two pots of coffee weren't much of a remedy. What the hell had he done over the weekend? The last thing he remembered was the gal from Archives stopping by his apartment and making a pitcher of margaritas. He was blasted before she arrived but thought he was sober enough to have at least one drink and then play kissy face with her.

God, he hoped she left before he passed out and soiled himself. It was the end of his career if she recorded his sorry-ass passed out like a skid-row drunk. He hoped the extra world credits he tossed her way for services rendered each week were also enough to keep her mouth shut. Maybe he would do something nice for her today providing he sobered up enough to figure out what she might like.

He was about ready to have his identification scanned for entry into the building when one of Raul's agents walked up to him. "Mr. Ekstrom, could you come over here with me? This is very important."

Klaus was in no mood to play games but the look in the agent's eyes told him this wasn't a request, it was a demand.

They ducked into a small office off the main lobby. Once inside, the agent locked the door and then contacted his boss.

"Mr. Hakala, I have Mr. Ekstrom in room 3Z."

"Good, I'll be right down."

Klaus was losing patience. "Is this some kind of joke? Do you know who I am? And what's with a room designated 3Z? What the hell does the Z stand for?"

Klaus didn't let the agent answer any of his questions. He got up from the chair and started for the door which was an old, manually operated by key type. He turned the knob to open the door, but nothing happened.

"Would you get the hell over here and let me out? If you don't, I swear to god this will be your last day at Phoenvartis."

"Sir, please sit back down. Mr. Hakala will be here in a minute. It's very important that he talks to you before you go upstairs."

Klaus started to pound on the door hoping someone in the lobby would hear him and open the door.

"Mr. Ekstrom, this room is soundproof. The walls and door are triple-layered with a soundproof material. You can set off a bomb in here and no one outside will hear, feel or smell it."

"That's just wonderful. Get Hakala on the communicator for me. I want to fire him the same time I fire you."

At that moment, the door opened, and Raul walked in carrying a medium-size, leather suitcase. He looked at Klaus from head to toe and said, "You look better than I expected."

Ekstrom started to open his mouth to read Raul the riot act but only got as far as, "Mr. Hakala, who the hell..."

"Mr. Ekstrom, the representative from the World Council is

here. He came in a day early and already spent about six hours touring our facility. I believe he is one of the twelve high council members."

Ekstrom fell back into the chair he got out of two minutes earlier. He wanted to process what Hakala said but his migraine headache stood in the way of any logical thoughts or deductive reasoning. He opted instead to ask questions but stopped when Raul held up a finger and said, "Let me finish."

"This guy's name is Sedgewick Slice. I've checked him out as far as I can. He has the highest security clearance possible. In fact, when I entered his identification number for verification, the system did everything but say, "Warning, don't screw with this guy."

"As I said, we spent about six hours together. This guy knows a lot about Phoenvartis. In fact, he is so well versed on Phoenvartis I would say he must have some clandestine agents here feeding the World Council information." Raul paused for a moment to catch his breath and then continued. "He was particularly interested in the ReLife cloning project. He and I spent over two hours in the lab. He visually tore the place apart. He looked at everything at least twice and asked hundreds of questions. Frankly, I don't know why he bothered. I don't know that much about the project and I'm sure he already knew the answers to his own questions.

"Okay, I don't think we have much time, so listen-up, Mr. Ekstrom. This Slice character hasn't arrived yet. I'm sure he will be here today but for some reason, he hasn't shown yet. Everyone in the building knows about his visit. I'm sure my agents who intercepted him on his first visit spread the word. You need to get your act together and quick. You look like hell and still smell of booze. You need to get presentable."

Klaus opened his mouth to say something but again Raul cut him off.

"First, I want you to contact your assistant and tell her you'll be upstairs in fifteen minutes. Mr. Todd, standing over there, is going to take you into an adjacent room and put you through a cleansing station. He also has a *pick-me-up rub* for you. It will bring you back to Earth and make you feel damn good for the rest of the day. By the time you leave this room, you'll look, smell and act like your normal shitty self. Also, we have a fresh and clean suit and shirt in the suitcase for you. No time for questions now. You and I can discuss this entire situation after the day is over. Now, go with Mr. Todd and listen to what he tells you before leaving this room."

Raul turned and left the room by the door he entered through. Mr. Todd grabbed Klaus by the arm and led him into the adjacent room. As Raul described, the room had everything in it to make Klaus feel and look better. Klaus started to take off his clothes but called his assistant first to tell her exactly what Raul instructed him to say. As he spoke to her, Mr. Todd opened a sealed packet and removed the drug-laced pad from it. He rubbed it across Klaus's exposed arm skin and then disposed of the used pad. The drug entered Klaus's system through hundreds of pores and immediately attacked the toxins in his body. By the time he finished the conversation with his assistant, his head was clear, and he felt energetic enough to run a marathon.

Klaus appreciated what Raul was doing but he had a ton of questions for his security director. The first one would be what did he mean by "you look better than I expected?" The second question would be, who authorized this room and what the hell was it used for? With luck, he would still be the CEO at day's end and could ask Raul these questions. If Slice didn't like what he saw and heard at Phoenvartis, the building maintenance department might have a former CEO on its staff.

Ten minutes later, Klaus Ekstrom looked and smelled like a

top-notch executive. His thinking was lucid enough to once again put two or more thoughts together at the same time. The suit and shirt Raul picked out fit perfectly and looked very professional. He would have to compliment Raul about his choice in clothes. He might even thank Raul for what he did this morning providing he was still the CEO after Slice's visit.

"Mr. Ekstrom, please come over here and let me look at you. Okay, turn around slowly." Mr. Todd examined Ekstrom like he was purchasing a new, ultra-expensive vehicle.

"You look good, Mr. Ekstrom, and I'm sure you feel a lot better. Couple of things before you leave. Raul wants you to walk directly upstairs to your office. Put a big smile on your face, say hello to a couple of employees and act as though you don't have a worry in the world. Also, don't let anyone know that you're the last person at Phoenvartis to know about Sedgewick Slice's visit. If anyone asks you about Slice, respond with a non-answer. I recommend something like, 'his visit is just routine,' or 'we're elated to have a member of the World Council take time from his busy schedule to visit us.' Do you understand these instructions?"

Klaus didn't like being told what to say and do. But in this case, he was glad someone took the time to think this situation through and put together a game plan which included dialogue.

"I understand, Todd, I mean, Mr. Todd." Klaus owed this guy enough to be respectful and refer to him as Mister. Besides, Todd looked like he could be one mean son of a bitch if you didn't follow his instructions precisely.

"Good, let me open the door for you. Two last things. Mr. Hakala will meet you in your office in about thirty minutes, and zip up your fly."

Klaus didn't have to look down; he could feel the open door in his crotch area. He zipped up and started to his office, following Mr. Todd's instructions to the word. Other than the instructions, only one other thing got his attention. Who was Mr. Todd? Klaus was sure he had never seen this guy around Phoenvartis. Klaus made a mental note to find out about him.

Smiling and saying hello were difficult for Klaus. Both things were far removed from his normal personality. Somehow, he accomplished both and made it to his office without letting on that he was scared out of his mind by Sedgewick Slice's arrival and probing interest in Phoenvartis. He smiled at his assistant, Helga, which was very unusual and asked her into his office.

"Helga, do I have any messages this morning?"

"Just a couple, Mr. Ekstrom." Helga handed over the message chip from Ekstrom's main contact number and sat back to wait for further instructions from her boss. Ekstrom scrolled through the message chip looking for anything from Sedgewick Slice. Finding nothing, he looked closer at the other messages. Most were from executive committee members. He could see that the same committee members had tried to reach him several times this morning. These guys could wait. Right now, he had more important matters to handle.

"Helga, has anyone by the name of Sedgewick Slice stopped by my office this morning?"

Helga knew exactly who her boss was asking about. Not only was the name Slice unusual but everyone in the building knew he was the visitor from the World Council.

"No, sir. The only person who stopped by the office was Mr. Hakala. He asked that I contact him as soon as you came in this morning."

"Okay. Have you seen or heard of anyone wandering around this morning who might be our visitor?"

"Absolutely no one, Mr. Ekstrom." Helga intentionally forgot to mention the dozens of contacts she received from employees in her gossip circle. These were a dozen women and two men who were either executive assistants or mid-range executives. All had worked together for years. They were the eyes and ears of the company and nothing happened at Phoenvartis without their first-hand knowledge. With their key positions within the company, they were able at times to manipulate the direction of the company to achieve their own goals. Trivial things, like getting someone fired who they didn't like, were within their sphere of power.

Being the assistant to the CEO, Helga was the unofficial leader of this group. When the first dribble of news leaked out about Sedgewick Slice, the members of Helga's group went into high gear passing information back and forth. They wanted to be the first employees to figure out what Slice was doing at Phoenvartis. And could they use the information from Slice's visit to better their position or pay?

Klaus sat back and considered what to do next. He couldn't think of anything worse than not knowing what to expect from Slice. It would take every ounce of energy he possessed to remain calm and deal with the unknowns of Slice's visit.

"Helga, Mr. Hakala will be here within a few minutes. Don't make him wait; get him into my office right away. Then contact the executive committee members who have been trying to get ahold of me this morning. Raul and I are going to have a meeting with them. As a matter of fact, contact all the committee members regardless of whether they contacted me or not. Let's get the entire committee in on the meeting. Any questions?"

"Only one, Mr. Ekstrom. What should I do with the other people trying to contact you? As you can see there were several."

"Helga, speak to each of them and find out what they want. Use the excuse that I'm in conference and can't be disturbed. If anything sounds important to you, come and get me. Otherwise, I'll contact each of these people later."

For the next fifteen minutes, Klaus Ekstrom sat in his office thinking about what to do next. It didn't take long for him to realize there wasn't much he could do. The future of Phoenvartis was now in the hands of others, especially Sedgewick Slice. Until Slice showed up and gave him some type of direction, Klaus was nothing more than a defrocked executive. He would sit around, afraid to make any decisions or use the power of his position.

In the background, he could hear Helga speaking with the people who contacted his office earlier. The gruff and hoarse voice she used as one of the most powerful people at Phoenvartis now had a mellow edge to it. This didn't surprise Klaus one bit. Slice's visit was affecting everyone. He was walking on pins and needles and she was less authoritative. In fact, he could detect a hint of pleasantness in her voice.

Raul Hakala strolled into Klaus's office. He was the one employee who seemed to thrive in stressful situations. His military background prepared him well for challenging situations like Slice's surprise visit. He was at his best and seemed to enjoy responding to ambiguous and threatening situations. His leadership of men came to the forefront when everyone else was trying to figure out what to do.

"Klaus, have you heard from Slice yet?"

"No, not a word. How about you?" At any other time, Ekstrom would have said something to Raul about not addressing him as "Mister". But this didn't seem important now with his career and the future of Phoenvartis in jeopardy.

"Same here. I've had my contacts scouring the city and the surrounding area, but so far, not a thing. If Slice is still in Zurich, he's doing an excellent job of hiding.

"Well, what the hell are we going to do? I can't shut down

the company just because we don't know where Slice is and we're waiting for him to show up."

"For now, Mr. Ekstrom, I suggest you sit still and let me try to find out what Slice is up to. If he doesn't show up until tomorrow, then it's back to business as normal. I know today is going to be hard but be calm and don't do anything irrational or abnormal. Remember, Slice may want to see how you respond to his unannounced visit and disappearing act. Don't give him a reason to change things here or replace you. Understand?"

Klaus shook his head up and down in agreement. Raul's theory that Slice might be testing him hit a raw nerve. Besides being very insightful it was very logical the more he thought about it. Thank God, he had someone like Raul around to consider every possible tactic of the enemy regardless of how absurd or irrational it may seem.

"Raul, I asked Helga to set up a conference with the executive committee. Several of them have been trying to contact me this morning. I'm sure they want to know what the hell is going on. I'd like you to be in on that meeting."

"No problem, Mr. Ekstrom. But let's make sure we keep the meeting short. I've got a lot to do today and can't afford to be chitchatting or trying to answer questions which can't be answered yet. By the way, is there anything you should tell me which might influence Slice's visit? Possibly something which you are keeping under wraps which could be embarrassing to you or the company if it came out?"

Raul was fishing. He hoped that Ekstrom would say something about the woman from Archives or other compromising situations he might be trying to hide.

Ekstrom put a solemn look on his face. He stared into space as though he was seriously considering Raul's question and wanted to answer it with total honesty. This gave him time to wonder what exactly Raul knew about his personal life. Did he know about his drug use and what many people would consider sexual deviancy? And could his big mouth be another knife in his back? He always did have the problem of saying too much to the wrong person at the wrong time. One day he may learn that boasting about his position and power created unnecessary risk. Also, prematurely broadcasting the successful future of the ReLife program had already got him in hot water with the executive committee and World Council. He could only hope that he had passed out the previous night before divulging confidential information.

"No, I don't think so, Raul. What you see is pretty much what I am."

It was difficult for Raul to sit facing this man without either laughing or calling him a damn liar. Ekstrom's denial of any prohibited, unsavory and possibly illegal activities was a giant pile of bullshit. Raul knew it and Ekstrom knew that his security director didn't believe him.

"By the way, Mr. Hakala. I wanted to ask you about Mr. Todd. Who is he and what is room 3Z?"

"Klaus, I would describe Mr. Todd as a professional fixer. There are only a couple of people in the world with his talents. He takes bad situations which have gotten out of control and fixes them. He either puts them back together so they seem normal or neutralizes them so there is no evidence they existed in the first place."

"I'm not sure I understand what you are saying, Raul."

"Very well, let me be perfectly blunt and to the point. I stopped by your apartment the other night and found you passed out and in bad shape. This was after I spent five or six hours with Sedgewick Slice. I was going to fill you in on Slice's visit, but you weren't in any condition to hear what I had to say. I turned the music down, closed your door and left." Raul's small lie about why he stopped at Klaus's apartment fit perfectly with what he was about to say.

"It didn't take me long to realize things were spiraling out of control and headed toward a major catastrophe. I needed help and needed it fast. I used Todd once before, so I knew he could be an asset in straightening out this mess. After describing the situation, he instructed me on setting up the 3Z clean room, and what to do until he arrived in Zurich. I've asked him to stay in Zurich for a while until we know for certain what Slice is going to do."

"Interesting, very interesting, Mr. Hakala. I'm impressed with how you responded even if it sounds like a very expensive solution. By the way, I hope you weren't too offended by my appearance last night."

"I've seen a lot worse, Mr. Ekstrom. And, yes, Mr. Todd's services are expensive, but he's worth it. You might also be interested to know that Mr. Todd may have been a former World Council member. It's just a rumor but could explain why he can move freely around the world and is so knowledge-able and talented. If Slice doesn't show up soon, I'm going to ask Mr. Todd for his evaluation of what Slice is up to. I'm sure his worse guess will be better than anything we can come up with."

As Klaus processed everything Raul had to say, Helga stepped into his office. "Gentlemen, I'm sorry to interrupt but there's a man on the communication network from the Beobachter. I think it's the same guy who wrote the recent article about our company's cloning project. He wants to talk with you, Mr. Ekstrom, about our visitor from the World Council."

"Mr. Ekstrom, let me talk with him." Seeing no reluctance from Klaus, Raul instructed Helga what to do next. "Helga put him on Mr. Ekstrom's receiver; voice only, no visual."

Klaus nodded his approval to Helga to follow Raul's instructions.

"Mr. Ekstrom here. What a pleasure to have a member of the Beobachter contact me. What can I do for you sir, and with whom am I speaking?"

"Hello, Mr. Ekstrom. Thank you for speaking with me. I'm Boris Turrick and I'd like to ask you about the World Council member who is at Phoenvartis. I was wondering why he is at your company and what repercussions his visit will have on the cloning project? Can I get your..."

Raul, pretending to be Klaus Ekstrom started laughing, so hard that Boris stopped asking his question.

"Mr. Ekstrom, did I say something funny? If I did, don't keep me in the dark. Let me know...."

Raul cut off Boris again. "Mr. Turrick, I think you have some erroneous information. You need to get better contacts at Phoenvartis." Before Boris could challenge his last comment, Raul went on.

"The reason I'm laughing, Boris, is that we're trying to figure out the same things you're asking about. I was hoping you could give me the answer to why the World Council member is in Zurich and what he wants to know about Phoenvartis."

"I don't understand Mr. Ekstrom. Are you saying that the World Council member ..."?

For the third time, Raul cut him off and said, "Boris, let me do this for you. I'm very busy today but I'm going to send over my personal assistant to see you and answer all your questions to the best of our ability. He's sitting here with me now and heard everything we said to each other. His name is Mr. Todd and I am now instructing him to be honest and forthwith when you interview him. Where and when can he meet you, Boris?"

Raul could tell Boris was caught off guard. He never expected an offer to interview an emissary from Ekstrom's office. Before he could think clearly about the offer, Boris gave Raul a time and location to meet Mr. Todd.

After the communication ended, Boris wondered if he had done the right thing. The conversation with Ekstrom went too easy. Phoenvartis had never been this open about their internal affairs. Why would they change their public relations policy now? Maybe his interview with Mr. Todd would answer this question in addition to the many others he already prepared for Ekstrom.

"Why did you do that, Raul?"

"Klaus, it's time to take care of Boris what's his name. We don't have the time now to figure out who from Phoenvartis is leaking information. So if you can't eliminate the informant then the next best thing is to eliminate the person who wants the information. Mr. Todd is exactly the guy to take care of this."

"Good God, Raul, you make this sound like the overthrow of a government by assassination."

"Klaus, Mr. Todd will do whatever he thinks is best to end Beobachter sticking their nose into our business. Forget that you and I discussed this. Believe me, you have more important things to worry about."

Klaus knew Raul was right, but his plan sounded a little too evil. All he could hope for was that Mr. Todd handled Beobachter effectively without killing anyone.

"Okay, Raul. Let's do it your way."

"Good. Klaus, tell Helga to get the executive committee on your communication network and let's get this over with."

It took only forty-five minutes to brief the executive committee on Slice's visit and speculate on what he wanted from Phoenvartis. Having Raul involved in the meeting was an unexpected benefit for Klaus. Raul's detailed report on what Slice did during his visit and what transpired since was good enough to calm the committee members. They wanted to know more but Raul convinced them that there was nothing more to report. He assured them that they would be updated on any new developments. Klaus couldn't remember the last time the executive committee was so agreeable and kept their arguments and opinions to a minimum.

"Okay, Klaus, I've got to go and take care of things. Remember what I said about staying calm and don't do anything irrational. You know how to reach me. I'll be back at the end of the day."

CHAPTER TWENTY

HEADACHES FOR EVERYONE

THE NEXT TWO days were littered with unexpected events.

The follow-up article by Boris Turrick about the World Council member visiting Phoenvartis was never published. Sophia couldn't understand what happened. She gave Boris all the inside information on Sedgewick Slice. All he had to do was some investigative reporting and then write the article.

She was very surprised to find out that Boris no longer worked at the Beobachter. When she tried to find out what happened to him, her questions hit a stone wall. The public relations person at the newspaper would only say, "our company policy is not to release any information about current or former associates."

She struggled to think of something she could do to find out about Boris. Not because she cared about his welfare. Rather, she wanted to know if his leaving Beobachter had anything to do with her leaks about Phoenvartis? Did someone find out how he was getting inside information? And most important, was that someone trying to figure out who she was and how she could be so well versed in Phoenvartis business?

Sophia racked her brain to remember every detail about interacting with Boris. She hadn't given him her name or position at Phoenvartis. But she dropped enough clues about herself so that some clever investigator could backtrack to her identity. She had to assume the worst. Someone not only stymied Boris's reporting about Phoenvartis but also was trying to identify her. God forbid Boris was subjected to a memory brain scan. If he had, there was a good chance he was a babbling idiot now and her days at Phoenvartis were numbered. She would never get the opportunity to earn a huge bonus for making the CR47 available to the Black Cross. In fact, her days as an undercover operative were over unless she could dramatically change her appearance before the next undercover job.

Sophia prayed that the worst-case scenario about Boris wasn't true and his departure from Beobachter was due to a personal or business reason like finding another job. At the same time Sophia was praying to a supernatural being which she didn't believe in, Mr. Todd and Raul Hakala were meeting at Phoenvartis.

"Mr. Hakala, the Beobachter reporter was very cooperative. He needed an incentive or two to start talking, but did quite well after he lost a couple of teeth. He described his source as a female in her thirties, well-built with long black hair. From the way he described her facial features, I would guess that her ancestry was southeast European. Does this help identify your leak?"

Raul wasn't pleased that Todd described his method of obtaining information from the reporter. He was paying Todd for information, not a lesson on torture.

"Yes, Mr. Todd, I believe it does. You've saved me a lot of wasted time." Raul's mind raced ahead to how he should handle this revelation. There was no doubt the girl in Archives was the source of leaked information to the Beobachter. But why? Why was she intent on having the company's business made public? What did that accomplish and who did it benefit?

Getting rid of Boris shut off the leak problem but left a bigger problem. The girl from Archives was sleeping with the company's CEO and a key executive. Raul had to assume she was gathering information from both. Again, the primary question was "why"? What was her goal and where was the information going? The easy thing to do would be to drag her in and question her. But Raul had a feeling she was much too clever and experienced to confess to anything. He knew as soon as she left his interrogation she would disappear and any hope of figuring out what she was up to would go with her. Plus, she might expose her relationships with Klaus and Rollie before leaving town. That would be very embarrassing for the company. For the time being, Raul decided to keep an arm's length from her. This would give him time to establish her identity, where she came from and what she planned to do at Phoenvartis.

"Mr. Todd, have you had a chance to think about Sedgewick Slice's disappearance?"

"I have, Mr. Hakala, and I'm afraid I don't have any insight or new revelations for you. I am truly surprised that Slice didn't make another appearance at Phoenvartis. If you told me everything about his initial tour of the company, then I cannot understand why he hasn't come back for another visit. I would have, and I think you would have also. It doesn't make a lot of sense to me."

"Have you been able to track him down, Mr. Todd?"

"I can't help you with that. My contacts don't know where he is. He might be still here or in England or anywhere in the world. You would think a large, boisterous man with a huge mane of red hair and matching bushy beard would be easy to keep track of, but obviously not. But I did find out that Slice's forte is handling difficult jobs for the World Council. It seems he prefers assignments which no one else wants and loves surprising people with his quirky methods. It sounds like you got a large dose of his unconventional ways when he toured the company."

"I certainly did and I'm in no hurry to see him again. Which raises the next question, Mr. Todd. Do you think he'll come back to Phoenvartis?"

"Yes, there's no doubt in my mind he'll be back. But I don't know when. About the only thing I can recommend is to conduct business as normal. Don't try to predict his next move and keep a vigilant eye watching for his reappearance. I know that is easier said than done, but you don't have a choice. You are, whether you like it or not, at his mercy."

Raul was memorizing the important things Mr. Todd said. His comments about Sedgewick Slice were placed immediately into the total recall memory basket in his brain. He needed to update Klaus on Slice's activities even if they were only Todd's opinions and predictions. This wasn't going to calm Klaus down entirely, but it might help him get his mind back on running the company. He needed to push the important projects ahead without any more unnecessary delays.

"Do you have any other thoughts for me, Mr. Todd?"

"No, I don't think so. You know how to reach me, and you have my world credits account. As we agreed, I will be looking for the deposit to my account by week end." Both men stood and shook hands without exchanging any accolades or parting pleasantries. Raul wondered how Todd was going to keep a large deposit of world credits hidden from the government. He realized this was a waste of his time. If anyone could manipulate the world credit system to his advantage, it was Todd.

Raul walked Mr. Todd out of the building and then headed

to his office. The first thing he did was get updated by his agents on the assignments they were given two days before. All their assignments centered on the ReLife project. Specifically, who was entering and exiting the CR47 lab and what visual recordings were made of the lab and surrounding area in the last few weeks. What he had not delegated to any of his agents was investigating the girl from Archives. This was too sensitive and could have major consequences for the company. He would handle the Sophia probe. If necessary, he would hire outside investigators who could be trusted and had specific skills, sources, and talents.

As Raul and Mr. Todd were wrapping up their business, Rollie and Claude were finalizing their ReLife project schedule. Now that Slice had apparently gone home, they could get back to their original night schedule. Access to the lab in the evening allowed uninterrupted experimentation with the CR47 incubator.

"Claude, are your mice still doing okay?"

"From every test I've run, they seem to be as normal as any mice on the planet. How's the mutt?"

"Same thing with the puppy, Claude. He seems perfectly normal. Actually, I'm getting kind of attached to him, so I hope he lives a long and normal life."

Both men sat motionless, staring into space wondering the same thing. Why were some clones normal and others an abomination? There had to be something they were overlooking which could explain such contrasting results. They needed to find the clue to successfully replicating life and do it fast. Rollie had a bad feeling about where their secretive ReLife experimentation was headed. Sedgewick Slice was a warning signal. Someone or something else was closing in on them. It wouldn't be long before time ran out and their sabotage was exposed. They had to beat this unknown person or thing to the finish line and determine the feasibility of ReLife.

"Okay, I'll see you tonight around eleven."

As Claude left Rollie's office to head home and get a couple of hours of sleep, Raul was meeting with his agents. Each of them had assignments related to the CR47 lab. What he just heard damn near catapulted him out of his chair into a rage. It was taking every ounce of energy to maintain his composure even though he knew his face was glowing red.

"Let me see if I understand correctly what you two have told me. Mr. Zeggler, you disabled the access reader into the CR47 lab about six to seven weeks ago. And Mr. Murphy, you took the CR47 lab recorders off-line about the same time. Is that an accurate recap of what you just said?"

Zeggler and Murphy nodded their heads. They knew Raul was pissed off, so they weren't going to make things worse by talking.

"Well, gentlemen, that's great. Can you answer one question for me? Why the hell didn't you tell me about this before today? Someone please explain fast because your actions are beyond my comprehension."

Neither man wanted to look like a fool and answer the boss's question, but they were backed into a corner. Until one of them offered up a flimsy excuse they were staying in the corner.

"Mr. Hakala, we were told by Mr. Sweats to do these things and he claimed that Klaus Ekstrom approved the changes. He said there was a possibility that the access and recording systems might be creating enough interference to alter the results of the CR47 testing. So they had to be shut down until it was determined if this was true or not."

"Well, why didn't you confirm this with me, Murphy?"

"As I recall, sir, he made it sound like you already knew about these changes."

"Did he specifically mention my name? Did he say that your boss or Raul Hakala knew about these changes?"

Murphy looked at Zeggler for some type of guidance or support. Raul could tell by their facial expressions that Rollie had not used the security director's name to sell the idea of shutting down both systems. Most likely, Rollie made some vague reference to their boss. That was all it took for the two agents to assume everyone, including their boss, approved of the changes.

Zeggler answered with a lie. "Sir, to be honest, we don't remember exactly what Mr. Sweats said. It was several weeks ago."

It was bad enough that these two fell for Sweats' charade but now they were lying about it.

"Gentlemen, one last question. When I asked you two days ago to review the current access and recorder logs, what did you think I was asking you to do? Why didn't you tell me then about no logs available for the past six weeks?"

Murphy hung his head and sheepishly answered. "We thought you were asking for us to check the logs from a couple of months ago."

Raul spun his chair around, put his feet up on the wall credenza and gazed out the only window in his office. He was afraid that if he kept looking at Murphy and Zeggler he would say or do something he would regret. On one hand, his two agents were idiots for not confirming everything Rollie told them to do. On the other hand, Rollie's story was good. It sounded completely believable. How would two security agents know if power systems like the access reader and recorders were having a deleterious effect on the CR47 testing?

Add in the CEO's approval and these two fools would have done anything Rollie asked.

There wasn't anything Raul could do to salvage what his agents screwed up. Without turning back to face them, Raul gave them instructions before kicking them out of his office.

"Gentlemen, I want you to know that by not double-checking Mr. Sweats' story you have set back a very important investigation by weeks. From this point on, you will confirm any special requests or anything outside of normal procedure with me. If you fail to do this, you're done at Phoenvartis. Do you understand what I just said?"

Both men responded with "Yes, sir." Raul continued.

"Tomorrow, you will put the CR47 access and recorder systems back on-line. I don't want you to tell anyone what you've done. In fact, you will not say anything about disarming those systems six weeks ago, and you will not say anything about what we discussed this afternoon. If any of what we discussed today leaks out, you can start looking for new positions. Any questions?"

Both men answered, "No sir," and were out of their chairs and heading for the office door before Raul could say, "Get out."

Raul thought to himself, "what a day." He had taken one step forward by identifying the Archives girl and then fell back two steps because of two gullible agents. What should he do now? Or, what could he do now? Rollie had outwitted anyone wanting to know what was going on in the CR47 lab. But disarming the lab systems did prove one thing. Rollie was up to something, something big.

He had to give Rollie credit. His cover story was bullshit, but it was believable, especially to non-scientists. There was no use accusing Rollie of intentionally using this ploy to sabotage the cloning project. Accusing him of anything would be nothing more than circumstantial evidence and guesses. Not one fact pointed directly to subversive activity. Yes, Rollie won this round but tomorrow was a new day. Raul hated to lose, even to a friend.

Raul decided to break with his normal routine and go home early. He had enough for one day. If he stayed and heard worse news, he might do something crazy. An hour on the boxing punch bag and a long hot bath were exactly what he needed. He didn't want to hear or see anything about Phoenvartis until tomorrow morning.

Had he stayed at Phoenvartis and took the time to review the CR47 recordings from six to seven weeks earlier, he might have stumbled on the evidence he needed to prove Rollie and Claude were sabotaging the ReLife project. He might have found the recordings from the night they produced seven abnormal clones and five normal ones. Producing clones when the CR47 was supposedly broken and in need of two replacement parts.

Raul's disgust with his staff and departure from his normal routine fit perfectly with Sedgewick Slice's next move.

CHAPTER TWENTY-ONE

IS HE THE DEVIL OR A LEPRECHAUN?

"HELLO, Mr. Sweats and Mr. Ekstrom. I was hoping you two would be here tonight."

Rollie and Claude were surprised by the interruption from someone they had never seen before. Standing before them was a short, plump gentleman with shocking red hair and a shaggy beard to match. His rosy cheeks peeked through the massive red beard and highlighted eyes which were so pale they appeared to lack any color. Rollie could see the stranger's clothes were expensive but they were ill-fitted and hung on him like a tent.

Rollie and Claude didn't know whether to stand up or stay seated at the lab table. Both opened their mouths to say something but were so stunned by the stranger's appearance nothing came out. One moment they were alone and the next they had a visitor. For such a wide man, he moved without making a sound. Rollie found this unusual and wondered if he was losing his hearing. It was either that or this guy was a leprechaun with magical powers. He sure as hell looked like one.

"Sedgewick Slice, gentlemen. I'm sure you heard I was here a few days ago. Thought I'd come back and talk to the guys who know the most about the ReLife project. Can you fill me in on where the cloning project stands?"

"Good to meet you, Mr. Slice." Rollie had come to grips with Slice's appearance and regained his composure. "Could I see your identification first, Mr. Slice?"

"Very professional, Mr. Sweats. I was wondering if either of you would want me to prove who I claimed to be." Slice then flashed his holographic identification so Rollie and Claude could verify his identity.

When Rollie was satisfied, he said, "Please have a seat, Mr. Slice. I'd be happy to bring you up to date on ReLife."

"As you know, the ReLife project has stalled temporarily due to numerous factors. Currently, we are waiting on two replacement parts for the CR47 incubator. Without these parts, we cannot do any additional testing and...."

Rollie stopped in mid-sentence when Slice held up his hand like the universal sign for stop.

"Mr. Sweats, I didn't come here to hear the cockamamie story you and Claude have been telling Klaus and everyone else. I know there isn't anything wrong with the CR47 unit. For some reason, you two have stalled the ReLife project and I'd like to know why. What is really going on, gentlemen? Just so you know, anything said here tonight will stay between us and the World Council. You don't have to worry about Klaus or the executive committee finding out."

Claude started to fidget in his chair and kept looking at Rollie, waiting for his partner to say something. Rollie was debating if Slice was telling the truth or lying. How could he know there was nothing wrong with the CR47? And what made him believe the project was being intentionally sabotaged? Rollie had to decide to either believe Slice or call his bluff. He drew upon his experience as a good poker player and decided to acknowledge Slice's accusations.

"Mr. Slice, Claude and I want the ReLife project to be successful. It would be the next major technological and medical breakthrough in history. Plus, the company and everyone involved in the project would be world-renowned heroes overnight. But Mr. Slice, there's something wrong with the CR47. Of the tests we've run, about 70% of the cloned animals have ended up failures. You wouldn't believe the atrocities that have come out of that machine."

Rollie stopped to think about what he wanted to say next and see if what he already said had any effect on Slice. Slice hadn't moved a muscle or changed his facial expression since Rollie began his truthful explanation.

"We have been stalling the project, so we could figure out where the problem is or conclude that cloning is not 100% safe with the CR47. We've made some progress but still need more time. That's the bottom line, Mr. Slice."

All three men sat motionless, each contemplating what to do or say next.

"Thank you for being honest, Mr. Sweats. Let me ask you a question. Did Raul Hakala tell you what I recommended?"

"Yes, he did, but I don't understand what your comments meant. Raul isn't very scientific, so he had a tough time relaying your recommendations."

"That's what I was afraid of." Slice took a small, leather notebook from his coat pocket and opened it to a blank page. With an antique writing pen, he wrote something on the blank page and then passed it over to Rollie.

Mr. Sweats, this is exactly what I recommended. I can't guarantee these things will get the ReLife project jumpstarted, but I think there's a good chance one of these items is your nemesis."

Rollie looked at the paper and read the items Slice had written. Each of them was straight forward and easily understood. He passed the paper and waited for Claude to read what was written.

"Gentlemen, do you have any questions about what I've written?" Both men responded by shaking their heads back and forth.

"Gentlemen, do you have any questions about anything we've discussed?" Rollie wanted to ask Slice a hundred questions like how he got into the building and approached the lab so quietly. He decided this was not the appropriate time to be cutesy with a guy like Slice. There was something about this guy which scared the hell out of Rollie.

"Good, then you have two more weeks to resolve the ReLife project. At the end of this time, you'll either have fixed the CR47 problem or decided cloning is not possible now. If you decide the latter, then the ReLife project will be turned over to someone else."

Slice paused to let what he said sink in with the two scientists sitting across the table.

"I strongly suggest you get the CR47 incubator running correctly and figure out how to clone with 100% accuracy, 100% of the time."

Slice stood up and slammed his fist on the table. "No more screwing around gentlemen! Get the damn thing working, otherwise, terrible things are going to happen."

Slice turned and started to walk out of the lab room. When he got to the entrance, he stopped and turned back to the scientists. "Mr. Sweats, you need to be more careful about who you see outside of work." A sinister smile slid across Slice's face and he said, "Oh, by the way, tell your brother M.C. and Grandma LeeLee I said hello." Before Rollie could make any type of response, Slice walked away and faded into the darkness of the hallway.

CHAPTER TWENTY-TWO

SPREADING FREEDOM

DATE HATTORI WAS GAINING wealth beyond his wildest dreams.

In less than nine months he established a thriving business selling his cloaking device. Gangsters, revolutionaries and assorted other criminal groups were his primary customers. A considerable number of common folks also contacted Date to buy a cloaking device. How they found out about the device was a mystery. The only theory which made any sense was that average people learned of the device from seedy, lowlife members of society. Date accepted this explanation because he knew every town and village had its gangster element. And everyone in the town knew who the gangsters were and what crimes they excelled at.

Making the first sale of the cloaking device was difficult and took longer than he expected. At first, he approached several criminal organizations in and around the Asian continent with no luck. Most of these groups wouldn't talk with him because they thought he was either a government informant or simply crazy. Whoever heard of a cloaking device? They knew of only one way to avoid the world government tracking system. That was by surgically removing the kidney with the embedded tracker. They had used this method for decades with moderate success. If the operation wasn't botched by a drunk doctor and the operating room was somewhat sterile, the patient had a 50-50 chance of surviving. The opportunity for a young man or woman to live free of the government's surveillance grid was worth the surgical risk. And the allure of being a rich criminal unknown to the government attracted thousands of willing risk-takers.

The first customer to try Date's cloaking device was a crime lord by the name of Trang Mau. Mau controlled the criminal activities within a 1200 square-mile region of the central highlands of Vietnam. There was very little which took place in this region he didn't know about and approve. He took a little bit of squeeze from every transaction. It didn't matter if the transaction was criminal, like selling dope or sex girls, or a normal business transaction like selling fruit in the marketplace. Mau got his cut, or the transgressor got something which hurt like hell and he remembered the rest of his life.

For only thirty-five years old, Trang Mau was a very practical man. He knew that if Date's cloaking device worked it would cost him much less than paying for hundreds of failed surgeries. Besides, Date's device was easy to use and humane which was very appealing to new recruits. Any young person wanting to join a crime family would rather work for Mau than some other crime lord who required the life-threatening surgery.

There was one last reason Mau decided to test and ultimately buy Date's cloaking devices. Dealing with any member of his crime syndicate who became a problem child was very easy. All he had to do was take the offender's cloaking belt and destroy his phantom tracker sitting in a small container of circulating blood. At that moment, the offender reappeared on the government's monitoring grid. Of course, the government would investigate this reemergence on the grid. Usually, the disciplinary action meant a poverty level existence for the offender. The threat of being taken off Date's cloaking system worked better than any other threat Mau used in the past to control his men and stop defections.

The news of Trang Mau using Date's device spread like wildfire. Hardly a day went by without some criminal element contacting Date about purchasing his device. The criminals were willing to pay handsomely for the device and Date was more than willing to take their payments. Common folks who did not belong to a crime organization paid what they could afford. In some cases, it was a family heirloom with more senti- mental than economic value. At other times, Date accepted foodstuffs or livestock which he returned to the villagers as gifts from an unknown benefactor. On a couple of occasions, he provided a cloaking device without any compensation.

Payment was never in world credits because this could attract government attention. Authentic samurai swords and battle gear were a preferred payment type. All the samurai antiques went into Date's hidden museum concealed under the hill of boulders behind his farmhouse. His collection grew and before long he had one of the best and most valuable collections of samurai military hardware in the world.

He also accepted hard goods which he could use or sell on the black market. Everything from kitchen utensils to precious jewels were accepted for cloaking devices. But fraudulent iden- tification items were by far the most valued things he got in exchange for cloaking devices. These items included hundreds of different holographic identifications, eye iris and fingerprint overlays. With these counterfeit items, he could switch identi- ties as easily as changing clothes. And he could roam around the world conducting business without any chance of being stopped and asked to explain his travel.

With a booming business, he had very little time to tend his fields. He spread the rumor in the village that he was too heart-broken by his wife's death and getting too old to continue farming full time. He then took on two villagers to work his fields and gave them half of the harvest. This was the first time anyone in the village had leased out their fields in a share-cropper business arrangement. The remaining villagers didn't know what to think of this arrangement and waited to see if it worked. It was appealing to the elderly farmers who wanted to retire but didn't have any younger family members to pass their farms on to.

Date's customer base was growing exponentially, and it was difficult keeping up with the demand. If all he had to do was produce cloaking devices, he might be able to keep up, but other concerns were eating up his valuable time. Vetting poten-tial customers was the most demanding concern. He had to make sure the identity and credentials of new customers were verified. Otherwise, he might sell to a government agent or snitch and end up exposed and prosecuted. He wasn't worried about the financial consequences of being caught as he had stockpiled enough wealth to live lavishly for the rest of his life. But shutting down his operation would have dire consequences for the millions of people who hated the World Council. These were the people Date wanted to support so they could live free of government intervention.

Date thought back to the limited schooling he had as a young man. The schools were all under the rule of the central government and taught the same propaganda no matter where the school was located. One class was on the evils of capitalism. A comparison between capitalism and an economy created and controlled by the World Council was taught in detail. He remembered the teacher pointing out all the negative things associated with a company making a high-demand product in a free market. These evils included hiring temporary employees to work long hours at slave wages and continually increasing the price of the product until it was beyond the reach of the common man.

He had no intention of following the capitalistic evils pointed out by that teacher years before. His capitalistic company wasn't going to hire workers because he feared exposure by a loose-lipped employee. And, he wasn't going to raise the price for his cloaking device based on demand. His pricing was based on how much he liked the customer. People who Date thought were respectful and friendly got the best price. Those who were egotistic and rude got the worst prices. It was a simple formula, one which fit well with his understanding of Bushido, the samurai code.

Having production problems was an on-going thorn in his side. When he couldn't take it any longer, he sat in his museum admiring the beauty and functionality of the samurai military antiques. His problems faded away and he could daydream about becoming a samurai working for a great lord.

CHAPTER TWENTY-THREE

I DON'T CARE WHAT YOU BELIEVE

"YEAH, WHO IS IT?"

"Mr. Hakala, it's Murphy. I'm sorry to wake you but I think I saw Sedgewick Slice leave the building. In fact, I'm sure it was him. He turned around at the front door and waved to me before leaving."

It was 3 a.m. in the morning and Raul wasn't happy about being awakened from a sound sleep. It was rare for him to sleep this long and hard with a collage of dreams running one after another through his head. As much as he would like to remember the dreams, Murphy's surprise announcement took priority and quickly cleared his head.

"Murphy, run out into the street and look for Slice. If you see him, bring him back into the building. Make up some reason for bringing him back, like he didn't sign out correctly. I'll be there in ten minutes."

Before Murphy could ask a bunch of useless questions, Raul shut off the communication and ran to the bathroom to relieve himself and get dressed. Damn, he forgot to ask Murphy which direction Slice headed when he left the building. If he had thought quicker, he could have driven in that direction and tried to spot Slice.

Sedgewick Slice was about a half mile from Phoenvartis when he heard someone running toward him from one direction and a hover vehicle approaching from the other direction. He had just removed his disguise and disposed of the red beard, hair, eyebrows and belly pillow. He turned his coat inside out and walked onto the sidewalk to stand in the public transportation corral. He made a point of standing under a high-intensity lamp. Any passersby would see a slightly built, elderly gentleman with short silver hair and nothing on his face other than glasses.

As the hover vehicle passed by, the driver gave Slice a once over and then drove on to meet the man running on the sidewalk. They rendezvoused about fifty feet from Slice, spoke for a minute in the street and then drove off together heading back toward Phoenvartis. Slice was somewhat amazed that the security director and Agent Murphy could respond so fast to his surprise appearance and disappearance at the Phoenvartis office building.

As the hover vehicle faded into the night's blackness, Slice smiled and started to walk toward his next destination. If he could be anywhere now, he wished to be inside the hover vehicle. He'd give anything to eavesdrop on the conversation going on between Raul Hakala and Murphy. If not hilarious, he was sure it would provide a few good laughs.

"I can't believe that son of a bitch disappeared again into thin air. Where could he have gone? Murphy, are you sure you checked the side streets?"

Murphy was absorbed with looking out the hover vehicle's windows searching for Slice. He didn't turn around to answer his boss's question. "Yeah, I looked everywhere, the best I could. Being the middle of the night didn't help any. Slow down a little so I can get a good look into these alleys."

Raul knew the game was over. Slice was gone and slowing down to a crawl wouldn't change that fact.

"Murphy, tell me exactly what happened tonight."

This time he looked at his boss to answer. "There's not much to tell. I saw him leave the building and he waved to me. That was the first and only time I saw him."

"Were you on duty all night?"

"Yes, Mr. Hakala, I started at 6 p.m. Slice didn't come through the front entrance where I was stationed. If he got into the building during my shift, I don't know how the heck he did it."

"Is there any possibility he entered the building before you started your shift?

"It's possible, Mr. Hakala, but I'm sure the agent I relieved at 6 p.m. would have told me and contacted you. After his first visit, everyone was given specific instructions on what to do if this Slice guy showed up again."

As Raul guided the hovercraft toward Phoenvartis he was formulating a theory about Slice's latest visit. He didn't have any doubt that Slice had been in the building for at least a couple of hours during the evening. Somehow, he got by the entrance guards unnoticed. He could have left the building without being seen but decided to make sure everyone knew he had been there by waving to Murphy. But, why did he want his visit made public? Better yet, what was he doing inside the building?

"Murphy, has there been anyone working in the building tonight?"

"Ah, let me think. A couple of people from the training department came in for an hour but they left around 10 p.m.

Other than those people, I can't remember any other people working tonight. Oh, wait a minute, the agent I relieved told me that Mr. Sweats and Claude Ekstrom were working in the lab. As far as I know, they are still in the building."

A thin smile spread across Raul's face. He felt like he had won the world government lottery drawing. How interesting that Rollie and Claude happened to be working in a lab with disabled surveillance systems when Slice showed up. Sedgewick Slice, the sneaky son of a bitch from the World Council who had been digging for something at Phoenvartis. The same Sedgewick Slice who enjoys messing with people's minds and pretends to have special, mystical powers. No, it wasn't a coincidence that Slice picked this night to make his second and probably last appearance at Phoenvartis. Raul was betting Rollie and Claude had something to do with getting Slice into the corporate offices for a late-night meeting. There was only one way to determine if his guess was right or wrong.

"Murphy, I'm heading upstairs to talk with Rollie and Claude. Don't bother me unless Slice shows up again and wants to ask for forgiveness." Murphy nodded even though he had no idea what Raul's comment meant. Was it a sarcastic remark or was there really a reason why Slice would ask for forgiveness? Then again, what did he do to be forgiven for? His brain was too overtaxed by the evening's events to figure out his boss's remark.

"Well, well, well, if it isn't the Bobbsey twins. Hard at work boys?" Raul didn't wait for either Rollie or Claude to answer. "You have no idea how good it does my soul to see you two working so hard to fix the ReLife systems. By the way, guys, did Mr. Slice have anything interesting to say?"

Rollie could feel Claude tense up at the mention of Slice. Thankfully, he kept quiet waiting for Rollie to respond. After Slice's visit, the last thing he needed was a grilling from Raul but there wasn't anything he could do about it. He knew from being around Raul for several years, the best thing to do was answer his questions directly and factually.

"Yeah, Slice dropped by for a while to find out the status of the ReLife project. To be truthful, Raul, he wasn't very happy with the report we gave him. He gave Claude and me two more weeks to reach a final determination on ReLife. If we can't make it work or give up, he's going to give the project to someone else."

Raul didn't know whether to believe Rollie or not. He wasn't expecting Rollie to be so forthcoming. The last thing he expected to hear was Slice's criticism of the ReLife project status and the two stumblebums in charge of it. He decided to push a little farther to test Rollie's honesty.

"Rollie, how the hell did you get Slice past the security checkpoint at the front entrance and then up here?"

Rollie looked at Raul closely waiting to see if his question was real or a joke of some kind. He could tell by the look on his face he wanted an honest answer. He wasn't screwing around or being sarcastic.

"Raul, we didn't have anything to do with Slice coming up here this evening. Actually, he was so damn quiet coming into the lab he scared the living crap out of us."

"Aw, come on Rollie. You are the only two in the entire building working on the most important project the company has now. The monitoring systems are down in the lab thanks to you two. Somehow, Slice walks right by my agent downstairs and then makes a beeline directly to you. Do you expect me to believe he dropped by to say hello to you two? And, it was only a coincidence that you two were here? That's bullshit, Rollie, and you know it. You guys knew Slice was coming tonight and didn't bother to tell anyone else, like me or your boss, Klaus."

"Raul, I'm not in the mood for this. I don't care what you

believe. Claude and I had no idea Slice was coming up here. Do you think we wanted him here? What could he possibly contribute to help us with the ReLife project? As I told you, he gave us two more weeks to get the damn thing done. If not, well, Claude and I are done with ReLife. Now unless you have something important to say or can help us in some way, please leave. We've got a ton of work to complete.

The fire in Rollie's eyes and his flushed cheeks told Raul there was a good chance he was telling the truth. Raul was starting to believe that Rollie and Claude were surprised by Slice's appearance just like Murphy in the entrance lobby. He knew there had to be more to the Slice visit than giving Rollie and Claude a two-week ultimatum. During the few hours he spent with Slice, the man never stopped talking. With the two main scientists on the ReLife project, Slice had to have said more than what Rollie claimed. These two were holding back something from their conversation with Slice but now wasn't the best time to flush it out of Rollie. He would have to wait until Rollie was more amenable to his prying.

It made perfect sense that Slice wanted to talk face-to-face with the ReLife lead scientists. But what was all the cloak and dagger stuff about? Why did the guy show up after normal business hours and move around the building like a Ninja warrior? His stealth tricks were not only weird but very unprofessional. And whoever heard of a dignitary visiting an important ally and snubbing its leader? Klaus was going to be furious that Slice was in Zurich for a couple of days and couldn't find time to at least drop by and say hello. It was obvious he didn't want Klaus's input on the ReLife project. But being so discourteous and disrespectful toward Klaus was over the top. What kind of message did that send to the Phoenvartis employees, vendors and community leaders?

Slice's lack of professional decorum was the farthest thing

from Rollie's mind. If given a choice, Rollie would have jumped at a chance to be snubbed by Slice. His visit added to their workload and put them under an extreme amount of stress by assigning a due date for the project. Even though Slice recommended a couple of solutions to correct the cloning failures, these were unproven theories which would take days or longer to examine. And on top of everything else, Slice dropped a couple of bombshell remarks about Sophia, his brother M.C. and grandmother LeeLee.

There was only one thing Rollie knew for sure. He wasn't going to tell Raul or Klaus about Slice's recommended solutions or comments about his personal life and family. He needed a lot more time to consider these things.

Raul turned and started for the lab exit. "I'll see you later. I suspect Klaus will want to see you two in the morning."

Rollie hated to see Raul leave pissed off but sometimes friends have disagreements. He knew their friendship was strong enough to survive this minor dispute. Besides, the two of them needed each other as an ally.

"Rollie, what did Slice mean by ...?"

Rollie held up his hand to stop Claude from finishing his question. "Claude, we have too much work to do now. We can talk tomorrow about Slice and other things. By the way, did you hear Raul say he knew the monitoring systems were down?"

Claude got the hint and realized everything they said or did in the lab was being recorded or would be very soon. Raul made a major mistake by letting them know that he found out about their sabotage of the monitoring systems. If he had kept that fact to himself, he might have heard Rollie and Claude discussing all the other things Slice said during the lab visit. Now, the lab was off limits to any sensitive discussion topics.

"One question, Rollie. Are you coming in early tomorrow morning to meet with Klaus?"

"Claude, I don't know." With a certain amount of exasperation in his voice, Rollie added, "It seems to me that for the next two weeks we belong to Sedgewick Slice. Klaus, Phoenvartis, the executive committee and what we want are all secondary to what Slice wants."

CHAPTER TWENTY-FOUR

MAYBE WE HAVE A CHANCE AFTER ALL

"WHAT DO you mean Slice was here last night?"

Raul rubbed his face. It was a forced habit of disgust when he had to repeat himself.

"Klaus, Sedgewick Slice was here last night. Here, in Phoenvartis. Here in the CR47 lab. Here, talking with our cloning experts, Mr. Sweats and Claude. Right here, in good old Zurich, Switzerland."

Both men were on edge. Klaus had just come into work to be confronted with the Slice visit. Raul was getting irritated with everyone and everything related to Slice. They each had a million thoughts racing through their minds. Unfortunately, these thoughts ended up as questions rather than conclusions or facts which could be turned into constructive steps forward.

"I'm sorry, Mr. Ekstrom. I didn't mean to be disrespectful. I've been up since three this morning running around town chasing a ghost and then came here to play who's a liar with Rollie and Claude." Raul took a cigar from the wood box on Klaus's desk not wanting to smoke it but rather play with it. He had never done anything like that before without asking permission. But now, it didn't seem to matter if Klaus approved or not. Raul was fed up and in his own little world where he could do whatever he wanted.

Klaus could tell his security director was close to coming apart, so he reached over the desk and lit the cigar for Raul. After a couple of puffs, Raul seemed more relaxed, so Klaus began the conversation again.

In a fatherly tone, Klaus asked, "Raul, tell me what happened here last night."

For the next forty minutes, Raul took Klaus through the entire night, step-by-step, without any interruptions. He made a point of telling Klaus about the disabled lab monitoring systems even though his agents were complacent participants in Rollie's sabotage. By the time he was done, Klaus was upset with everything Raul said but hid his disgust well by lighting and smoking a cigar. Of all the things which pissed him off, Sedgewick Slice's snub and dismissive attitude were at the top of the list. He vowed to retaliate and get back at that little prick if it was the last thing he did in life.

"Raul, it's time to contact Rollie and Claude. I'd like to hear what those two have to say. Would you find them and get them in here, so we can all meet?"

"No problem, Mr. Ekstrom and again, I'm sorry for acting like such a jerk earlier."

Klaus gave Raul a limp salute indicating he accepted his apology and appreciated the effort he put into the entire Slice affair.

Raul headed to his office to catch up on his department's daily report and find Rollie and Claude. Unknown to him, the two cloning experts were still at Phoenvartis. They were in the cloning lab tinkering with the CR47.

"Claude, I think that son of a bitch Slice pointed us in the right direction to figure out why the incubator has been acting erratically. Come over here and look at this."

Rollie was ready to call it quits and head home to sleep when he noticed something peculiar about the gauge which measured pressure within the CR47 and the lab room. Each time he rebooted the CR47 to start its initiation sequence the pressure gauge, known as the AAC, gave the same reading regardless of what was going on in the lab. Rollie noticed this oddity when he started an initiation phase at the same time Claude opened the lab door to return from a visit to the men's room. When Claude came into the lab the AAC should have moved slightly to reflect a change in the room's pressure. It didn't. It stayed the same. Rollie then went through three or four more reboots with the same results. The AAC was giving false readings, which in turn might be affecting the operation of the CR47.

"Watch this, Claude."

Rollie started a reboot of the CR47 and then opened and closed the lab door several times. He then turned on the air-conditioning blower in the room. If that wasn't enough, he flooded the room with a fire suppressant which dissipated within thirty seconds. The AAC maintained its same reading no matter what Rollie did to intentionally change the pressure in the room.

Claude's eyes grew to the size of saucers. "Heilige scheibe." Anytime Claude spoke German all Rollie had to do was look at him. "Sorry, I mean holy shit. Do you know what this means Rollie? We've been using false data to tune the CR47 before each cloning experiment. No wonder some of the cloned animals came out of the incubator looking like monsters."

"Let's not jump ahead of ourselves, Claude. We have a good lead on what's wrong with the CR47, but we still have a lot of experimentation to do to verify this theory. Let's face it, this might not be the only thing wrong with the incubator. If the AAC is malfunctioning, what else is wrong?"

"Good point, Rollie. But I must say, this looks very promising."

From behind them, someone asked, "What looks so promising Claude?"

Rollie and Claude stood up from crouching in front of the AAC gauge and found Raul and Klaus standing just inside the lab door.

Klaus didn't wait for his nephew to answer the question. He was more interested in what Slice was up to a few hours before. "I understand Mr. Slice met with you two last night. Would you mind telling me what he had to say?"

"He said we had two weeks to either get the CR47 working correctly or give up on the cloning project. And if we give up, then the project will be turned over to someone who can get the CR47 working. In other words, you, me and Claude are halfway out the door. Raul, you might survive, but the rest of us are gone unless cloning becomes a reality."

The conversation came to a screeching halt. All the questions Klaus thought of asking before getting to the lab vanished. His only concern now was his job. The great salary, cushy apartment, latest hover vehicle and fulfilling his peculiar sexual appetite would end with the loss of his job. It had taken him years to climb the corporate ladder and become a CEO. All the training, education, and backstabbing would amount to nothing if the ReLife project faltered under his watch. Before he could stop grieving for himself, Rollie added an encouraging comment.

"On a brighter note, Claude and I might have found out tonight why the CR47 is malfunctioning. That's what Claude was talking about when you two walked into the lab."

It was now evident that Rollie and Claude had been sabotaging the ReLife project. How would they know the CR47 had been malfunctioning? For weeks, they claimed two parts in the CR47 needed to be replaced. If the incubator needed parts and wasn't operational, how did they discover a problem with the CR47 during the night? Obviously, they had been lying for whatever reason. Klaus could have nailed them on the lies and sabotage, but it didn't seem all that important now.

"Rollie, I have a couple of questions for you. How convinced are you that you found the problem and can get this goddamn thing working?"

"I'm 100% convinced that the AAC gauge has been malfunctioning and that has negatively affected our cloning experiments. What I'm not sure of yet is whether the AAC malfunction is the only thing wrong with the CR47. There might be other problems."

Rollie knew he had admitted to weeks of lying to his boss and sabotaging the ReLife project. But, like Klaus, it didn't seem to matter. The only thing which mattered was moving forward and getting done within the two-week time frame.

"Is two weeks enough time for you and Claude to get ReLife project working?"

"Mr. Ekstrom, it doesn't matter if two weeks is enough time or not. That's all Slice gave us."

"True, very true. What can I do to help you?"

What a shocking change in Klaus's management style. Rather than making demands he was asking an employee what he could do to help. Rollie had been formulating what needed to be done in the next two weeks so he answered Klaus's question immediately.

"Klaus, I need Raul to get a couple more recorders into the lab and I'll indicate where they should be focused. Claude and I need real-time access to all the lab and CR47 recordings any time of day. We need a full-time technician who has a mechanical engineering background. Don't give me anyone with less than ten years' experience. I also need someone to run errands. This person doesn't need any special training other than a track record of being 100% reliable. Also, he must be able to take orders without complaining and asking a bunch of questions. And I need you and Raul to be open to any other requests which might come up as we move forward."

"Those requests are all doable, Rollie. Is there anything else?"

Rollie debated whether to bring up the last thing on his list. It was going to sound ridiculous, but he decided to go ahead and ask for it. "Mr. Ekstrom, I need an animal trainer or scientist who has a lot of experience teaching apes or monkeys to communicate using sign language. I've read about a woman in central Africa who has devoted her life to this sort of thing. If you can have someone track her down, I want to talk with her before she comes to Phoenvartis."

Everyone in the room was confused by Rollie's last request. What possible connection could there be between talking apes and cloning? For now, it was good enough to let Rollie worry about that link.

"I'll do the best I can, Rollie. By the way, can I cancel the order for the two defective parts you placed with the CR47 manufacturer?"

Rollie chuckled at Klaus's smart-ass question. "I think we already did that, Mr. Ekstrom."

Now it was Klaus's turn to chuckle as he and Raul walked out of the lab. Unfortunately for Rollie and Claude, his chuckle wasn't humor based.

CHAPTER TWENTY-FIVE

THREE WOMEN, A DOG, AND ONE BED

AFTER ALMOST TWENTY HOURS, Rollie left Phoenvartis and went home to get some sleep. It had been a long, eventful night and morning. First, Slice showed up with a boatload of suggestions, ideas, and threats. Then, the malfunctioning AAC gauge was discovered. Klaus followed with an appearance at the lab to ask stupid questions and plead for a quick resolution to the CR47 problems, so his job wasn't in jeopardy. And, before Rollie and Claude left Phoenvartis several requests including a talking monkey expert were assigned to Klaus and Raul.

To Rollie, it had been twenty incredible hours. On his walk home, he had replayed every crucial moment of the past day. As he put his palm to the door entry reader, Rollie couldn't help marveling at the number of lies and hidden agendas which were exposed within a short period. It was as though everyone wanted to play some of their best cards to display their power and authority. Even with all these admissions now in the open, Rollie couldn't help but think there were more buried below the surface waiting for the right time to be exposed.

Normally, the puppy greeted Rollie with panting, jumping and a few mad dashes around the apartment. This time, he was nowhere to be seen or heard. He could feel someone else in the apartment and hoped this person wouldn't interfere with his planned nap. He didn't have enough energy to entertain or contend with whoever was waiting for him in the bedroom.

"Hi. You don't look so good." A nude Sophia was lying crosswise on the bed with her head and chest slightly elevated and supported with a crooked arm. Next to her was the puppy, half asleep and enjoying Sophia's gentle petting. The sunlight shining through the bedroom's one window was just enough to highlight her long and lean body, jet black hair and porcelain skin. Rollie thought how perfectly she was posed. Professional advertising people would pay a lot of world credits to replicate a sensual image like this to help sell their product.

"Hi to you, too. Yeah, I don't feel real great either." Rollie let his clothes fall to the floor and laid down next to her and the dog.

"How long have you been here? And aren't you supposed to be at work?"

"I told the boss I haven't been taking lunch breaks every day, so I was going to take a couple of hours off this afternoon. I'll have to go back in about an hour."

Sophia could feel Rollie's body starting to relax and feared he would fall asleep before she could ask him a few questions about the ReLife project.

"I hear you had a visitor last night. The rumor mill has it that the guy from the World Council showed up again and you and Claude spent time with him."

Rollie was too tired to discuss Slice's visit with Sophia but the mere fact that she brought it up raised a red flag and put him on the defensive. Even in his weary state he immediately thought about Slice's warning to be careful of the people he associated with outside of work. Was he referring to Sophia or someone else? He didn't like the answer he provided to his own question.

Slice had to be referring to Sophia. There was no one else he saw on a regular basis. But why was Sophia a threat? Yes, she had some odd beliefs like reincarnation and was obviously hiding parts of her background, but those things were circumstantial and didn't make her a threat to his life or career. Or did they? Slice's observations about other things had been too accurate to ignore the warning about Sophia. He needed to put his feelings for Sophia aside and admit she might be an operative who wanted something from him. The physical intimacy with her was great but it couldn't squash his overriding feeling that something was wrong with her and their relationship.

"Yeah, Mr. Slice showed up last night. I got to say he's quite a character. He had Claude and I laughing our asses off."

"About what?"

"I don't know. He's just a really funny guy. Damn near everything that comes out of his mouth is funny."

"So he didn't ask you about the cloning project?"

"He asked about the cloning project, but he also wanted to be updated on several other projects."

"Wow. That's a lot different than the way the rumor mill has painted his visit. What I've heard is that Slice only wanted to know about the cloning project and that's why he met with you and Claude and no one else."

"The rumor mill has it wrong, Sophia." Rollie paused for a moment thinking of a way to end this conversation and move on to something important, like sleep.

"The only negative thing I told him was the girl in the Archives department is doing a lousy job and needs to be fired."

At first, she didn't know if she heard Rollie correctly. Why would he tell Slice to fire her? She rolled over, so she could see his face. The broad smile on his face told her the comment was nothing other than more of his sarcastic wit. It was a type of humor she didn't understand. What was with these North Americans and their love of teasing people? For now, she had to ignore his stupid remarks and play along.

Sophia gave Rollie a light slap on the chest and said, "That's really funny, Rollie. Thank you so much for mentioning me to the World Council guy."

"It was the least I could do for my favorite girl. Hey, I hate to be a killjoy, but I've got to get some sleep. Can I contact you later tonight?"

"Make it tomorrow, Rollie. You need a lot of rest so let's talk tomorrow."

Even though he was exhausted, he had led her away from questions about Slice and the ReLife project. As he squeezed one of her ass cheeks he leaned over and kissed her with as much passion as he could muster. She pretended to be concerned with his welfare and returned his kiss. As Rollie passed into dreamland she crawled out of bed, got dressed and left the apartment. It was now almost three in the afternoon and she would have to act fast to arrange seeing Klaus this evening.

For some reason, Rollie chose to answer all her questions with a lie. He either didn't trust her or was too tired to explain the encounter with Slice. There wasn't much of a choice. She believed that Rollie intentionally avoided her probing questions. In the next few days, she would need to determine if he was still a viable source of information. If not, their relationship would change to something other than what it was now. For now, she had only one source of information about Slice and the ReLife project. It was Klaus, the pervert. And the thought of sleeping with him to get straight answers about ReLife made her want to puke.

As Sophia sent Klaus Ekstrom a coded message to rendezvous at his apartment after work, Rollie was in a trance-like sleep carrying on a garbled communication with Grandma LeeLee. She sat on her porch in rural Macon, Georgia, staring into the cornfields which surrounded her house. Although her eyes were open, she was oblivious to the sights and sounds around her. The only thing she could see and hear was her grandson Rollie, half-a-world away. In her mind's eye, she saw him in a bed with a small, four-legged creature. There was a red, wispy stain next to him in the bed. From its size and curves, Grandma LeeLee knew it was a woman. An evil woman who intended to use and harm her grandson.

"Grandma LeeLee, what should I do with the body parts you sent in the antique wood box?" Anyone listening to Rollie in his apartment would have heard nothing but mumbling. It was like the speaking in *tongues* of the outlawed Pentecostal Christian sects. To LeeLee, the question was as clear and concise as if Rollie was sitting next to her on the front porch having a mid-afternoon, lemonade-drinking jaw session.

"Rollie, keep them hidden for now. It won't be long before you will use them in His name."

As Grandma LeeLee finished answering Rollie's question, a car pulled into her driveway and stopped next to the front porch. M.C. Sweats, Rollie's brother, and his girlfriend got out of the car and waved to the old woman rocking back and forth on the porch. LeeLee had no idea her other grandson and his friend were close by. But she could feel a wave roll through her connection with Rollie and hinder their communication.

"Grandma, do you know Sedgewick Slice from the World Council?"

"No, I don't think so. Does he know me?"

"What did you say, Grandma?" M.C. heard LeeLee's disjointed answer to Rollie's question about Slice and thought she was talking to him. When she didn't look in his direction or acknowledge his question, M.C. walked in front of his grandmother and looked at her glazed-over eyes. He could tell she was asleep even though her eyes were open, and she was rocking in her chair. His grandmother had always been a little weird and did strange things, but this ranked near the top of the list.

Before Rollie answered his grandmother, he could feel two back-to-back waves roll through their connection. "Grandma, he claims to know you and M.C. but I think he was lying to me."

"Rollie, your two friends seem to be good, God-fearing souls. I must go now. I love you. Guard yourself against the evil ones in your life."

The connection was broken. Grandma LeeLee awoke to find M.C.'s face less than three inches from her own. He was staring directly into her eyes. The concerned and confused expression on his face was so odd she almost broke out laughing.

"Grandma, are you okay? You've been gibber-jabbering ever since we got here. Do you remember what you were dreaming about? Here, take a sip of lemonade and cool off."

LeeLee remembered exactly what was said during her dream talk with Rollie. She appreciated M.C.'s concern but there was no reason to tell him the truth. Her two grandsons didn't get along well enough to mention either one's name and reignite their feud.

"Oh, hello M.C. I must have dozed off for a while. See, this is what old people do. Fall asleep on porches and talk to themselves." LeeLee let out one of her famous deep throat chuckles and then turned her attention to M.C.'s friend.

"Is this your girlfriend, M.C.? My, such a beautiful young lady. What's your name sweetheart?"

Grandma LeeLee acted like the perfect host for the next hour even though her thoughts were still on Rollie. She prayed that he understood everything she said during their connection. He was a bright, young man so there was a good chance he would figure out her comments regardless of how ambiguous they were. She had delivered God's message so there was no reason to continue to fret about Rollie's welfare. She focused 100% of her attention on M.C. and the new girlfriend who was just like the other tramps M.C. got involved with through the years. She wondered if M.C. would ever learn good from bad when it came to women.

In Zurich, Rollie slowly regained consciousness and opened his eyes. Sprawled in front of him was the pooch, still sound asleep. Behind him laid Sophia who was caressing his head with a gentleness he never knew she possessed.

"Welcome back. I was beginning to worry about you."

Rollie's eyes doubled in size and he flipped over to face a woman who was not Sophia. Lying next to him, fully clothed and with a big, inviting smile on her face was Gretchen. The same Gretchen who had served him dinner at the Raven's Lair restaurant. She looked exactly as he remembered her; long golden hair, light blue eyes, and a pleasant yet impish facial expression.

Before he could ask her what she was doing in his apartment, she said, "Were you having a bad dream? Whatever you were mumbling and screaming about sure sounded serious. That's why I came into your apartment when I found the door unlocked. I heard you yelling and thought you were getting beat up or something bad was happening. I was surprised when I found you asleep, thrashing about in your bed. I laid down next to you to see if I could calm you down."

Rollie's surprise at finding Gretchen was still wearing off.

"What are you doing here, I mean, why did you come over in the first place?"

She lowered her eyes with schoolgirl modesty. He could tell she was embarrassed and preferred not to answer his question if there were a way to avoid it. There wasn't. "I'm not sure. I guess I wanted to see you."

It was Rollie's turn to be embarrassed. It wasn't often that a woman chased after him. It was a wonderful boost to his ego. He would remember this for many years.

"Well, I'm glad you came over and rescued me from my demons." It was easier blaming his loud, frightful outbursts on demons than trying to explain that he was communicating with his grandmother, the most loving, God-fearing person he knew.

"Hey, are you hungry? Why don't we go out and get something to eat?"

"That's sounds great. I've got to work tonight but not for another couple of hours."

"Okay, give me a minute or two to get cleaned up."

Rollie started to get out of bed when he remembered he didn't have any clothes on. He only had a bed sheet covering his naked body. He wasn't sure how he got under the sheet. A playful smile spread across his face when he thought that Gretchen might have found him nude. Whether she had seen him in the buff or not didn't matter. He modestly wrapped the bed sheet around his body and walked into the bathroom like a penguin.

As he got ready, several thoughts ran through his head. First, he was glad his apartment building didn't have a doorman and the front entrance door lock had been broken for years. He then thought of how nice it would be to be seen in public with a woman. The cat-and-mouse game he played with Sophia was sophomoric and getting old. Lastly, he wondered how many men went to sleep with one woman and woke up with another in their bed. He couldn't help but think that he now belonged to a very select group of men who could claim such a feat.

But there was one thing which overrode and crowded out all his other thoughts. Was Gretchen one of the good souls Grandma LeeLee referred to during their connection? If so, who was the other? The only other choice Rollie could come up with was Fido. If anyone knew if dogs had souls, it would be Grandma LeeLee.

As he reached for the bathroom door, a scary thought raced through his head. Was Sophia the evil one Grandma LeeLee warned him about?

CHAPTER TWENTY-SIX

BD DOESN'T TASTE THAT GOOD AFTER ALL

"MR. SANTANEZ, we've asked you to come to the government office today to discuss a critical issue which has come to our attention. It seems that you have been accused of being a revolutionary and spreading seditious propaganda about our benevolent government."

Poppy Santanez was stunned by the accusation from one of the two women sitting across the table from him. His accuser's name badge identified her as Martina, a homely, overweight woman of approximately fifty years of age. Her traditional medium-length hairstyle, no makeup, and government-issued clothing identified her as a career government bureaucrat. Poppy had met many like her before. Her life revolved around the government. It was her child and husband. She needed no friends or family to confide in or love. Dishing out government punishment to the citizens within her district was all she needed to fill her life with meaning.

Poppy waited for Martina or the other woman to say more about his supposed treachery. Neither of them moved a muscle or spoke. They stared at Poppy without batting an eyelid. They wanted him to make the next move; either agree with the accusation or deny it.

Poppy began to laugh. At first, a weak chuckle. It gradually increased in intensity until it was a deep, uproarious laugh from his gut. He could tell the women were not prepared for this reaction. They were used to suspects who acted like scared little rabbits, fumbling over their denials and begging for mercy. Martina's face went from stoic to rigid as though it was chiseled from marble. The other woman who was much younger kept looking out of the corner of her eye at Martina without facing her. She wanted Martina's leadership to control this interview.

"Do you find this funny, Mr. Santanez?"

Poppy pretended to try to catch his breath, so he could answer Martina. What he was really doing under the facade of laughter, was racking his brain to think of what this old hag might be referring to. At times, he had voiced his disapproval with the government, but it was usually said to himself when he was mad. He could not remember one time when he voiced openly negative remarks about the government. He had been around too long to make a stupid mistake like that. The world was filled with snitches looking to turn someone in to one of the government's regulatory bureaus for a few extra world credits.

"I'm sorry, but you have to be playing a prank on me. Please tell me who put you up to this. Was it one of my neighbors or work companions?"

"Mr. Santanez, you're here to answer my questions. I'm not here to answer yours. Why don't you tell me the anti-government things you have done or said, and we'll all go home to our families."

"Miss, I love my government. Why would I say anything against it?" Poppy almost choked on his words of praise for the government. He hated everything about Papa government as he was beginning to hate the socialist pigs sitting across the table from him.

"Mr. Santanez, I don't know why you would degrade our wonderful government. But the facts indicate that you have spread anti-government propaganda with the intent to overthrow our leaders and bring down the structure of our society."

"Miss Martina, that is not true. Who makes these accusations against me?

Martina flipped through the file she had on Poppy, double checking her sources and information.

"Mr. Santanez, I don't normally divulge my sources or the names of people making a complaint, but in your case, I don't see a good reason for keeping these names secret. There are so many of them, I think it's time for you to hear what citizens say about you. Are you ready for this or would you rather tell me what you have been doing against the government? It would be to your benefit to freely admit your infractions rather than forcing me to bring them out in the open."

Poppy leaned back in his chair waiting to see how far Martina's bluff would go before she backed off. To his surprise, Martina said, "Okay, let's see. So far, I've received complaints from the Perez family, Tordo Ulinda, Mr. and Mrs. Ortize, Carlos and Maria Turlousa, the Escalara family, the ..."

Martina went on for another twenty to thirty seconds listing the people who complained about Poppy's anti-government beliefs and activities. When she stopped, Poppy looked at her and asked, "Who the hell are those people? I don't know any of those people. Come on, this must be a joke. Now tell me, who's put you up to this?"

"Mr. Santanez, why do you deny that you don't know these people? They all know of you. You have offended every one of them with your anti-government rhetoric. And, worst of all, you have corrupted their children by infecting their minds with capitalistic theories. You have been preaching that individualism is more important than helping fellow citizens."

When Martina said the word "children", Poppy had the first clue. Now he might be able to piece together why he was being accused of hate speech against the government. His memory flashed back several months to the BD dessert incident on his porch. Was it possible that his grandson, Ramon, had told someone about the night Poppy took his BD dessert and gave it to his sisters to show how the government steals a person's labor? It was the only explanation which made any sense. But Ramon was a smart young man who was warned often about repeating to others what happened within the confines of his family house. Poppy had difficulty believing it was Ramon. The list of people accusing him of sedition against the government was too extensive to be due to Ramon.

Poppy shook his head back and forth giving the inquisitors the impression he still didn't know what they were talking about. There was a good chance the BD incident was the basis for this interrogation. But who was the leak in the Santanez family and how could so many people have heard about what Poppy did with the BD that evening?

"Miss Martina, I'm sorry. I have no idea who these people are and what you are talking about. You need to give me more information before I can comment on anything."

Martina's face turned a pale shade of crimson and the carotid artery in her neck stood out and pulsated with each beat of her heart. She was irritated with Poppy's responses. When she slammed her fist on the table, Poppy and the co-interrogator were surprised enough to lift slightly from their chairs.

"Mr. Santanez, if you want to be difficult that's fine with me. Your denials and lack of cooperation will be taken into consideration when a penalty is determined for your crimes against the state."

Martina stopped to let her threat sink into Poppy's brain. She hoped that he would start a confession but that didn't happen. "Mr. Santanez, do you know two girls by the names of Louisa and Christina?"

Poppy thought, "Oh no, not the girls." What did these two innocent children do to cause such a major inquiry by the state? They weren't old enough to understand the underlining political message of the BD incident. If they didn't understand the message, how could they repeat it to anyone? How could they corrupt anyone's mind against the government by simply repeating what happened at the Santanez home on BD night?

"Yes, Madame, they are my granddaughters. But what can these two children have to do with the accusations you have made against me?"

"So, you deny knowing what they have done?"

Poppy was sick of playing a cat-and-mouse game with Martina. Her attitude was shameful. How dare she treat an elderly person like a criminal. His years of working like a slave on the land made it possible for bureaucrats like her to enjoy a higher standard of living than his and most other citizens.

Poppy lost his temper and stood up. He leaned over the table, stared into Martina's eyes and through clenched teeth said, "Yes, I deny knowing what dreadful things an eight and ten-year-old have done. I find it hard to believe that a couple of little girls can do anything which could bring the government to its knees. So, Martina, let's knock off the bullshit and tell me what these two hardened criminals have done." Poppy was furious, and he was yelling rather than speaking his words. "You're a servant of the people, Martina. I'm one of those people. At least have enough respect for me to be honest. What do you think they have done?"

This guy had things completely backward. She wasn't a servant of the people. She worked for the World Council.

Everyone worked for the government, including this old man. Her position within the government hierarchy gave her certain privileges which were unattainable by this old man and his family. He obviously didn't realize what an honor it was for peasants like himself to serve and support her and the other government officials.

Where had he learned such capitalistic nonsense? Her baiting him had paid off. He lost his temper and exposed his true feelings about the government. This was a man who hated his government and needed to be taught a lesson to rid his mind of such rancid thinking. There was no question that Mr. Santanez was a cancer within his family and community. The complaints against the children were secondary to dealing with Mr. Santanez.

Martina smiled at her ability to trap anyone into confessing anti-government beliefs. She stood up, walked away from the table and with her back to Poppy, stared at the ceiling for a couple of minutes. From past interrogations, she knew how infuriating this was to detainees.

Poppy took her departure from the table as a sign he had either won or at least battled her to a draw. With an over-inflated sense of victory, he went in for the kill. "Well, are you going to tell me or let me go home to my family?"

Martina spun around and pushed a button on her hand-held recorder controller. "Mr. Santanez, this is precisely what your family doesn't need from you."

A holographic recording began to play against the far wall. In it were Poppy's two granddaughters and few of their playmates. Poppy's granddaughters positioned their friends in front of tables, near each other, and then gave each child a bowl, spoon, and cup. For the next few minutes, Poppy watched his granddaughters reenact, almost to the word, what happened on his porch months earlier during the BD incident. One of the girls played the role of Poppy and the other stood in for their brother, Ramon. Without realizing what they were doing, the girls had made a game out of the BD incident. The kids laughed and enjoyed themselves thoroughly during the entire recording. They went through the game a couple of times before tiring of it. The recording ended when some unknown adult entered the picture, broke up the party and sent the children home.

Poppy felt like he had been hit across the back with a tree limb. He returned to his seat and hung his head. He was filled with so many different emotions he was at a loss for what to say or do. The only thing he knew for certain was that he had let his family down. He should never have voiced his displeasure with the government in front of the younger members of the family. Now, he and his family were at the mercy of Miss Martina and her heartless cohorts.

He didn't care about his own welfare but penalizing the members of his family was unacceptable. Why should they pay for his egotistic bravado of teaching Ramon a lesson about the pitfalls of socialism? He tried to clear his mind and focus on a simple question. How was he going to get out of this mess?

"Well, Mr. Santanez, did you recognize anyone in this recording?" Martina didn't wait for a confirmation of the obvious. "Did you recognize what your granddaughters were doing in this recording? Were they reenacting something which may have happened at the Santanez home? It always amazes me, Mr. Santanez, how observant children are. I like to think of them as sponges and mirrors. They suck in everything going on in their world and then reflect it back into society. Don't you agree with me, Mr. Santanez?"

Without looking up, Poppy said, "Yes, Madam Martina."

"Yes what, Mr. Santanez?"

At first, Poppy didn't know what she was asking but then

realized she was looking for a total confirmation of her authority, thoughts, and opinions.

This time he looked sheepishly at his inquisitor and said, "Yes, Madam Martina, you are right about everything."

"I thought you would eventually see it my way, Mr. Santanez. What should we do with you, Mr. Santanez?"

"Madam Martina, do whatever you want with me. I was the only person who criticized the government. No one else in my family did anything bad. Please don't penalize them because of my stupidity. I beg of you, Madam Martina."

"Well, Mr. Santanez I have been thinking about your sentencing for some time now. After I watched this recording a few weeks ago, I knew you and possibly some other members of your family were guilty of anti-government thought and sedition. All I needed was to hear you admit your guilt and see how forthcoming and regretful you were. Unfortunately, Mr. Santanez, getting the truth from you was like pulling teeth. And, from what I saw and heard in the past couple of hours you are light years away from being sincerely regretful."

Poppy opened his mouth to say something in his defense, but Martina held up a hand to stop him.

"You've had your say, Mr. Santanez. The only person who needs to speak now is me."

"At first, I thought it might be worth the time and expense to send you to a re-education camp to learn about our wonderful and benevolent government. But, after your background check came back, it was evident you are incapable of changing your opinion about anything. This includes the World Council which protects, houses and feeds you and your family. You, Mr. Santanez, are the perfect example of the old saying, you can't teach an old dog new tricks. Mr. Santanez, I sentence you to spend the rest of your life without a monthly allotment of world credits. Also, the monthly allotment of world credits for the remaining members of your family will be reduced by 25% for the next two years. Be thankful, Mr. Santanez, that I have a weakness for your kind. Goodbye, Mr. Santanez."

Poppy was stunned by the severe penalty. And, she had a weakness for his kind! What the hell did that mean? He debated whether to leap across the desk and beat the living crap out of her or leave like a dog with its tail between its legs. In a split second, he decided to attack the bureaucratic bitch. How much worse could his penalty be if he killed her? He was on a death march now without a stipend of world credits.

As he catapulted out of his chair, something caught him in midair and escorted him from the room. Two large goons had ahold of him by each arm. They dragged him into the street where he was left face down.

How could he be so unlucky in one day? If he had killed her, he would have been locked up and sent away, never to deal with the humiliation of telling his family about the dire future they faced. Now, he had to figure out how to break the news to the family he loved so dearly. The family who he tried to lead with respect and honor. The family which he let down and sentenced to poverty and possible death. They barely scrimped by now on their allocation of world credits. How could they survive with fewer credits?

Inside the government building, Martina looked over to her young trainee. "My dear, that's how you handle anti-government revolutionaries. I feel good with the outcome. Let's go and celebrate."

The younger woman looked at Martina with admiration and said, "That was incredible. I can't wait to ask you a couple of questions about your interviewing techniques."

As the two government interrogators left the building laughing and joking about persecuting another anti-government type, their victim, Poppy Santanez, walked home. About four miles from his destination, he fell to the ground and started to cry. He wept by the side of the road until a truck returning from the Amazon basin stopped and gave him a lift home. The dozen men in the truck were all friends and co-workers he had known for decades.

Poppy crouched in one corner of the truck bed and buried his head in his arms. His co-workers knew he was distraught about something but thought it best to mind their own business. Finally, one of the men couldn't ignore Poppy any longer.

"Poppy, what is wrong, my friend?"

Without looking up, Poppy knew the question was asked by Emmanuel, one of the kindest men in the district.

Poppy didn't want to burden Emmanuel with his problems, but he needed to talk to someone. He didn't expect a solution to his problem but maybe talking with a friend would help in some way.

"I have let my family down, Emmanuel. Because of my inflated ego, I have condemned them to a life of poverty and persecution."

"What do you mean my friend? It can't be as bad as that."

For the next several minutes Poppy explained what happened at the government building. There was no reason to hide or taint any of the facts. The government published a monthly list of condemned revolutionaries like Poppy which detailed their crimes and sentences.

"Emmanuel, they are only little girls. They don't even know what they're doing. The game they invented was a reenactment of something they saw me do. They thought it was funny because they got to eat their brother's BD."

"I know my friend. Many times, life is not fair." After a slight pause, Emmanuel continued. "Poppy, I might be able to help you. Here, I want you to take this card and contact the number listed on it. Will you do that Poppy?"

Poppy looked at the small card. On it, written by hand, was a contact number only. No names or addresses were on it. "Who is this, Emmanuel?"

"A friend, Poppy. Just a friend. He has helped many people with problems like yours. So, promise me that you will contact him."

Poppy stared into Emmanuel's eyes attempting to see beyond what he had already been told about this mysterious friend. The eyes he peered into offered no more clues, so he answered with, "I promise to contact this person, Emmanuel."

That evening, Poppy pretended to be sick and went straight to bed without dinner. He spent hours lying in bed trying to conceive a plan for telling the family about how he got them sentenced to a sub-poverty existence for the next two years. He didn't care about his future. If he died because of no government assistance, so be it. The family would be better off without him. Before he fell asleep, he contacted the number Emmanuel gave him and left a message which consisted of his name, number and a brief description of his plight. "I have been condemned to a life without world credits."

Two days later Poppy had recovered from his fictitious illness and was ready to tell the family about the punishment they faced. He waited until dinner was over and the children were bedded down for the night. As he was ready to bare his soul, there was a knock at the door.

"Poppy, there is a man here to see you."

He didn't know whether to be thankful or not for the interruption. He rose from his chair and meandered to the door expecting more bad news. Standing outside the door was an Asian gentleman who Poppy guessed to be in his fifties or sixties. For his age, he had yet to grow one gray hair among the thick black mane on his head. He was short and stout. Poppy could see by the way he filled out his clothing, the man was familiar with hard work and had a muscular physique to prove it.

"Mr. Santanez, my name is Date Hattori. You left a message for me the other day. I understand that you are in a predicament which I might be able to help you out of. Do you have time to take a walk with me and talk?"

Poppy felt an instant bond to this man. He could tell by the weathered face and rough hands he was a man of the earth like himself. There might be an outside chance this man was a government snitch but the way he carried himself spoke of honor rather than deceit.

"Yes, let's talk, Mr. Date. I'm sorry, I have forgotten your last name already. I've had a lot on my mind lately."

"That's what I've been told, Mr. Santanez. Don't worry about my name. Date is good enough. Get a jacket. It's a little nippy out here tonight."

For the next two hours Date and Poppy walked the dirt roads and alleys of the small town. It was obvious from the one-story, wood shanties and roving dogs prowling for their next meal, this town was teetering on the brink of economic failure. This area always needed to be economically propped up by the central government. Without an infusion of government *make-work* programs, it would become a ghost town within a few short months.

By the time they returned to Poppy's home, the future looked brighter for both men. Poppy was the new distributor for Date's cloaking device in his region of the Amazon basin. Over the next two days, Date instructed Poppy on how to use the cloaking device to deceive the government. His step-by-step training was based on his own use of the device. It made the government believe Poppy was an old derelict, cast aside, and living at the mercy of his family and anyone else who would give him hand-outs.

As the distributor, Poppy would provide a needed service and product to rebels, foes of the government and anyone who wanted to drop off the monitoring grid. His income would far exceed what he and the family lost by being penalized for trumped-up charges of sedition against the government.

Before leaving the Amazon, Date attended a family meeting where Poppy explained to his wife, two sons, and their wives what happened during the past week. The family heard how two government compliance officers humiliated, tried and sentenced Poppy to a slow death by eliminating his allocation of world credits. Poppy tried to avoid dragging the granddaughters into the discussion. But it eventually came out that their make-believe game based on the BD incident was the cause of the government investigation.

As expected, the family became very upset when the 25% reduction in their world credits was brought up. The men were aggravated but held their peace until the rest of the story was told. The women were near hysterical knowing a reduction in world credits would be catastrophic. At this point, Date entered the discussion and explained how the loss of world credits was going to be compensated for and exceeded by Poppy's new position. Date avoided being too specific about what Poppy would be doing. The less the family knew the less likely they or the children could divulge sensitive information which might be funneled back to the government.

To convince the family that his plan was legitimate, and their standard of living wouldn't suffer, Date handed over the keys to a home he purchased on the other side of town. This home wasn't only nicer and in a better neighborhood but was fully stocked with a four-month inventory of food. Also, he gave each of the wives a world credit account number under a fictitious name. Each account had enough world credits to easily surpass the 25% they were to be docked by the government in the next two years.

"Mr. Hattori, we don't know what to say." It was one of Poppy's sons expressing his gratitude. "You have saved my father's life and helped the entire family rise above this miscarriage of justice."

"It's been my pleasure."

"I have one question, Mr. Hattori. Why must we move to another home and leave my parents behind?"

"Your father, mother and I have discussed this at length. We feel it is better to separate you from your parents, so you know very little about what your father is doing for me. You still have young children and we don't want to take the chance they might overhear and repeat something which must remain secret. It is for the safety of everyone involved. The only thing you need to do is go on with life as you have in the past. Don't tell anyone what your father is doing and enjoy the extra food and world credits. Remember, the less you say to people outside the family, the safer you will be."

"Are we allowed to see our parents, Mr. Hattori?"

"Yes, but try to keep it to no more than a couple of times a month. When you do, always come to your parent's home. Again, for everyone's safety, your parents are not allowed to visit you in your new home. Do you all understand what is expected of you?"

Everyone around the table nodded in agreement with Date's simple rules. For the rest of the evening, Date joined the Santanez family in a celebration of their future. When he left around midnight, he and Poppy walked outside for five minutes and said their goodbyes.

"Mr. Hattori, I can't tell you enough how you have saved

my family. I am so deeply indebted to you. Is there anything I can do for you?"

Date and Poppy gave each other a respectful and manly embrace. When they separated, Date looked at Poppy and said, "Poppy, you don't understand yet the part you are playing in changing the world. One day you'll understand what I am talking about. For now, do everything I taught you and do it with caution and secrecy. Sometime in the future, you might be asked for a favor in return for what I have done for your family. I'm not sure what the favor will be or who will ask it of you, but it will have major consequences and affect many people you will never meet in your lifetime."

"Mr. Hattori, I am your servant. I look forward to paying back my debt to you."

CHAPTER TWENTY-SEVEN

THERE'S GOING TO BE ONE LESS TIGER SOON

"MR. SUN, I have given you my report. There is no more to add. My information is direct from the CEO at Phoenvartis. You can either accept what I have reported or, or... do whatever you want with it. Frankly, I don't care."

"Calm down, Catherine. No one is questioning your information or methods. All I asked was, have you verified the CEO's information with the other mark. I believe he is the head of the ReLife project."

"This is the last time I'm going to say this. The head of the ReLife project, Rollie Sweats, is working around the clock to get the CR47 unit working. I rarely get to see him. When I do, he says about ten words and then falls to sleep. For now, you'll just have to take the CEO's information at face value."

Sophia, known as Catherine to the Black Cross, had no intention of telling Mr. Sun that she suspected Rollie Sweats of withholding information from her. The last couple of times she had seen him produced no additional, new information. And his answers to some of her questions contradicted what Klaus Ekstrom told her.

In addition, her reporter friend at the Beobachter news service was pulled out of the Limmat river after a mysterious disappearance several weeks before. The local police declared his death a suicide, but Sophia knew better. To her, the evidence pointed to a professional hit. It was intended to get rid of a cancerous nuisance who was divulging too much information about the inner workings of Phoenvartis. Whoever was protecting the company from negative publicity had no qualms about using the ultimate penalty of murder.

With one of her contacts suspecting her as a mole, it was only a matter of time before the other contact came to the same realization. When that happened, the game was over. It was now a race to see if she could use the CR47 to clone whoever the Black Cross wanted or meet the same fate as the Beobachter reporter laying in the city morgue. The risk was as high as the potential reward. Unfortunately, there was only one way to collect the huge bonus promised by the Black Cross. She had to continue as a deep *mole* and hope for the best.

Sophia knew Rollie suspected her as a mole, but she had no idea there were so many others who knew of her deceit. Grandma LeeLee, Raul Hakala, Sedgewick Slice, and Mr. Todd were on to her and waiting for the right time to use this information.

By chance, Raul saw her on a recording entering Rollie's apartment buildings. The doorman at Klaus's apartment then confirmed Raul's suspicions about the girl from the Archives department. Boris Turrick, from the Beobachter, gave Mr. Todd enough information about the Phoenvartis informant to figure out her identity. Slice obtained the leak's identity in some mysterious way. Grandma LeeLee was the only one who knew Sophia was more than a corporate mole. Even though her information about Sophia came from Above, she still felt sorry for this young woman. How could someone so intelligent and beautiful be so consumed with evil to leave a trail of death and destruction everywhere she went?

"So, if I understand you correctly, the CR47 should be up and running very soon. Is that correct, Catherine?"

"Yes, Mr. Sun, that's what I've been saying for the past half hour."

"When do you think we'll be able to use the CR47?"

"Too soon to know. My best guess is three to four weeks from now. Do you know who you want to clone, Mr. Sun?"

"Yes, Catherine, we have several samples from a host." Catherine found Sun's answer very interesting and revealing. Sun wasn't smart enough to know of the term host, so he must have picked it up from someone with a scientific background. She guessed that the Black Cross must have scientists or consultants with enough knowledge about cloning to use correct terminology. If she hadn't spent so much time with Rollie and Klaus learning about the ReLife project, Sun's response would have been ignored.

She never thought of a couple of DNA samples like a severed finger or skin sample as a host, but the word was a simple and direct description for creating a new living organism. She also found it interesting that Sun had referred to a single host, not multiple hosts. The Black Cross knew exactly who they were going to bring back into this world from the past. If she had to guess, the host was someone from their organization's seedy past. It might be one of their former leaders killed by government troops putting down a minor rebellion somewhere in the world.

"Mr. Sun, I have to go. Be prepared to move on a moment's notice and make sure you have the bonus world credits to pay me. No bonus, no access to the CR47. Do I make myself clear?"

"Yes, I understand, Catherine. Keep me updated on anything new from your bed buddy, the CEO of Phoenvartis.

Goodbye." Mr. Sun disconnected before Sophia had an opportunity to respond to his sarcastic remark with a demeaning salvo of her own.

Krieger sat in his run-down warehouse room, smiling to himself and thinking how clever he was to put a verbal sword into her. He loved agitating her. He could imagine how furious Catherine must be now. Her fiery temper was surely boiling over. He wished he could be in Zurich watching her throw a fit.

"Funny, really funny, Mr. Sun. After this is all over, I'm going to find you and put you where the sun doesn't shine. Pun intended you prick." Sophia was so humiliated and irritated by his comment she was talking out loud to herself. When the anger lessened, she looked around the Archives office to make sure no one had entered without her knowledge. The last thing she needed was for a Phoenvartis employee to stumble into her conversation with Mr. Sun and overhear some of the incriminating things she said to and about him. She made a note to herself never to talk again with Sun on Phoenvartis property. The risk of being exposed as an anti-government sympathizer was too great.

She knew that Mr. Sun had purposely made the caustic remark about her and Ekstrom. He probably thought he was being funny or witty. But if he knew the unspeakable things Klaus demanded of her sexually, he might not be so flippant with the smart-ass comments.

Rollie's lovemaking was gentle and caring, giving more than he expected to receive. Klaus was demeaning, physical and lewd. Each time she saw Klaus he demanded a new perverted sex act of her. Their sex was full-blown sadism now with Sophia being more damaged with each rendezvous. It now took her several days to physically recover from an evening with Klaus.

If Rollie had not cut her off from ReLife updates, she

would have done everything possible to avoid Klaus. But he was her only reliable source of information now. She would have to go along with his sadism for a while longer until the CR47 was operational and the Black Cross could use the incubator. After that, she made herself a promise to exterminate the two men who abused her; Klaus and Mr. Sun. She would leave Rollie alone even though he was making her life difficult. At least his actions were not designed to hurt her.

As Sophia daydreamed about how she intended to torture Klaus and Sun to death, both men were daydreaming about her. Klaus was cherishing his last meeting with her and thinking of the next perversion to put her through. And Mr. Sun, also known as Krieger of the Black Cross Tiger cell, was imagining how she would explode with anger after he cheated her out of the world credit bonus for using the CR47.

CHAPTER TWENTY-EIGHT

PROBLEM ISOLATED, NOW PROVE IT

SIX DAYS after Slice's visit, Rollie and Claude were convinced the CR_{47} problems were due to only one malfunctioning AAC gauge. They ran hundreds of electronic, mechanical and electrical tests on the incubator. Everything pointed back to the faulty gauge. Because the AAC was a universal gauge, Rollie had Helmer Stanke bastardize another piece of equipment for a functioning gauge and installed it into the CR_{47}. With the good and bad gauges hooked up in parallel, Rollie and his crew watched the different readings between the two gauges as conditions changed within the room and the incubator. There was no question that the AAC gauge which arrived with the CR_{47} from the manufacturer was defective.

Rollie was surprised that Klaus added Helmer Stanke to the ReLife project for a couple of weeks. Besides Helmer being a talented engineer, he was also a key executive in the company and led several important departments. The financial success of Phoenvartis was tied into each of Helmer's pet projects. For Klaus to reassign him to Rollie's team spoke volumes about the importance of the ReLife project. Or maybe it spoke more to Klaus's fear of losing his job.

Claude and Helmer weren't the best of friends, but they learned to tolerate each other for the success of the project. Helmer loved to pull pranks on Claude and joked non-stop with the young, nerdy German. Claude tried his best to trade humiliating, sarcastic quips with the senior vice president but his attempts were empty and often embarrassing. On several occasions, Rollie and Helmer couldn't stop themselves from laughing at Claude's lame put-downs. They were so pathetic compared to Helmer's cutting wit. As the days went by, Helmer cut back on his sarcastic remarks because Claude was such an easy mark.

"Guys, it seems to me that the only problem with the CR47 is the AAC gauge. When the defective gauge was in the unit and we tried cloning, about two-thirds of the animals turned out as monstrosities. The faulty gauge forced the CR47 to pressurize its cabin incorrectly. When this happened, the chromosomes of the host mutated enough so the resulting clone was an abomination. Do you two agree with this hypothesis?"

Helmer and Claude nodded in agreement. As an afterthought Helmer needed to ask, "Rollie, why did a few of the clones turn out okay if the AAC was malfunctioning?"

"Good question, Helmer. I've been thinking about this and I think the answer is simple. Some of the clones turned out okay because the pressure within the cabin was at or close to what it should have been. In other words, even though the AAC was defective, it was defaulting to a reading which was close enough to the correct reading to produce a normal clone. It was only when there was something going on in or around the CR47 that the AAC would malfunction. Then the allowable margin of error was exceeded, and the cabin pressurized incorrectly. The result was an abnormal clone. Does this answer your question, Helmer?"

"Yeah, it sounds like a very viable explanation. I guess there is only one way to test your hypothesis, Rollie. We need to run at least a couple dozen new clone tests with the good AAC and then run a few with the defective AAC."

"You're right, Helmer. That's the only way we'll know for sure if the AAC is the root of our problems. But I got to tell you, I'm not looking forward to intentionally producing more defective and pathetic creatures."

"None of us are. But I'm not sure we have a choice. It has to be done."

Helmer looked back at Rollie who was now in deep thought about something. "What is it, Rollie?"

Helmer's question finally registered with Rollie. He looked up and explained what he was thinking about. "There might be another way to prove the AAC was malfunctioning when the clones were abnormal."

"What's that, Rollie?"

"Claude, how many test mouse clones did you produce before one was successful?"

"At least a dozen, Rollie."

"Did you keep a log on all of them?"

"You know me, Rollie. I make a log of everything I do, using the approved WCSM testing methodology."

"Guys, we have Claude's log showing the dates and times he tried to regenerate a mouse clone. We know which ones were unsuccessful and which one turned out perfect. Why not compare his cloning log to the CR47 data recorder? The data recorder captures everything including the reading from the AAC gauge. We should be able to detect a pattern in faulty AAC readings when the clones were abnormal versus the normal one.

"That seems like a reasonable thing to do. But it might take a lot more time than we have available."

"You're right, Helmer. Backtracking through Claude's log and data reports will definitely be time-consuming." Rollie stared into the air at nothing. His thoughts were aimed at finding another way to get the information they needed without creating more creatures from Hell.

"Well, think about this. Before we had Raul's people disable the recording system in the CR47 lab, we cloned several animals. Although most of them turned out abnormal, some of them were perfect specimens. As a matter of fact, my dog is one of the perfect clones. I wonder if Raul's system was positioned so it recorded what the AAC gauge was reading for each clone; good and bad. If we can retrieve those recordings and see the AAC gauge before and during each cloning test, we might be able to verify our hypothesis."

"Other than the first cloned mouse, I had no idea you guys successfully cloned other animals."

"No one did, Helmer. We couldn't tell anyone about the other successful clones because there were so many unsuccessful tests. We knew something was wrong with the CR47, but we didn't know what. And we were afraid that disclosing the successful clones would lead to premature human cloning which would have been a disaster. Even thinking about what human cloning would have produced before the CR47 was fixed sends shivers up and down my spine."

"Wow, it sounds like there've been a lot of shenanigans going on behind the scenes."

"Someday, I'll tell you the entire story. You won't believe what Claude and I had to do to delay the ReLife project, so it wasn't misused. Anyhow, we're wasting time. I think we should resurrect those recordings and see if they show close-ups of the AAC. Helmer, why don't you take this assignment? A fresh set of eyes looking at the recordings would be more objective than Claude or me looking at them.

"No problem, Rollie. After we end this meeting, I'll go to Raul and see if he'll help find those recordings."

"Good. They should be about seven or eight weeks ago. To tell you the truth, I've been surprised that Raul didn't find these recordings before now. If he did, he's kept quiet about them even though they prove the CR47 wasn't really broken."

"Well, I'll know immediately when I ask Raul to pull up the recordings if he has seen them before. Not that it makes a lot of difference now."

"Okay, great, Helmer. In the meantime, Claude and I will go ahead with new clone tests. We can't afford to wait and see if you and Raul can find the recordings. Even if you find them, they might not show the AAC gauge well enough to read during the test clones."

Rollie looked at his fellow scientists to see if they agreed with his plan. He could tell Helmer was keyed up and ready to start his assignment, but he wasn't sure if Claude felt the same way. There was something about Claude's facial expression which struck Rollie as odder than normal.

"Claude, do you have anything to add?"

Whatever Claude was daydreaming about evaporated with Rollie's question. He cleared the phlegm from his throat and snorted a couple of times before saying, "No, not a thing, Rollie. Let's get on with it. The sooner we prove what caused the CR47 to malfunction, the better my life is going to be."

Rollie and Helmer didn't know exactly what Claude meant by this, but figured it couldn't be anything too exciting. His reputation as an odd, little nerd who dressed and acted weird was reason enough to ignore comments about his personal life. If anything, Claude probably meant that he was looking forward again to getting eight hours of sleep each night. But this time, Claude's comment was more ominous than Rollie or Helmer could have guessed.

"Okay, good! Claude, you start collecting more host samples to test. Helmer, you track down the recordings we spoke about, and I need to go and talk to a woman about an ape."

Helmer started laughing thinking Rollie was screwing around. This was the second time Claude heard Rollie mention apes and monkeys, so he found nothing humorous about the comment. But he did wonder about what Rollie was up to and why he was being so secretive about it.

"Claude, lighten up, my man. Rollie is only trying to get a date for tonight."

This time, Rollie laughed at Helmer's wisecrack. Claude's strait-laced, solemn facial expression didn't change one bit.

CHAPTER TWENTY-NINE

THE MONKEY WOMAN

"INGRID, have you got the communication to the Congo set up?"

"Yes, Mr. Sweats. Ms. Weeks is expecting your call in exactly..." Ingrid looked at the time on her Communications and Production Station (CPS) to get the right time. "In exactly twenty minutes."

When Rollie returned from his morning briefing with Claude and Helmer he found his executive assistant, Ingrid, preparing for the day's activities starting with his call to the monkey scientist in equatorial Africa.

"Ingrid, tell me her background again. I don't want to insult her or screw up this conversation."

"Let me pull it up." Rollie took a chair next to her so he could look over her shoulder as he sipped on some weird coffee-based drink. Before she started, Rollie wondered whatever happened to black coffee like Grandma LeeLee served each morning with a healthy batch of corn cakes, hog fat, and syrup. He could still smell the rich aroma of her coffee as it percolated on the stove. But the best part was finding a few coffee grounds at the bottom of each cup. He loved to roll the grounds around in his mouth before washing them down with the last swallow. He promised himself to one day enjoy another of her delicious breakfast meals after his life returned to normal, if that day ever came.

Ingrid began to read and summarize out loud Weeks' background and experience when it came up on the CPS halo screen.

"Ms. Weeks is 67 years old. Her first name is Calderon. She was born in the old United Kingdom and was the only child of Trish and Thurmond Weeks, scientists who attempted to find a cure for the FISS plague. Being one of the few girls born during the plague made Calderon a celebrity. Her parents were constantly harassed for interviews and special requests from the government to examine the child. It got to the point where Calderon was spending more time at government medical and research facilities than at home with her parents. Finally, Thurmond Weeks decided this unwanted attention was intolerable. He moved the family out of London to a very remote area of the world.

Providing the little girl with a normal childhood experience was the primary reason for moving. But spreading the Christian gospel was more important. The Weeks were true believers in the Christian religion and felt it was their responsibility in life to make sure everyone heard the word of Jesus. Unfortunately, the anti-religion sentiment of the World Council was very strong. Openly preaching any religious doctrine was considered heresy against the state and its citizens. In a few short years, the government would legally ban all types of religious promotion and activity. Any religious followers and advocates defying this edict were penalized with the loss of world credits."

Ingrid stopped and looked over to Rollie. "With me so far?"

"Go ahead. We only have a few more minutes."

"Okay, this is where things get dicey. It seems the Weeks family didn't do their homework very well before moving to tropical Africa and ended up walking right into a tribal war. There were several tribes killing each other off as quickly as they could. Some thought the conflict was economically based due to the recent discovery of platinum in the area. Others thought it was a continuation of tribal feuds going back hundreds of years.

Anyway, Calderon's parents were killed within thirty days of relocating to the former African state known as the Congo. Calderon, who was ten at the time, was taken in by one of the warlords and made one of his concubines. This report doesn't say explicitly but implies that the fair skin, blonde Calderon was a huge prize for the warlord. Surprisingly, Calderon blended in quite well with the warlord's extended family. Over time she became the number one female in his household.

The tribal war eventually tapered off and Calderon turned her attention and inquisitive nature to the local wildlife. She had an immediate affection for the apes and monkeys of the area. This became her love and specialty. She spent the next four decades researching, and at times, living with these creatures.

She was very lucky that the population of all the different monkeys and apes in the area was on the upswing. As a reward for her loyalty, the warlord imposed a death penalty on anyone caught poaching these animals. Also, the FISS plague reduced the human population which in turn led to less farming and harvesting of the forest. The jungle slowly expanded, which gave the primates more room to roam and forage for food.

Calderon became an expert in primate behavior and discovered that the FISS plague did not affect their species. Their male-female birth rates maintained a balanced ratio and their overall birth rate increased as the habitat expanded. With little formal education, Calderon went to work to discover why humans were affected by the FISS plague when monkeys and apes were not. In an ironic twist of fate, she ended up carrying on her parents' professional work to find a cure for FISS."

Ingrid took a drink, caught her breath and went on. "Here's what you might be very interested in. The locals in the area swear that Calderon can talk to the apes. They don't mean that she has an intuitive relationship with them, or they have learned a few hand signals from her. They truly believe that she can communicate, by voice, with her primate friends. Many people have seen her grunting and groaning back and forth with them as she displays the same body movements.

"There have been countless reports of Calderon asking her primate friends to do this or that and they comply. It's as if they understand her requests perfectly. In one situation, Calderon asked and then demanded an alpha male ape to make amends with another male ape who was ostracized from the troop. The alpha male ape whined and complained like a little kid but eventually welcomed the rogue ape back into his family. Regardless of whether this is true or not, everyone agrees that she is closer to apes than humans.

"Well, that's about it, boss. The only other thing is that she never married even though her warlord partner died almost twenty years ago. Interesting woman, don't you think?"

Rollie was in deep thought about Weeks' bio. He wondered whether this woman might help discover the expectations and limitations of the CR47. There was no question she had the background he was looking for, but the part about her parents being religious missionaries concerned him. Even though they died when she was quite young, she was probably indoctrinated to believe that only a divine spirit can create life. The question was whether she still held this belief, and could she make allowances for the benefit of mankind? In the next hour, he would find out if her strict religious upbringing would find cloning morally objectionable. If so, could he convince the monkey woman that God created life, whereas cloning only extended it?

"Uh, what did you say, Ingrid? I was thinking about something."

Ingrid smiled and thought it best not to make the same lame observation again. "I said, you better get in your office, so I can make the communication with Ms. Weeks."

Rollie walked into his office and checked his appearance in the private bathroom mirror. He looked a little tired but good enough. There was no reason to look like a male model. After all, his conversation was with a woman who knew more about primates than humans.

"Good morning, Ms. Weeks. I hope I'm not interrupting your day too much. They tell me you are the world's most noted authority on primates and that's exactly why I am calling. I need your help, Ms. Weeks."

Rollie hoped he didn't hit her with too much information in his opening greeting. He guessed that being upfront and honest with a woman of science and research would lead to her cooperation.

"Good morning to you too, Mr. Sweats. Just so you know, I know a lot about apes and monkeys but not much about human primates."

Ms. Weeks and Rollie started to laugh. The conversation was off to a good start because of Rollie's foul-up of not including humans in the primate group. He now knew that she had a sense of humor.

"My mistake, Ms. Weeks. For some reason, I don't put humans in the same class with animals. And that isn't meant to be a negative observation about primates. It's the exact opposite. I find human behavior so outrageous at times that putting us in the same category as jungle animals is an overgenerous ranking."

"I agree with your assessment, Mr. Sweats. But I must tell you that apes and monkeys display outrageous behavior too. And by the way, you can call me Callie, which is easier to say than my given name."

Ms. Weeks' request to be called by her nickname was another good sign the conversation was trending in the right direction. "My pleasure, Callie. And please use my nickname which is Rollie."

There was a slight pause in the conversation while each participant evaluated what had been said so far. Before he re-opened the dialogue, Rollie looked at the picturesque background behind Callie and thought how different it was from Zurich. The bright sun, swaying palm trees and lush vegetation everywhere reminded him a little bit of his homeland in Macon. He loved the Universal Communication Network's vision mode. Its holographic imagery was so vivid and spectacular it made Rollie feel like he was sitting on Callie's porch enjoying the warmth of the day and all sights the Congo had to offer. Using a technology Rollie never understood, the UCN also transmitted the smells from the Congo. In all, the total experience was almost as good as being with the person you were communicating with.

Rollie refocused and remembered he was several thousand miles away. "Rollie, you mentioned that you need my help. What can I do for you?"

"Callie, my assistant Ingrid already told you that we work for a major research corporation in Zurich called Phoenvartis. I'm not going to bore you with all the major breakthroughs and new products we have created through the years. I'm sure you have either read about our products or used them."

Before Rollie could go on, Callie cut in with, "Rollie, after I talked to Ingrid, I did a little research on your company and I can say you are being quite modest. The list of products and accomplishments your company has made available to the world is very impressive."

"Callie, we try very hard to make the human experience a little easier and enjoyable." Rollie wondered where that description of Phoenvartis came from. It sounded like a sales ad promoting suntan lotion or cosmetics. He could only hope she either ignored what he said or took it in the spirit of nervousness from getting to know each other.

"Callie, we have been working on another breakthrough for the past couple of years which will have a major impact on humanity. We are very, very close to perfecting human cloning. With only a few cells from a host human, we'll be able to regenerate new life. The ramifications will be beyond description. Failed body organs will be easily replaced with new ones. Accident or burn victims will be made whole again by regenerating a new appendage or organ. Great thinkers and the most productive of our species will be able to extend their contributions to mankind. And, God forbid, if another plague like FISS occurs, we will be able to outmaneuver and checkmate it until a cure is found."

"That sounds very interesting, Rollie. Have you thought about the negative consequences of regenerating human life?"

"I know there will be some, but to be honest, we haven't spent a lot of time thinking about the negatives. And I must believe the positives, like those I just mentioned, will far outweigh the negatives."

"I hope you're right, Rollie. If I were you, I would give some serious thought to the negatives before you perfect and release the cloning system. My experience has been that it's the unexpected results of scientific experiments which end up dictating the feasibility of a new product. You might think cloning only has an upside for humanity but there might be something negative about it which is hiding in the weeds, so to speak. It's just waiting to rear its ugly head and take down the entire project. In other words, one negative might be so overwhelming that it overshadows and negates all the positive things about cloning.

"Do you have something in mind, Callie?"

"No, Rollie. I've never been good at predicting the future. But I have to believe there is someone at Phoenvartis who is talented and shrewd enough to see the potential bad side of cloning."

"Callie, I'll give it some thought and consideration. My biggest problem, however, is that the World Council is pushing hard for this project to be completed. I don't think they give a damn about the possible negatives associated with human cloning."

"Ah, yes, the World Council. They do tend to be pushy and show up at the wrong time quite often, don't they Rollie?"

"Yes, they are demanding. That's for sure." Rollie didn't like how the conversation got off track from the outline he prepared in his head. He needed to get her off the negatives of cloning and back to why he needed her expertise. The faster she realized cloning was going to happen with or without her help, the more likely she would agree to participate.

"Callie, here's why I contacted you. Within the next day or two, I expect our cloning machine to be working perfectly. And within a few weeks, it will be producing exact physical replicas of humans. What we don't know is what to expect from the newly created replicants. Will they be mentally, physically, and emotionally the same as their hosts? Will they have the same personalities and intelligence as the host, or will they be different? Will the age of the clone match up with their mental development and personality? Will they act like a human or some other species? Callie, the bottom line is we have no way of predicting what will be in the hearts and heads of these clones."

"Those are all interesting questions, Rollie. So tell me, how can I possibly help you answer those questions? I assume you think I can."

"Yes, I do. I'd like to clone an ape or monkey who you knew intimately. I want you to tell me if the replicant is acting like or different from the host primate you use to know. Also, is the replicant of the same status within the troop as he was when he died? And does the replicant recognize you and does he realize he has been reborn, so to speak? If it's true you can talk to primates, then you should be able to get a read on the cloned animal."

Anticipating her next question, Rollie went on to describe why he wanted to clone primates before humans. "Callie, it's better to determine the answers to these questions initially using primates instead of humans. Primates are intelligent, but their brains are not as complex as humans. My guess is that primates will be more honest and anxious to answer questions about their own cloning compared to humans. Rather than taking the major step into human cloning, this will be a prudent, intermediate step. I'm hoping these animals can clue us in to what will happen with humans."

"Don't forget the best reason to start with apes, Rollie."

"What's that, Callie?"

"An unsuccessful primate clone will be easier to explain or sweep under the rug than a defective human clone. You don't need the negative publicity of a failed human clone."

"You're right, Callie. That is certainly a consideration. I would rather explain to the public a monkey clone gone bad as compared to a defective human clone. A human abomination coming out of our cloning unit would be catastrophic to the project."

"Rollie, I need a while to think about this. Now, I'm torn. I would love to bring back one or more of my favorite primates. It would be great to interact with the replicants as I did with their hosts. As a matter of fact, there was a silverback ape who was my favorite and I'd love to have him back. But I don't know how I feel about this from a morality standpoint. It seems like you might be treading into an area reserved for the Almighty. Can I have a day or two to think about your project?"

"Callie, I can give you until Wednesday at this same time. That will give you two full days to consider my request. Of course, should you decide to take part in this experiment, all your expenses will be paid, and you will receive a handsome sum of world credits for being a consultant. Also, your replicant primates will be yours to keep and take back to the Congo or do whatever you think is best for them."

"Your generosity is appreciated, Rollie, even though I don't need the credits. If I decide to participate it will be because... because I've talked myself into it for personal reasons."

"Fair enough. Please let me know what you decide even if your answer is "no". Callie, it was a pleasure speaking with you and I hope to hear from you soon."

"I promise to call, Rollie, regardless of what I decide. Goodbye."

Rollie sat at his desk replaying in his head the entire conversation with the monkey woman. For every reason he could raise for her to accept the offer and help the ReLife project, he could think of a reason she wouldn't help. He wondered if he could have added something to the conversation or presented the project differently, so she would have agreed right away to help. He finally concluded there was a 50-50 chance of her helping.

Rollie spoke Ingrid's UCN number into his micromic and said, "Ingrid, could you get ahold of Klaus's office and see if he can see me sometime this afternoon. Tell his assistant Helga I want to update him on the ReLife project."

"I'll do it right away, Rollie. How did things go with Ms. Weeks?"

"I'm not sure, Ingrid. She's considering my request and will decide in the next 48 hours. By the way, you were right. She is an interesting woman."

Ingrid smiled to herself and thought, "he was listening to me after all."

CHAPTER THIRTY

PLASTIC SURGERY THE HARD WAY

"WHAT THE HELL HAPPENED TO YOU?"

Rollie walked into Klaus's office to find his boss with his arm in a sling, a black eye and numerous scratches crisscrossing his face.

"Oh, I had an accident."

Klaus was not a good liar. Even his pulverized face couldn't hide the dishonesty of this explanation. Rollie laughed to himself. There was only one explanation which made sense. Someone had kicked Klaus's ass and did a damn excellent job of it. His big mouth had finally found the wrong end of someone's fist. Whoever was the assailant didn't care one iota that Klaus was the powerful CEO of Phoenvartis.

Rollie decided to have some fun. "Did anyone else get hurt in the accident?"

Klaus reached for a cigar but realized he had only one good hand. "Rollie, will you unwrap this for me and light it?"

While Rollie clipped the cigar's end and got it going, Klaus answered Rollie's question. "As a matter of fact, there was another injured person. It was a woman." Klaus had such a wry smile on his face it seemed like he was happy someone else was hurt. He leaned back in his chair and blew the first ring of smoke into the air. The blank stare in his eyes revealed how much he relished remembering how the woman was injured. Rollie always knew Klaus as a jerk, but now he saw him for something much worse; a sick sadist.

Rollie expected Klaus to lie about who beat him up but didn't expect a woman to be the assailant. Rollie knew Klaus wasn't muscular or athletic, but a woman? He must have run into one tough lady who had some type of fighting experience. What started out as an amusing anecdote about Klaus's private life was now a strange exchange with a disturbed person.

Rollie thought it best to end this bizarre conversation but asked one more question before he could stop himself. "How bad was she hurt?"

Klaus bellowed out a plume of smoke and looked at Rollie. "She'll survive. Won't be too attractive for a while, but she'll recover.

"Rollie, enough chit-chat. Let's get down to business. What's going on with the ReLife project? Are we going to make the two-week deadline?"

For the next twenty minutes, Rollie updated Klaus on ReLife. He explained the assignments Claude and Helmer were pursuing and his discussion with the monkey lady. Throughout his entire update, Rollie couldn't help wondering about the identity of the female who went toe-to-toe with Klaus.

"Unless there are some unforeseeable obstacles, we should make the two-week deadline."

"That's great, Rollie. Make sure that monkey woman stuff doesn't delay the final human tests of the CR47. If she doesn't want to help us, then that's the way things are. Do you understand, Rollie?"

When Rollie didn't answer immediately, Klaus added in a forceful tone, "There's too much riding on successful human testing to let a sideshow like ape testing get in the way. Remember that your career rides on meeting the two-week deadline." Rollie knew Klaus was concerned with only one person's career— his own.

"I get it, Mr. Ekstrom." Rollie was going to plead his case why the ape testing was so important but decided against saying anything more. It was obvious that Klaus didn't care about the emotional and psychological state of human clones coming out of the CR47. His first concern was their bodies. If there were psychological problems, he would worry about that later. Of course, if the human clones had severe psychological problems Klaus would point the finger of blame at Rollie's group.

"If you haven't got anything else, Rollie, I have a meeting in a few moments so please show yourself out." Getting beat up hadn't changed his impolite behavior one bit.

"Sure thing, boss. I'll be in touch."

Rollie whistled a muted catcall at Helga as he passed by her CPS station. She played along and said something in response, but he was too far down the hall to hear exactly what it was. He made a note to himself to bring a micro recorder to the next meeting with Klaus. He could see that Klaus would deny any knowledge or responsibility for human clones who were a psychological mess. At their next meeting in a day or two, Rollie would lead Klaus into another conversation about the importance of this type of testing. And unless Klaus had a change of heart about this issue, he would condemn himself on the micro recorder. If Rollie lost his job because of this issue, then he was taking Klaus with him.

After Rollie left, Klaus dialed into his apartment's recording system. He sat back to watch and listen to the brawl he had the night before with Sophia. God, she was a tiger. Where did she learn to fight with such ferocity? It took all his strength to beat her into submission, rip off most of her clothes and take her several unusual ways.

The recording was so exciting that he thought of going to her apartment for another heated session. He shut off the recorder and attempted to stand without wincing in pain from the injuries spread across his body. The welts, open wounds and throbbing bruises made him reconsider the idea of seeing his love tigress before his body had a chance to heal. Besides, she was most likely incapable of taking him without excruciating pain and passing out. He dropped the idea when Helga announced, "Mr. Ekstrom, a Mister Slice from the World Council would like to speak with you."

Klaus snapped to attention, forgetting the pain from his injuries and the desire in his loins. There wasn't time to apply makeup over his damaged face and take his arm out of the sling. He would leave his communicator in the speak mode only so Slice wouldn't be able to see his condition. He snubbed out his cigar and spoke out loud, "Communicator on."

On the floor below, Rollie turned the corner to find a locked and unlit Archives Department. He tried to peer through a window but couldn't see anything other than rows and rows of reference discs. They contained the entire history of Phoenvartis and most of the technological advancements from the four free zones. Anything you wanted to know about the company, its products, employees, finances and a bevy of other topics could be found in the disc library. The information in Archives was available to the key managers and executives of the company. It was all self-serve and could be accessed remotely by each executive. As the head of the Archives Department, Sophia's job was to maintain the discs, add new data to the files and help locate specific archival information when an executive could not find it.

This area was designated *high-security clearance* which limited access to only key personnel. Also, two or more authorized employees had to be in Archives at any given time. The only person at Phoenvartis who could be in Archives alone was Sophia, the head of the department. When Rollie tried to gain access using his identification, he was denied entry. What Rollie didn't know was an automatic message was sent to Raul's department. It alerted them that someone was trying to access a closed and highly restricted area.

"May I help you, Mr. Sweats?"

Rollie turned around and came face-to-face with a woman who he had seen many times before on the company campus. He had no idea who she was or what she did for the company. Her face was about ten inches from his and Rollie wondered if she had a vision problem. Whatever the reason, he felt very uncomfortable being this close to her and stepped back to put some distance between them. Within a few seconds, she narrowed the gap again and was so close he could hear her breathing.

"I was trying to see if the Director of Archives might be in her office."

"Oh, didn't you hear? Sophia had a terrible skiing accident and won't be back to work until next week at the earliest. If there is anything you need from Archives, Mr. Sweats, I'd be happy to help you find it."

Rollie took another step back, disregarded the woman's offer and asked, "Is she in the hospital, Miss...?"

"I'm sorry, my name is Claudette and I fill in on this floor when someone is sick or taking time off. I've been at Phoenvartis so long that I know what everyone on this floor does. I'm what you may call a ...."

Rollie blanked out the rest of what Claudette jabbered about and filled in the rest of the sentence. She was a busybody who knew what everyone on the floor did because she never stopped prying into everyone's business. He thought she was probably in high demand as a fill-in because she was reliable and well known in the company. And she did have a sunny disposition which made her easy to approach and ask favors of. The more he talked to her the more he felt sorry for her. He guessed she had few friends outside of work. She was single but married to the company. It was her life and without it, she would go stark raving mad.

"Ah...I'm sorry, what did you ask me, Mr. Sweats?"

"Claudette, I was asking about the Director's condition. Is she in the hospital and how bad was the accident?"

"I didn't talk to her when she called in this morning, but the lady she talked to said Sophia could hardly talk. It was like she had a mouth full of marbles. Apparently, she spent all night in the hospital but was discharged this morning. That's about all I know, Mr. Sweats." With a big, sincere smile on her face, Claudette asked, "Are you sure I can't help you find something? You know that's my job and I've been doing it for, let's see now, it's been ..."

Rollie tuned out Claudette's gibberish and walked away. As he got to the lift to go to his floor, he could still hear her muted voice. My god, does that woman ever shut up? He would have to remember what a gossip monger this woman was in case he ever wanted to spread a rumor throughout the company within a short amount of time.

"Rollie, wait up."

Rollie turned around and found Raul heading his way. He was half walking and running down the aisle from the Archives Department. When he got to Rollie, he asked, "Did you try to get into the Archives Department?"

"Yeah, I needed some information, but it looked closed. So, I tried my identification just for the hell of it."

"That triggered an alarm in my department, Rollie. I happened to be on this floor, so I responded to it. That red-headed woman who gets in your face when she talks told me you were at Archives and headed this way."

Rollie started laughing. Apparently, he wasn't the only person at Phoenvartis who thought Claudette's conversation boundaries were unusual. "She's really something, isn't she?"

Before Raul could respond, Rollie asked, "Have you seen Klaus today?"

"No, I haven't. Why do you ask?"

"Raul, walk with me to my office. I want to run something by you."

The two men walked to the end of the hall and got on the lift. As they rode to the floor with most of the executive offices, Rollie began explaining his meeting with Klaus. He gave Raul the same briefing on ReLife which Klaus received an hour earlier. He didn't bother saying anything about the monkey woman because he wanted to get to Klaus's physical condition as quickly as possible.

"Raul, someone kicked the crap out of Klaus. His arm is in a sling and his face looks like it went through a sausage grinder. He moved so gingerly around his office I bet his entire body is black and blue. He tried to make me believe it was an accident, but I'm sure that was a lie. There's no question he fought with someone."

"Did he say who he got into a fight with or where it happened?"

"No, not specifically. All he said was the other injured person was a woman. And here's the strange thing. I could tell he was happy that the other person got hurt. In other words, he enjoyed beating up a woman."

"A woman? Are you joking?" At first, Raul didn't know what to think of Rollie's story about Klaus and his physical condition. He was about ready to end the conversation and go see Klaus for himself when the woman from Archives popped into his head. Was she the other injured person?

There was no doubt in his mind that the Archives woman could give an out of shape guy like Klaus a damn good thrashing. He could tell that beneath her charm and sexuality there was a woman who was physically solid as a rock. The way she carried herself was a tip-off she was not your normal debutante who spent her childhood at a girl's finishing school. No, she grew up a tomboy who enjoyed rough-housing with the boys. She learned early in life how to inflict pain on anyone who looked at her the wrong way or said something demeaning.

It wasn't a coincidence that Rollie took a detour route after leaving Klaus's office. He must have suspected the woman from Archives was Klaus's sparring partner. And when he found the Archive Department closed for the day his suspicions grew.

Raul wondered how much Rollie knew about his lady friend's relationship with the CEO of Phoenvartis. Was it all suspicion until today or did he know he was involved in a three-person sexual liaison? Raul didn't give a damn about who was sleeping with whom. All he wanted to know was why this woman was involved with both men. It certainly wasn't because she enjoyed being beat up. She was getting something from these relationships and Raul hoped it wasn't confidential company information. He needed to discover her ulterior motive and do it fast.

Within a couple of minutes of talking with Raul, Rollie decided that there was no reason to hide his suspicion about Sophia being the woman Klaus assaulted. Telling Raul would probably lead to exposing himself as one of her lovers and a violator of company ethics policy, but it was a chance he had to take. Things were getting out of hand and it was better to trust Raul than saying nothing and feel horrible if someone ended up getting killed.

Now that Gretchen was in his life, he intended to end his relationship with Sophia. He needed to find a way to do it. Regardless of what she might be doing behind his back with Klaus, he still felt a deep affection for her and wanted to let her down easy. And if they could remain friends, that would be even better.

Rollie opened his mouth to tell Raul his suspicions about Sophia and Klaus when Ingrid cut him off.

CHAPTER THIRTY-ONE

SURPRISE, SURPRISE

"MR. SWEATS, Ms. Weeks from the Congo would like to speak with you."

"Ingrid, tell Ms. Weeks I'll be right with her."

Rollie turned back to Raul only to find him gone. In a few short moments, Raul had scampered off. Rollie guessed that he was on his way to see Klaus and verify Rollie's story. Rollie was only half right. Raul headed to the Archives Department to find the woman he spoke to earlier. He wanted to know exactly why the Archives Department was closed. If there was anyone who knew the answer to that question it would be the woman who stood too close during conversations.

Rollie walked into his office to answer Callie's communication. It had only been a few hours since their first conversation. To Rollie, it was very important that they know beforehand how a clone may act compared to its host. And Callie was one of the few people on Earth who might be able to predict a human clone's behavior based on a study of cloned apes.

She initially asked for two days to figure out how she felt about helping with the ReLife project. But now she was getting back to him in less than a day. He tried not to read too much into this quick response. It could be that she only wanted to ask a couple more questions to help make her decision.

"Callie, I didn't expect to hear from you this soon. Have you reached a decision already?"

"I guess I have, Rollie. I'm not going to bore you with all the details of how I made my decision, but it came down to this. In principle, I'm opposed to what you are doing. I think it's morally and spiritually wrong. You are treading into an area which is reserved for the Almighty. In my humble opinion, only God has the right to create life."

Callie paused waiting for Rollie to respond with a comment or question. When he said nothing, she continued. "Rollie, I'm a throwback to a time when most people believed in a Creator of heaven, earth, and man. I'm in the minority now. Very few people believe as I do. Those who happen to agree with me keep their beliefs to themselves to avoid retribution from the government. Personally, I could care less whether the government knows I'm religious. Or I should say a religious nut, which is the term the government likes to use when describing people like me. What I'm trying to say is that you need a religious nut like me on your team. Someone needs to point out the potential repercussions and pitfalls of playing God."

Rollie made sure she was finished before he responded. "So you agree to come here and take part in the cloning project as we discussed before?"

"Yes, Rollie. My objections to what you are doing are trumped by my belief that you need a moral compass for this project. I know you're going ahead with or without me. So I thought it best to see if I could help spiritually rather than look back years from now and regret that I did nothing."

"That's great, Callie. I can't promise we'll do everything you suggest but I know we can use your help. I know your involvement will be invaluable. And just so you know, I have a grandmother who is a religious nut like you."

"Rollie, I could tell by the way you talked to me that you have been around someone who knows the Lord."

Rollie didn't know if she was exaggerating for the sake of the conversation or not. It might be possible that Grandma LeeLee's spirituality had rubbed off on him and was obvious to other believers.

"When do you want me there and what should I bring?"

For the rest of their conversation, Rollie explained the travel arrangements and what type of DNA samples she should bring along. He stressed the importance of having multiple host samples and what type of samples were the easiest to clone. For the sake of expediency, Rollie decided to rent a private transport to fly Callie to Zurich. Not only would she be able to get to Zurich faster but there would be plenty of room for everything else she needed to bring. This would include host samples, tools, and equipment needed to teach and translate primate languages.

As Rollie continued his conversation with Callie, Raul was at the other end of the building speaking with Klaus's assistant.

"Helga, can I go in and see Klaus? This is pretty important."

"You better wait, Raul." Without saying another word, she pointed to her CPS halo screen and rolled her eyes toward it. Raul got the message. He followed her finger to the line which showed Klaus's communication was coming from Ickleford, home of the World Council. It didn't take a genius to figure out who Klaus was talking to. Raul looked at Helga, thanked her for the tip-off with a nod of his head and then took a seat in the waiting area. He might as well wait and see what developed. Klaus was going to need someone to talk to after his conversation with Slice. And Raul wanted to know what the red-haired little prick wanted.

Inside Klaus's office, things were off to a shaky start. "Mr. Ekstrom, is there a reason why you haven't turned on your vision mode?"

"No, no, I guess I forgot to turn it on, Mr. Slice."

"Well, please turn it on. I always like to see who I'm talking to. It's more personal, don't you think?"

Both men were surprised with the image on their halo screen when Klaus activated his vision mode. Slice had been told by his informant that Klaus was in rough shape, but he never expected to see the mess staring at him now. Klaus was almost unrecognizable compared to his company identification. One eye was completely closed with a huge bump surrounding it. The other eye was flooded with blood which contrasted vividly with the black and blue coloration of the nearby skin. It was obvious that Klaus's nose was broken and would need to be forced back into place. The other facial injuries were minor; a cut bottom lip and several bloody scratches on his cheeks. Klaus's contorted face reminded Slice of an old black and white boxing movie he saw years ago as a boy. One of the boxers was beaten savagely by an opponent using gloves packed with steel ball bearings.

Klaus looked at his halo screen expecting to see a full, oval face covered with a flaming red beard and a head topped with a massive tuft of curly red hair. Raul's description of Slice as a man who could pass for a leprechaun wasn't anything like this guy's appearance. Klaus was staring at an elderly gentleman with a pasty complexion covering a narrow rectangular head. He was almost bald and the remaining hair circling the sides of his head had long ago turned silver. This man wore nothing on his face other than a pair of antique, wire-rim glasses. These were the same type of glasses which people wore to costume parties or when they wanted to draw attention to themselves.

Corrective eye surgery had long ago put the eyeglass industry out of business.

Klaus was ready to ask the elderly gentleman on the halo screen who he was.

"Ah, there you are, Mr. Ekstrom. Looks like you've had an accident. I would recommend that you have that nose put back in place before it sets up and has to be re-broken to straighten out."

Klaus decided to play along with whoever this guy was. "Nice to finally meet you, Mr. Slice. I wish we could have met a week ago, but apparently your schedule was too busy." Klaus wanted to add a scathing remark about Slice's unprofessional behavior of shunning the leader of Phoenvartis but decided to keep his thoughts to himself. Things were already too tense between the World Council and Phoenvartis when it came to the ReLife project.

"How can I help you, Mr. Slice?"

"I wanted to check in and see if the ReLife project is on schedule. As you know, you have one week left and there will be no extensions."

Klaus was thankful he had seen Rollie earlier and got a complete update on the ReLife project. He passed on the information from this update to Slice almost word for word. He even included Rollie's attempt to get the monkey woman to Phoenvartis to predict the psychological make-up of human clones. This was the only time during the conversation where Slice seemed genuinely interested in what Klaus said.

When he finished, he asked, "Do you have any questions, Mr. Slice?"

"Not one, Klaus. Everything you told me is very encouraging. But you haven't answered the most important question. Are you going to make the two-week deadline? Or, do I have to start thinking about making personnel changes at Phoenvartis to get the ReLife project completed?"

Klaus couldn't help thinking back to Raul's distasteful description of Slice as a prick. Raul was right. This guy was a first-class jerk and now he was thankful Slice hadn't bothered to introduce himself during his visit to Phoenvartis.

"We will make the deadline, Mr. Slice. I guarantee it."

"Good, very good, Klaus. I'll hold you to that." Both men stared at each other waiting for the other to say something which might betray his real thoughts.

"It was good speaking with you, Klaus. I'm sure it won't be the last time. Remember, take care of that nose. And by the way, there's a good chance that a little less play time will result in fewer accidents."

Klaus's halo screen went blank. He continued to sit at his desk thinking over what Slice had said. The World Council member had been straightforward about the successful operation of the CR47 incubator by the assigned due date. His parting comment about a little less play will result in fewer accidents was unexpected and haunting. Did Slice know about Sophia and their tumultuous and perverted affair? There was a good chance he did. That meant someone at Phoenvartis was feeding him information.

Several thousand miles away in Ickleford, Sedgewick Slice sat at his desk thinking about the conversation with Klaus Ekstrom. Overall, he was quite pleased with the results. The information he received from his informants had turned out to be accurate. Claude was right about Klaus sneaking into Phoenvartis in the morning looking like the bad end of a traffic accident. His contact at the Black Cross finally figured out who the Phoenvartis informant was and sold her name to Slice. And Claude's update on the progress of the ReLife project matched perfectly with what Klaus described.

The only new information was Rollie Sweats' attempt to hire a monkey expert. Slice didn't know how he felt about this. From the standpoint of trying to predict how human clones will act, it was a great idea. But it could be a giant waste of time and money. Just because a cloned ape acts the same or different from its host was no guarantee that humans would react the same. Even if they didn't, it was an interesting theory to pursue.

"Mr. Ekstrom, Raul is waiting to see you."

"Send him in, Helga." Klaus reached for another cigar, so Raul could get it going for him.

Raul walked into Klaus's office and found a man beat about the head exactly as Rollie described.

"I ran into Rollie downstairs and he told me you had a bad accident. Thought I would come up and make sure you are okay. Anything I can do for you, boss?"

"Yes, could you light this cigar for me?"

"No problem." Raul took the cigar, snipped off the mouth-end and fired it.

After a couple of puffs, Klaus looked at Raul and said, "I just spoke to your friend at the World Council."

Raul knew who Klaus's sarcastic remark was about but acted dumb, so Helga didn't get in trouble.

"Who's that, Mr. Ekstrom?"

"Mr. Slice. Sedgewick Slice. I've got to say Raul, your description of him as a prick was spot on."

"If you don't mind telling me, what did he want?"

"He wanted an update on the ReLife project. Besides that, he wanted to tell me what would happen if we don't make the two-week deadline. Klaus flicked the ash off the end of his cigar and took another puff. "Raul, I got the distinct opinion that he really enjoyed threatening me if the deadline wasn't made."

"That doesn't surprise me in the least, Mr. Ekstrom. During

the four or five hours I spent with him, it was evident how much he enjoys using his power."

"Raul, the other thing I noticed was that he wasn't interested in anything I had to say. The only time he seemed interested was when I described Rollie's idea of getting a monkey scientist to help predict how clones will act. Everything else seemed like old news to him."

"That's exactly how I felt when he and I toured the cloning facility. In fact, I answered one of his questions with an intentional lie just to see how he would react."

"What did he do with your lie, Raul?"

"He tried to hide his surprise, but I could tell he knew I was lying."

Both men sat thinking about what had been said so far. Klaus was the first to say what both men were thinking. "Raul, we have a mole here at Phoenvartis who is feeding information to Slice."

"You're right, Mr. Ekstrom. Actually, that might not be such a terrible thing." Raul went on to explain his unusual comment. "Once we figure out who it is then we can use that person to our advantage. In other words, we can relay misinformation to Slice if we want."

"That's an interesting thought, Raul. But in the meantime, we better start looking for the mole."

"Will do." Raul wasn't going to say anything about his belief that Sophia was the mole. He was hoping Klaus would bring her out into the open when he tried to explain away his physical condition. And, there was the outside possibility that Sophia wasn't the only mole.

As Raul got up and started to leave, Klaus said, "Hey, I thought you said Slice looked like a leprechaun with a red beard and hair."

Raul froze and turned back to Klaus. "Pardon?"

"The guy I spoke to didn't have red hair or a beard. And he certainly didn't look like a leprechaun."

"Really?"

"Yeah, the guy I talked to was almost bald with silver hair on the sides of a narrow face. Raul, you better go back and do more research on what a leprechaun looks like." Klaus laughed at his own witty remark and turned his halo screen back on.

Klaus started shuffling through his halo messages as Raul left the office. Raul had a new mystery to analyze. Why was Klaus's description of Slice so much different than his own?

After saying goodbye to Helga, he stood in the hallway looking outside to the street below. From five stories up, everything below looked miniature. As he stood there watching the people and hover vehicles move back and forth, the street lights came on. It was only 6 p.m., but there was a dark overcast blanketing the city. A broad smile crossed his face. He remembered the frail, elderly gentleman standing under the street lamp the night he and agent Murphy searched for Slice. Now he knew how Slice moved around without being recognized. Raul couldn't help admiring the ingenious little prick.

CHAPTER THIRTY-TWO

I THINK IT'S FIXED, BUT...

"MS. WEEKS, how nice to finally meet you. Was your trip here okay?" Rollie gave his guest a once over and instantly took a liking to her. His first impression was a tough old bird who gave straight answers to tough questions. She probably never tried to sugarcoat anything no matter how much it might hurt someone. The truth was more important to her than feelings.

"Everything was fine. The trip was perfect and my accommodations here are more than satisfactory. Your assistant, Ingrid, has done a marvelous job taking care of me."

"Great. I don't mean to be pushy, Callie, but we only have five days left to get the CR47 working and the first human clone completed. So, I'm going to get my assistants up here to meet you and then put together a time and action plan for you."

"Ingrid, can you contact Claude and Helmer and ask them to come to my office; done." The voice recognition of his CPS station turned on when he said **Ingrid** and off when he said **done**.

"As I was saying, we'll put together a T & A for you which should give us plenty of time to get a couple primate clones done. Then it's up to you to communicate with the clones and determine their similarities or differences from the host primates. Also, I need you to point out any other observations you make about the clones. I wish I could tell you what to look for but I'm going to leave that criteria to you. It could be something as minor as a nervous twitch to a major personality change in the clone which was nonexistent in the host. It's up to you to provide a complete evaluation of the clones. Don't hold back on anything you observe, feel or suspect about the clones. This is one of those times when more information is better than less."

"Rollie, you do understand this could take a while? Talking with apes and monkeys isn't as easy as sitting down with your best friend and having a polite conversation."

"I guessed that, Callie. I was hoping it would be easy for you, but common sense told me that attempting to communicate with any wild animal was difficult. Callie, do the best you can. That's all I can ask of you." In a way, Rollie regretted asking Callie to do her best. He was sure that she was the type of scientist who always gave 110% to any task she chose to take part in.

"Rollie, do you mind if I smoke?"

"Not at all, Callie. Be my guest."

To Rollie's surprise, Callie took a pipe out of her safari jacket, filled its bowl and fired it.

"I still enjoy a pipe full every so often even though it's a filthy habit. My former partner got me started smoking a pipe and I enjoyed it so much I never gave it up. My parents would roll over in their graves if they knew I smoked; especially a pipe." Callie paused to take another draw of smoke and blew it out before continuing.

"What's surprising Rollie, is that my smoking drove the apes crazy. Believe it or not, they tried to get me to quit. My favorite ape, Maxine, would say things like, "that not good for you" and "I don't like smell." It upset them so much I stopped smoking in front of them. They were like doting parents who hated to see their child do something harmful."

"That's interesting, Callie. I would have never expected a primate to be so concerned with the welfare of a human."

"Primates form intimate relationships and are very protective of family members. That's not to say they won't punish a member who does something detrimental to the troop. I've seen troop members ostracized and once I watched the patriarch of the troop kill a member who repeatedly broke the rules."

"Wow, that's spooky the way they act like humans. They must have accepted you into their troop if they were concerned about the effects of smoking on your health."

"It took several years before they accepted me as a friend and started to treat me like an honorary member of the troop. I was allowed to share their food and groom them but there were other things which were off limits, like holding the infants. They trusted me but only to a certain point."

"That's fascinating, Callie. Maybe one day you can tell me more about the time you spent with the monkeys and apes."

"It would be my pleasure. Oh, before I forget, what arrangements have been made to house the primates? And, how are you going to get the clones from the cloning machine to the secured rooms where they will be housed?"

"Here's what we've done, Callie. After the clone is generated, a weak sedative gas will be introduced into the CR47 incubator. This will cause the clone to fall asleep long enough to transport him to the secured laboratory. Each clone will have its own house. There are also a couple of research rooms within the lab. They are large enough for you to conduct your experiments and accommodate your equipment. After our meeting with Helmer and Claude, I want you to go to the primate laboratory, check it out and let me know if you want any changes made."

Over Callie's shoulder, Rollie spotted his two co-workers. "Speak of the devils." Rollie waved his assistants into the office. "Callie, let me introduce you to the two gentlemen who have been helping on the ReLife project. These guys know more about cloning than anyone else on the planet."

"Callie, this is Claude Ekstrom, a very talented scientist who has been instrumental in the ReLife project. He also happens to be the CEO's nephew, but don't hold that against him." Callie and Helmer chuckled at Rollie's sarcasm. Claude gave it a forced, half smile.

"And this guy is Helmer Stanke, a vice president here at Phoenvartis. He has been assigned temporarily to the ReLife project. He loves to kid around and play practical jokes, so keep a close eye on him."

Claude and Helmer shook Callie's hand as Rollie explained why they were meeting this woman. "Gentlemen, Callie is the primate expert from Africa you have heard me talk about. She has brought a couple of DNA samples with her of deceased primates who she studied and lived with. In other words, she knew these primates as well as knowing a brother or sister. Our first human-like clones will be these primates."

"Rollie, that's really interesting, but I still don't understand what we can learn from primate clones."

"Claude, I left out one important fact about Callie and her study of monkeys and apes. Gentlemen, this woman can talk to primates. Maybe not as concise and free-flowing as the four of us are talking now, but damn close. The goal is for her to talk with the primate clones. This assumes, of course, that the clones remember the language Callie taught the hosts. If they remember the language, then Callie's job is to evaluate the clones psychologically compared to the hosts she knew before they died."

"Oh, I get it." Rollie could tell by Claude's nervousness that he now understood the concept behind Callie's assignment. He was happy to see Claude's nervousness didn't lead to his embarrassing habit of clearing the phlegm from his sinuses by snorting like a wild boar.

"So Callie will be testing the primate clones for intelligence, memory recognition, personality deviation and things like that?"

"Exactly right, Claude. I'm hoping Callie's research will give us at least a cursory understanding of what may happen psychologically with human clones."

"Thank God one of us has been thinking about more than just the clone's body." Besides complimenting Rollie for thinking about all the ramifications of cloning, Helmer's remarks were more introspective than his normal sarcasm. "I guess it doesn't make a lot of sense to create a replicant who has no personality or has a sub-marginal intelligence or some other psychological flaw. Claude and I have been so wrapped up in getting the replicant body done correctly, we completely overlooked the person inside. Very smart, Rollie."

One look at Claude told Rollie he hated being spoken for by Helmer. It wasn't that Helmer's comment was wrong, it just irritated the hell out of him that it came from someone he considered a pompous ass.

"Don't thank me yet, Helmer. It's a long way from theory to practical application. Anyhow, let's get going, guys. Callie, I'm going to have Ingrid take you to the primate lab, so you can check it out and start setting up your equipment. Like I said earlier, let me know if you need any physical changes made. When Claude, Helmer and I are done with our update meeting, I'll come to the primate lab and show you how to use the visual and audio recording system. I think it would be a good idea to record all your talks with the cloned primates. In fact, you should record every minute they are in the lab. Do you agree?"

"Absolutely. I have a feeling I'll be replaying the recordings quite often."

"Callie, we still need to put together a T & A for you. Let's do that this afternoon. I'll get it to Helmer and Claude, so they know what you are doing and when. Oh, I almost forgot. Tonight you and I are going to dinner with Raul Hakala, who is the D\director of security. We've never had wild animals the size of apes in this facility, so I want to make sure Raul is onboard with how we are housing these animals. If we had more time, I'd move the entire primate lab off campus, but we don't have that luxury."

"Sounds like we have a lot to do today, Rollie, so I'll go with Ingrid and see you later. Gentlemen, I look forward to working with you and let's pray that God is in our corner."

The original members of the ReLife team watched as Callie Weeks left the office and walked down the corridor with Ingrid to the primate lab. Each of them had a different opinion of Callie's comment about asking God for help. They kept their opinions buried. Now wasn't the time to debate the existence of a supreme spiritual being.

"Guys, let's sit down at the conference table and see how close we are to doing a couple of primate clones for Callie."

"Helmer, you go first. What has your research into Claude's mouse cloning and the AAC gauge revealed?"

"Rollie, I took Claude's log and compared it to the CR47 data reports and came up with a big, fat zero. From what I can tell, the AAC was sending the same inaccurate reading to the data recording unit in the CR47 for every mouse clone. As a result, there is no difference in what the data reports show for the unsuccessful mouse clones versus the one good clone."

"Damn. So what you're telling us is that the AAC gauge was so screwed up that any successful clone was just..."

"It was luck, Rollie. Sheer, unadulterated, luck."

"Did you bother to look at the video recordings of when Claude and I did a dozen different clones?"

"I did, and you wouldn't believe what I saw. By chance, one of the recorders was focused on the AAC gauge. Each time you guys started the CR47 to do a clone, the AAC gauge started jumping all over the place. If I didn't know better, I'd say it was short-circuiting. Then, the gauge would stabilize and lock on the same reading throughout the entire cloning process. You and I know that this is damn near impossible. That gauge should have been moving slightly as the pressure in the room and incubator changed. To make sure I wasn't seeing things, I pulled the data reports and matched them to the visual recordings. As I suspected, there was no correlation between the gauge readings from the video recordings to the data reports."

"Unbelievable! So if I understand you correctly, any successful clones Claude and I ended up with were, again, due to luck."

"That's exactly what I'm saying. The pressure system defaulted to a setting which was close enough to the real pressure to allow the CR47 to create a successful clone."

"That's frigging wonderful." Rollie closed his eyes and shook his head in disgust. He knew what was coming next but the thought of bringing it up made his stomach turn somersaults.

Hoping against hope, he asked, "Do either of you have any good news?"

"I do, Rollie." Claude's comment surprised both vice presidents.

As Rollie and Helmer watched, Claude took a couple pieces of paper from his lab coat and spread them on the table. He looked them over and gave a couple of his famous sinus snorts while holding the bridge of his nose.

"Helmer, I don't know if you know this, but you talk to yourself. Every time you hit a brick wall backtracking through old recordings and data sheets, you voiced your disgust to whoever was close by. I was usually around to hear your complaints, so I knew things weren't going very well."

"How is that good news, Claude?"

"It isn't, Rollie. What I'm trying to say is that Helmer's complaining convinced me to go ahead and do new clones using the new and old AAC gauges. I know you and I were supposed to do them together, but you get so depressed seeing deformed clones that I went ahead without you."

Rollie wanted to lean over the table and kiss Claude but decided to keep himself in check until he heard the results of the new cloning. "Claude, I can't stand the suspense. What were the results?"

Claude scanned his notes again and then began. "Gentlemen, I did fifteen new clones. Twelve with the good AAC in place and three with the defective AAC hooked up to the CR47. When I used the defective AAC, I made sure the readings were intentionally off from what my hand-held monitor indicated. Every one of these replicants came out of the CR47 unit deformed."

Rollie wanted to jump for joy but then remembered what the previous deformed replicants looked like.

"What about the good AAC clones, Claude?" Helmer and Rollie were now on the edge of their seats waiting for Claude to answer this question.

Claude loved seeing Helmer squirm with dire anticipation.

He wished he could think of a way to prolong his answer for hours, so Helmer would agonize more.

Claude gave a couple more sinus snorts which he knew pissed off Helmer and said, "All twelve good AAC clones were successful. Now, you know that fifteen experimental clones are not an adequate scientific test, so I recommend..."

Claude and Rollie were no longer listening to Claude. They were too busy celebrating the good news from the nerdy member of the ReLife group. After smiling, laughing and congratulating each other with back-slapping, Rollie offered Helmer one of his rare and expensive stogies from the Caribbean. He then removed a bottle of very old Irish Whiskey from his desk, broke the seal and poured three small glasses of the scarce liquor. All the while, Claude was still rambling on about how more testing was needed to register confirmed accreditation per WCSM standards.

"Claude, stop blathering and come over here." Claude sauntered to Rollie's desk like he was going to a beheading rather than a congratulatory mini-party.

"Gentlemen, raise your drinks so I can make a toast. Gentlemen, here's to us, to Maxine and to an ambitious guy named Claude who may have saved our jobs." Rollie and Helmer slammed down their entire glass of whiskey. Claude sipped and made funny faces at the smell, taste and burning sensation on his lips and in his throat.

"Rollie, who the hell is Maxine? Is she your girlfriend?"

"You're going to meet her in a day or two, Claude. She's going to be a girlfriend to all of us."

"What is that supposed to mean, Rollie?"

"It means that tomorrow we are going to clone an ape; a female ape named Maxine."

CHAPTER THIRTY-THREE

SECRETS UNVEILED

ROLLIE LEFT his office to meet with Callie in the primate lab. He was still overjoyed with Claude's surprise announcement that the CR47 performed perfectly in fifteen new clones. He understood Claude's reluctance to jump into a primate clone without further testing, but time was running out. If need be, Claude could continue his testing after the first and second primate clones. It was more important getting Callie talking to cloned primates than more verification and testing of the CR47.

Helmer headed to the CR47 lab to double check all the systems for tomorrow's cloning and make sure the lab was on lock-down for the evening. The last thing the ReLife team needed was an intruder sabotaging the CR47.

Claude went to his office to write an official protest to primate cloning before satisfactory testing was completed per WCSM standards. Rather than leave the addressee's block empty, he listed the recipients of his protest letter to be the World Council, Klaus Ekstrom, Phoenvartis Directors and To Whom It May Concern. He had no intention of sending the letter until after the primate clones were completed and Callie had a day or two to communicate with the replicants. If anything went wrong during this period, his I-Told-You-So protest letter would be sent immediately to the addressees.

Upon entering the primate lab, Rollie was surprised by the number of shipping containers sitting around waiting to be unpacked.

"Callie, it looks like you brought most of Africa with you."

Callie jumped and turned around quickly to face Rollie. "Oh, my God, you scared me, Rollie. Don't do that again, you'll give me a heart attack. What did you say?"

"I asked if you brought most of Africa in these shipping containers. I had no idea there was so much equipment needed to communicate with monkeys and apes."

"I probably brought more than I need but I thought it best to be safe rather than sorry. If I forgot something, it would be impossible to get it here in short order. After all this stuff, I only had enough room to pack two shirts, another pair of jungle trousers and a toothbrush. So if you plan to go to a fancy restaurant tonight make sure it's dimly lit. Otherwise, I'll stick out like a sore thumb."

The more he spoke with her, the more he loved her matter-of-fact attitude and wry sense of humor. "Don't worry about being fashionable, we're going to a restaurant where there is no dress code. The only thing they request is a healthy appetite to eat the home-made food which is delicious."

"I look forward to it. What time are we going?"

"Well, it looks like you have a lot to do here, so I'll stop at your hotel around 7 p.m. In the meantime, I better get Claude and Helmer down here to help you unpack and set up this equipment."

"What's the rush, Rollie?"

"I've moved up the primate cloning to tomorrow. After you

left, Claude informed us that he ran several test clones and all of them were successful, even the ones he intentionally altered." Callie suspected that Rollie's carefully chosen phrase, "intentionally altered," was a subtle way of saying deformed and atrocious.

"Callie, I am very confident that we've figured out what was wrong with the CR47 incubator and fixed the problem. I wish we had more time to test the incubator, but we don't. So I want to do at least one primate clone tomorrow and get you working with the replicant. If the first clone looks good and we have enough time, we'll do the second one. We're flying by the seats of our pants on this Callie, so let's hope for the best."

"How many days do I have to work with the clones before my report is due?"

"You're not going to like this, but we need at least a preliminary report within three days."

From her furrowed brow Rollie could tell she wasn't pleased. "You must be joking. Are you serious?"

"I'm afraid I am."

"Well, if that's the case, you better get the hell out of here and let me get back to work. And get my helpers down here quick."

"As Rollie headed out of the primate lab Callie yelled to him, "By the way, the lab is good enough for what we're going to do. And, don't hope for the best, Rollie. Pray for it."

Rollie smiled and considered how much this woman acted like his Grandma LeeLee. That was why he had an immediate affection for her.

By luck, Rollie was wearing one of his few shirts which had a micromic embedded in the collar. He activated the device and asked Claude and Helmer to help Callie in the primate lab after they finished whatever they were working on. Rollie then called Raul to see if they could meet at his office.

"I'm kinda busy now, Rollie. We're going to dinner tonight. Can it wait 'til then?

"No, Raul. This is too personal to discuss in front of our guest from Africa."

"Okay, give me a few minutes to finish what I'm doing, and I'll meet you at my office."

Fifteen minutes later Raul entered his office to find Rollie staring out the only window. He was watching the midafternoon activities of the city. The backdrop of the snow-covered Alps helped to ease the anxiety of what Rollie wanted to tell the security director.

"Sorry I'm late. Sometimes, supervising takes a little longer than planned. What's going on?"

Rollie didn't bother to turn around. He figured it would be easier to bear his soul without facing Raul. "Raul, I tried to tell you this yesterday, but we were interrupted before I could get it out. I believe that Klaus beat up the girl from Archives. I can't prove it, but it's too much of a coincidence that he came to work looking like a rotten piece of fruit and the girl from Archives called in claiming she's had an accident and won't be in for several days."

Raul sat in one of his office guest's chairs, reached for a real Caribbean cigar and fired it. Normally, he smoked the imitation tobacco products which contained no harmful chemicals. But he could tell this conversation was going to be filled with a rare blend of honesty and understanding. A real cigar seemed appropriate for the occasion.

"I think the same thing, Rollie. You know the two of them have been seeing each other, don't you?"

Raul's question came as a surprise but not a complete surprise. In the back of his mind, Rollie wondered about Sophia's faithfulness. It was unrealistic for him to think she wouldn't see other men. The fact that they couldn't be seen in public because of the company non-fraternization policy was enough of a reason for her to go out occasionally and enjoy the Zurich nightlife. He couldn't expect her to be his personal sleepover companion.

But what would compel her to see a man like Klaus who had to play by the same non-fraternization rules? There was only one reasonable explanation. Sophia wanted something from each of them.

Rollie sat down in Raul's desk chair and leaned back in it as far as it would go. "No, Raul, I didn't know that. I suspected she was seeing someone, but I didn't know it was Klaus. How long have you known about this?"

"A couple of months, Rollie."

In a sheepish monotone, Rollie asked, "She wants something from both of us, doesn't she?"

"I'm afraid so, Rollie. I'm sure she wants information about the ReLife project, but I don't know what she plans to do with the information. I'm certain she isn't freelancing. Someone has hired her to get the information. And whoever hired her is very, very interested in cloning."

Rollie sat back and tried to replay from memory everything he said to Sophia about the ReLife project. There was no question he said more than he should have. He had violated the company policy about secret projects and could be terminated immediately. He wondered how much that dweeb of a boss, Klaus, had told her.

"Rollie, do you think she would tell you what she's up to if you came clean and told her everything we know about her?"

Rollie shook his head slightly from side to side to clear his head and think through what Raul asked. "I don't know. How much do we really know about her?"

Raul snorted a half laugh. "I guess not that much, Rollie. We know she's an agent for someone. She's very bright and sexy and is one tough bird. Someone has taught her how to fight and do it well. I'm guessing she's from somewhere in eastern Europe. I suspect her real name isn't Sophia and she isn't living at the address she provided when hired. I've already checked that address, and no one has ever heard of her there. Oh, and one last thing. She provided the information for the Beobachter article about the company's cloning project."

"Why did she do that, Raul?"

"I'm not sure, Rollie. Maybe things were moving too slow for her and she wanted to stir the pot and see what happened. I simply don't know.

"Rollie, what do you know about her?"

Rollie replayed every conversation he had with Sophia trying to uncover something over and above what Raul already knew. "Let's see. This is going to sound stupid, but she knows a good from a bad cigar." He paused for a moment concentrating as hard as he could. "She did have an interest in my work, but it didn't seem pointed at any particular project I was working on." Rollie thought a little longer about what he just said and added, "No, that's not true, Raul. She did ask about the puppy I brought home from work. She wanted to know where I got it from."

"What did you tell her?"

"I ended up telling her the truth. I told her the puppy was a clone. God, what a dumb-ass I am."

"Rollie, there's nothing you can do about it now. What else can you remember about the time you spent with her?"

"There were a couple more things. I always had the feeling she was well educated. I wouldn't be surprised to find out she was raised in a family of privilege. Just the way she spoke and moved and knew so many things about the finer things in life. As an example, she once told me how better wines are made as opposed to wines for average people. I found it interesting that she knew the winemaking process, but more so, how she referred to average people as though they belonged to a class beneath her."

"Raul, the more I think about her the more convinced I am that she is a master manipulator. The first time I met her, or I should say saw her, was in a tavern. I stopped to have a late-night dinner before going home. As I was reading the daily edition of the Beobachter, I could feel someone's eyes on me. I looked up and across the room was this gorgeous woman, dressed entirely in black, staring at me. She was with two other women who were yapping away nonstop. The woman in black, who I figured out months later was Sophia, ignored her companions and stared a hole right through me. Even though nothing was said between us, her inviting eyes were so intense I became embarrassed and left the restaurant with my dinner. In retrospect, there's no question in my mind that she made herself available to me and I took the bait for the companion-ship and sex."

"Interesting. Rollie, few men could have ignored Sophia. Let's face it, she's very attractive and alluring. Is there anything else you can think of?"

"This is going to sound very weird, but my grandmother LeeLee doesn't trust her and thinks she is evil."

"What in God's name are you talking about? I thought your grandmother is in North America?"

"She is, Raul, and that's why this sounds bizarre. I'm embar-rassed to tell you this, but my grandmother can communicate with me by some type of psychic-sensory communication. It usually happens when I'm sleeping. I can hear and see exactly what my grandmother is thinking and saying. I know how goofy this sounds but it's the truth. Anyhow, my grandmother warned me about Sophia a few weeks ago, and that's when I started to sidestep her questions about my work. Unfortunately, I wasn't subtle about it so I'm sure Sophia knew I was brushing her off."

Raul leaned forward, trying to see if he could spot any evidence of deception in Rollie's story about his grandmother's psychic abilities.

"You're telling the truth, aren't you?"

"Yeah, I'm not making this up. She really does talk to me by telepathy. I have no idea how she does it, but this has been going on ever since I was a child."

"Wow. That is weird." Raul started laughing.

"What's so funny, Raul?"

"I was just thinking what a great new product your grand-mother's psychic telepathy would make. After we get the ReLife project up and running, we can work on bringing your grandmother's talent to the marketplace. Wouldn't that be mind-boggling? Think about it. New from Phoenvartis International, the *psychic-communicator*. Be the first in your neighborhood to talk to anyone, anywhere on Earth, using only your mind."

Rollie rolled his eyes. "I don't think my grandmother would approve. Besides, she credits God for everything in her life and I'm sure this is no exception. I doubt that grandmother would ask the Almighty to grant Phoenvartis the exclusive rights to this special gift. Especially when 90% of humanity doesn't believe in Him."

"I know, Rollie. I was being a smart-ass; trying to lighten the conversation a bit."

"Raul, what are we going to do? I mean, what are you going to do? God, I don't know what I mean. I'm at your mercy, so I guess it's up to you to figure out what to do with Sophia."

Rollie slammed his fist on Raul's desk in disgust. He was frazzled and fed up with this entire discussion. But most of all, he was disgusted with himself. How could he have been taken in by a fraud? Someone who undermined the entire ReLife project for some devious purpose. Had he been so wanting of love and affection that he allowed himself to be manipulated by this temptress? He got up and walked over to the office cooler for a cold drink.

"Rollie, we're going to do exactly what this woman least expects. We're going to kill her with kindness and hope like hell she cooperates with us."

Rollie turned toward Raul and waited for him to explain.

"Rollie, you're a good person with a good soul. I'm betting that she knows this and has at least a small bit of respect and affection for you. I'm sure she would slit Klaus's throat without a second thought. But, you're different. I don't think she'll betray you unless she is forced to. So let's treat her with respect and kindness and see if she'll cooperate with us. We don't have a choice. If I get tough with her, she'll either disappear or clam up."

"Okay, that sounds reasonable, but how are we going to do this?"

"Rollie, I figure we have about three days before she comes back to work. It's going to take that long before her face starts to look good enough to be seen in public. There's no sense trying to find her apartment because it will take at least that long. Anyhow, you are going to leave a nice bunch of roses in her office with a mushy note saying how much you've missed her and hope she feels well. Don't include too much in the note, we don't want her to think you want something from her. End the note with something like, "looking to hear from you soon." Raul thought for a moment more and added, "Write a p.s. Say that I let you into her lab to leave the flowers. She is going to wonder about that, so we might as well get in the open right away."

"Then what do we do, Raul?"

"I'm not exactly sure. I still need some time to think this one through. But when she contacts you, make plans to see her. In fact, we might want you to take her out in public. I'll tell you what to do in the next day or two. Sound reasonable?"

"Raul, I'll do whatever you think is best. I have enough on my mind with the cloning scheduled for tomorrow."

"Tomorrow? Are you doing a human clone tomorrow? That was damn..."

Rollie interrupted his associate and confidant before he had a chance to veer off onto a tangent. "No Raul, we're doing two primate clones tomorrow. One is an ape and one is a monkey. That's why I want you to meet Callie Weeks tonight at dinner. She is the world's leading expert on primates and supposedly can talk to them. Also, I want you to check out the rooms we've built to house the primates to make sure they are secure enough to hold them."

"How long will the primates be here, Rollie?"

"Definitely not more than two weeks. Callie has three days to analyze them and submit her report to me. There's a good chance it will be less than a week, but the worst-case scenario is two weeks."

"Okay. If you don't mind me asking, what is the purpose of doing monkey clones?"

"I'm trying to get an idea of what to expect with human clones. What will their personalities be like? How intelligent will they be? Do they remember their past? Things like that. We've spent so much time worrying about their bodies we haven't given much thought to their personalities and psychic make-up."

"Sounds smart to me, Rollie. Okay, what time do you want me at the Raven's Lair to meet the monkey woman and where exactly are their cages?"

For the next five minutes, Rollie answered Raul's questions and gave him more information on the upcoming primate clonings. When he left Raul's office, he felt more at peace with the Sophia situation. He was still apprehensive about the ultimate outcome of confronting her but at least they had a plan. It would either work or backfire in their faces. Regardless, it felt good to clear his conscience and tell someone about her before something horrible happened.

CHAPTER THIRTY-FOUR

DO YOU BELIEVE THE MUSCLES ON HER?

ROLLIE AWOKE a 6 a.m. and prepared for a busy and suspenseful day. He didn't bother to wake Gretchen who came by after her shift ended at 11 p.m. The first clone was scheduled for 9 a.m. so Rollie wanted to be at the lab by 7 a.m. and give the equipment a final examination. He knew that Helmer had done the same thing the previous night, but another review wouldn't hurt. Plus, he wanted to check the nightly security logs and recordings to make sure no one entered the cloning lab to sabotage the equipment.

The evening at the Raven's Lair was a pleasant opportunity for everyone to get to know each other. Raul let everyone know that he thought the enclosures for the primates were secure and would be fine for a couple weeks. He got a laugh out of his dinner companions when he declared that his opinion was based on the years spent as a professional zookeeper.

Rollie couldn't pass up an opportunity to zing his friend. "Raul, living in a cage at a zoo doesn't qualify you as a zookeeper." Everyone had a good belly laugh in response to Rollie's sarcastic wit.

Raul and Callie got along great from the first minute. In fact, after talking for about a half hour the two of them realized they had met years before in the Congo. Raul had been hired by Callie's mentor and lover to train some of his military officers. From what they could remember, it had been over twenty years since their introduction.

Rollie asked the maître'd to sit them in a section not assigned to Gretchen. He knew having her hovering around their table would be too much of a distraction. This dinner was too important to the ReLife project to have one eye on the conversation and the other on his girlfriend. As Raul and Callie left the tavern, Rollie pretended to go to the men's room so he could explain to Gretchen why they sat in a different section.

"I already figured out why you were sitting over there. I want you to know that you still owe me a tip, buddy boy."

"Oh, you'll get tipped when I see you later." They smiled with desire at each other's playful flirtation and went their separate ways.

Their lovemaking that night was every bit as good as the fantasized sex they each planned. By the time they were done, a good night's sleep was in order, so they could recharge their energy level to handle the next day's activities.

At about 5 a.m., Rollie received a message telepathically from Grandma LeeLee. It was short and graphic. As with many of her messages, Rollie found himself in a large field with waist-high shrubs, prairie weeds, and flowers. This time he was holding hands with an attractive blonde girl and they were running for their lives. Behind them was a twenty-foot snake, big and evil enough to grab and eat them alive. Rather than covered with smooth, scaly skin, this snake was covered with a rainbow of different colored hair. From its head back, there was black, brown, red and silver hair growing from its back and sides. It moved through the underbrush faster than Rollie and his mate could run. Just before the snake swallowed the two to them in one gulp, Rollie woke up.

He rubbed the sweat from his brow and walked into the kitchen to make a cup of black coffee. Neither Gretchen or the puppy bothered to wake up and see who was stirring. He took out an extra ounce of liquid caffeine and dumped it into the coffee maker. He usually didn't like to use liquid caffeine because it made his heart race all day long. But today was extremely important and he needed to be acutely aware of everything happening at once. The caffeine would heighten his senses, so he could process a great deal of information quickly.

He thought about the message from Grandma LeeLee and wondered what underlying message she was trying to communicate. The likely choice for the blonde girl was Gretchen. The snake represented some type of danger to him and his girlfriend. But what did the multi-colored hair on the snake represent? It was an odd way to depict evil and danger. But he knew that eventually this clue would reveal itself just like every other clue from his grandmother.

Thirty minutes later Rollie walked into Phoenvartis. He was surprised to find Raul standing at the front security desk.

"Good morning, Raul. What got you out of bed so early?"

"Based on what I heard last night at dinner, I think it would be wise if I'm here for the experiments." One of Raul's agents was close enough to overhear their conversation, so Raul purposely substituted the word "experiments" for cloning. The fewer people who knew about the primate cloning the better.

Rollie motioned for Raul to follow him. "Raul, I want to review the CR47 lab recordings from last night to make sure we didn't have any uninvited guests. Can you send them up to my office?"

"No problem. Do you suspect foul play overnight?"

"Raul, considering the weird things that have happened

around here lately, I think reviewing the recordings is a prudent thing to do."

"You're probably right, Rollie. Do you need any help?"

"No, I can handle it. I'm going up to the CR47 lab now for a visual inspection and then I'll go to my office to look at the recording. If I ask the computer to look for unexpected noises and movements in the lab, I should be able to complete my review within ten minutes."

"Sounds good. Let me know if you need anything. Otherwise, I'll see you in the CR47 lab around 9 a.m."

Rollie could tell by the way Raul was acting and looking at him that something else was on his mind. "Raul, I can see the smoke coming out of your ears. What's up?"

"I shouldn't tell you this now, but I found Sophia."

"You're kidding, how did you do that? Is she okay? Did you speak to her? When did ..."

"Slow down, Rollie. The only thing I know is where she lives. I haven't seen or talked to her. And before you ask, it was dumb luck that I stumbled onto her residence. I played a hunch and it paid off."

"Well, what are we going to do, Raul?"

"Nothing other than what we've planned. Tonight, we'll put the roses and note in her office and wait for her to come to you. But I've decided that you should take her out in public once she contacts you. Rollie, you better get going and prepare for the clonings. We can talk later."

"Okay, I'll see you at 9 bells."

An hour and a half later, the six key members of the ReLife project assembled in the CR47 lab. The only non-employee of Phoenvartis was Callie. Otherwise, the team included Raul, Rollie, Claude, Helmer, and Klaus Ekstrom. Even though the welts and black and blue marks on Klaus's face had started to shrink he still looked terrible.

"Callie, this is Klaus Ekstrom, our boss, and CEO of Phoenvartis." Callie extended her hand to Klaus but wasn't sure she wanted this freaky looking guy touching it. "Mr. Ekstrom had a slight accident this week."

"Sorry to hear that, Mr. Ekstrom. I'm sure in another week or two you'll be back to normal." Callie didn't believe that, but it sounded genuinely sympathetic.

"Okay, let's get started. Callie, you have the two host samples with you? Callie nodded in agreement.

"Which one do you want to start with, Callie; the monkey or the ape?"

"Let's do the monkey, Rollie." Callie removed a sealed box from the refrigerator and began to open it. "Actually, this particular primate is a male chimpanzee. He was forty-two years old when he died of natural causes. He was the alpha male of his troop and fathered twelve children by six different female chimps."

"How long ago did the chimp die, Callie?"

"It's been about two years, Claude. I usually cremate the animals if they die on my property, but this chimp was buried in a crude wooden box. I was surprised to find the body in decent shape when I exhumed it. By the way, the chimp's name was Mike."

Callie removed a five by five-inch frig-pack from the box and opened it. Inside were skin and hair samples which Callie had surgically removed from the chimp. The frig-pack, another innovative zone product, kept the chimp sample moist and cold during its trip from the Congo to Switzerland.

As Claude turned on the CR47, Helmer prepared the host sample drawer where Mike's skin and fur would be placed.

"Callie, bring the sample over and put it right here." Helmer pointed to exactly where he wanted the sample placed. He then adjusted it slightly before closing the host sample drawer.

"Rollie, put your eye to the iris reader to verify authorization." Rollie leaned forward so his face was within two inches of the iris reader. The reader scanned his eyeballs to make sure he was authorized to use the incubator. A small green light came on to verify Rollie's authorization. Claude then entered a series of initialization codes into the CR47 control panel which began phase 1 of the cloning process.

"Well, that's it for now. The CR47 is reading the host sample's DNA and chromosomal structures to make sure a replicant can be produced. We have about forty-five minutes before this phase will be done and we'll know for certain whether the host sample is acceptable or not. Why don't we go and get something to drink? By the way, I need a volunteer to stay here and make sure phase 1 happens without a hitch."

"Rollie, I'll stay. I haven't seen this thing work before so I'd like to get some first-hand experience with it."

"Helmer, you're elected. We'll see you in a while"

"Rollie, I'm going to go back to my office. Keep me updated on how things go today." For being such an egomaniac, Rollie could tell Klaus was embarrassed by his appearance. Rollie didn't try to talk Klaus out of going to his office. The less time he had to be around this sicko, the better.

Thirty minutes later, Rollie received an urgent communication from Helmer. "Rollie, you better come up here. The CR47 is throwing up on itself. There's a blinking red light and a code is scrawling across the control panel."

Five minutes later Rollie, Callie, Raul, and Claude arrived at the cloning lab to find the CR47 acting exactly as Helmer described. Rollie had no idea what the "SR12-N16" message on the control panel meant. He was ready to access the operating manual for an explanation when Claude announced, "Shit, the CR47 rejected the host sample."

Rollie wanted to ask Claude if he was sure about the code

but knew it was a waste of time. Claude was a perfectionist with a foolproof memory when it came to technical data. If Claude said the SR12-N16 message meant host sample rejection, then that's exactly what the manual would say.

"Claude, do you know why the sample has been rejected?"

"There are a couple possibilities, but the most likely explanation is pollution. The sample has been contaminated by something. This prevents the diagnostic phase from reconstructing the chromosome and DNA structures accurately."

"Is there anything we can do about it?"

"Not a damn thing, Rollie. This sample is bad and will be unacceptable to the CR47 until the end of time."

"That's just great. Well, Callie, you better get out the second sample and let's hope it's good."

Callie went through the same preparation with the second sample as she did for the first. "Gentlemen, this sample is from a great ape named Maxine. I was very close to Maxine. Her mother died when she was a baby, so I was allowed by the troop to raise and nurture her. If I hadn't been around, the troop would have cast her aside and let her die. Anyhow, by the time she was an adult, we treated each other like sisters. She was killed by poachers when she was twenty years old. The only thing I recovered from her body was this hand. We don't know what the poachers did with the rest of her body."

Callie raised the large, black hand which was fifty percent larger than the size of an average human hand. She walked it over to the CR47 and placed the hand in the host sample drawer. Rollie, Claude, and Helmer once again went through the authorization and initialization procedures.

"Well, who wants to babysit this time?"

"I'd like to be here." Rollie was reluctant to allow a non-Phoenvartis employee stay alone with the cloning equipment but he knew that Callie was more trustworthy than anyone else on the team. There was something about this woman which gave Rollie total confidence in her loyalty and devotion.

"That's fine, Callie. Do you know how to contact me?"

"No problem. I talk into this little gizmo and tell it who I want to contact. Right?"

"That's right. But, to be on the safe side, five minutes after I leave, give me a practice call. Okay?"

"Will do, Commander." Rollie could tell her comment wasn't vicious in any way. She was developing a fondness for Rollie and showed it by poking fun at him.

Twenty minutes later Raul and Rollie were moving through the food line in the cafeteria. "Raul, we had a visitor last night in the cloning lab."

"What do you mean, Rollie?"

"When I did an auto review of last night's recording the computer stopped at 3:10 in the morning. On the screen was a faint shadow on the lab floor. The shadow was made by someone looking through the glass walls from outside the lab. At first, I didn't think too much about it and figured it was a cleaner from the janitorial staff. But then the shadow moved back and forth across the lab floor for a couple minutes. Whoever made the shadow was very interested in the cloning equipment in the lab."

"Did you see who it was?"

"No. Somehow this person avoided the recorders, which isn't easy to do. That's another reason why I think our intruder was up to no good. But there was one clue which might tell us who this was."

"What's that, Rollie?"

"I noticed a blurred reflection on the stainless-steel side of the CR47. As the shadow on the floor moved back and forth, this reflection moved right along with it. I zoomed in on the reflection, but it was still too blurred to recognize the intruder."

Rollie reached for a piece of cherry pie before continuing. "Raul, can your recorder system enhance the reflection, so we can see it better?

"Possibly. We have an extensive software library designed to do that, but the results are usually hit-and-miss. I'll get Zeggler right on it. He's a whiz when it comes to the recorder system. By the way, let's keep this to ourselves." Rollie nodded in agreement.

Exactly forty-five minutes after leaving the cloning lab, Callie contacted Rollie. "Rollie, I think the CR47 is done. A green light came on and the screen says **Phase One Complete; Begin Phase Two as Outlined In blah, blah, blah."**

"We're on our way, Callie." As the four team members headed back to the lab Rollie laughed to himself. He found it humorous that she used the word "blah" instead of the technical jargon. She wasn't one for getting hung up doing everything by the book. When it came to technical correctness, she was the exact opposite of Claude.

When everyone reconvened at the lab, Helmer and Claude double and tripled checked everything to make sure the CR47 was ready to clone Maxine.

"Looks like we're ready to begin the next phase, Rollie."

"Okay, guys. Put in the codes and let's get this show on the road." Rollie's frivolous comment wasn't close to how he really felt about the primate cloning. In the back of his mind, he knew this might be the beginning of a major advancement in human development. It might lead to extended human life and the aversion of horrible deaths due to disease and injuries.

Claude pushed the Start button and the CR47 came to life. For the next three to four hours a replicant named Maxine would be reconstructed in the incubator. For the ReLife team members, this would be the longest couple of hours of their lives.

"Why don't each of us take a shift keeping an eye on the CR47? Callie, you take the first hour; Claude the second; Helmer the third and I'll take the last hour." Rollie looked at the CR47's counter and estimated the time when the clone would be finished. "Why don't we all plan to be back here at 3:20 p.m. Claude, would you pick up the special gurney we had made to move the replicant. It's in the monkey research lab. Any questions?"

Hearing nothing from the team, Rollie commended everyone for a job well done thus far and then headed to his office. He wanted to get a quick nap but knew the extra dose of caffeine would most likely keep him awake. Laying down, however, might help to take the edge of uncertainty and stress off his mind.

Two hours later he awoke from a fitful sleep. At first, he was disoriented until he recognized the room as his office. He got up from the couch and went to the bathroom to throw a couple handfuls of cold water in his face. For the next forty minutes, he reviewed all his visual and verbal contacts. The only ones he considered important were from Klaus and Gretchen. Klaus wanted an update on the cloning and Gretchen wanted to meet him for dinner. He was disappointed there was nothing from Sophia. He didn't expect anything from her yet but couldn't help thinking about her well-being. There was a part of himself which was still attached to her and that part wanted to nurse her back to health.

When Rollie returned to the cloning lab at 3 p.m., he was startled by the size of the thing in the incubator. The interior of the CR47 was designed to accommodate two large-size men. This thing barely fit within the width of the incubator.

Helmer saw Rollie come into the lab and notice the blank

expression on his face. "Rollie, come over here and look at Maxine."

Both men stood next to the incubator, looking through its shatterproof glass. The thing inside bore a striking resemblance to themselves. Neither had ever been so close to a wild animal of such grandeur. Everything about this animal was magnificent. Of all the marvelous features of this animal, Rollie noticed the fingernails first. He couldn't get over how similar they were to his own.

The face drew his attention next. The forehead, cheeks and eye sockets were humanoid in likeness. Other than the entire face being flattened, the only difference was a wider nose with immense nostril passages. Rollie guessed the nostrils were specifically designed to take in enough air to keep the ape's body running at peak efficiency.

"Can you believe the muscles on this beast? Maxine won't need to spend any time at the fitness complex."

"Helmer, I'd be scared to death meeting one of these things in the wild. Callie must have nerves of steel."

"There's my baby!"

Helmer and Rollie turned to see Callie enter the lab and rush over to the incubator. "My god, she looks exactly like my Maxine. Do you guys see that small bump over her right eye? She's had that ever since she was born." Callie thought for a moment. "Born the first time, that is."

Within a few minutes, Claude and Klaus joined the rest of the team in the lab. The count-down timer still showed twelve minutes before the clone was done. This time would be used to put the finishing touches on Maxine like hair and skin.

Other than the initial comment made by each team member when they first saw Maxine, not much else was said. Everyone was so taken in with the nobility of this animal, making comments seemed unnecessary.

When the countdown timer hit zero an automatic sedative mist was released within the incubator.

"Okay, guys. Let's get the gurney over here and load Maxine."

"How much time do we have before the sedative wears off, Rollie?"

"Should be about twenty minutes, Callie. Do you agree with me, Claude?"

"I did some quick calculations based on her weight and I estimate about seventeen minutes."

"Rollie, let's make sure we get her to the lab before she wakes up. Even though there are restriction guards on the gurney I'm not sure how she'll react if she wakes up being rolled through brightly lit hallways. Being resurrected outside the jungle will be very traumatic for her."

"Raul, will you call one of your guys and have him put one of the lifts off limits for the next thirty minutes? If we don't have to wait for a lift between floors that will save a couple of minutes."

"I'm a step ahead of you. Already did that. Also, we secured the hallways and put them off limits."

"Way to go, Raul."

As Rollie finished talking, the lid to the incubator popped open. The suddenness surprised everyone and froze them in position.

Callie was the first to recover and realize they were now racing against the clock. "Okay you guys, let's get her on the gurney. Rollie and Helmer, you grab her under the arms and lift. Try to keep her head propped up. Claude, you support her under the midsection, and I'll lift her feet. Klaus, we need you to make sure the gurney doesn't move. If we can't lift her, we'll have to roll her onto the gurney. Okay, on the count of three, everyone lifts. Ready? One, two, three."

With a sudden burst of energy by everyone, Maxine was lifted onto the gurney. Rollie hadn't heard that much grunting and groaning since football training camp. The only minor blunder was that Claude got his arms wedged under the ape. With some help from Helmer and Callie, he pulled them out without getting hurt.

"Holy crap she weighs a lot."

Callie walked around the gurney touching, petting and examining her friend. "Helmer, Maxine is a big girl. She weighs about 225 pounds which is unusual for a female ape. Rollie, she looks good to me. Help me put a sheet over her before we put the restriction bars in place."

Within thirty seconds the team members pushed Maxine's gurney out of the CR47 lab on the way to the primate research lab. Only Klaus hung back so he could go back to his office.

"Klaus, will you secure the lab?"

"Yeah, no problem, Rollie. As an afterthought, he added, "Just make sure that thing doesn't get loose."

Callie and Rollie looked at each other thinking the same thing. "What a jerk."

CHAPTER THIRTY-FIVE

MAYBE THIS AND MAYBE THAT

"ROLLIE SPEAKING."

"Rollie, this is Sophia."

Rollie was caught off-guard. He wanted to hear from her but when it finally happened, he wondered if it was a good idea. He didn't want to say anything stupid or let on that he knew she wasn't hurt in an accident. He needed to keep his temper in check and not think about the beating Klaus gave her.

"How are you, Sophia? I've been trying to contact you but..."

"Rollie, I want to thank you for the beautiful flowers. The different colored roses arranged in a rainbow pattern was a very nice touch."

"I wish I could say I thought of it, but I overheard Ingrid talk about it one day. One of her girlfriends got a rainbow arrangement and thought it was wonderful."

"Well, I do too." Some of Sophia's words were difficult to understand. Her pronunciation of each word was slurred and spoken much slower than normal. Rollie thought there was a good chance her jaw was wired shut.

"When did you put the flowers in my office?"

"Two days ago, Sophia. Raul helped me get into Archives. Sorry, I guess you already knew that."

"Yes, that's what your note said. You're lucky to have a friend like Raul."

"Sophia, can you turn on your visual? I don't care what you look like. I mean, I care, but I'd feel a lot better if I could see your face."

"Not now, dear. I still look terrible and I'd be very embarrassed if you saw me like this. Give me a couple more days, okay?"

"Okay. But please promise to let me know when I can see you. Promise?"

Before Rollie could say anything, she was gone. He couldn't remember her ever calling him "dear." Anytime in the past when she used an endearing term it was done sarcastically or joking around. This time it was sincere. Garbled or not, he could hear the heartfelt honesty in her voice. He was honored by her affection but knew it would make breaking up extremely difficult.

It then occurred to him that Sophia must be coming to work at night. She could have seen the flowers remotely on the halo system, but his note was in an envelope. She had to be in Archives to read the note. Unless someone read it to her. That seemed hard to believe, but for some reason, he couldn't shake the thought.

He continued to think about this mystery until he was interrupted by Ingrid. "Rollie, Callie needs to talk with you."

"Thanks, Ingrid."

"Callie, what's going on?"

"Rollie, can you come to the primate lab? I need to show you something."

"Any problems, Callie?"

"I'm not sure, Rollie. That's why I want you to see this. I want your opinion."

"Okay, I'll be right down. Can I bring Raul with me?"

"Another set of eyes might be beneficial. Sure, why not?"

It had been almost two full days since Maxine was cloned. Rollie intentionally left Callie alone to work with the cloned primate. He figured the fewer interruptions, the faster she could evaluate the replicant and submit her report. They were on a tight schedule and she needed to focus on Maxine's mental state.

"Raul, where are you now?"

"I'm in my office."

"Meet me at number five in a couple of minutes. I just heard from Sophia."

Neither man bothered to say goodbye. It was off to the lift, posthaste.

Rather than get on a lift with other Phoenvartis employees Raul and Rollie waited for an empty lift car. It was a short trip to the subterranean fourth floor so Rollie gave Raul a synopsis of the conversation with Sophia.

"She thanked me for the flowers and note. I asked her to turn on her visual, but she refused; said she was too embarrassed to be seen. When I asked to see her in person she said maybe in a few days. She did promise to contact me when we could get together. Her words were so garbled I wouldn't be surprised if she has a broken jaw and had to get her mouth wired shut. That happened to a couple of guys I played football with and they sounded just like her." Rollie stopped and thoughtfully selected his next words. "Raul, I think she misses me. I'm pretty sure she has some type of genuine affection for me."

"You sound surprised, Rollie. You're a great guy. Of course, she has feelings for you."

"It seems strange that an undercover snitch could develop an emotional tie to someone like me. Well anyhow, that's it."

Raul was in deep thought as he leaned against one wall of the lift. His head went back and forth as though he were having a tennis match with his thoughts. Finally, one side or the other in his head won a match point.

"So, if she's seen the flowers and read the note, then she came in to work; probably at night, so very few people would see her. I'm surprised that my guys didn't say anything about a beat-up woman coming in at night. Then again, it's amazing what can be done with theatrical makeup these days. I'm going to check the data logs to see if her identification has been used in the last 48 hours. Which reminds me. Zeggler is still working on that reflection off the CR47. It's definitely a person but that's about all he knows so far."

"Raul, what are we going to do about Sophia?"

"Nothing changes. Wait and move ahead as we planned. It's going exactly as I wanted. So we wait. When she contacts you the next time, make sure you invite her to go out in public. She might not want to go because of her appearance, but the mere fact that you want to take her out will help build the bridge we need to get her help."

"Okay." Rollie hung his head in disgust. "I'll be glad when this cloak and dagger stuff is over."

"You have to be a little more careful in the future about who you get romantically involved with, my man."

"You're right. I sure learned a lesson this time. By the way, Callie wants to show us something. Have you got some time?"

"Sure. Have you seen Maxine since the cloning?"

"No, this will be the first time. I've been trying to stay out of Callie's hair, so she can get her evaluation done on time."

The primate lab was labeled "Energy Transfer" with a large "Restricted" sign on the door. The intent was obvious; to dissuade nosy employees from trying to gain access. To get into the lab Raul and Rollie had to go through a double door, inter-locking vestibule. The first door opened when Raul's eyeballs were scanned and approved as an authorized entrant. The second door would not unlock until the first door closed and locked. A secondary security measure was also required before the inner door opened. A DNA sample was taken from the surface of Raul's skin and compared to the approved sample on file. The DNA reader worked on the same principal as eyeball, fingerprint and voice readers. No two people had the same chemical makeup within their skin cells.

The two Phoenvartis executives entered the primate lab to find it dimly lit. Only about a third of the overhead lighting was being used. At the far end of the lab, within a glass-enclosed room, sat Callie and Maxine. Callie was holding Maxine's hand, gently stroking it like a mother trying to soothe the ills of a young child. Maxine heard the men first. Her entire body tensed, and she let out a low growl.

Rollie could see the ape's clenched teeth and fire in her eyes. There was no question Maxine didn't want the men inter-rupting her time with Callie. When Callie figured out why her primate friend was agitated, she started petting and grooming her head. After a couple of minutes Maxine calmed down and started grooming Callie's head. Callie stood up, whispered something in Maxine's ear and then gave her a peck on the lips. Even from twenty yards away, Rollie could see Maxine's schoolgirl joy and embarrassment when she was kissed.

Callie left the glass enclosure and walked over to Raul and Rollie. "Thanks for coming, guys. The way Maxine reacted to you being in the lab is exactly how an ape will react to people she doesn't know."

"Now I know why it takes years to form a bond with these creatures."

"You're right, Raul. I got the same treatment from Maxine's troop when I started to study them."

Callie turned and walked over to a table where she picked up several papers. Each paper had a series of numbers and bullet point notes written on it. "Guys, come over here and have a seat. What I'm going to show you are selected clips taken from the past two days with Maxine. They start when she first wakes up in the lab and go until about one hour ago. Just like the old silent movies, superimposed at the bottom of each clip is what she and I are saying to each other. If you look in the upper right-hand corner of the recordings, you'll see the date and time stamp. Any questions before I begin?"

Hearing nothing from her guests, Callie started with the first halo clip. "Guys, this is when Maxine first wakes up after being cloned. For the next fifteen minutes, she walks around her enclosure touching and feeling everything. At first, she feels the glass barrier and then pounds on it. You can see the confusion in her eyes at waking up in a strange environment. It would be like you and I going to sleep in our homes but waking up on another planet, light-years from Earth. I'm going to skip forward to when she acknowledges my presence on the other side of the glass."

Rollie watched as Maxine squats on the enclosure floor and stares at Callie. "At this point, I purposely let Maxine begin our conversation. You can see her first words at the bottom of the clip."

M: "Callie, where we?"

Callie uses a strange combination of grunts, groans, hand

signals, head and body movements to respond to Maxine's question.

C: "We far from jungle. Place we no been before."

M: "Where trees and friends?"

"Here she is asking about the other members of the troop."

C: "No trees. Friends at home."

M: "Maxine see friends?"

C: "Yes. Many sleeps from now."

"Guys, apes don't understand the concept of time like we do. Instead of using minutes, hours and days they relate time by how many nights they sleep."

"I'm going to skip ahead again. Watch what happens when I light a cigarette."

M: "Callie bad. Not good. Stop."

"That was a test. I was testing her memory and her feelings for me."

"Callie, I have a question. Does Maxine remember being killed by the poachers?"

"Good question, Raul. So far, it hasn't come up. I don't want to bring it up because it leads to other perplexing questions about identity."

"What do you mean, Callie?"

"Think of it this way. If you are a clone and remember being killed or dying, then how do you account for your existence? It's not going to make any sense to you. On one hand, you're dead and on the other hand, you're not. You could go crazy trying to figure this out. Sure, I would be there to explain it to her but I'm not sure she could grasp the concept of being a replicant. I want to stay away from this issue unless she brings it up."

Callie's answer to Raul's question about death made perfect

sense to Rollie. "Yeah, I'm not sure any animal other than a human could understand being engineered back to life as a replicant."

"Okay, let's move ahead with another clip. Now, here is something I found interesting. You see Maxine take a bite of banana and then makes a funny face."

M: "Bad banana. Not from jungle."

M: "Callie not laugh."

"I don't get it, Callie. What is Maxine saying?"

"She somehow can tell the difference in taste between a banana from the Congo and one that is store-bought here in Zurich. She's not an enthusiastic fan of the farm-raised bananas. And did you see the face she made? I started laughing which made her mad. She thought I was making fun of her."

"Unbelievable! She's like a little kid, isn't she?"

"Rollie, in many ways she does act like a human child. But at times, she'll act as mature as any adult human. After years of working with her, I'm able to determine when she'll be child-like and when she'll be more mature."

For the next twenty minutes, Callie played a collage of different clips with the accompanying primate-talk translated into English. Every clip showed some type of behavior by Maxine which Callie thought was important. To enhance the behavior, Callie related most of it to how Maxine handled similar situations in the jungle. There were examples of comedy, sadness, anger, and thoughtfulness. In total, the wide variety of behaviors equaled an ape with a well-rounded personality.

"Gentlemen, that's about all I have to show you. From what I can tell, Maxine's clone is an intelligent, thoughtful and level-headed young female ape. It might be too early to tell conclusively but she seems to have the same memories as host Maxine. Her physical reactions are the same as the host. And quirky traits like biting her toenails are the same as the original Maxine."

Callie paused long enough for Raul to ask, "That's good, isn't it?"

Rather than answer verbally, Callie sighed, hunched her shoulders and nodded her head up and down.

Rollie could tell that they had reached the negative part of the presentation. "There's something wrong, isn't there, Callie?"

"Yes, and I don't know what to make of it. That's why I asked you to come down here. Let me show you one last clip. Watch closely because it happens very fast."

On the halo screen, Maxine is seen sitting on a fake, horizontal tree log within her enclosure. She is eating a piece of fruit and casually looking around. It's very possible that she is watching Callie on the other side of the shatterproof glass. Without any forewarning, she smashes her right hand on the log. She then wipes her hand across the log and goes back to eating the fruit and looking at whatever has her attention on the other side of the glass. Throughout the entire incident, she doesn't give one hint of interest in what was on the log or why she bashed it.

"Did you see that? Let me play it again for you."

Rollie and Raul asked to have the clip replayed two more times. After the last time, they looked at each other in puzzlement.

"Callie, I'm not sure exactly what we were supposed to see but it looks to me like Maxine kills something on the log."

"That's exactly what she does, Rollie. She kills a bullfrog as nonchalantly as scratching an itch. The host Maxine would never have done that. The real Maxine would have ignored the frog. On a rare occasion, she might have played with the frog by moving it along with her finger until it hopped away."

"What is a frog doing in her enclosure, Callie?"

"Raul, I've put a few things into her enclosure to simulate a jungle setting. There are several types of grasses and vegetation she likes to eat and live in. There are some fake trees which look like the ones she had in the jungle. And, to recreate the sounds of the jungle I put in about a half dozen bullfrogs. In the jungle, frog croaking and other insect sounds are soothing to the apes. The noise makes them feel safe and at night it's a lullaby. In fact, when the noise stops the apes know there is danger close by."

"So, Maxine killing a frog doesn't make sense?"

"You're right, Rollie. It's out of character for an ape, especially Maxine."

"What do you make of this, Callie? Is it possible it may be an anomaly; something that will never happen again?"

"I hope so, Rollie. But what she did is so out of character I have my doubts. Killing that frog might be a precursor to some bigger problem. I don't know what to think. I'm going to keep an eye on her and see if anything like this happens again. In the meantime, I would recommend that you delay the human cloning until I can figure this out."

"Callie, I appreciate your concern but that's not going to happen. All you've told me is that something might be wrong with the Maxine clone. It might be her personality, values or psyche. If there is a problem, it might even be something related to genetics. Maybe something was slightly skewed during the cloning. I think you get the point, Callie. There are too many "ifs" and "maybes". The only way I can delay the human cloning is if I have definitive proof that there will be significant problems with every human clone. A problem which will ultimately lead to some tragedy or catastrophic event."

"Rollie, you realize that you're playing with fire. I know there is something wrong with Maxine. She is not the same Maxine I befriended in the jungle. There is something not right with her. I don't know what it is but there is something. Please take my recommendation seriously and delay the human cloning."

Rollie got up and walked around the lab considering everything he had heard. Callie and Raul followed his every move and waited for his thoughts.

"Callie, let me ask you a question. If I told you today to pack your equipment and leave, would you take the cloned Maxine back to the Congo?"

It didn't take long for Callie to realize Rollie's question was loaded. By answering honestly, she provided conclusive ammunition for the human cloning to proceed as scheduled.

"Yes, Rollie, I would take her. What choice would I have? I love that animal, imperfect or not. Would you toss aside a loved one when he gets sick or handicapped?"

"No, Callie, I wouldn't. And I'm glad to hear that you would take her back to the Congo. Otherwise, we would have to .... Well, never mind what we would have to do with her."

Rollie came back to the table and sat down. "Callie, your report is due by the end of tomorrow. I recommend you put your suspicions in the report. Make it as factual as possible and don't go on a political witch-hunt. If you want to include a couple possible theories about why Maxine is acting this way, that would be okay. Otherwise, try to be objective and put in the good things you've observed in the cloned Maxine."

"Will that stop or put a hold on the human cloning?"

"I doubt it. But it will put everyone on notice that extra time should be spent researching Maxine and other primate clones before proceeding with a human clone. That's the best we can do now, Callie."

"Okay. You told me upfront that my participation in the ReLife project would be considered by many as superfluous interference. I guess it's unreasonable to expect everything to come to a screeching halt because of my suspicions. How much more time have I got to study Maxine and see if there is a problem with her?"

"The human cloning starts in two days, Callie. That doesn't mean you must stop evaluating Maxine. As far as I'm concerned, you have up to two more weeks with her. After that, we'll get you and her back to the Congo. Sound fair?"

"Sounds good, Rollie. I'll do my best to make a conclusion on this issue. Let's hope it's only my imagination and Maxine's erratic behavior is due to not being in the jungle with her friends. See ya later, guys."

Neither Raul or Rollie said much as they meandered through the halls of Phoenvartis. Both were replaying the meeting with Callie and thinking about what they learned and what was yet to be learned about cloning.

As they approached Rollie's office, Raul said, "Well, what do you think?"

"I wish Callie worked here full time. She is very good. She's one of a kind. I mean, how many people do you know who can befriend a dictator and a great ape?"

"I agree that she is special. But that's not what I meant."

"I know, Raul. I'm in a total quandary now. On one hand, I know we should delay the human cloning until more time is spent with Maxine. But I've got only a couple days to get a human clone and save the members of the ReLife project from termination. I feel like a marionette being danced across a stage by forces beyond my control."

"Go spend the night with Gretchen. That will take your mind off this mess." Raul smiled and winked at Rollie as he turned to walk away.

Rollie smiled back and thought, "how does that SOB find out these things?"

CHAPTER THIRTY-SIX

THE PRICE OF CLONING ESCALATES

"ROLLIE, I'd like to thank you for putting another monkey wrench in the ReLife project. Why in God's name would you send out that monkey woman's report to everyone and their brother? The irritation in Klaus's voice belied the fact that he was aware of his pun.

"I didn't know there was a limitation on who her report could be sent to." Rollie could barely keep looking at Klaus when he made such a dishonest statement. He expected Klaus to be upset when Callie's report was distributed without approval. Especially when it contained speculative assertions about the emotional health of the cloned ape. The implication that the same issue would occur in cloned humans sent Klaus into orbit.

"Who else did her report go to besides Phoenvartis executives and the Board of Directors?"

"Those are all the people I asked Ingrid to send the report to." Regardless of the limited distribution, Rollie was sure the report was unofficially passed on to hundreds of other people.

Within a couple hours of release, he suspected that the World Council also had a copy and was studying it.

"This is another stalling tactic, isn't it?"

"Mr. Ekstrom, I admit that further observations should be made of Maxine before human clones are attempted. But I can assure you that a planned delay was not my intention. You and I know that Mr. Slice gave us a total of two weeks to do human clones. He made it empirically clear there would be no time extensions or acceptable excuses for changing that timetable. The bottom line is that we are scheduled for human cloning in approximately 40 hours."

"Well, at least you haven't screwed that up. Make sure it happens. In fact, I want to be there. And I want that monkey woman out of here today."

Rollie stood up, leaned forward and braced himself on Klaus's desk. "That's a mistake, Klaus. She is the only one who can determine once and for all if there is something wrong with the cloned ape. The damage has already been done by her report. Let her keep working and see if she can negate that damage. She might be able to establish a plausible explanation which will explain away her fears. What have we got to lose? Even if she conclusively determines there is a flaw in the primate clone, the human clone will be done beforehand. And that's exactly what Slice wants."

"She has one week, Rollie. Then get her out of here. And by the way, here are the remains of who the World Council wants cloned." Klaus reached down behind his desk and retrieved a 10-inch square thermal box which he handed to Rollie.

Rollie was taken by complete surprise. He had already decided to use host samples taken from the city morgue. If the World Council wanted these samples used, then they must have come from someone very important. Someone who had a great deal of influence in the past with the World Council.

"Whose remains are these?"

"I have no frigging idea; just use them and don't worry about who the host is. Now, get out of here."

Rollie had been taken down a notch before by Klaus, but this was over the top. He was furious. One day he promised himself to get back at Klaus for the insults, backstabbing and sicko behavior of beating up women. This was the first time Rollie left Klaus's office without jesting with his assistant, Helga.

As Rollie made his way to the cafeteria for an anti-anxiety drink, several people within and outside of Phoenvartis were busy planning, scheming and jockeying their futures in a post-cloning world.

One of these was Claude, who had finished reading Callie's report for the second time. As he anticipated, there was a possible flaw in the cloned primate. Callie's report pounded that point home repeatedly and summarized her suspicion with a recommendation to delay human cloning. Claude brought up the protest letter he wrote before the primate cloning and made a few changes to it. The revised protest letter made it clear he was opposed to primate cloning from the first time he heard of it. Even though he could see Rollie's time at Phoenvartis was coming to an end, he debated whether to send out the letter. He put the letter back in his "to send" file and decided to wait until the human clones were done.

On the other end of the building, Raul was sifting through files collecting anything he considered important. He needed information which could be used for protection and blackmail when he left Phoenvartis. Until he could find another security or paramilitary job, he needed a source of world credits or some other form of income. The easiest way to survive would be to sell confidential Phoenvartis information to whoever would pay for it.

As a secondary measure, he planned to alter the building's entry and security systems, so he could come and go as he pleased after being fired. Plus, the communications system was already embedded with *bugs*, so he could listen in on any important conversations or meetings taking place within the building. He expected to have unfettered access to Phoenvartis for at least a month or two after departing. It would take them at least that long to find the eavesdropping devices.

Raul had been in enough conflicts to know when the tide of battle was turning against him. It was a feeling of pending defeat before a shot was fired or a casualty was suffered. He had learned the hard way to turn tail, disappear and then regroup when this feeling came over him. Listening to this inner voice had saved many lives, including his own. He now had this same feeling about his employment at Phoenvartis. Besides, his informant, Mr. Todd, was dropping hints that major changes were about to happen at Phoenvartis. Few of the current staff would survive. The end of his career at Phoenvartis was near and he wanted to be completely prepared for it.

In a better Zurich neighborhood, Sophia was sitting in her spacious living room looking at herself in a mirror. The facial swelling, blood in her left eye and scratches were almost unnoticeable. She was still walking with a limp but could hide it with enough pain-blocking drugs.

An hour earlier she had spent ten frightful minutes speaking with Klaus Ekstrom. He begged and pleaded to come over to her apartment. He used every excuse he could think of to get her permission. At first, he had a get-well gift for her. Then, it was to offer an apology. His last reason was to discuss the lease on her apartment— the apartment he paid for. Sophia refused, which turned the conversation into a full-fledged argument. It ended with Sophia saying, "Klaus, I'll kill you if you come here."

Two minutes after hanging up on Klaus, Krieger from the Black Cross called.

Sophia didn't try to hide her rotten mood. "Yes, Mr. Sun. What do you want now?"

"Well hello to you too, Catherine. I wanted to get an update on the cloning project. That's all."

"I'll have news for you tomorrow or the day after. Are you ready at your end?"

"Catherine, we have the host samples and can have them to you in 8 hours."

"What else, Mr. Sun?"

"We have the world credits ready to transfer to your account."

"Good, I want a 25% deposit before I do your clone. No deposit, no clone."

"Catherine, that wasn't part of the deal. It was 100% payment upon delivery of the clone."

"I changed the terms, Mr. Sun. Frankly, I don't trust you."

Krieger was furious. He hated being outwitted; especially by a bitch like Catherine. Fortunately, she was only asking for 25%. He could live with that. "You drive a hard bargain, Catherine. The 25% will be in your account tonight."

"Good. Again, no deposit, no clone. Understand?"

"You should know I'm a quick study, Catherine. By the way, the hospital did a wonderful job of putting you back together." Krieger started laughing and Sophia, aka Catherine, broke the connection. After two disgusting conversations with pigs, she decided to reach out to Rollie the next morning.

In the Phoenvartis cafeteria, Rollie was finishing his anti-anxiety drink. The drink acted exactly as advertised. He was starting to relax and let the positives of his life crowd out the negatives. He looked at the bottle he was drinking from and started to laugh to himself. The name of the drink was "Mellow

Yellow," which perfectly described its color and effects. He was about ready to get up from the table and go to his office when his micromic came on.

"Hello Callie, I was thinking about coming down and seeing you."

"Oh, good. I wanted to see what feedback you've gotten on my report and tell you the latest about Maxine. I think I've figured out what made Maxine kill the frog."

"It's 4 p.m. now. Can you wait until 5?"

"Sure, no problem. Come down when you can. Maxine and I are playing now. It usually takes her about an hour to get tired or bored."

"Okay, see you in a while."

Rollie left the cafeteria and went to his office to review contacts and store the thermal box in his refrigerator. For the first time during his tenure at Phoenvartis, he locked the refrigerator. As much as he hated the thought of cloning anything from the World Council, he didn't want to be accused of intentionally losing or destroying their host samples.

"That was quite a report you sent out, Rollie."

Rollie looked up to see Helmer come into the office, sit down and light a cigar.

"Has Klaus seen it?"

"Yes, sir, my friend. He wasn't a happy boy. But I was able to talk him into another week here for Callie to work with Maxine."

"I sure hope she can establish an explanation for Maxine's unusual behavior. I have been getting tons of contacts about this report. You and she sure stirred up a hornet's nest."

"Yeah, I know. But there's nothing I can do about it now other than hope this odd behavior was an anomaly. Hey, you haven't seen Maxine since the incubation, have you? I'm going down to see Callie right now. Do you want to come along?"

"Sure, let's do it." Helmer put out his cigar and the two executives headed to subterranean floor number four.

Once they were in the transport lift, Helmer asked, "Rollie, are we still on for the human cloning?"

"Yes. Not tomorrow morning but the next day at around 8 a.m."

"Helmer, can you keep something to yourself? Never mind, that was a stupid thing to ask. Get this. Guess who the host is?" Rollie didn't wait for Helmer to venture a guess.

"We're cloning someone associated with the World Council."

Helmer's head snapped around to face Rollie. "What? Are you joking? How the hell did that happen?

"All I know is Klaus gave me a thermal box containing remains which came from the World Council."

"Holy shit. It's got to be someone important. And you have no idea who it is?"

"I don't have a clue. But if I had to guess I'd say it's someone who Slice wants to resurrect."

"That's probably a good guess. We'll just have to wait to see who it is."

Both men approached the primate lab door and started the security procedures to get through the interlocking doors. When the second door opened and both men stepped into the lab, they froze and didn't take another step forward. About fifteen feet from them was Maxine sitting on the floor next to Callie's prone body. Maxine looked up with weepy eyes at the two men.

Without moving an inch, Rollie spoke slightly above a whisper, "Callie, Callie, can you hear me?"

Callie didn't move even when Maxine rubbed her hand across the woman's forehead.

"Helmer, slowly back into the interlocking door vestibule."

When both men were in the vestibule, Rollie closed the door and contacted Raul.

"Raul, I hate to bother you, but we have a problem in the primate lab. I think Callie is dead."

Rollie listened to what Raul said and then answered. "I don't know, Raul. It might have been Maxine, but who knows. Maxine is sitting right next to the body and we're going to need a tranquilizer gun. Have you got one?" After a momentary pause, Rollie ended the conversation. "Okay, I'll see you in a couple of minutes."

Rollie looked at Helmer. "Raul is on his way. Let's wait in the hallway."

"Jesus, Rollie, do you think Callie is dead? Is it possible that Maxine killed her?"

"I hope Callie only passed out and Maxine is protecting and comforting her. But we're dealing with a wild animal. A wild animal that has already exhibited some unusual behavior compared to her host."

"Isn't her enclosure secured? How did she get out?"

"Helmer, I have no idea. For all we know, Callie may have let her out or forgot to secure the door when... Oh hell, I don't know. I'm not very good at being a Sherlock Holmes. Raul will figure out what happened. Right now, we need to focus on the human cloning."

At the far end of the hall, the lift door opened, and Raul and a couple of his agents got off. Raul was carrying what appeared to be a tranquilizer gun. His agents had several pieces of equipment including a large net, rope, and sack of bananas. Rollie explained in detail what he and Helmer saw when they were in the lab.

"Okay, here's what we're going to do. Helmer, you stay here. The rest of us are going into the interlocking vestibule. I'm going to peek into the lab and see where Maxine is. If she is still sitting next to Callie, I'm going to put a couple of darts in her and duck back into the vestibule. Zeggler, don't close the lab door. Keep it open so I can get back in fast. I'm guessing it will take about two minutes for Maxine to go under. When she does, we'll go in, put her in the net and slide her across the floor to the enclosure. Any questions?"

Hearing nothing from his companions, Raul led the way into the interlocking vestibule. When he went through the second door Maxine was still sitting next to Callie holding her hand. Raul fired twice and ducked back into the vestibule making sure the door was locked. For a couple minutes, it sounded like a tornado was on the loose in the lab. Glass shattered. The vestibule door took a direct hit from something bouncing off it. Maxine was wreaking havoc in the lab turning over and throwing anything which wasn't tied down. As Raul predicted, the noise stopped about two to three minutes after it started.

"Okay, I'm going in. Don't follow until I say it's okay."

Raul and Zeggler had to force the vestibule door open. Directly on the other side was Maxine, out cold and lying face up. Her breathing was labored but otherwise, she looked like a healthy ape at sleep. Raul took out his real gun and hurried over to Callie. Her skin was lukewarm to the touch and Raul couldn't find a pulse.

"Okay, you guys, come in."

The first thing Raul and the two agents did was step around and move back from Maxine. Even in her semi-conscious state, she was imposing enough to be threatening.

"Okay, let's get her over to the enclosure." Raul spread the net on the floor next to Maxine and instructed each guy on how to lift her. With less effort than when she was removed from the CR47, the four men lifted her into the net. Each man grabbed a side of the net and started to pull it toward the enclosure at the far end of the lab.

As Raul opened the enclosure door, Maxine's eyes popped open and she grabbed an agent's leg. She growled and rolled over dragging the agent to the ground. When she put her hands around the agent's head and started to squeeze, Raul put a blast through Maxine's brain.

Rollie stood at attention watching the ape spasmodically contort before death took her. He had no idea what to do, who to call or what to say. Raul made sure Maxine was dead and then he and Zeggler helped their fellow agent.

Raul took a quick lap around the lab looking for clues and evidence. "Everyone out of the lab. Don't touch anything on the way out. Zeggler, secure this room after we leave. No one other than the medical examiner is to enter this room. Until I tell you otherwise, I want someone posted in the hallway 24 hours a day. Don't tell anyone about what you saw here this evening." Raul knew this was a waste of his breath. He figured everyone at Phoenvartis would know about the two deaths within an hour. "Okay, everyone out."

Raul stayed alone in the lab for about five minutes. When he exited, he walked over to Rollie.

"Are you okay? You looked a little peaked."

"I'm okay. Helmer took off. He was feeling sick."

"Someone altered the lab recorders which tells me there is a good chance Callie was murdered. I highly doubt that Maxine had anything to do with Callie's death. I've got to call my friend at the medical examiner's office and get him down here. I'll talk to you later, Rollie. By the way, when you go home or back to your office make some notes on what happened here. The sooner you record your observations the more accurate they will be. The medical examiner is going to need a statement from everyone."

Raul left to make his call and Rollie slid down the hallway wall to a sitting position on the floor. He was mentally exhausted. Seeing a dead body was one thing but watching the brains blown out of Maxine's head was indescribable and something he never wanted to see again. How could anyone, like Raul, spend years in combat seeing such horror?

After calling the medical examiner's office, Raul rushed to his office to review the primate lab recordings. He had lied to Rollie about someone destroying the lab recordings during the time Callie was killed. He suspected she was murdered and with a little luck he would see or hear who was responsible.

It took about ten minutes for Raul to piece together Callie's murder from the lab recordings. The murderer had left behind one important clue which identified him as the guilty party. After Raul stumbled onto the clue, he sat back in his chair, smiled and said to himself, "I never thought you were so resourceful. You little turd." He made a copy of the recording immediately preceding and during the murder and then deleted that segment from the archives. He disabled the lab recorders, so everyone would think the system failed for some reason before Callie was killed.

Raul finished sabotaging the evidence as Rollie fell into his office desk chair. After a minute or two, Rollie found enough energy to make a copy of the primate lab recordings for the last two days. This time frame overlapped with Callie starting to work on why Maxine killed the frog. He figured it was better to have too much video and audio data rather than too little.

He got up to go home but only got halfway to the office entrance. He went back to his desk and brought up the primate lab recordings again. For the hell of it, he did a search back to 4 p.m. and started the recording. For the next twelve minutes, he watched Callie feed, play and talk to Maxine. Throughout this entire time, Maxine was in her enclosure. At 4:12 the recording went black and stayed that way.

He agreed with Raul. Someone had manipulated the recordings and then killed Callie. There was a good chance the murderer let Maxine out of the enclosure to make her the primary suspect in Callie's murder.

Rollie left Phoenvartis and headed home for some well-deserved sleep. As he walked the Zurich streets, he repeatedly thought about why and how Callie was killed. He had already eliminated Maxine as a suspect. He wasn't an animal psychologist, but the way Maxine looked as she sat next to Callie's body suggested a grief-stricken friend. Plus, the way she went berserk when tranquilized reminded him of a ferocious guard dog trying to protect its master. The murderer had to be a human, someone Callie knew and would have invited into the lab without trepidation.

But why would anyone want to kill Callie? She was a terrific lady. Maybe a little headstrong but that was no reason to kill her. And, bringing to light a possible flaw in Maxine's personality was another ridiculous reason for murder. There had to be something about Callie's research which scared the bee-Jesus out of whoever was responsible for her death.

Rollie planned to review the primate lab recordings after a good night's sleep. Hopefully, he could pick out what Callie had seen in Maxine's behavior to explain the killing of the frog. He wished he had asked Callie whether her discovery exonerated Maxine or pointed to a psychological problem. Without that one clue, his investigation was going to be twice as difficult. The odds were against him because he didn't know the real jungle Maxine. Plus, Callie probably hadn't put the subtitles on the recordings so Rollie would know what she and the ape were talking about. This was going to be an almost impossible task, but what choice did he have?

His puppy greeted him at the door and then ran around the apartment until he was out of breath. Rollie fed him a couple pieces of the turkey sandwich he made for himself and then tried to play ball with him. He only had enough energy to throw the dog's favorite ball a couple times. The puppy could have retrieved the ball a couple hundred times but Rollie needed sleep more than play with his buddy.

Rollie fell into bed and was asleep within five minutes. The puppy was wide awake but laid still, content to be with his master.

A telepathic communication with Grandma LeeLee started immediately. She had been waiting for him to enter the psychic state where he was receptive to her messages. Her message was simple and to the point. **"Don't clone the World Council host samples. Use the samples received in the antique maple box with the "H" chiseled into the cover."** This same message repeated itself over and over for the next eight hours of sleep. The only thing which changed was the way the message was presented. In one scene, the World Council host samples were destroyed by fire. In the next scene, they were thrown into a bottomless pit. They were destroyed thirty to forty unusual ways during the night. There was no question the samples were from a host Grandma LeeLee and her God considered evil.

Using the host samples from LeeLee was also presented in several different ways. In one scene, a smiling Grandma LeeLee was sitting in her favorite rocking chair on the porch of her Macon home. In her lap was the maple box with the engraved "H." Grandma LeeLee slowly spoke the words, **"Use This Now"** over and over. In another scene, Rollie saw an army of angels flying through the heavens. The lead angel, who was carrying the maple box, is surrounded by dozens of angels triumphantly blowing horns of victory. The message of using LeeLee's box is very clear.

"Rollie, Rollie, wake up darling."

He could hear a woman's voice pleading with him, but he couldn't see her. How could he hear her voice when he was now underwater trying to swim to the surface? The more he struggled to reach air and safety the louder and more desperate her pleas became.

"Rollie, wake up. You're having a bad dream."

He broke the surface of the water and his eyes opened to find Gretchen and the puppy staring down at him. His skin and clothes were coated with a heavy layer of sweat; or was it water?

"Oh, thank God. You scared the hell out of me. Do you remember what you were dreaming about?"

Slowly, reality took over. He recognized his apartment, his girlfriend and dog. He reached out and held Gretchen's hand to make sure she was real, and he wasn't dreaming any longer.

"What did you say, Gretchen?"

"I said, do you remember what you were dreaming about?"

Rollie lifted himself onto his elbows so he could get a better look at her and everything in the room.

"Yes, I guess I do. My grandmother wants me to do something for her."

Gretchen was puzzled. She knew Rollie had a grandmother and the woman was eccentric but what was he talking about?

"It's nothing, Gretchen. I guess I'm still in La-La Land."

Gretchen wiped the sweat from his forehead and gave him a glass of ice water.

After a couple of sips, he handed the glass back to her and said, "Callie was killed last night."

Gretchen didn't know if he was serious or still dreaming.

"Who is Callie?"

"The woman Raul and I were with a couple nights ago at your tavern."

"What? That nice looking, older woman? Are you sure you're awake? Did that..."

"I'm awake, Gretchen. She was either killed by a replicant ape or someone murdered her and made it look like the ape was responsible. I'm guessing she was murdered, and it wasn't the ape."

"My God, Rollie. Who told you this?"

"Helmer and I found her dead in the lab."

"Oh, I'm so sorry. I know you thought she was special. What, what are you going to..."

"What time is it?"

"It's about 9:30. What time do you have to be at work?"

"I should have been there about two hours ago. Listen, I've got to get going. I'm sure the examiner and Raul will want to talk with me, plus I've got a lot of preparation work to do for tomorrow's test. Let's plan to have dinner tomorrow night. I'll fill you in on everything then. Okay?"

Gretchen took Rollie's head in her hands and kissed him on the forehead. "Let me know when and where and I'll be there. And, be careful, okay?" Gretchen playfully squeezed and shook his head to make sure he understood how concerned she was for his safety.

As she left the bedroom on her way out of the apartment, Rollie called, "Keep the Callie thing to yourself, okay?"

He wasn't sure she had heard him until she exaggerated her walk and wiggled her butt.

CHAPTER THIRTY-SEVEN

MILKWEED AND CONFESSIONS

AS ROLLIE ENTERED PHOENVARTIS, Raul was escorting a couple of men through the lobby to the front doors. Both men carried large satchels like the doctor bags in old black and white movies from the 20th century. To Rollie, their bags plus shabby, wrinkled clothes added up to government lackeys.

Rollie waited at the security desk for Raul. When he finished with his guests, he spotted Rollie and came over to talk with his friend.

"Glad you could make it today. Those guys were from the medical examiner's office. They wanted to talk to you but I'm not going to call them back. You can talk to them later."

"Did they figure out who killed Callie?"

"You're jumping way ahead, Rollie. This is the beginning of their investigation. What they know so far is that Callie was hit very hard in the temple. She had a huge black and blue contusion on the left side of her head. We didn't see it because it was hidden under her hair. Anyhow, they had the body removed and taken to the morgue, so they can do an autopsy. It will be several days before they reach any conclusions. In the meantime, one of Zurich's finest will be doing the investigation."

"You mean a cop?"

"No, this guy is an investigator attached to the medical examiner's office. There aren't many places that have police departments with detectives any longer."

"Do you think he'll find out who killed her?"

"I don't know, Rollie. I have no idea whether he's competent or not. The medical examiner speaks highly of their investigators, but that's his opinion. As a precaution, I'll be running my own investigation."

"Good. That makes me feel better. By the way, where is Maxine's body?"

"I think it's on the way to be cremated."

"That's a mistake, Raul. At least her brain should be kept and examined for any anomalies, like a tumor. Can you stop the cremation?"

"I'll try. But I can't guarantee it. Even if I can stop it, who is going to remove her brain? The medical examiner won't do it. Will you do it?"

"I'll find someone, Raul. If need be, I'll do it. See if you can delay the cremation, okay?"

The two men parted. Rollie headed to his office and Raul went to his. Trying to stop the cremation of Maxine's body was way down Raul's priority list. There was still a lot of work to be done in preparation for becoming a former Phoenvartis employee.

As Rollie sat down to review his communications, an incoming call from Sophia flashed on his network board. The events of the last twelve hours had been so disturbing he didn't feel like talking with her but knew it had to be done. There was good reason to believe he might not get another chance.

"Hello, Sophia. How do you feel?"

"I'm much better, Rollie. Thanks for asking. Are you doing anything tonight?"

"Not yet. I've got to prepare for a big day tomorrow, but I should be able to get the prep work done by the end of today. Are you asking me to dinner?"

"Yes sir, I am. The lady in black will meet you at the Schwarzenbach Tavern at seven o'clock. Until then, my dear."

The reference to the lady in black had been an ongoing, endearing code phrase between the two lovers. It marked the beginning of their relationship. It would also mark the end of their liaison if she wore it again to the Schwarzenbach. The selfish side of his personality hoped she would wear the black outfit because she was so damn sexy in it. But that might also mean she thought they were still an item. Either way, he needed to make sure that she understood they were done.

It was now noon and he had six hours to get everything done before his dinner with Sophia. His priority was meeting with Claude and Helmer to make sure everything was ready for the human cloning. He also had to put Grandma LeeLee's host samples into the World Council thermal box and reseal it, so it appeared exactly as Klaus received it. What he should do with the World Council host samples was another dilemma. He needed to give this some deliberate thought and not make a rash decision. In the meantime, he would hide them in his office. Any extra time before dinner would be devoted to reviewing the primate lab recordings. This could take days, even a week or more. He was looking for a needle in the haystack. But it was so important to determine what flaws, if any, clones had in their personalities.

"Ingrid, are you out there?"

"Yez sir, master. Eyes out here."

Rollie laughed at her portrayal of a long-past slave from old

America. Every so often she came up with an unexpected antic funny enough to put a smile on his face.

"Ingrid, you're watching too many of those old black and white movies; no pun intended. Would you get ahold of Claude and Helmer and ask them to be in my office at one o'clock for a pre-clone meeting?"

"Will do. By the way, I forgot to tell you how sorry I was to hear about Callie."

"Thanks, Ingrid."

"Hang on a minute, Mr. Sweats."

In the background, Rollie could hear a muffled conversation taking place. "Mr. Sweats, there is an investigator here to see you. Says he is from the medical examiner's office."

"Okay, send him in and tell Claude and Helmer 1:30 instead of one o'clock."

Into Rollie's office walked a young man with long blonde hair hanging down past his shoulders. It had been years since Rollie had seen a man with such long hair. Rather than wearing the typical food stained, wrinkled clothes of most government workers, this guy was dressed like a male model. His suit was precisely tailored with a beautiful white shirt and matching tie. The tie was another thing Rollie couldn't remember men wearing except in old movies. The investigator's height of about six and a half feet and broad shoulders reminded Rollie of a football tight end.

"Mr. Sweats, my name is Jason Milkweed. I'm with the medical examiner's office and I'd like to ask you a few questions about the death of a... a Ms. Weeks."

Rollie knew Jason was waiting for a wisecrack about his last name. With a name like Sweats, there was no way Rollie was going to attack this guy's last name. Without comparing any personal history, Rollie knew the two men shared years of ridicule, badgering, and torment from neighborhood kids attacking their odd last names.

But the investigator's last name wasn't the most unique thing about this young man. Rollie couldn't get over this man's appearance. His baby face reminded Rollie of the faces painted on angels in old Russian and Greek Orthodox churches. It was unblemished, rosy-cheeked and more feminine than male. Rollie stared at the man with a boy's face as he shook his hand.

"Mr. Sweats, can we get started? This shouldn't take long."

"Uh, sure. Have a seat. Would you like something to drink or smoke?"

"No thank you, sir. Do you mind if I record this interview? I talk with so many people it's hard to keep straight what each person has said."

"No problem. I'd rather have it recorded than write a statement."

"Good. Thank You. Mr. Sweats, can you tell me what happened yesterday between the hours of, let's say, 3 p.m. and 6 p.m.?"

For the next twenty minutes, Rollie walked Jason Milkweed through everything he could remember leading up to, during, and after Callie's death. During his entire statement, Milkweed didn't make one comment, ask one question or change the expression on his face.

When Rollie finished, Milkweed asked, "Mr. Sweats, tell me again why there was an African ape in your building. I'm not sure I understand why you were cloning an ape as opposed to any other animal."

Rollie spent another five minutes putting in layman's terms the similarity between primates and humans. He then explained Callie's ability to talk to monkeys and how invaluable it was in getting feedback from a clone. He tried to avoid mentioning how Maxine was a precursor to understanding possible psychological problems in human clones.

"Interesting. Who determined if the ape's enclosure was secure enough to hold her?"

"We built the enclosure to Callie's recommendations. Raul Hakala then approved the construction for safety and security." Rollie embellished his answer somewhat by claiming that Callie provided detail specifications for the enclosure. For some reason, he felt like Milkweed was pointing a finger of blame at him for an inferior way of housing the great ape.

"A couple more questions, Mr. Sweats. First, tell me again why you went down to see Ms. Weeks in the lab and why Mr. Stanke went with you."

"I ran into Helmer by coincidence and asked if he would like to see Maxine. He hadn't seen the ape since she was taken out of the cloning machine and wheeled down to the primate lab." Rollie paused for a moment trying to remember what else Milkweed had asked. "Sorry, what else did you ask me?"

"I wanted to know why you went to the lab at that particular time."

"Ah, yes. I went because Callie asked me to. She wanted to discuss some recent observations she made of Maxine's behavior."

"What were those observations again?"

"I don't know, Mr. Milkweed. She didn't tell me when I spoke to her before going to the lab and she was dead when I got there." Rollie was starting to get irritated with Milkweed. His questions and demeanor were structured to entrap Rollie in a lie or conflicting answers.

"One last question, Mr. Sweats. You said earlier that Mr. Hakala stayed behind in the lab after you and Helmer left. How long did he stay in the lab?"

"I'd say about three to four minutes."

"Could it have been ten to fifteen minutes?"

"Absolutely not. Five minutes at the max."

"What was he doing in the lab?"

"I thought you had one more question!" Milkweed didn't react to Rollie's sarcasm in any way. He just waited for Rollie to answer.

"I have no idea what he was doing in the lab."

"Didn't he tell you when he came out?"

"Mr. Milkweed, I already answered your question. Listen, I have another meeting now with some coworkers who I can see standing in the hall. So if you have any more questions send them to me verbally or in writing and I'll respond when I can. Nice meeting you."

Rollie stood up and walked around Milkweed to invite Claude and Helmer into his office. He had enough of Milkweed and hoped his rude behavior would be crystal clear to the investigator. Milkweed followed Rollie to the door to leave but not before he said, "Mr. Stanke, good to see you again."

As soon as the ReLife team sat down, Claude asked, "Who was that?"

"An investigator from the medical examiner's office."

"What did he want?"

"He's investigating Callie's murder."

"Murder? I thought the ape killed her. Are you saying she was killed some other way?"

"That's why he was here, Claude. His job is to answer that question. Helmer, I see you have already spent some time with Mr. Milkweed."

Helmer chuckled a little. "Yeah, I spent a delightful hour with Milk-Bone, Milk Toast or whatever his name is. By the time we were done, I wanted to punch him in the nose."

"Same here. He has a way of pissing off a person. But I have to admit that he has more between those ears than a pretty-boy face."

Before Rollie got the meeting started, Helmer couldn't help himself and had to throw a barb at Claude. "Claude, you'll be hearing from Milk Toast. He asked me about you, and I recommended that he interview you as soon as possible."

Helmer made his comment straight faced and with so much conviction that even Rollie thought he was telling the truth.

"What? Why would he want to talk to me? I wasn't with you guys when you discovered Callie's body. I haven't been in that lab since..."

Claude rambled on and on about having to meet with Milkweed. His face reddened and beads of sweat broke out on his forehead. He gradually lifted out of his chair as he denied, agonized and swore an oath of innocence in the Callie murder case. He was so upset that he started to stutter and went into one of his famous sinus-clearing, snorting fits. His last statement before Rollie interceded was, "No damn way am I going to talk to that guy."

"Claude, calm down. Helmer was putting you on for God's sake."

When Claude realized he was the butt of another Helmer prank, he swore, ranted and raved about the unprofessional staff at Phoenvartis, particularly Helmer and Rollie. The more he complained the more Helmer and Rollie laughed. The three ReLife team members created so much commotion that Ingrid came into the office to make sure everyone was okay.

Finally, things calmed down enough so Rollie could get the meeting called to order. For the next two hours, the ReLife team went through an extensive checklist making sure everything was in order and ready for the human cloning. Rollie was very impressed with the amount of work Claude and Helmer had put into the preparation. Apart from a couple of minor details, it appeared that everything was ready.

"Okay, guys. That's about it. You've done an excellent job getting ready for this. I'll talk to Raul and make sure a double sentry is put on the CR47 tonight. Get a good sleep tonight and I'll see you around 9 tomorrow morning."

Rollie watched Claude and Helmer leave his office. He got a chuckle out of seeing Claude leave far ahead of Helmer. This was another grudge Claude would add to his Helmer shit list and carry around for years to come. Other than Claude getting steamed about a fictitious meeting with Milkweed, Rollie thought this was one of the best meetings he ever attended.

As he got ready to call Raul and then switch the host samples, a thought crossed Rollie's mind. Out of the blue, he realized Claude did not ask any questions about the host samples. Where they came from. Did Rollie have them? He was such a perfectionist he couldn't have overlooked such an important detail in the cloning procedure. It was obvious Claude already knew the answer to those questions. Rollie wondered who filled Claude in on where the host samples came from.

Rollie devoted about an hour and a half to review the primate lab recordings. He reviewed them at three-quarter speed. At a slower speed, Rollie felt he would have a better chance of seeing Maxine's elusive behavior which explained her odd behavior. By 6:15 p.m. he hadn't seen anything unusual, so he shut off the playback and left the building to meet Sophia.

Rollie arrived at the tavern a few minutes early. He went in and was about to get a table for two when he spotted Sophia sitting at the back of the dining area. She was at the same table as the first night the two of them had played eye-tennis, flirting back and forth across the dining room. As he approached her table, he could see she was wearing the sleek black dress outfit he thought was so sexy.

"Hi, how are you?" Rollie reached out and held Sophia's hand as he gave her a peck on the cheek.

"I'm fine, Rollie. It's good to see you. It seems like years since we've been together."

Rollie was surprised at how good Sophia's face looked. He could see that she was wearing heavy makeup, but it was only hiding the remaining black and blue marks and blood under the skin. The swelling had receded, and her face was back to its original shape.

"Yes, it seems like a long time. So much has happened since I saw you last."

"I understand that you lost a member of your team. I heard that it was the woman from the Congo who can talk to monkeys."

Rollie looked into her eyes. "How do you know that?"

"My dear, there is an underground rumor mill at Phoenvartis that you wouldn't believe. If you know the right people you can find out just about anything."

"You're kidding. Who's in it?"

"I'll only tell you that it starts right at the top." Rollie thought for a moment. The top was Klaus's office. There was no chance it was Klaus, so it had to be his assistant, Helga.

"Helga? Are you kidding? She's the leader of a gossip group?"

"Not a group, Rollie. It's a gang. They not only spread and filter information around the company, they also wield a lot of power. I know of two people in the last year they had fired for trumped-up reasons."

Rollie didn't know what to say. He was befuddled. There was no question she was telling the truth. What surprised him was how efficient this gang was in keeping their activities hidden from the company's executives.

"What other surprises do you have for me, Sophia?"

"Well, let's see. An investigator is investigating the primate scientist's death. Tomorrow morning there is a human cloning scheduled. One of Raul's men is trying to figure out who was snooping around the CR47 and is seen as a reflection on the side of the incubator. By the way, that was me. I came into work a couple nights and got the urge to look at the CR47. I had never seen it before. There are some other things, but they can wait. I'd like to eat something first."

Rollie was stunned. He kept staring at Sophia thinking he might be asleep, and this was a bad dream.

His thoughts finally cleared, and he called the waitress over. Sophia ordered a meal but Rollie ordered a double shot of Irish whiskey, straight up with no chaser.

"You have been a busy little girl. I'm going to be honest with you, Sophia. What you've told me is correct. What I don't understand is why you are telling me these things."

"Time is running out, Rollie, and you're the only person I trust. I need to ask a favor of you."

"Before you say anything more, I need to tell you a few things." Rollie paused for a couple of seconds to make sure Sophia was willing to listen to what he had to say.

"Sophia, Raul and I know that you have been seeing Klaus and he is the one who beat you up." Rollie waited for Sophia to respond but all she did was lower her head in shame and then take a drink of water.

"Here's the thing which we are very concerned about. We know you are working undercover for someone. We don't know who or what you're trying to do. But your position as Director of Archives is a cover for your real job which is collecting information for someone."

Sophia began playing with her silverware, stalling for time to think about how to answer Rollie's accusations.

"I guess this is as good a night to confess as any. Yes, I'm working for an ultra-right wing, anarchist group called the Black Cross. I believe their mission is to topple the World Council, but I don't know for certain. I'm doing it for the credits, Rollie. No other reason, just the credits. Enough credits to live the rest of my life in luxury, anywhere I want."

Sophia paused and put her hands over Rollie's closest hand. "I want you to join me, Rollie. Come with me and let's see the world, have fun and forget about the World Council, all its lackeys and the problems it creates for decent folks. Rollie, life is too short to be constantly fighting against the bureaucracy. I'm sick and tired of wondering if you're next to be shut off from credits because you want a little freedom."

The waitress delivered Sophia's meal and Rollie's drink. The meal looked and smelled wonderful, but Sophia's hunger had subsided with her confession.

"Rollie, do you want this? I'm not hungry any longer. I need a drink."

"Here, take this one and I'll get another." Rollie called the waitress over and ordered two more double shots of Irish whiskey. He was sure that either he or Sophia would drink the extra one.

After they downed most of their drinks, Rollie said, "Sophia, I can't join you. It sounds very inviting, but I don't want to be on the run for the rest of my life. I have a large family and too many personal ties to walk away and disappear." Rollie finished his drink and sucked on an ice cube while he gave more thought to Sophia's proposition. Sophia considered saying something about Rollie's new girlfriend but decided it would sound vindictive no matter how she made the comment.

"Sophia, this Black Cross group obviously wants more than

the information you are providing. Will you tell me what they want?"

"Rollie, it's best that I keep that to myself for now. If I tell you then you become an accomplice to what I'm doing for the Black Cross and I don't want to put you in that position. If you change your mind about leaving with me, I'll tell you what I have to do for them."

Even though her response made sense, Rollie still wanted to know what her mission for the Black Cross entailed. "Sophia, answer one question for me. Will anyone get hurt because of what you're doing for the Black Cross?"

"Rollie, no one you know will get hurt." Sophia knew this might not be entirely true. In the short term, no one at Phoenvartis would get hurt. But there was always the possibility that whoever they wanted cloned might cause trouble and end up hurting a lot of people. Sophia decided not to say anything more because it would be nothing more than a guess.

"That's kind of an open-ended answer."

"Rollie, I can't see the future. It's the best answer I can give you today."

Rollie shrugged realizing he wasn't going to get any more information from Sophia. Each of them had another drink and talked about less serious subjects like the puppy, oddball characters at Phoenvartis and the good times they shared.

"Rollie, will you walk me home?"

"Sure. Let me get a thermal shell for your dinner and we'll get out of here."

"Good idea, I'm sure I'll get hungry later."

Five minutes later, Rollie and Sophia left the tavern. They strolled along the river walk enjoying the sights on an unusually warm night. About a block from the tavern, Sophia took Rollie's arm as though they were new lovers still in the infatuation stage of their relationship. Neither of them verbalized any of the thoughts racing through their heads.

Rollie speculated that this might be his last intimate moment with Sophia. And, it might be the last time he ever saw her. He still wondered about her mission for the Black Cross. He hoped she was telling the truth about any evil it might produce.

Sophia loved walking with Rollie, even if he was a former boyfriend. Just being seen in public with a handsome man made her feel important. Maybe there was a tinge of feeling loved also.

Sophia anticipated Rollie's reluctance to run away with her. She put the odds of him agreeing at less than 20%. She was disappointed but not emotionally destroyed. Experience had taught her that there were other Rollies in the world and with some luck, she would find one. After receiving the 25% down payment from Krieger at the Black Cross she had enough credits to stay lost in luxury for quite a few years. Maybe not the rest of her life but at least fifteen years. To be safe, she transferred the credits several times between accounts. This would prevent anyone from ever finding and taking them. Using a complicated algorithm, the credits would transfer every month or so to keep anyone looking for them confused and off the scent.

A half hour after leaving the tavern, they arrived at the Opulenz apartments. This was one of the premier apartment buildings in Zurich. In English, its name meant opulence. It was an appropriate name for the elegance. Rollie knew Sophia wasn't paying for this lifestyle. Someone else was footing the bill. It might be part of her deal with the Black Cross. It would be easy for Raul to find the name of her benefactor if he hadn't done so already.

At the entrance to the building, Sophia turned Rollie and

gave him an extended hug. Even though he wanted to see her expensive apartment, he didn't ask to be invited in. Likewise, Sophia thought it best to part on the street and not create a situation in her apartment which might be awkwardly seductive.

"Sophia, please be careful and if you ever need anything, call me." He knew she was too dangerous to partner with, but the adventurous part of his personality would miss her.

"Rollie, give the puppy a big kiss for me and good luck tomorrow." She gave him a kiss on the lips and then headed to the entrance. The doorman opened the door for her, and she was halfway inside when she turned back to Rollie. "Rollie, remember that things are not always as they appear." She then walked out of sight.

Rollie stood there for a moment wishing she would return and explain her last comment. He turned and started the fifteen-minute walk to his apartment.

In the darkness across the street, a well-dressed man smoked as he watched Rollie and Sophia part ways. When Rollie was out of sight, he walked over to the Opulenz, entered, and took the lift to Sophia's floor. It was time for the two of them to get together.

CHAPTER THIRTY-EIGHT

OFF TO A GOOD START IN A BAD WAY

THE NEXT MORNING, Rollie and Helmer arrived at Phoen-vartis at the same time. As they walked through the courtyard, Helmer was talking nonstop as if he were on an adrenaline high. Rollie had seen the same emotions from football players who acted like they were possessed by the devil until they got on the field and hit an opponent.

"Rollie, do we have clothes for the clone? How do we know what size clothes the clone wears? Where is the clone going to sleep? Have we planned meals for the clone? We forgot these things, didn't we? And, another thing, is there going to be a doctor...?"

"Calm down. I have a robe for the clone to wear until we know what size he is, and I can send Ingrid to buy some clothes. If he is around my size, he can wear some of the extra clothes I have in my office. I've planned for the cafeteria to provide three well-balanced meals each day for our guest. And Raul had the primate lab updated last night with a bed, dresser, toiletries and a full complement of kitchen utensils if he needs them. There's already a shower and cooler unit in the lab. In fact, there's a vibration tub also, in case he wants to unwind and get a muscle massage."

"Helmer, why don't you and I go to the cafeteria and get a Mellow Yellow. You definitely need to calm down and I could also use a sip or two."

By 8 a.m., the anti-anxiety drink had done its job and brought Helmer back to Earth. The two men left the cafeteria and went to their offices to check communications and give instructions to their assistants.

Rollie removed the thermal box containing the host samples from a locked cabinet in his office. The night before, he booby-trapped the opening of the thermal box with a hair from his head. The hair was still in its original position indicating the box had not been opened or tampered with since he put it in the cabinet.

"Ingrid, I'll be in the CR47 lab for the next hour or so. Take messages and don't interrupt us unless atomic laser war breaks out."

Ingrid got the message. She knew how serious the next four to five hours would be for everyone who worked at Phoenvartis. The rumor mill kept her well informed on the human cloning scheduled to begin within the next hour. She smiled at him and said, "Good luck, boss."

Rollie didn't give a minute of thought to why Ingrid wished him well. After his discussion with Sophia the night before he figured Ingrid knew exactly what was about to happen in the CR47 lab. In fact, he wouldn't be surprised if she knew more than the ReLife team.

By the time Rollie arrived at the cloning lab, everyone was there except for Klaus.

"Good morning everyone." Rollie waited for Raul, Claude and Helmer to acknowledge his welcome. "Okay, guys. I guess this is it. Let's get started. It's almost 9 a.m., so Klaus may or may not show up. Claude, if you and Helmer will start the authorization and initialization phases, I'll get the host samples out and load them in the sample tray. Raul, do you have anything we should know about before starting?"

"I've got some news for you, but it can wait. Let's move forward and..... break a leg, everyone."

Claude turned back to Raul with a puzzled look on his face.

"Claude, break a leg is what actors say to each other before opening night of a play."

Claude furrowed his brow. He still didn't understand the meaning of the phrase. He turned back to the CR47 and started the initialization phase as he mumbled to himself.

Rollie turned his back to everyone and opened the thermal box. He removed the host samples which consisted of a severed forefinger and clumps of human hair. He walked these items over to the sample tray and placed them in their designated spots. When the tray was closed, the samples were hidden from view.

Five minutes later everyone had completed their assigned tasks and stood back from the CR47.

"Claude, the honor is yours. If you would, please push the Start button."

In a rare display of emotion, Claude smiled at being chosen to start the incubator. When he realized his emotions were on display for everyone to see, he tried to hide his smile with a short coughing fit.

The CR47 came to life and codes started scrolling across the information panel. The team members stood there for a good ten to fifteen minutes making sure the green light didn't turn to a red trouble light.

"Everything looks good, guys. Let's take observation shifts as we did with Maxine. Who wants to go first?"

"I'll take the first shift, Rollie." After Claude, Rollie volunteered for the second shift followed by Raul and then Helmer.

"Okay, it's 9:20 a.m. now, so everyone meets back here at around 1 p.m."

Other than Claude, everyone left the lab. Rollie wanted to go back to his office and continue reviewing the lab recordings but was stopped in the hall by Raul.

"Rollie, let's go to the cafeteria. I need to talk with you."

After selecting something to drink, the men sat at a table by themselves, several tables away from any snooping ears.

"Have you seen the early edition of the Beobachter or listened to the news this morning?"

"No, Raul. But I have the feeling I should have."

"Here, look at this."

Raul spread the front page of the Beobachter in front of Rollie. Even though it was in German, Rollie could make out enough of the headlines to realize the lead story was about a massive explosion and fire at the Opulenz apartments.

"My God, that's where Sophia lives."

"I know, Rollie. Don't you remember that I found her place about a week ago?"

"That's right. I forgot. What else does this say?"

Raul was fluent in German, so he read the highlights of the article.

"A massive explosion was reported by the doorman at about 9:30 p.m. last night. The explosion was followed by an intense fire which destroyed all the apartments on the third and fourth floor. Even with the automated sprinkler system, it took the fire department several hours to extinguish the fire. The cause of the fire is unknown, and a final list of victims has yet to be compiled and released. Two people of interest are being held for further questioning. One of these is..." Raul pointed to the name in the article.

In bold, capitalized letters was the name **Klaus Ekstrom, CEO of Phoenvartis**.

Rollie's eyes went back and forth between the print and Raul. Raul already had close to ten hours to digest and think about the consequences of this event. Rollie was in an early phase of doing the same thing. His first thought was to blame himself for not going up to Sophia's apartment. If he had, she might still be alive. It was so predictable that something bad would happen between Sophia and Klaus. How could he have ignored all the warning signs? He should have taken at least some precautionary steps to make sure she was returned safe and sound to her apartment.

"No wonder Klaus wasn't here this morning. Raul, I blame myself for this. I could have walked her to the apartment rather than drop her at the entrance to the apartment building. What a stupid thing for me to do."

"Yeah, you could have taken her to the apartment and gotten yourself blasted to smithereens. Besides, we don't know yet that Sophia was killed. Wait for the official report from our buddy Milkweed before hanging yourself from the nearest lamppost. Okay?"

"Yeah, fine. But it sure doesn't look good for Sophia."

"What did she have to say last night, Rollie? Even if she's dead it's still important I know who she was working for. In fact, whoever it was might be responsible for her murder."

"You're right. She's working for a revolutionary group called the Black Cross. They offered her a ton of World Credits to do something, but she wouldn't tell me what it was."

"Why wouldn't she tell you?"

"Because I turned down an invitation to run away with her. She said that if she told me what they wanted her to do then I would become an accomplice and be subject to prosecution. Or maybe she meant I'd be subject to retaliation by the Black Cross. Frankly, I don't know what the hell she meant."

"Interesting. Damn, I wish she had at least given you a clue to what she was up to."

"Raul, the only thing that makes sense is they want something involving the ReLife project. I don't know exactly what, but what else could it be? There's nothing else going on at the company which is even close to the importance of ReLife."

"You're right. What else did she have to say?"

"That was about it. Raul. No, wait. She knew about the death of Maxine and Callie. And she told me about a group of non-executives within the company who wield enough power to get people fired. Supposedly, the ring leader is Klaus's assistant, Helga."

"Rollie, both of those things are old news. I'm surprised you didn't know about this group."

Rollie felt like an idiot not knowing about Helga's group. "I must walk around with my head in the clouds."

"Did she say anything else?"

Rollie gazed into the air and tried to squeeze out the last bit of information. He was forgetting something. Then it came to him. "One last thing. Sophia was the reflection in the CR47. You know the reflection in the stainless steel?"

"Really? What was she doing in the lab?"

"She claimed that she came in a few nights and was curious about the cloning equipment. She wanted to see it, so she went to the lab and that's when the recorders picked up her reflection."

Raul thought for a moment, twisting and turning this bit of information. "What a bunch of bullshit. She might have been curious about the CR47, but she wasn't looking at it because of curiosity. She was looking because her mission for the Black Cross has something to do with ReLife. Think about the care she took to avoid the recorders. If it wasn't for the reflection no one would have known she was there. You are right, Rollie. The Black Cross wants to get its hands on the CR47. At least, that's my guess."

"Wow. You think they will try to take it?"

"Could be. Or they want access to it for their own purpose. Either way, I'm putting round-the-clock guards on the lab, starting tonight."

After speaking with Raul, Rollie was mentally drained. In less than an hour he discovered his boss was a suspect in a murder case, his ex-girlfriend was probably dead, and a radical group was planning some type of espionage involving the ReLife equipment. And to top it off, he was most likely the last person at Phoenvartis to become aware of the gang of thugs who manipulated the system for their own benefit.

He needed to lie down and rest before everyone reconvened in the cloning lab. Maybe another mood-altering drink from the cafeteria plus a couple hours' sleep would make the world a little brighter. He bought a Lyfte carbonated drink and headed to his office. The drink contained a combination of drugs and natural ingredients which altered the parts of the brain responsible for depression. One bottle of Lyfte would be enough to change his brain balance from depressive to happy and positive.

At 12:30 p.m., Ingrid woke him from a slumbering sleep. The Lyfte plus sleep had worked. He felt much better, ready to attack whatever the future held.

Rollie was the first to arrive at the lab. He greeted Helmer who was on the last watch. "How's it going?"

Helmer had a big smile on his face which was an obvious, non-verbal answer to Rollie's question. "Look for yourself, Rollie."

Even though Helmer's body language screamed success,

Rollie was still apprehensive as he approached the CR47 and looked through the shatter-proof glass. Seeing Maxine in the incubator had been impressive. This was incredible. Lying prone in the CR47 was a perfectly formed man of over six feet in length with shoulder length hair and naked as a jaybird. Rollie estimated the replicant's age at late-forties.

Rollie was mesmerized by this new human. He knew what the CR47 was supposed to do, but seeing a finished human clone took his breath away. Of all the people at Phoenvartis associated with ReLife, he was the main person responsible for what he now viewed. He had conceived the idea of ReLife, figured out how to make the incubator work and babysat the entire project from start to finish. In an odd way, he considered himself the father of this replicant.

Within a couple of minutes, Raul, Claude, and Helmer were standing quietly next to Rollie viewing the replicant.

Rollie broke the silence. Everyone on the ReLife team knew what had to be done next but Rollie thought it best to repeat the instructions. "Okay, guys. Let's get ready to transport our new friend to the primate lab. Same procedures as we used for Maxine. We'll put him under for ten to fifteen minutes. I don't want him waking up in a hallway or in the incubator. The lab will be scary enough to wake up in but at least it's been remodeled to feel like the inside of a house."

"Claude, will you and Raul bring the stretcher over to the side of the incubator? Same lifting procedure as we did with Maxine. Two guys lifting his shoulders, one on his feet and one under his midsection."

When the CR47 shut down, everyone on the team performed exactly as instructed. When the clone was on the stretcher and ready for transport, Raul said to the team, "God Almighty. Do you believe this? I wonder who he is?"

Claude was wondering the same thing. Mr. Slice had told

him the clone was going to be a woman. If this was a female, it was the first one he had seen with male genitalia. Something was wrong, and he needed to contact Slice. But first, he needed to play along and act like the rest of the team members who were excited and full of themselves.

PREVIEW OF THE RELIFE PROJECT;
BOOK 2 - WORLD WAR

DISSATISFACTION with the World Council has led to economic depression and mass protests. The World Council is frantic to find the missing host samples which can reproduce their former leader who they believe can salvage their grip on society and reign of terror. Their representative, Sedgewick Slice, is desperate and resorts to kidnapping, torture and murder to find the missing samples.

Rollie Sweats realizes that Grandma LeeLee's clone is a legendary Founding Father of the old United States. The president's heavy consumption of red wine doesn't hinder his ability to learn the last 350 years of history and revive his leadership skills.

Rollie and Raul Hakala know that they have very little time left at Phoenvartis. They fear that their lives are in jeopardy from the crazed Sedgewick Slice. With a small group of accomplices, Rollie and Raul flee Zurich and head to a safe-haven where they can plan their future.

Although Grandma LeeLee has died, she and The Almighty have a different plan for Rollie and his group. They are to become the major force in the fight against two evil forces, the World Council and Black Cross.

War erupts. All three factions vying for world domination are led by a larger-than-life clone from the past. It's a struggle of economic, political and spiritual ideologies. Freedom and capitalism battle against socialism and fascism.

Follow this exciting confrontation to the surprising conclusion by reading The ReLife Project – World War, Volume 2. Revised February 2019

Dear reader,

We hope you enjoyed reading *2156*. Please take a moment to leave a review, even if it's a short one. Your opinion is important to us.

The story continues in *World War*.

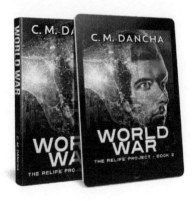

Discover more books by C.M. Dancha at https://www.nextchapter.pub/authors/cm-dancha

Want to know when one of our books is free or discounted? Join the newsletter at http://eepurl.com/bqqB3H

Best regards,

C.M. Dancha and the Next Chapter Team

ABOUT THE AUTHOR

C.M. Dancha lives with his wife and puppy in Florida. After retiring, he decided to "put-to-paper" the characters and stories which had been percolating in his head for over 40 years. His first 6 books were published in the past four years with another 7 novels scheduled for release in the next 4 years. Upcoming books will run the gamut from a religious, action-adventure trilogy to murder mysteries featuring his favorite protagonist, Mick Danger.

2156
ISBN: 978-4-86745-854-9

Published by
Next Chapter
1-60-20 Minami-Otsuka
170-0005 Toshima-Ku, Tokyo
+818035793528

18th April 2021

Lightning Source UK Ltd.
Milton Keynes UK
UKHW010635290421
382834UK00001B/292

9 784867 458549